IN HER
RIVAL'S ARMS

BY
ALISON ROBERTS

MILLS &
BOON

Published in Great Britain 2014
by Mills & Boon, an imprint of Harlequin (UK) Limited,
Eton House, 18-24 Paradise Road, Richmond, Surrey, TW9 1SR

© 2014 Alison Roberts

ISBN: 978-0-263-91314-9

23-0914

Harlequin (UK) Limited's policy is to use papers that are natural, renewable and recyclable products and made from wood grown in sustainable forests. The logging and manufacturing processes conform to the legal environmental regulations of the country of origin.

Printed and bound in Spain
by Blackprint CPI, Barcelona

Alison Roberts lives in Christchurch, New Zealand, and has written over sixty Mills & Boon® Medical Romance™ novels.

As a qualified paramedic she has personal experience of the drama and emotion to be found in the world of medical professionals, and loves to weave stories with this rich background—especially when they can have a happy ending.

When Alison is not writing you'll find her indulging her passion for dancing or spending time with her friends (including Molly the dog) and her daughter Becky, who has grown up to become a brilliant artist. She also loves to travel, hates housework, and considers it a triumph when the flowers outnumber the weeds in her garden.

For the Maytoners, with love, in recognition of the
magic you have all brought into my life. xxx

CHAPTER ONE

No WAY WAS he a genuine customer.

Suzanna Zelensky had no need to call on any intuitive powers she might have inherited from her bloodline. Even the dark silhouette of this stranger, caused by the slant of late afternoon sunshine through the window behind him as he stepped further into her domain, radiated a palpable scepticism. He wanted nothing to do with anything this business represented. The impression wasn't all that uncommon in the gypsy shop Spellbound and it was almost always emanated by males, but they were invariably dragged in a by a female partner.

This man was alone and yet he moved with a determination that suggested he had a good reason for entering her world. Alarm bells rang with enough force to make the back of Zanna's neck prickle. Who was he and what did he want?

She had seen him well before he'd had the chance to see her. Had caught a clear glimpse of his face in that heartbeat of time from when he'd come through the door until he'd stepped forward into that shaft of light. Strong features with a shadowing to his jaw that accentuated uncompromising lines. A harsh but compelling face. This man wouldn't just stand out from a crowd.

He would render those around him virtually invisible. He was different. Beautiful…

Having other customers to attend to was fortunate. Zanna had time to think. A chance to consider the implications of this unusual visit and an opportunity to gather her emotional resources. She turned back to the teenage girls.

'You'll need a burner to use the essential oils as aromatherapy. We have a good range over here.' The heavy silver bangles Zanna was wearing gave the movement of her arm a distinctive, musical accompaniment.

She could feel him looking at her now. A predatory kind of appraisal that should have raised any hackles she possessed but instead, disturbingly, she could feel a very different kind of response. Her skin prickled as though every cell was being stirred. Coming alive.

'How do they work?' One of the girls was reaching for a burner.

'A small candle goes in the base.' Zanna risked a quick glance behind her, maybe because she had sensed she was no longer under scrutiny. Sure enough, the man was moving, staring at the objects on display. For a moment, Zanna stared blankly at the object in front of *her*. What had she been talking about?

'You put water in the bowl above it,' she managed, 'and sprinkle a few drops of your chosen oil on the water. As it heats, the scent is carried in the vapour.'

'What do these ones do?' A dark-haired girl picked up a tiny bottle.

'Those ones are designed to complement zodiac signs. They increase your personal powers.'

He was watching her again. Listening? Quite likely, given the increase in the strength of scepticism she could sense. Scathing enough to bring a rising flush of heat to her neck. Zanna had always loathed the fact that she blushed so easily and she particularly didn't appreciate it right now.

'I'm Sagittarius,' the blonde girl announced. 'Can I open the bottle and see what it smells like?'

'Sure.' Zanna moved away as the girls tested the oils. Despite being acutely aware of the movements of the stranger within the shop since he'd entered, she had made no direct acknowledgment of his presence. As far as he was concerned, he had been totally ignored, which was not a practice she would normally have employed with any potential customer. They couldn't afford to turn away business.

But this man wasn't a customer. The dismissive rake of his glance across shelves of ornate candle holders and chalices, stands of incense and display cases of Celtic jewellery, even before the flick of a finger against a hanging crystal prism that sent rainbow shards of light spinning across the ceiling, had confirmed that his mission did not include any desire to make a purchase.

He didn't look like someone who might have been drawn in for the refreshments available either. She could imagine him ordering a double-shot espresso to go, not lingering over herbal teas and organic cakes and cookies. Had he even noticed the blackboard menu as he'd raised his gaze? Had he been caught by the play of light on the ceiling from the prism or was he inspecting the intricate pattern of stained glass in the fanlights above the main windows?

He was moving away from her now, towards the selection of crystal stones in a basket near the window. He was tall. She knew he was over six feet in height because

the circular feather and twine dreamcatchers suspended
from the ceiling brushed the top of his head as he walked
beneath them. His hair was black and sleek, the waves
neatly groomed, with just enough length to curl over the
collar of a well-worn black leather jacket. His jeans fitted like a glove and the footwear was interesting. Not
shoes—boots of some kind. Casual clothing but worn in
a way that gave it the aura of a uniform. Of being in com-
mand. A motorbike helmet was tucked under one arm.

Zanna could almost taste the testosterone in the air
and it made her draw in a quick breath and take a mental step sideways.

Maybe those alarm bells had been ringing for a more
intimate purpose. Perhaps her intuition had been over-
whelmed by the raw sexual energy this man possessed.
A subtle but determined shake of her head sent a lock
of waist-length copper-coloured hair over one shoulder.
She brushed the errant tress back calmly as she moved
towards the stranger.

'Can I be of any assistance?'

Dominic Brabant almost dropped the stone he was
weighing in a careless hand. He'd only seen the profile
and then the back view of this woman when he'd entered the shop because she'd been busy with her customers. He'd had a good look at that back, mind you, while
wrestling with the annoyance that two silly schoolgirls
presented such an effective barrier to having a private
conversation.

He could wait. He'd learned long ago that patience
could be well rewarded.

Maybe he would go to one of the small wooden tables, screened by bookshelves, and order one of the teas
described on the blackboard menu.

A ginger tea for its energising properties, perhaps?

No. He had more than enough energy. The motivation for being here in the first place had been validated in those few minutes he'd had to take, standing out there in the street, untangling the overload of memories and emotions. He could feel it fizzing in his veins and gaining strength with every passing minute. It had to happen. Fate had provided the opportunity and it felt like the inspiration had always been there, just waiting to be unleashed. The desire to succeed was more powerful than any that had preceded his achievements so far in life.

This was personal. Deeply personal.

He blew out a breath. Maybe a soothing chamomile tea might be the way to go. He couldn't afford to make this any more difficult than it had to be. And he wasn't even sure that this was the woman he needed to speak to. She might simply be a shop assistant who was paid to wear that ridiculous dark purple robe and improbable hair that had to be a wig. Nobody had real hair that could ripple down their back like newborn flames.

It was just part of the image. Like the flowing clothes and heavy silver bangles. The assumption that she was probably large and shapeless under that flowing fabric and that the hair under the wig was steely grey was blown away somewhat disconcertingly by the sound of her voice at close quarters.

The witch—if that was who she was, according to the information he'd been provided with—was young and the lilt in those few words created a ripple that was reminiscent of the silky fall of that wig.

He cleared his throat as he turned to meet her gaze. 'I'm just looking at the moment, thanks.'

A flash in her eyes let him know that she recognised

the ambiguity as he continued to look at her rather than what was for sale in the shop.

The sustained eye contact was unintentional. This wasn't the time to intimidate anyone—especially someone whose co-operation might be essential—but the proximity of the window gave this corner of the shop much more light than the rest of the candlelit interior. Enough light to see the copper-coloured rims around those dark, hazel eyes and the dusting of freckles on pale skin. And the hair was *real*. Or was it? Nic had to suppress an outrageous desire to reach out and touch the tendril caught on the wide sleeve of the robe. Just to check.

'Are you looking for something in particular?' Zanna held the eye contact with difficulty. The hint of a foreign accent in the stranger's deep voice was only faint but it was as intriguing, not to mention as sexy, as her earlier observations. The feeling of connection was more than a little disturbing. How could such an intensity be present so instantaneously?

And, yes…he was looking for something in particular.

Something he had promised when he'd been only six years old.

When I'm big, Mama, I'll be rich. I'll buy that big house next door for you.

Disturbingly, he could almost hear an echo of his mother's quiet laugh. Feel her arms holding him. The sadness that would always give her voice that extra note.

'Merci beaucoup, mon chéri. Ce sera merveilleux!'

'No.' The word came out more forcefully than he'd intended. He summoned at least the beginning of a smile. 'Nothing in particular.'

His eyes were dark. Almost black in this light. Inscrutable and unnerving. Resisting the instinct to look away was almost unbearable. The strength of will this man possessed was a solid force but she couldn't afford to lower her guard until she knew what his motives were in coming here.

He was bouncing the crystal in his palm. Zanna had the uncomfortable notion that it wasn't just the rock he was playing with. He had a purpose in coming in here. He wanted something from her. He wanted...*her*?

The ridiculous notion came from nowhere. Or was she picking up a well-hidden signal?

Whatever. It was strong enough to make her toes curl. To send a jolt right through her body, sparking and fizzing until it melted into a glow she could feel deep in her belly.

Desire? Surely not. That was a sensation she thought she might have lost for ever in the wake of the London fiasco with Simon. But what if it was? What if something she'd feared had died had just sprung to life again? She couldn't deny that the possibility was exhilarating.

It was also inappropriate. She knew nothing about this man and he could well represent a threat, both to herself and the only other person on the planet she had reason to cherish. Knowing she had to stay in control in the face of the power this stranger had the potential to wield over her physically was going to be a challenge.

And that was just as exhilarating as knowing she was still capable of experiencing desire. These last weeks, alone in both the shop and the house, had been lonely. Stifling, even.

The challenge was irresistible.

'You're holding a carnelian crystal.' She was pleased to find she could keep her tone pleasantly professional.

If she gave him something concrete to dismiss maybe he would reveal his true motive for being there. 'It's considered to be a highly evolved mineral healer that can aid tissue regeneration. It enhances attunement with the inner self and facilitates concentration.' She smiled politely. 'It opens the heart.'

'Really?' He couldn't help his sceptical tone. His own concentration had just been shot to pieces and he was still holding the stone.

Did some people really believe in magic?

Like they believed in love?

He released it to let it tumble back with its companions in the small wicker basket. He wasn't one of them.

'Excuse me.' The teenage girls had given up on the essential oils. 'What's in all those big jars?'

'They're herbs.'

It was hard to turn away from the man and that was a warning Zanna needed to listen to. A few moments to collect herself was a blessing but the task was made more difficult because the girls were staring at the man behind her now, their eyes wide enough to confirm her own impression of how different he was.

'Common ones like rosemary and basil,' she added, to distract them. 'And lots of unusual ones, like patchouli and mistletoe and quassia.'

Zanna never tired of looking at her aunt's collection of antique glass containers. They took pride of place on wide, dark shelves behind the counter, the eccentric shapes and ornate stoppers adding to the mysterious promise of the jars' contents. They had always been there. Part of her life ever since she'd arrived as a frightened young girl who had just lost both her parents. As grounding as being here, in the home she loved.

'They can be burned for aromatherapy or drunk as teas. They can also be used for spells.'

'*Spells.*' The girls nudged each other and giggled. 'That's what you need, Jen. A love spell.' They both sneaked another peek behind Zanna and Jen tossed her hair.

'Have a look at the book display,' Zanna suggested, unhappily aware that her tone was cool. 'There's some good spells in that small, blue book.'

'You have got to be kidding.'

The deep voice, unexpectedly close to her shoulder, startled Zanna and made her aware of another jolt of that delicious sensation. Cells that had already come alive caught alight. She could actually imagine tiny flames flickering over every inch of her skin.

'Got some eye of newt in one of those jars?'

Here it was. The first open evidence that this man was not a genuine customer. Zanna turned, her smile tight. 'No. We find that currants are a perfectly acceptable substitution these days.'

The giggles suggested the girls were oblivious to the tension that Zanna could feel steadily increasing. She cast a quick glance at the grandfather clock near the inner door of the shop. Only another ten minutes or so and she could close up and stop wasting her time with customers who either had no intention of buying anything or schoolgirls who couldn't afford to. At least the girls were enjoying themselves. The stranger wasn't. She could sense his irritation with the girls. Why? Was he waiting for them to leave? So he could be alone with her?

The flames flickered again but it was beyond the realms of possibility that the strength of the physical connection she could feel was being reciprocated. He wanted her for something, though… Of *course*…why hadn't she thought of that the moment she'd seen him come in, looking as though he had ownership of whatever—and *whoever*—was around him? As if he had the power to snap his fingers and change her world? To give her exactly what she wanted most.

Or to take it away.

Zanna stilled for a moment. Could he have come from the offices of the city council? They were as keen as the owner of the dilapidated apartment block next door that this property be sold and both the buildings destroyed in order to make a fresh development possible. There'd been veiled threats of the council having the power to force such a sale.

There was no sound of movement behind her either. Just a deep silence that somehow confirmed her suspicion and made her apprehensive.

Maybe the girls picked up on that. Or perhaps they'd seen Zanna look at the clock.

'Have you seen the time?' one of them gasped. 'We're going to be in *so* much trouble!'

They raced from the shop so fast the door banged and swung open again. Zanna moved to close it automatically and, without really thinking of why she might be doing it, she turned the sign on the door around to read 'Closed'.

She turned then. Slowly. Feeling like she was turning to face her fate.

And there he was. Relaxed enough to have one hip propped against the counter but watching her with a stillness about him that suggested intense concentration. Zanna felt a prickle of that energy reach her skin and she paused, mirroring his focus.

Something was about to happen.

And it was important.

His smile seemed relaxed, however. Wry, in fact, in combination with that raised eyebrow.

'You don't really believe in any of this stuff, do you?'

'What stuff in particular?' Zanna's heart picked up speed. If he was admitting his own lack of interest, maybe he was going to tell her why he was really here. 'There's rather a lot to choose from. Like aromatherapy, numerology, crystals, runes and palmistry. And the Tarot, of course.' Mischief made her lips curl. 'I would be happy to read your cards for you.'

He ignored the invitation. 'All of it.' His hand made a sweeping gesture. 'Magic.'

'Of course I believe in magic. I'm sure you do as well.'

The huff of sound was dismissive. *'Pas dans un million d'années.'*

The words were spoken softly enough that Zanna knew she had not been intended to hear them but the language was instantly recognisable. He was French, then. That explained the attractive accent and possibly that aura of control, too. She might not have understood the words but the tone was equally recognisable. Insulting, even. *Why* was he here—when he felt like this?

She'd had enough of this tension. Of not knowing.

'Are you from the council?'

As soon as the words left her mouth Zanna realised how absurd they were. It wasn't just because he was French that he had that quality of being in charge. A confidence so bone deep it could be cloaked in lazy charm. This man didn't work for anyone but himself. To suggest he might be a cog in a large, bureaucratic organisation was as much of an insult as dismissing everything that science was unable to prove. No wonder she could sense him gathering himself defensively.

'I beg your pardon?'

'You've come about the house?'

His hesitation spoke volumes. So did his eyes. Even if she had been close enough, those eyes were so dark already she might not have picked up the movement of his pupils but he couldn't disguise the involuntary flicker.

She'd hit the nail on the head and, for some reason, he was reluctant to admit it. Another possibility occurred to Zanna. He could be a specialist consultant of some kind and perhaps this was supposed to be an undercover inspection, in which case she might have been well advised to simply play along with the advantage of her suspicions. But this was too important to risk playing games. Honesty couldn't hurt, surely?

Disarming…*charming* this man, even, might get him on side. *Her* side.

'The historical protection order,' she said. 'I've been expecting someone to come and want to see the house.'

'Ah…' He was holding her gaze and, for a heartbeat, Zanna had the impression he was about to tell her something of great significance. But then his gaze shifted and she could sense him changing his mind. He nodded, as though confirming his decision. 'Yes,' he said, slowly. 'I *would* like to see the house.'

Should she show him? How dangerous would it be to be alone with this man? But what if he did hold the key to saving this place? How good would it be to have its safety assured by the time Maggie got home? She owed her beloved aunt so much and a protection order would be a gift beyond price.

For both of them.

Zanna took a deep, steadying breath. And then she mirrored his nod. 'I'll have to lock up,' she told him. Moving to collect the key from behind the counter took her even closer to him and she felt that odd curl of sensation deep within again. Stronger this time. That heady mix of desire laced with…danger.

She was playing with fire.

But, oh…the heat was delicious.

'I'm Zanna,' she heard herself saying. 'Zanna Zelenksy.'

'Dominic Brabant.' It was only good manners to extend his hand and his smile disguised the satisfaction of confirming that she was the person he'd been hoping to meet. 'Nic.'

'Pleased to meet you, Nic.'

The touch of her hand was as surprising as hearing her voice had been. That familiar *frisson* he noted would have been a warning in years gone by but Nic had learned to control it. To take the pleasure it could offer and escape before it became a prison.

Not that he'd expected to find it here. Any more than he'd expected this opportunity to appear. Fate was throwing more than one curveball in his direction at the moment. But how was he supposed to handle this one?

He watched as Zanna dipped her head, holding her hair out of the way, to blow out the numerous candles burning on the counter. With swift movements she divided and then braided the hair she held into a loose, thick rope that hung over her shoulder. Pulling a tasselled cord around her neck released the fastening of the purple robe. Skin-tight denim jeans appeared and then a bright orange cropped top that left a section of her belly exposed. There was a jewel dead centre. Copper coloured. It made him remember her extraordinary eyes. And as for her skin…

His gut tightened in a very pleasurable clench. The notion of her being a witch was too absurd. He was quite certain he would be unable to discover a single wart on that creamy skin.

Anywhere.

Mon Dieu… His body was telling him exactly how he would prefer to handle this and it didn't dent his confidence. It was a given that he would win in the end because he had never entertained the acceptance of failure since he'd been old enough to direct his own life, and this new project was too significant to modify.

Could what was happening here work in his favour?

Be patient, he reminded himself. He needed to go with the flow and see what other surprises fate might have in store for him.

The ripple of anticipation suggested that the reward would be well worth waiting for.

CHAPTER TWO

STONE GARGOYLES SAT on pedestals, guarding the steps that led to the shop's entrance. While Zanna fitted an old iron key into the lock and turned it, Nic took another stride or two onto the mossy pathway beneath massive trees.

Having already admitted his interest, he didn't have to stifle the urge to look up through the branches to get another look at the house. Zanna's distraction was fortunate because it gave him a few moments to deal with a fresh wave of the turbulent emotions that memories evoked.

It had to be his earliest-ever memory, running down a brick pathway just like this, summoned by the creak of the iron gate that announced his father's return home. Being caught in those big, work-roughened hands and flung skywards before being caught again. Terrifying but thrilling because it was a given that nothing bad could happen when Papa was there.

He could hear the faint echo of a small child's shriek of laughter that blended with the deep, joyous rumble of the adult.

Piercing happiness.

Nothing bad *had* happened while Papa had been there. Life had been so full of laughter. Of music. The sounds of happiness that had died when Papa had been snatched away from them.

The memory slipped away, screened by filters the years had provided. And he could help them on their way by focusing on the house and using his professional filter—an extensive knowledge of architecture and considerable experience in demolishing old buildings.

It really *was* astonishing, with the unusual angles to its bays and verandas that gave it the impression of a blunted pentagon. It was iced with ornate ironwork, intricately moulded bargeboards and modillions and, to top it all off, there was a turret, set like a church spire to one side of the main entrance, adding a third storey to the two large rooms with rounded bay windows.

A secret, circular room that begged to be explored.

Especially to a small boy who had gazed at it from over the fence.

The shaft of remembered longing was as shiny as that moment of happiness had been. The filters were like clouds, shifting just enough to allow a bright beam to shine through. Bright enough to burn.

The emotion behind this current project would be overwhelming if he let it surface. Not that his mother was here to see it happen but that only made it more important. This was going to be a memorial to the one woman he'd ever truly loved. To the man she'd loved with all her heart. To the family he'd had for such a heartbreakingly short breath of time.

He swallowed hard.

'It's amazing, isn't it?' Zanna had joined him on the path. 'The most amazing house in the world.'

A leaf drifted down from one of the trees and landed

on Nic's shoulder. Zanna resisted the urge to reach up brush it off.

'It's certainly unusual. Over a hundred years old. Queen Anne style.'

Had she been right in guessing that he was a specialist in old houses? 'How do you know that?' she asked. 'Are you an architect?'

'Used to be. Plus, I've done a lot of study. The style was taken up in the 1880s and stayed popular for a long time. The Marseilles tiles on the roof make it a bit later because they weren't introduced until about 1901.'

The brief eye contact as he glanced at her was enough to steal Zanna's breath for a moment. The connection felt weird but gave her hope. He knew about old houses. Would he fall in love with *her* house and help her fight to save it?

'I didn't know about the Queen Anne style until recently,' she confessed. 'I had to do some research to apply for the historical protection order. It's all about the fancy stuff, isn't it? The turret and shingles and things.'

It didn't matter if he didn't admit that consideration for protection was the reason he was here. Zanna was asking the question partly because she wanted him to keep talking. She loved his voice. It reflected the dark, chocolate quality of his eyes. And that faint accent was undeniably sexy.

'It was also known as free classical,' he told her. 'The turret *is* a bit of a signature. Like those dragon spikes on the roof ridges. It looks like it was designed by an architect with a strong love of fairy-tales.'

'Or magic?' Zanna suggested quietly.

He shook his head, dismissing the suggestion, but the huff of his breath was a softer sound than she might have expected. 'Typical of New Zealand to adopt a style and make it popular only after it was considered passé by the rest of the world.'

'So you're not a kiwi, then?'

'By birth I am. My mother was French. A musician. She came across a kiwi backpacker who'd gone to Paris to trace his own French ancestry. She found him sitting in a park, playing a guitar, and she said she fell in love with him the moment she heard his music.'

Why was he telling her this? Were memories coming at him so hard and fast they had to escape? No. Maybe it was because he'd had more time to process these ones. They'd been spinning and growing in his head and his heart for days. They'd inspired this whole project.

'She came back here to marry him and I was born the same year. He…died when I was five and I got taken back to France a year or so later.'

Turning points. When life had gone so wrong. He couldn't fix that, of course. But he could honour the time when it had been perfect. Not that he could share any of that with Zanna. Maybe he'd already said too much.

'I still have a home there,' he finished. 'But I also live in London.'

Zanna's eyes were wide. 'I've lived here since *I* was six. My parents got killed in a car accident and my aunt Magda adopted me. I've only recently come back, though. *I've* been in London for the last few years.'

The point of connection brought them instantly that little bit closer and Nic was aware of a curl of warmth but then, oddly, it became an emotional seesaw and he felt disappointed. So they'd been living in the same city, oblivious to the existence of each other? What a waste…

Another leaf drifted down. And then another. Zanna looked up, frowning.

'I'd better get some water onto these trees. It's odd. I didn't think the summer's been dry enough to distress them.'

'Maybe autumn's arriving early.'

'They're not deciduous. They're southern ratas. They don't flower very well more than once every few years but when they do, they're one of our most spectacular native trees. They have bright red, hairy sort of flowers—like the pohutukawa. The street was named after them. And the house. But they were here first and they're protected now, which is a good thing.'

'Why?'

'The trees are big enough to make it harder to develop the land—if it's ever sold.'

'You're thinking of selling?' Maybe this mission would end up being easier than expected. Done and dusted within a few days, even. Strange that the prospect gave him another pang of…what *was* that? Like knowing that he'd lived in the same city as Zanna without knowing about it. Not quite disappointment…more like regret?

Yet he knew perfectly well that the world was full of beautiful women and he'd never had trouble attracting his fair share of them. What was it about Zanna Zelenksy? Her striking colouring? Those eyes? The strong character?

She certainly wasn't feeling it. Her face stilled and he could see a flash of strong emotion darken her eyes.

'Not in my lifetime. This is my home. My refuge.'

Refuge? What did she need to run and hide from? Was there a streak of vulnerability in that strength? Yes…

maybe that was why his interest had been captured. But Zanna ignored his curious glance and began walking down the path.

'It's part of the city's heritage, too,' she flung over her shoulder. 'Only the council's too stupid to recognise it. They'd rather see it pulled down and have some horrible, modern skyscraper take its place.'

It wouldn't be a skyscraper.

It would be a beautiful, low building that echoed the curve of the river.

The Brabant Academy. A music school and performance centre, funded by the trust that would bring brilliant musicians together to nurture young talent. A serene setting but a place where dreams could be realised. A place of beautiful music. And hope for the future.

Nic followed her along the path. Heritage was often overrated, in his opinion. A smokescreen that could hide the truth that sometimes it was preferable to wipe out the past and put something new and beautiful in its place.

And this was one of those times. A final sweeping glance as he reached the steps leading to the main entrance of the house revealed the cracked weatherboards and faded shingles. Peeling paint and rust on the ironwork. Poverty and neglect were stamped into the fabric of this once grand residence and it struck deeply engrained notes in Nic's soul.

A new memory of his father surfaced.

'Why on earth would we want a grand old house that would take far too much money and time? We have everything we need right here, don't we?'

The tiny cottage *had* contained everything they'd needed. It had been home.

The shock of moving to the slums of Paris had been all the more distressing. The smell of dirt and disease and...death.

Yes. The hatred of poverty and neglect was well honed. Memories of the misery were powerful enough to smother memories of happier things so it was no surprise that they were peeking out from the clouds for the first time ever. Maybe he would welcome them in time but they were too disturbing for now. They touched things Nic had been sure were long dead and buried. They had the potential to rekindle a dream that had been effectively crushed with his mother's death—that one day he would again experience that feeling like no other.

The safety of home. Of family.

Zanna found she was holding her breath as she turned the brass knob and pushed open the solid kauri front door of her home.

First impressions mattered. Would he be blown away by the graceful curve of the wide staircase with its beautifully turned balustrade and the carved newel posts? Would he notice that the flower motif on the posts was repeated in the light switches and the brass plates around the doorknobs—even in the stained glass of the windows?

Maybe he'd be distracted by the clutter of Aunt Maggie's eccentric collections, like the antique stringed instruments on the walls above the timber panelling and the arrays of unusual hats, umbrellas and walking sticks crowding more than one stand on the polished wooden floorboards.

He certainly seemed a little taken aback as he stepped into the entranceway but perhaps that was due to the

black shape moving towards them at some speed from
out of the darkness of the hallway beneath the stairs.

Three pitch-black cats with glowing yellow eyes. Siblings that stayed so close they could appear like one
mythical creature sometimes. She could feel the way
Nic relaxed as the shape came close enough to reveal
its components.

'Meet the M&Ms.'

'Sorry?'

Zanna scooped up one of the small, silky cats. 'This
is Marmite. The others are Merlin and Mystic. We call
them the M&Ms.'

'Oh…' He was looking down at his feet. Merlin, who
was usually wary of strangers, was standing on his back
feet, trying to reach his hand. He stretched out his fingers and the cat seemed to grow taller as he pushed his
head against them.

Artistic fingers, Zanna noted, with their long shape
that narrowed gradually to rounded tips. If Aunt Maggie were here, she'd say that this man was likely to be
imaginative, impulsive and unconventional. That he'd
prefer an occupation that gave him a sense of satisfaction even if it was poorly paid.

He'd said he used to be an architect. What did he
do now? Consulting work with organisations like the
historical protection society? It certainly seemed to fit.

Those artistic fingers were cupped now, shaping the
cat's body as they moved from its head to the tip of the
long tail. Merlin emitted a sound of pleasure and Zanna
had to bury her face in Marmite's fur to stifle what could
have been a tiny whimper of her own. She could almost
feel what that caress would be like.

It was Mystic that started the yowling.

'They're hungry,' Zanna said. 'If I don't feed them, they'll be a nuisance, so would you mind if we start the tour in the kitchen?'

'Not at all.'

She led him into the hallway—shadowy thanks to the obstructed light and the dark timber panelling on the walls. What saved it from being dingy was the large painting. A row of sunflowers that were vivid enough to cast an impression of muted sunshine that bathed the darkest point.

She knew that Nic had stopped in his tracks the moment he saw it. Zanna stopped, too, but not physically. Something inside her went very, very still. Holding its breath.

It doesn't matter what he thinks. What anybody else thinks...

The involuntary grunt of sound expressed surprise. Appreciation. Admiration, even?

Okay. So it *did* matter. Zanna could feel a sweet shaft of light piercing what had become a dark place in her soul. Not that she could thank him for the gift. It was far too private. Too precious.

Opening the door to the sun-filled, farmhouse-style kitchen—her favourite part of the house—accentuated the new pleasure. The knowledge that Nic was right behind her added a dimension that somehow made it feel more real. Genuine. Even if nothing else came of this encounter, it had been worth inviting this stranger into her world.

The surprise of the stunning painting had only been a taste of what was to come. Nic had to stop again as he entered the huge kitchen space, blinking as he turned his head slowly to take it all in. It should be a nightmare scene to someone who preferred sleek, modern lines and an absence of clutter. It was only a matter of time before he experienced that inner shudder of distaste but at least he knew it was coming. He would be able to hide it.

Cast-iron kettles covered the top of an old coal range and the collection of ancient kitchen utensils hanging from an original drying rack would not have been out of place in a pioneer museum. The kauri dining table and chairs, hutch dresser and sideboard were also museum pieces but the atmosphere was unlike any such place Nic had ever been in. Splashes of vivid colour from bowls of fruit and vegetables, unusual ornaments and jugs stuffed with flowers made the kitchen come alive.

The shudder simply wasn't happening. Instead, to his puzzlement, Nic found himself relaxing. Somehow, the overall effect was of an amazingly warm and welcome place to be. It felt like a place for…a family?

Abandoning his helmet on the floor, he sank onto a chair at one end of the long table as Zanna busied herself opening a can and spooning cat food into three bowls. When she crouched down, her jeans clung to the delicious curve of her bottom and the gap between the waistband and the hem of her orange top widened, giving him a view of a smooth back, interrupted only by the muted corrugations of her spine. He could imagine trailing his fingers gently over those bumps and then spreading them to encompass the curve of her hip.

Oh…*Mon Dieu*… The powerful surge of attraction coming in the wake of those other bursts of conflicting and disturbing emotions was doing his head in. He needed distraction. Fast.

Maybe that curious object wrapped in black velvet on

the table, lying beside a wrought-iron candelabra, would do the trick. Lifting the careful folds of the fabric, Nic found himself looking at an oversized pack of cards.

Witchy sort of cards.

The shaft of desire he was grappling with morphed into a vague disquiet. It was very rare to feel even slightly out of his depth but it was happening now. There was an atmosphere of mystery here. Of eccentricity that had an undercurrent of serenity that had to come from someone who knew exactly who they were. Or some-*thing*, perhaps, because he couldn't be sure whether the vibe was coming from Zanna or the house.

Weird...

'We keep them wrapped in black.' Zanna's voice was soft. And close. Nic looked up to see she had a pair of wine glasses dangling by their stems in one hand and a bottle in the other. She held it up in invitation and he nodded.

'Sure. Why not?'

The wine was red. Blood red. His disquiet kicked up a notch.

'Why?' he asked.

'It just seemed like a good idea.' Zanna wasn't meeting his eyes. 'A glass of wine is a nice way to wind down. We could go into the garden, if you like.'

He followed the direction of her gaze. French doors provided a glimpse of a bricked courtyard between the kitchen and a tangle of garden. An intimate kind of space.

'I'm fine here.' Nic cleared his throat. 'I meant why do you wrap those cards in black?'

'It's a neutral colour that keeps outside energy away.' Zanna had filled her own glass and she sat down at right angles to Nic.

'It's black magic, right? Witchcraft?'

The flash in those extraordinary eyes was enough to make Nic feel unaccountably apologetic.

'I don't believe in witchcraft,' Zanna said, her voice tight. 'And calling any of this black magic is an insult to my aunt. Her family can trace its roots back to the sixteenth century. They travelled around and made their living by things like fortune-telling. Aunt Maggie has a very strong affinity with her heritage. I've grown up with it and I love Maggie enough to respect it. I see it as another dimension—one that adds some colour and imagination to life and can help people cope with the hard stuff.' She closed her eyes and sighed. 'Sorry...I get a bit defensive. We've had people try and twist things into something they're not and then use it against her. Against us.'

Nic said nothing. He had a feeling he knew who those people might be. But they were out of the picture now. He was the one who got to decide how things would be handled from now on. Except that he had no idea. Yet. He stared at the cards.

'I've always thought of it as a load of rubbish,' he admitted. 'The fortune-telling, that is.'

'Depends on how you look at it.' Zanna reached out and touched the pack of cards with her fingertips. 'It's about symbols. They demand an active response. You have to think about how you really feel and trying to relate to an unexpected symbol like the picture on a card can make you consider a totally new dimension to a problem. I like to think of them as a tool for self-knowledge. A way of centring oneself, perhaps.'

'Seeing the future?' He couldn't help the note of derision but she didn't seem to take offence.

'I don't believe the future can be seen…but I don't believe things are necessarily fated to happen either. There
are choices to be made that can radically alter the direction you take in life. Big choices. Little choices. So many
that you don't even notice a lot of them but it pays to be
aware. Some people think they have no control and they
blame others when things go wrong. If you've made an
active choice and things go wrong, you can learn from
that experience and it's less likely to happen again.'

Like falling in love with the wrong person…

Inviting a complete stranger into your home…

'If you don't believe the future can be seen, how can
you tell a fortune and say something's going to happen?
Like a new job or overseas travel or…' he snorted softly
'…meeting a tall, dark, handsome stranger?'

Was that a reference to himself? Was he *flirting* with
her? Zanna knew the rush of heat would be showing in
her cheeks. Did he know how good looking he was?
Probably. Nobody could be out there looking like that
in a world full of women and not find it incredibly easy
to get whatever he wanted. Maybe toying was a better
word, then. It made her remember the way he'd been
looking at her when he'd been playing with that crystal
in the shop. It made her remember the way he'd made
her feel. That reawakening of desire.

How far could that go?

How far did she want it to go?

'Okay…' She avoided meeting his eyes. 'First off, I'd
probably say that there was an opportunity of a new job
or travel or something. You might not have been thinking about it but the idea would be planted and you'd be
more open to new ideas because of that suggestion. You
might recognise an opportunity and then you'd have a

choice. Something would change. You'd either take that opportunity or be more content to stay where you were.'

'Do you tell your own fortune?'

She smiled. 'Occasionally. If I have a problem I want to think through. I prefer to have Aunt Maggie read my cards, though. It's great fun and the best way I know to have a really meaningful conversation. That's how this whole business started. Way back, before my time here, but I've had plenty of people tell me about it. They came to have their cards read and Maggie became a magnet for anyone with a problem. And she's such a warm and loving person she would offer them tea and cakes at the same time and it all just grew into a way she could make her living.'

She took a sip of her wine and Nic couldn't look away. He watched her bottom lip touch the glass and the way her throat rippled as she swallowed. He picked up his own glass to find it contained a surprisingly good red wine.

'Back then,' Zanna continued, 'before the city centre spread and the houses gave way to office blocks and hotels, there were streets and streets of cottages. Houses that had big gardens with lots of fruit trees. People kept chickens. Mr Briggs down the road even kept a goat. So many people. This was the big house but everyone was welcome. They all adored Maggie and this place was like a community centre. I remember it being like that when I was young.'

'But the houses have gone. There's no community now.' Okay, it was sad but things changed. Progress happened.

'Some of the people still come back and talk about the old days. They can't believe that the house and Maggie are just the same as ever and they love sharing the memories. She always promises she'll still be here the next time they come.'

She wasn't here now. If she was, Nic might have been tempted to ask to have his cards read so that he could see if she was as amazing as Zanna made her sound. Had she really helped solve problems for so many people?

'Can you read the cards?'

Her eyes widened. Surprise or shock? 'I've grown up with them…yes… I'm not as good as Maggie but I can certainly read them.'

'Would you read them for me?'

The hesitation was obvious. 'Are you sure you want me to?'

So that they could have a really meaningful conversation? So that he could sit here a while longer and put off thinking about why he was really here? Maybe even find a solution to his own problem?

Nic held her gaze. Long enough for a silent message that had nothing to do with fortune-telling. He wanted more than his cards read and that want was getting stronger by the minute.

'Yeah…' His voice was husky. 'I'm sure.'

CHAPTER THREE

HE HAD NO IDEA, did he, how much could be revealed in a reading? He was drinking his wine, leaning back in his chair and watching curiously as Zanna went through the ritual of lighting the five fat candles on the arms of the candelabra and opening a drawer to extract a tiny bottle of lavender oil that she sprinkled on the black velvet square.

'To cleanse the space,' she explained.

'Right…' The corner of his mouth quirked but his gaze had enough heat that she could only handle the briefest contact.

Was it what she was doing that had captured his attention so intently or was he watching *her*? Adding the impression to wondering what she was about to find out about *him* made her feel oddly nervous. She needed another mouthful of her wine.

'The first thing I need to do is pick a card to represent you as the significator.'

'The what?'

'Significator. The querent. The seeker of knowledge.' This was good. She could hide her nerves by doing something she knew she was good at. She spread the cards, face up, in front of her. The sound Nic made was incredulous.

'But they're beautiful… They look like artwork re-productions.'

'This set is based on one of the oldest known packs. Tarot cards have been around for five hundred years. The first known cards were painted in Italy during the Renaissance. Back around the second half of the fif-teenth century.'

Was he impressed with her knowledge? Why did she *want* him to be? Zanna glanced up but Nic was staring at the cards. Many pictures depicted people and each card had a title.

'I don't like that one,' he muttered. 'I hope Death isn't going to appear in my line up.'

'The meaning isn't necessarily literal. The death card means that something must come to an end. Whether or not it's painful depends on the person's capacity to ac-cept and recognise the necessity for that ending.' The words came easily because they'd been learned many years ago. 'Sometimes you have to let go of an old life in order to take the opportunity of a new and more ful-filling one.'

'That's very true.' Yes, he was impressed. 'Something I've always lived by, in fact.' There was a question in his eyes now. Or was it an accusation? 'Do *you*?'

Zanna blinked. This wasn't supposed to be about her. She retreated into card lore as she looked away. 'The cards are designed to portray a story. Kind of the rites of passage of an archetypal journey through life. Every-body faces the same sorts of challenges and problems—the same as they did five hundred years ago. People don't change and it's often a surprise to find how similar we are to those around us. Every situation is different but the challenges can be the same.'

'You don't really believe you can predict the future, do you?'

This time, Zanna was able to hold his gaze. 'I believe that particular choices and situations have led to where one is in life and the response to that position presents future choices and situations. Understanding why and how some things have happened is the best way to cast a more conscious influence on the future.' She gave herself a mental shake. 'Are you over forty years of age?'

That made *him* blink. 'Do I *look* like I'm over forty?'

A bubble of laughter escaped. 'You could be a well-preserved specimen. How old *are* you?'

'Thirty six. How old are *you*?'

'That's not the least bit relevant. You're the one I need to find a card for.'

'Hey…I answered *your* question.' There was an unguarded tone in his voice. A peep at a small boy having a playground conversation perhaps. It gave her a soft buzz of something warm.

'I'm twenty-eight,' she relented. 'Oh, yes…This is definitely you.' She picked up the card. 'The King of Pentacles.'

'Why?'

'He represents a strong, successful individual with a gift of manifesting creative ideas in the world. He also represents status and worldly achievement and has the Midas touch.'

He looked taken aback. Did he think that wearing well-worn leather and jeans would disguise his obvious lack of any serious financial hardship? That jacket had been expertly tailored to fit so well and the nails on the ends of those artistic fingers were beautifully manicured. His casual appreciation of the special wine she had chosen had been another giveaway. She placed the chosen card on the centre of the black cloth. Then she scooped up the rest of the pack and began shuffling the cards.

'That's a lot of cards.'

'Seventy-eight.' Zanna nodded. 'The major Arcana that is the depiction of the journey and then the minor Arcana. Four suits of Cups, Wands, Swords and Pentacles. They represent elements and experiences.' She spread the cards in a fan shape in front of Nic, facing down this time. 'Formulate your question or think about a problem you want clarified,' she invited. 'You don't have to tell me what it is. Then choose ten cards and hand them to me in the order selected.'

She placed the cards in set positions in the form of a Celtic cross. 'This card over yours is the first one we look at. It's the covering card. Where you are at the moment and the influences affecting you.' She turned it over. 'Hmm...interesting.'

He was sitting very still. He might think this was a load of rubbish but he was unable to stop himself buying into it.

'Why?'

'Page of Wands. It suggests that it's time to discover a new potential. Also suggests restlessness at work. Something's not going the way you want it to.' She touched the card at right angles to the one she'd just read. 'This is the crossing card. It describes what is generating conflict and obstruction at the moment.' She turned the card face up.

The oath Nic muttered was in French but needed no translation.

'You're taking the pictures too literally,' she told him.

'The Hanged Man is a symbol. It suggests that a sacrifice of some sort might be needed. Maybe there's something that would be difficult to give up but it needs to go because it's blocking progress.'

He was giving her that odd look again. As though he was including *her* in whatever thought processes were going on.

'This is the crowning card,' she continued. 'It represents an aim or ideal that is not yet actual.'

'The future?'

'Potentially.'

'What's the Queen of Wands?'

Should she tell Nic that the Queen of Wands was the card that had always been picked as the significator for her own readings?

'She's industrious, versatile, strong-willed and talented.' Zanna kept her eyes firmly on the card. 'She's also self-contained and stable. She holds her great strength and energy within, devoting them to the few things to which she chooses to give her heart.'

The moment's silence was enough to make her realise that she didn't need to tell Nic about her own relationship to this particular card. He was joining the dots all by himself.

'It may not mean a person, as such,' she added. 'It could mean that it's time to start developing her qualities yourself. Things like warmth and loyalty and being able to sustain a creative vision.'

He wasn't buying that. He'd made his mind up, hadn't he, and she could sense his immovability when that happened.

The card depicting the immediate future suggested a dilemma to be faced with either choice leading to trouble and the card representing the kind of response that Nic could expect from others was one of her favourites—the Lovers.

Nic clearly approved of it, too. 'Now, why didn't that one show up for my immediate future?' he murmured. 'That would have been something to look forward to.'

The tone of his voice held a seductive note that rippled through every cell in Zanna's body like a powerful drug. She hadn't felt this alive for so long.

Maybe she never had.

Had this man come into her life to teach her to feel things she didn't know she was capable of feeling?

What would she do if he touched her with the kind of intent that tone promised?

Could she resist? Would she even try?

Maybe not. Zanna did her best to quell the curl of sensation deep in her belly. The anticipation. 'You're being too literal again. This card is the view of others. It could be that you're doing something to make them think as they do.'

She could sense his discomfort and it was disturbing.

He may not be who he seems to be. Take care...

She knew he might be dangerous. It was reckless to be taking pleasure from his company. From this anticipation of what might be going to happen, but maybe that was what was making this such a thrill. Adding something wild and even more exciting to this chemical attraction.

It was an effort to keep her voice even. 'This particular card might mean that you have to make a choice and it probably concerns love. It might be choosing between love and a career or creative activity. Or it could be that you're involved in a triangle of some sort. Or that someone's trying to get you to marry in a hurry.'

He was shaking his head now. 'I never have to choose between love and my career. I've never even thought about marriage and I avoid triangles at all costs.'

He walked alone, then? He was unattached?

The thought should have made him seem more attractive but something didn't feel right.

Zanna read a few more of the cards before she realised what was nagging at the back of her mind. It was too much of a coincidence that she felt so involved with every interpretation he was making. For whatever reason, Nic had included *her* in the question or problem he had brought to this reading.

Why?

'This card represents your hopes and fears.'

'The Fool? Who isn't afraid of making a fool of themselves?'

'The fear might apply to the fact that a risk of some kind is required. It suggests that a new chapter of your life might be about to begin but it needs a willingness to take a leap into the unknown. It fits with a lot of other cards here.'

'What's the last one?'

'That position is the final outcome. It should give you some clues to answer the question you brought into the reading.' Her own heart picked up speed as she turned it over. 'Oh...'

The tension was palpable. Nic didn't have to say anything to demand an explanation.

'The Ace of Swords means a new beginning,' she told him quietly. 'But one that comes out of a struggle or conflict.'

He drained his glass of wine. It was all rubbish. So why did it feel so personal? It was obvious that Zanna was part of his immediate future. That it was going to be a struggle to get what he wanted. But did she really need to be sacrificed?

The thought was disturbing. She was part of this place and it felt like a home. A kind of portal to those memories buried so far back in his own story. Nic looked away from the table, his gaze downcast. It was the first time he'd noticed the floor of this space. A background of grey tiling that resembled flagstones had been inset with mosaic details. Starburst designs made up of tiny fragments of colour that dotted the floor at pleasingly irregular intervals.

'It's not original, is it?' he queried. 'The floor?'

'Depends what you mean by original.' Zanna was refilling his glass. 'The old floorboards became unsafe because they were rotten. Maggie and I have always considered our creative efforts pretty original, though.'

'You made this floor?'

'Yes.' She topped up her own glass. 'Took ages but we loved doing it. In fact, we loved it so much we did flagstones for the garden, too. And a birdbath.'

Nic shook his head. Extraordinary.

'Maybe it's something to do with gypsy blood. Making do with what you find lying around. We dug up so much old broken china around here that it seemed a shame not to do something with it so we broke it up a bit more and used it for mosaic work.'

'Taking an opportunity, huh? Dealing with a problem.'

'Yes.' She was smiling at him as if he'd understood something she'd been trying to teach. The sense of approval made him feel absurdly pleased with himself.

'So you really do come from a gypsy bloodline?'

'Absolutely. It's only a few generations ago that my

family on my father's side was travelling. Maggie was my dad's older sister. My great-grandfather was born in a caravan.'

'Where does the name Zelensky come from?'

'Eastern Europe. Probably Romania. That's where my aunt Maggie's gone now. She was desperate to find out more about her family before she's too old to travel.'

The smile curled far enough to create a dimple. 'What's funny?' Nic asked.

'Just that Maggie's got more energy and enthusiasm than most people half her age have. She's the most amazing woman I've ever known and I never fail to feel enormously grateful that she was there to rescue me when I got orphaned.'

Suddenly Nic wanted to change the subject but he wasn't sure why. Maybe he didn't want to be reminded that she was vulnerable. That she'd been a frightened child. That this place was her home. Her *refuge*. Because it would give her an advantage in the conflict he knew was coming?

That was weird in itself. Nic didn't let emotions sway business decisions.

This was hardly a business decision, though, was it? It couldn't be more different from the luxury resorts he'd become known for designing and developing in recent years. And the impulsive decision to buy into Rata Avenue had unleashed so many personal memories. This had nothing to do with business, in fact. This was deeply personal. A step back in time to where he'd spent the most vulnerable years of his own life.

Was that why this house felt so much like home?

He cast another glance around the kitchen. No, this was nothing like the fragments of memory he still had.

The kitchen in the cottage had been tiny and dark and it had taken a huge effort from Maman to keep it sparkling clean. There was something about this space that tugged hard at those memories, however. Some of those old utensils, perhaps—like the metal sieve that had holes in the shape of flowers? He dropped his gaze to the floor. To the fragments of the old china embedded in the tiles.

Blue and white were prominent but many had small flowers on them. Like that one, with a dusty pink rose. He almost didn't recognise his own voice when he spoke.

'Where did you say you got all the china?'

'We dug it up. Some of it was in our own garden but most came from next door where the park is now. There was a cottage there that was even older than this place. The council acquired the land and demolished the cottage before I came here but it was a long time before the site was cleaned up so it was like a playground for me. I knew I wasn't allowed to go too close to the river but once I started finding the pretty pieces of broken china, I didn't want to. It was like a treasure hunt I could keep going back to. I think that was where my love of flowers came from.'

But Nic wasn't listening to her words. He wasn't even thinking of how musical that lilt in her voice was. He was thinking of a china cup that had pink rosebuds on it and a gold handle. He could see his mother's hands cradling it—the way she had when she'd become lost in her sadness. He could see the look in her eyes above the gold rim of the cup that matched the handle. He could feel the sensation of being so lost. Not knowing what to do to make her smile again. To bring back the laughter and the music.

'When I'm big, Mama, I'll be rich. I'll buy that big house next door for you.'

How could grief be so sharp when it had been totally buried for so many years?

Maybe it wasn't Zanna's vulnerability he needed to worry about at all. It was his own.

The pain was timely. He was here for a reason—to honour his parents—and he couldn't let anyone else dilute that resolution. No matter how beautiful they were.

'I should go.' He glanced at his watch. How on earth had so much time passed? 'It's getting late.'

'But didn't you want to see the house?' There was a faint note of alarm in Zanna's voice. 'There's still time before it gets dark.'

'Another time perhaps.' Except the words didn't quite leave his mouth because Nic made the mistake of looking up again.

The sun was much lower now and the light in the room had changed, becoming softer and warmer. Shards of colour caught in his peripheral vision as the light came through stained-glass panels and bounced off cut crystals that were hanging on silver wires.

It made that amazing colour of Zanna's hair even more like flames. Glowing and so alive—like her eyes and skin, and that intriguing personality.

There was no point in seeing the rest of the house but he didn't want to leave just yet. He might not get another time with her like this. Before she knew who he was or what he wanted. And being with her—here—might be the only way to get more of those poignant glimpses into his own past. As painful as they were, they were also treasure. Forgotten jewels.

Was it wrong to want more?

Quite possibly, but—heaven help him—he couldn't resist.

'Sure,' he heard himself saying instead. 'Why not?'

Maybe it hadn't been such a good idea to give Nic a tour of the house.

It might have been better to let him wander around by himself. But how could she have known that he would pick out the features she loved most herself? That the feeling of connection would gain power with every passing room?

He commented on the graceful proportions of the huge downstairs rooms, the ornately carved fireplaces and the beautiful lead-light work of the stained-glass fanlights. He knew more than she did about old houses, too.

'Those ceiling roses were more than a decorative feature.' With his head tilted back to inspect the central light surround, the skin on his neck looked soft and vulnerable. Zanna could imagine all too easily how soft it would feel to her fingers. Or her lips...

'They're actually ventilators. Those gaps in the plasterwork were designed to let out hot air.'

'Useful.' Her murmur earned her a glance accentuated by a quirked eyebrow. Could he feel the heat coming from her body?

No. It definitely hadn't been such a good idea to do this. Zanna froze for a moment at the bottom of the staircase. The rooms on the next level were far more personal. What would he say when he saw more of her handiwork? Could it take away that sweet pleasure that his reaction to the sunflower painting had given her?

He hadn't stopped moving when she did so his body

came within a hair's breadth of bumping into hers. Her
forward movement was an instinctive defence against
such a powerful force and there was only one way to go.

Up the stairs.

Maggie's room was safe enough. So were the spare
bedrooms but the bathroom was next and she stood back
to let Nic enter the room alone. Folding her arms around
her body was an unconscious movement that was both
a comfort and a defence.

So far, the features of this house had been expected.
Period features that were valuable in their own right.
Things that could be salvaged and recycled so they
wouldn't be lost and he wouldn't need to feel guilty
about their destruction.

But this…

Nic was speechless.

The fittings were in keeping with the house. The
claw-foot bath, the pedestal hand basin and the ceramic
toilet bowl and cistern with its chain flush, but everything had been painted with trails of ivy. The tiny leaves
on the painted vines crept over the white tiled walls
from the arched window, making it appear as though
the growth had come naturally from outside the house.
The floor was also tiled in white but there were small
diamond-shaped insets in the same shade of green as the
ivy. The interior of the antique bathtub was also painted
the same dark green.

'*C'est si spécial…*'

Reverting to the language of his heart only happened
when something touched him deeply but he didn't trans-
late the phrase as he walked back past Zanna. She didn't

move so he kept going towards the last door that opened off this hallway.

Directly over the shop, this room shared the feature of a large bay window but here it had been inset with a window seat that followed the semi-circular line. A brass bed, probably as old as the house, had a central position and the colours in the patchwork quilt echoed those of the tiles in the nearby fireplace.

The walls were lined with tongue-and-groove timber that had been painted the palest shade of green. Dotted at random intervals, but no more than a few centimetres apart, were reproductions of flowerheads. Every imaginable flower could be found somewhere on these wooden walls. From large roses and lilies to pansies and daisies—right down to the tiniest forget-me-nots.

'The hours this must have taken…' Nic murmured aloud. 'It must have cost a fortune.'

'It was good practice.'

Startled, Nic turned to find he wasn't alone in the room any longer. That feeling he'd had earlier of being potentially out of his depth had nothing on the way the ground had just shifted beneath him.

'*You* painted these?'

The shrug was almost imperceptible but the modesty was appealing. 'Maggie gave me an encyclopaedia of flowers for my twelfth birthday. I added one almost every day for years.'

'And the ivy in the bathroom?'

'That was a wet May school holiday.' Another tiny shrug came with the hint of a smile. 'Maggie said it would keep me out of mischief.'

He stared at her. 'Do you know how extraordinary you are, Zanna Zelensky? How *talented*?'

She simply stared back at him. As though he'd said something wrong and she was trying to decide what to do about it. The moment stretched but Nic couldn't break the silence. The air hummed with a curious tension but he had no clue as to what might have caused it.

Finally, she spoke.

'There's one room you haven't seen yet.'

His nod was solemn. His mouth felt dry and he had to lick his lips.

The turret. The one room he'd wanted to see inside for as long as he could remember. The child buried deep inside was about to have his dearest wish granted. But... what if it was a disappointment? If it was nothing more than, say, a storage area?

He forced his feet to start moving. To follow Zanna up the narrow, spiral staircase that led to the secret room beneath the witch's hat of the turret. If it was less than he hoped for, he'd cope. He had with every other childish hope and dream that had been crushed, hadn't he?

Opening the small door at the top of the stairs, Zanna walked ahead of him. She said nothing. She didn't even turn around as she walked over to one of the arched windows and stared out as if she was giving Nic some privacy.

And maybe he needed it.

Despite the now rapidly fading day, the light was still good in here thanks to the skylights in the sharply sloping, iron roof.

He was in an artist's studio.

Zanna's studio.

Works stood propped against the walls. A half-finished canvas perched on an easel and there was a strong smell of oil paints and solvents. The overwhelming first impression that struck Nic was the sheer vitality of the colours around him. Muted, sun-baked hues in what looked like a series of work based on old European town streets that made him think of Italy and France. More vivid colours were in the flowers, like the deep blue of hydrangeas and the scarlet shades of poppies. Black cats could be seen concealed amongst the blooms. A series of sketches that the M&Ms must have inspired lay scattered on a table. Black cats—sleeping, washing themselves, jumping and playing. Even her pencil lines caught a sense of movement and vitality.

For a long, long time Nic didn't speak.

He didn't need to ask if she'd been the one who had painted that stunning row of sunflowers that made a dark hallway downstairs glow but it would have been an easy way to break the silence.

He actually opened his mouth to ask the rhetorical question but, as he did so, he shifted his gaze to where Zanna was standing and there was something about her stance that made the words evaporate.

Was she even aware of him being here?

CHAPTER FOUR

GOD...THIS WAS so much harder than she'd expected it to be.

She'd wanted him to fall in love with her beloved home. To understand why it was so important to save it. And this room was an integral piece of the architecture of the old house...

But it was so much more than that. The house was the home of her heart—where she felt loved, *safe*—but this room...

This was the room of her soul.

Her absolute refuge. It wasn't just paint smeared over those canvas sheets. They all contained fragments of *who* she was.

Not that he could know how much of a risk she was taking right now.

Zanna stared through the window as the shadows deepened but she couldn't see the huge rata trees below as they became dark and vaguely menacing shapes. There were other pictures in her mind.

Her best friend, Brianna, who'd travelled to London with her three years ago, when she'd graduated from art school. The bottle of champagne they'd splurged on when Brie had scored that job in a big gallery.

The show opening where she'd met Simon and fallen in love for the first time in her life. It had been a given that they would be living together within weeks. Planning their wedding and the rest of their lives.

More champagne as Brie and Simon had conspired to get Zanna to have her own show and they'd toasted her sparkling future as an artist. Not that she could show the *craft* that she'd previously engaged in, of course. Anyone could paint cute cats and flowers but they would coach her into producing *real* art. The kind that the critics would take notice of.

Had they known what kind of notice that would be taken? The humiliation of having her work ridiculed so publicly?

Of course they had. They'd been laughing about it that day, hadn't they? When she'd come home to find them in bed together.

Such a long, lonely trip back to New Zealand but it had been the only thing to do. She'd needed to heal and there had only been one place for that—in the comfort zone of her past. Maggie and the house. The shop with its magic and *this* room—the studio Maggie had created for her because she'd believed in her.

Even with all that faith and love and the solid grounding of the link to her past, it had taken a long time for her to climb those stairs again. To pick up a brush and start the work she had to do because it was who she was.

And now she'd allowed a stranger in here.

A potential critic.

Maybe she'd read too much into his impressions when he'd seen the sunflowers in the hallway and her immature efforts in the bathroom and on her bedroom walls. He might be too polite to reveal his opinion now that he was faced with her real work but she'd know the instant she looked at his face.

And she couldn't put it off any longer. Good grief… it felt like she'd been standing here for ever and there hadn't been a sound behind her.

She could hear something now, though. A quiet footfall on the bare, wooden floorboards. A long, slow inward breath. The faint squeak of leather in motion. By the time she turned, he was so close that she would see exactly what he was thinking. Especially with the way a last ray of the setting sun was angling directly through the window.

The unexpected explosion of colour as that sunbeam caught Zanna's hair took Nic's breath away and something else ignited deep in his belly, making arousal an overwhelming force.

Those astonishing eyes were wide. Vulnerable. She was waiting for his reaction to her art, wasn't she, but how could he begin to put the emotions they evoked into words?

To do so would mean opening a part of himself that he never looked at, let alone shared with anyone. The place where abandoned dreams were locked away. Where there was unconditional love and the warm comfort of a place called home.

Where a sunset meant far more than the passing of another day because you could shut off the rest of the world and simply be with the people who mattered most.

Nic felt like he was being dragged into that place— that's how much of an effect this room and what it contained had had on him.

Had he really intended to persuade Zanna to sell this property to him so that he could tear the house down to make way for something new?

Yes. It had to go, didn't it? It was a part of a dark past for him. A symbol of a time when the world had spun on its axis for a small boy and started the downward spiral to unbearable misery.

But it was part of Zanna's past, too. Part of who she was and she was…amazing.

There was too much to think about and it was too much of an emotional roller-coaster.

Confusing.

Right now, all Nic could think was that he wanted to make it all go away so that he could simply be with Zanna. If he could spend more time with her, maybe it would all fall into place.

He had to try and find some words. He couldn't just stand here and stare into her eyes.

'I…I don't know what to say,' he admitted. 'It's… You're…'

Something in her eyes seemed to melt. Were tears gathering? No…her lips softened as well, though you couldn't call it a smile. She lifted her hand. Placed a fingertip softly against his lips.

'You don't need to say anything,' she said softly. She drew in a breath, her next words no more than a sigh as she released it. 'Thank you…'

His hand captured hers and held it as she took it away. He lifted his other hand, without thinking, to mirror her action and touch *her* lips. Of their own accord, his fingers drifted sideways until they reached the angle of her jaw, with her chin cradled by his thumb.

Repercussions simply didn't exist in this moment. He

had to kiss her. That would undoubtedly make the rest of the world disappear, at least temporarily.

His touch was light. He would have felt the slightest flinch or withdrawal and there could be no mistaking his intentions as he slowly lowered his head so maybe she was feeling the same overwhelming pull?

The conviction that—unbeknownst to him, anyway—choices had already been made?

He was going to kiss her.

Or maybe he was merely responding to *her* desire to kiss him?

Why did she want it so badly?

Because it was a fitting way to thank him for the unspoken gift of validating her work? Words couldn't have encompassed what she'd seen in his eyes—the way her paintings had made him feel.

Because she needed so badly to have him on her side? To present a case that would not only mean that the house would be safe from the council's determination to get rid of it but that financial help would be available to restore Rata House to its former glory.

Maybe it was simply because she wanted to feel desirable again. That somebody wanted what she had to offer. That that somebody was the most gorgeous man she'd ever seen would only make it more special. Was that wrong enough to be ringing alarm bells?

Good grief, she could actually *hear* those bells as Nic's mouth hovered over hers, so close that she could feel their heat.

But then they got louder and Zanna gasped. She felt her mouth graze Nic's lips as she jerked her head sideways.

'It's the phone… I have to get that…' She was already

moving. She could see the stairs. 'It could be Maggie and the phone lines in Romania are awful.' She raised her voice as she flew down the narrow staircase. 'I've been worried about her for weeks.'

The spell had been broken and maybe that was for the best.

The memory of how he'd felt when he'd been a heart-beat away from kissing Zanna could be shoved into that space where the other broken things were stored. It would help if he got out of this room.

Nic shut the door of the studio behind him. When he reached the bottom of the spiral staircase he could hear her voice drifting up from somewhere downstairs.

'Maggie? Is that you? Oh, thank *goodness*… How are you? *Where* are you?'

Yes. The phone call had been timely. He could use a few minutes here to try and clear his head. Her voice got fainter, making it easy to tune it out as he paced the length of the hallway and back again and then paused beside a wide window at the end to peer out.

Maybe he needed to find a reconnection to the real world?

He could see his new acquisition from here—the ugly apartment block. It would be no great loss to the world to put a wrecking ball through that architectural disaster.

On the other side of Zanna's house was the small park where his first home and other cottages had long since been removed. If he *could* get this land, there couldn't be a more ideal place for the music school—bordered by the river and blending seamlessly into the pretty park. Perfect.

The motivation for the project was as strong as ever.

Unshakeable, in fact. This was something he *had* to do but there was no denying that niggle of guilt. That doubts were brewing.

This house might be a symbol of crushed dreams for him but for a lot of other people it was a symbol of something far more positive.

A place that inspired creativity.

A place to have their problems solved.

A place that oozed warmth.

Love…

Maybe that was where the doubts were originating. For the first time, Nic was tapping into memories that were worth cherishing. Feeling things he had denied himself for longer than he could remember. Would that portal be damaged if he obliterated the past to make a clean slate?

Compromise. Maybe that was the key.

What if he made a gallery of beautiful photographs in the entrance foyer to the school to honour the house that had been on this site? With a plaque to record its history and importance to a community that had long gone?

People could still visit.

Zanna could make a new studio somewhere else. He could help her find one.

He was still standing there, lost in thought, when Zanna came back up the stairs. 'We got cut off,' she said. 'But it doesn't matter. At least I know she's all right. More than all right, it seems.'

'Oh?' The sound was polite. His mind might be clearer now but his body was drifting back into a haze of desire. He had to consciously keep his hands on the windowsill behind him so that they didn't move in the hope of touching Zanna.

This was more than the kind of physical attraction he was used to. Maybe she really *was* a witch and he was the victim of some kind of bizarre manipulation.

Even her voice seemed to cast a spell.

'I didn't realise how worried I'd been, not hearing from her for so long. It's no wonder the phone lines are a bit of an issue, though. She's been in Bucharest and as far as the border to Ukraine near the Black Sea.'

Her hands seemed to be trying to follow an invisible map of Romania. She was speaking quickly and tiny flickers of her facial muscles added to the impression of vitality. *Passion…*

Did she look like this when she was immersed in her painting?

'Anyway, one of her second cousins runs some kind of a B&B. There was another guest there. A man called Dimitry. He owns a castle, it has no plumbing but I think she's in love…'

How had they managed to exchange so much information in such a short time? Was her aunt just as passionate in the way she talked or did they have the kind of connection that allowed communication on a level that needed very few words?

'With the castle or Dimitry?'

'She says it's the castle but I suspect it's both.'

Not that it mattered. Or maybe it did. In either case, surely a new dream would need funding. It could be an ace up his sleeve if the offer to buy this property was generous enough to allow for a new studio for Zanna and some money for her aunt to put into a castle restoration project as well.

'So she might not want to come back?'

The glow faded with disconcerting speed from Zanna's face. He could almost see her withdrawing—as if she'd revealed too much or said the wrong thing. She was putting up some kind of defensive barrier. Dammit. He wanted to see her smile again. To hear the voice that made him think of a rippling stream. To watch those compelling movements of her hands and face. But he couldn't even see her face now. She had taken a step forward to stare at the shadows of the world outside beyond his shoulder.

'It's probably just a holiday romance. There hasn't been anyone in her life for as long as I've known her. She's just…lonely…for something *I* can't give her.'

Nic's breath caught as he heard the echo of her tone. He had to turn towards her.

Was Zanna lonely, too?

There was a harsher note in her voice as she spoke again.

'Ugly, isn't it?'

He blinked. 'What is?'

'That apartment block next door. It's had nothing done to it for decades. The only people that live in it are the occasional squatters.'

'Needs pulling down.'

'That would cost money.' There was still passion in her voice but this was the flip side of the joy he'd heard when she'd been talking about her aunt. There was an undercurrent of something dark now. Something he could recognise all too easily.

Hatred. Contained but deeply rooted in the fear that something precious was going to be taken away from her.

'The owner doesn't want to spend that money until he gets what he *really* wants.'

'Which is?' The question was no more than a quiet prompt.

'*This* place. Enough land to make it worthwhile.'

Nic chose his words with care. 'You know the owner?'

'It's a company. Prime Property Limited. They specialise in development, though why they picked this place is a mystery. They usually make millions by ruining some gorgeous beach by building posh resorts. It's run by a man called Donald Scallion and his son, Blake. The scorpions, Maggie and I call them.' She flicked him a glance that might have been apologising for her tone. 'There's been…trouble…going back a fair few years now.'

'I'm sorry to hear that.'

It wasn't hard to make that sincere. This would all be so much easier if so much damage had not been done. It had been a mystery to Nic as well why Prime Property had bought the apartment block in the first place but if they hadn't, he wouldn't have seen that file sitting on Donald's desk when he'd come over to discuss another one of those lucrative resort developments they had worked together on more than once. He wouldn't have seen the image of a house he'd only seen in dreams for decades.

No. They'd been nightmares. Glimpses of the absolute security and happiness of his earliest years. People he couldn't touch and the sounds of music and laughter that he couldn't hear because of the invisible barrier that was closing in and suffocating him.

Now that mystery had taken a twist. It was only days ago that Donald had had his own turn to be mystified.

'*Why on earth would you want it, Nic? It's a millstone.*

The land's not big enough for a decent hotel and next door won't sell. We've tried everything, believe me...'

Nobody had to know why. Not yet.

Even Zanna?

Maybe especially Zanna.

The sincerity of his words was still hanging in the air between them. They had diffused the strength of Zanna's anger. That hatred. Flipped it, even?

Yes...the way she was looking at him now suggested that she believed he could help her.

And maybe he could. The image of one of the cards that had shocked him flashed into his head. That hanged man. She'd explained that a sacrifice could be needed sometimes. Something that would be difficult to give up but needed to go because it was blocking progress.

Maybe she just needed to understand...

But how could he persuade her? It was getting difficult to think again as her gaze held his so unwaveringly.

The spell...or force of attraction or whatever it was was gaining power again.

He wanted to persuade her...

He wanted her to understand...

He wanted...*her.*

It was as simple—and as complicated—as that. Maybe everything else could just wait a while longer.

He spoke quietly. 'Try not to worry, Zanna. Things will work themselves out.'

He could see hope in her eyes now. More than that. Faith? In *him*?

That gave him an odd squeeze of something he couldn't identify. Made him want to stand taller. Be a better person?

He could make this right in the end somehow. He could give Zanna what she needed.

Somewhere else.

Somewhere better.

It felt like he was floating, rather than consciously moving closer to Zanna. Close enough to touch. To pick up where they'd left off before the interruption of that phone call but, this time, he moved with a deliberate, delicious intent.

The curl in her hair had been enough to hold the braid together without any kind of fastening, the long end twisted into a perfect ringlet. He slipped his fingers into the braid just above the ringlet and, surprisingly, he could drag them down without meeting any resistance. Her hair was so soft it was easy to tease the coils apart as he worked his way up the long braid. His head was bent close to hers so he could whisper in her ear.

'Maybe you're not the only one who can see into the future.'

He'd reached the base of the silky rope that was virtually separating itself now, so that when he pushed his fingers through the thick waves, they touched the soft skin behind her ears. Impossible not to caress it. Zanna's inward breath was a tiny gasp.

'And perhaps it's a good thing that your aunt is having a break,' he continued. 'That she's found happiness.'

'With a man she's only just met?' Zanna's eyes had drifted shut. There was a tiny frown on her forehead as if she was trying to concentrate and he could see the effort she made to swallow. 'She's old enough to know better.'

Nic's hand was cradling that slim neck, locked in place by a soft tangle of copper waves. He lifted his

other hand to trace the outlines of her face—drawing a
fingertip with exquisite tenderness over each eyebrow,
across her cheekbones, down the line of her jaw and,
finally, over her lips.

'And you, Zanna?' he murmured. 'Are *you* old enough
to know better?'

The touch of that fingertip was like the path of a slow-
burning fuse.

Oh, yes…she was more than old and wise enough
to know better. But there was a trail of fire that was
sending heat throughout her entire body. She'd kept her
eyes closed. Stifled a sigh that could have been one of
pure pleasure escaping but the touch on her lips was too
much. Her eyelids flickered open and it was a shock to
find Nic's face so close to her own. To meet the gaze
that was locked onto hers.

This man was a stranger. One who she might never
see again after tonight. Only hours ago the idea of a one-
night stand would have shocked her but that had been
before the reawakening of physical desire that was so
strong it was painful.

Deliciously painful.

She'd never felt it this strongly.

Maybe that was because she'd been so closed off since
she'd left London. But maybe it was because this man
had connected with her on a level that no one else ever
had.

He understood her work.

He *got* her.

It felt like they'd already connected on an intimate
level. What would it be like to make that connection
physical as well as emotional?

His eyes were darkened to black by a desire she recognised instantly because she was sharing it. Her lips parted to utter the word that should have been the only sane response to his soft query but no word emerged. Instead, her tongue touched that fingertip and her lips closed again, taking it prisoner.

Had he groaned, or had that sound of unbearable need come from somewhere inside herself? The tension was morphing into movement and Zanna braced herself for an explosive release of whatever was containing that shared desire. This kiss had the potential to be uncontrollable and bruising.

But when his lips touched hers, that first time, they did so with a softness that was heartbreakingly tender. A totally unexpected gentleness. A tiny gap of time and the pressure increased to soar into something as uncontrollable as she'd anticipated. A taste of something new and powerful enough to be frightening in its intensity but that tiny gap of time couldn't be erased.

It had only been a heartbeat of such gentleness but it had been long enough to win her trust.

She was lost.

Her bedroom.

It was the obvious choice, given that its door was open just down the hallway and it offered a surface where they could resume this amazing kiss without the distraction of having to stay standing.

Taking her hand by threading his fingers through hers, Nic led Zanna into the room with the painted garden of a thousand flowers. *Her* room. He felt the sudden tension in her hand that could have become hesitation and he lifted it smoothly to her neck, keeping their fingers locked as he kissed her again, his tongue dancing with hers. Then he released her hand, using his own to hook the hem of her top to lift it and peel it off over her head.

The scrap of orange fabric fell to the floor and Zanna felt his hands tracing the knobs at the top of her spine. Shaping the dip of her shoulder blades and ribs and then sliding around and coming up so that his thumbs slid over the curve of her breasts and grazed nipples already so hard they ached. The brief stroke sent an exquisitely painful jolt of sensation that went straight to another ache building much lower, in her core.

Did he sense that? She could feel the strength and purpose in those large hands as they went to the fastening of her jeans. He popped the stud but didn't touch the zipper, merely holding the waistband and pulling to separate the fabric. Zanna heard the groan of the metal teeth parting and then his hands were on her back again, sliding beneath the denim. Beneath the flimsy fabric of her knickers so that he was cupping bare skin.

Dear Lord…she had never done anything like this in her entire life. Sex with a total stranger.

Except he didn't feel like a stranger. Some sort of connection had been there from that first moment, hadn't it? The way he'd looked at her after he'd spent all that time looking at her paintings. A haunted—and haunt-*ing*—look. He'd been touched in a deep place.

A tender place. As tender as that first kiss that had won her trust had been.

Even after months together, Simon had never been able to touch her like this. To touch her body or her soul like this. But Nic *was* still a stranger. A gorgeous stranger who was, clearly, a very accomplished lover. This was new—and dangerous—but instead of making her want to run and hide, it was simply adding another dimension that made it irresistible.

Until now, she'd merely clung to him, the passage of time irrelevant. There was no going back. Zanna wanted it all.

And she wanted it *now*.

'Nic...'

The hoarse whisper was a plea that he couldn't refuse. Going as slowly as he might have liked was no longer an option as he felt her hands slide from his neck to fumble with the buckle of his belt.

He could give her exactly what she wanted. What they both wanted.

He caught her hands and held them. Tipped her back towards the bed and let her fall gently, catching her jeans as she slid through his hands to tug them free.

He stripped off his leather jacket, reaching into the pocket in the lining to extract the small, foil packet he knew was there. He saw the way her eyes widened. Did she think he carried a condom because he made a habit of spur-of-the-moment sex with a complete stranger?

The assumption would be wrong. He might have had the opportunity—more than once—but he'd never indulged in meaningless encounters.

Including now. How this had become so meaningful in such a short blink of time was beyond his comprehension but he wasn't going to waste a moment more than it took to shed his clothes by trying to think about it.

He didn't want to think about anything other than this amazing woman. How she would feel and taste as he made love to her. What he would see in those incredible eyes as he took them both into paradise.

CHAPTER FIVE

Spellbound...

Maybe there *was* some kind of magic in the air around here.

That could explain the vivid dream Nic had just woken from and the way his hand reached out to see if the woman he'd just been kissing so intensely in his sleep was actually real. To try and keep feelings he hadn't known existed pumping through his body for a bit longer?

But the other side of the bed was empty. Still warm but empty. As though someone had waved a wand and made Zanna simply vanish into thin air. The fragments of that dream became elusive and evaporated into the air as well. An overall impression of the last hours remained, however, and it had been—easily—the most memorable night of his life so far.

That pleasure also seemed destined to evaporate as Nic opened his eyes and blinked in the morning light. He was alone in a strange bed and he had potentially made a complicated mess of what should have been a straightforward business proposition.

He needed to buy this house and then put a bulldozer through it.

Admittedly, that would come after salvaging some

of the architectural antiques but there was no getting around the fact that he would be destroying this house.

Zanna's house.

Guilt took a hefty swipe at him out of left field. Something about this house had been absorbed enough to get under his skin. Or maybe it was something about Zanna that he'd absorbed.

Tasted and revelled in, more likely.

Mon Dieu...

Nic threw the bed covers back and pushed himself to his feet. He'd find that ivy-covered bathroom and take a quick shower. It would be helpful if he was fully clothed and couldn't smell Zanna Zelenksy on his skin before he initiated the conversation he needed to have with her.

The one where he persuaded her to sell him her house.

There was still no sign of Zanna as Nic went downstairs a short time later and he could feel the emptiness of the big old house. Not that it felt oppressive. However unhelpful it was to think about it, houses like this had real character and this one gave him a picture of an elderly and much-loved grandmother in a rocking chair, quite content with what life had to offer and waiting patiently, knowing that there were more good things to come.

Oblivious to the fact that there was a time for everything to die?

It didn't have to die, though, did it? Nic had the power to save a life here. The ridiculous notion was dismissed with a grunt. This was a *house*. If he wanted to wallow in the analogy of life and death, all he needed to do was focus on the birth of the new and beautiful creation that would take the place of this outdated dwelling.

Yes, Zanna would hate him for it but that wasn't his

problem, was it? It wasn't as if he'd ever see her again after his business was concluded here. His life was in Europe and New Zealand was a whole world away. There were countless other beautiful women in that world. He didn't have to forget about her—she could just join the ranks of others who had briefly touched his life in a memorable fashion.

Except she was nothing like any of the others, was she?

Her beauty was unique with that flame-coloured hair and those extraordinary eyes and milky skin. Her passion was unique, too. Her talent mind-blowing.

She's flaky, he reminded himself. Her unusual bloodline and upbringing put her on the outskirts of what rational people would find acceptable. An outcast, almost.

That wasn't helping to clear his head.

Nic knew what it felt like to be an outcast.

The kitchen was deserted but the French doors to the garden were open so Nic went outside. Into the bricked courtyard garden beyond the French doors. There was a wrought-iron table and chairs here and a clay chiminea that looked as though it was well used as an outside fire. A clear blue sky held the promise of a beautiful day but it was early enough for it to still be a little crisp. Following a brick pathway through an arch that was almost invisible beneath a riot of dark red roses, he turned a corner to find Zanna crouched in a large vegetable garden.

She was wearing those jeans again that clung to her long legs like a second skin but the orange top had gone today. Today's choice was a close-fitting, white singlet and, from this angle, Nic was getting a view of cleavage that took his mind straight back to the pleasures of last night. He wouldn't have thought it was possible but it had been even better the second time...

Layered over the singlet was an unbuttoned, canary-yellow shirt. Another flame colour to tone with her hair and that sharpened the memories of the heat that had been generated between them. The sleeves of the shirt were rolled up to her elbows and her hair was loose—the way he liked it best.

Whoa...the thought had an edge of possessiveness. Permanence, even. How disturbing was that?

And suddenly this had all the awkwardness of the morning after, with the need to escape without causing offence, compounded by the guilt of knowing he had infiltrated a rival's camp under false pretences.

He cleared his throat. 'Hey, there...'

'Hi, Nic.' Zanna stood up with graceful ease, a fistful of greenery in her hand. 'I was finding some parsley. I thought you might like some scrambled eggs for breakfast?'

One of the black cats appeared from beneath the giant leaf of a rambling pumpkin vine to rub against his ankle. Then it flopped onto its back, inviting a tummy scratch.

'I've never seen him do that before.' Zanna stepped carefully between the splashes of colour a row of marigolds made. The other two cats were close on her heels. 'Merlin really likes you.'

'You sound surprised.'

'He's very picky when it comes to people.' Smiling, she kept moving until she stood close enough for her body to touch his. Then she stood on tiptoe and lifted her face. Nic felt the bunch of parsley tickle his ear as she kissed him lightly. 'Just like me.'

The touch of her lips was a spell all on its own. For

a few seconds it was enough to wipe out the awkward-ness. Enough to shove that guilt into a mental cupboard and slam the door. Nic slid his hands beneath the yellow shirt and held Zanna's waist as he kissed her back. Disturbing echoes of warnings that he was only making things worse faded to nothing as he was sucked back into the present moment. The softness of those lips and the feel of her breasts against his chest...

Zanna felt the parsley slip from her fingers as the kiss took her straight back to last night.

The most amazing night of her life.

The strength of this attraction and her response to it was unnerving. Unreal. She could feel herself being dragged back into a place where nothing else mattered and no one else existed. Fighting the distraction was difficult but it had to be done. She knew she was risking too much, too soon, to trust how he made her feel. Not only that, she'd made a resolution out here in the garden—to talk to Nic about why he was really here. To be honest about how much they needed the financial help a historical protection order could provide.

To ask for his help...

'Eggs,' she murmured against Nic's lips. 'Scrambled,' she added a few seconds later.

'Mmm. With parsley.'

'It's here somewhere.' Zanna slipped free of his arms, crouching to collect the fallen sprigs.

They walked past the old apple and pear trees on the small lawn that divided the vegetable garden from the courtyard beyond the archway. The cats stayed as close as they could to her feet without getting stepped on.

'Look at that. The grass is almost dead. Which reminds me, I need to give the rata trees a good drink.

This is the best time of day to put some water on. Do you mind waiting a bit longer for breakfast?'

'You don't have to cook for me.'

'I'd like to.' Zanna looked up. 'There's something I'd like to talk to you about.'

He held her gaze. 'I've got something I'd like to talk to you about, too.'

Her heart skipped a beat. Could it be that they were on the same page? That she wouldn't even have to ask for his help because he already intended to offer it?

Leaving the parsley on the arm of a wooden bench seat, Zanna headed for the front of the house and Nic followed her. He needed a few minutes to think about what he was going to say and it was helpful to catalogue more of the degeneration of the building as they walked. The paint wasn't just peeling, it was clearly falling off rotten weatherboard. Guttering was hanging loose and he could see the remnants of broken roof tiles pushing more of it out of place. It wouldn't be that long before the house was uninhabitable.

The hose lay coiled like a solid snake near the outside tap. The sprinkler was inside a galvanised bucket with hose attachments and an old iron key. He held it up.

'Lost something?'

'No. It's the spare for the front door. Maggie's a great one for losing keys and she's convinced nobody would think of looking in the bucket. Leave it there. The sprinkler's all we need at the moment.'

She showed him where to place it. They stood under the rata trees amidst a steady drift of leaves and one of the cats took a swipe as a leaf fell nearby.

'Good grief…it's *raining* leaves.' Nic was staring up at the canopy of the tree. He shaded his eyes with his hand, already well into a damage-locating frame of mind but this was an unexpected bonus. 'What's *that*?'

'What?'

Nic moved to touch the trunk. Nearly hidden by the twisted bark was a large hole.

'If that hole was made by a beetle, I hope I don't come across it. It's *huge*.'

'There's another one.' Nic pointed further up the trunk. He stepped out of sight behind the tree. 'And there's more.'

'No wonder the trees are looking sick. They're infested.'

Nic's face appeared again. 'I don't think it's beetles.' Going back to the first hole at head level, he ran his fingers around its edge.

'These holes have been deliberately drilled,' he said quietly. 'And I'm guessing they've been filled with some kind of poison.'

Zanna could feel the blood drain from her face. 'Who would do something that awful?' she whispered. 'These trees are so special. A lot of people supported the bid to have them protected. There was quite a fuss about it and it was an election year so the city council had to take some notice.'

'How long ago did that happen?'

'Ages. Before I went to London. Maybe five or six years ago? Just after the apartment block was sold and we started having trouble, I guess.'

'If someone had been upset about the decision to have the trees protected and did something, it's more than long enough for poison to have an effect, even on such big trees. Let's have a look at the other one and see what we're up against.'

We?

Was this a declaration of whose side Nic was on?

The shock was wearing off by the time they returned to the kitchen but Zanna didn't bother collecting the parsley on the way past. She felt sick. Grief and anger twisted themselves into a painful knot in her belly.

'There's no hope for them, is there? Either of them.'

'I wouldn't think so.' Nic was watching her intently. 'Someone's done a thorough job.'

'What's it going to be next? Will they poison the cats to try and drive us away?'

He gave her an odd look. 'Nobody's going to poison your cats, Zanna.'

'You don't know that. They warned me that they'd win in the end.'

'Who?'

'The scorpions. Prime Property. The owners of the horrible apartment block next door. They want this land and, clearly, they're going to use any means they can to get it.'

He turned away from her and paced a couple of steps as though he didn't want to have any more to do with this situation.

Well…why would he? He'd been sent here to do a simple job and it was suddenly getting complicated and unpleasant.

What if last night had only been a one-night stand as far as Nic was concerned? If the prospect of emotional involvement sent him running for the hills? Maybe he was appalled at the thought of dealing with a weeping woman.

Zanna might be more than a little upset but she wasn't about to burst into tears.

She was angry. And it was too easy to turn at least a

part of that anger onto someone who wanted to simply walk away. What had happened to that *we* he'd mentioned?

When Nic turned back to face her, he knew his face was grim. This was the time to tell her a few home truths. That the trees would have to be felled. That the house was disintegrating around her. That the only sensible thing to do was to take an offer that would be generous enough to make it easy to move on to something that wouldn't generate increasingly stressful problems.

'No, they're not.' Tension made the words come out as almost a snap. 'They're not even in the picture any more. But—'

'How would *you* know?' Zanna's voice rose as she interrupted him. The flash in her eyes made him remember just how passionate this woman could be. And she was being threatened now, albeit in an underhanded way that had probably happened a long time ago. It might have had nothing to do with the Scallions' determination to acquire the property. Maybe there was someone out there who simply didn't like trees.

'Because...' Nic ran his fingers through his hair, blowing out a breath as he looked away from her again. 'Zanna...I...' He was struggling to think of what to say. *Because I own that apartment block now?* He could see exactly where that would go. She would see him as no more than the replacement of a Prime Property representative. Somebody determined to force her to give up her property. And she'd be right.

It would hurt her and...dammit, maybe it had to happen but he didn't have to like hurting her, did he?

And...maybe—just maybe—there was a way around this. A solution...

He could feel the way she was staring at him but the idea was embryonic and there was no point even suggesting it if it wasn't possible. He wasn't even thinking about her now. His mind was racing. He had a lot of work to do before he would know if this idea had merit.

Zanna could feel her eyes narrowing. He was looking for an excuse to get away, wasn't he? Fine. She had other people to worry about.

'How am I going to break this news to Maggie?' She didn't expect an answer. 'She'll be heartbroken. She'll feel like she has to come home and that'll spoil a trip of a lifetime for her.'

'Zanna… Listen to me. I—'

But she didn't want to hear any more of his well-intentioned reassurances. Not when he didn't actually care. Or have a clue how serious this was. She held up a hand as a signal to stop him speaking. She needed time to think. To get past this visceral reaction and plan what to do about it. A glance at the wall clock made the means of finding that time easy.

'It's nearly nine o'clock. You'll have to excuse me. I have to open the shop.'

She wasn't going to let him say anything, was she? His best intentions of letting her know that he wasn't the person she thought he was and that he had his own interests in this property were fading with every interruption.

'I've got things I need to do as well.' Nic followed her gaze at the clock, then he looked at the door.

Zanna shook her head. He really couldn't wait to get away, could he?

'Did you need anything else from me?'

A split second of searing eye contact reminded her of what he'd needed from her last night. What she'd needed from *him*. But it was gone so quickly she could have been mistaken.

'What?'

'The house. Did you need anything else?' He would need to file a report on the historical value of the house, wouldn't he? 'Like any documents or photos?'

Oddly, he blinked as if he had no idea what she was talking about. Then he closed his eyes slowly and nodded.

Of course. He was well down a new track mentally but Zanna still thought he was here on behalf of a historical protection society to document the merits of preserving this old house. And, thanks to the shock of finding the trees had been poisoned, she was so focused on the immediate issue that she would automatically block any suggestion of stepping back to look at the bigger picture.

Nic could see it very clearly and it gave him a completely different angle on which he might be able to base his pitch. He already had a dozen things buzzing in his own head that needed attention. They could talk later. When she'd had some time to calm down and he was armed with more information.

'Yeah… A few photos might be useful. I'll use the camera on my phone.'

Disappointment was just as strong as her anger. Painful, even. He would walk out the door any minute now and that might be the last time she ever saw him. She couldn't help the chilliness of her next words.

'That's not very professional, is it?'

'Sorry?'

'I would have thought that an official report would need more than that.' She gave an incredulous huff. 'How many jobs like this have you actually done, Nic?'

Good grief…how frustrating was this? He couldn't afford to tell her the truth now. She'd throw him out on his ear and he'd never get a second chance. 'I do know what I'm doing, Zanna.'

She'd annoyed him now. Oh, help… How had things changed so dramatically in such a short time? It seemed like only minutes ago that the world had stopped turning while they'd been kissing in the vegetable garden and now here they were, practically glaring at each other. This clearly wouldn't be a good time to ask for his help, then.

A flash of pure desperation made her open her mouth to do just that or at least to ask if she was going to see him again but Nic wasn't even looking at her. Was he trying to work out how to access the camera on his phone?

Words failed her.

What would she say? *It was nice to meet you* or *Thanks for last night and how 'bout you write a report that will help me save my house?*

Would he think that she'd offered him her body as some kind of bribe?

She could feel her colour rising. It was her turn to look away now. To eye the door as a means of escape.

'Well…you'll know where to find me if you need anything else, I guess. Just pull the front door closed when you're done. It'll lock itself.'

CHAPTER SIX

ZANNA HEARD THE ROAR of a powerful motorbike being revved a short time later as she finished lighting the candles on the counter.

So he was gone.

He'd made her feel so special.

Desirable.

Talented.

Loved…

A few hours. No more than a blip in a lifetime but she knew she would never forget those hours for as long as she lived.

They had been precious and they should be enough.

He'd given her two amazing gifts. He'd reawakened desire. So effectively that Zanna knew it was going to be possible to fall in love again. He'd shown her that there was an oasis in the desert it felt like her heart had become.

And he'd given her faith in her art again. Her real art.

Either one of those gifts were priceless. She should be feeling enormously grateful instead of this crushing sense of loss that she would never see Nic again. An almost desperate longing for more…

People came and went in the shop. Being so close to

the central city, there were a lot of hotels nearby and tourists were drawn to the anachronism of the old, dilapidated house that didn't belong where it was any more. They didn't buy much but at least the distraction was enough to stop her thinking so much about Nic.

The day still dragged, however, and Zanna had to try hard to keep focused. She smiled at the tourists and wondered if stocking a few souvenir items like kiwi toys and paua shells might help the profit margin. No. Maggie would hate that. She still mourned the time when Spellbound had been more about the tearoom and the people who'd come together here.

But they both had to make a living. More than make a living. Somehow, they'd have to find enough money to deal with the trees. To do something more than temporarily patch up the worst of the damage time was doing to the house. Manuka honey that was known for its medicinal properties wouldn't be so out of place amongst their stock. Zanna needed to ring her essential oil supplier among others today. Maybe one of them would know a reliable source for the honey.

By late afternoon, she'd had enough. The arrival of the teenage girls who'd been here yesterday made her spirits sink even further. They weren't genuine customers, any more than Nic had been. And they'd been in the shop when he'd arrived so it was impossible not to think of him. To cast a glance at the door with the forlorn hope that history might repeat itself and he would be the next person to appear.

'Jen wanted another look at that book of spells,' the dark-haired girl explained. 'The little blue one.'

'Knock yourselves out.'

It was quiet for a few minutes. Zanna breathed in

the lavender of the oil she had chosen today in the hope of calming her mind. It didn't seem to be working. She still felt churned up about the discovery of the poisoned trees. Maybe she should burn a bit of sage to eliminate any lingering negative energy. Except that it was more likely that a good part of that uncomfortable sensation was stemming from knowing she wouldn't be seeing Nic again and sage wasn't going to help.

'Hey, this is cool.' The girl sounded excited. 'You can make Stevie call you, Jen. Look—it's easy. First you just have to choose a colour that represents him.'

'How do I do that?' The blonde girl called Jen directed her question at Zanna rather than her friend.

'There's a colour chart in the book.' Zanna automatically went to help them, taking the book and flicking through the pages. 'Here. You choose a colour that represents his characteristics.'

'Stevie's orange for sure,' Jen declared, moments later. 'Able to make friends readily. Generally good-natured, likeable and social.'

Orange was her favourite colour. Would she pick it to represent Nic's characteristics? Likeable was too insipid a word to apply to him. With his beauty combined with that confidence and ability to display tenderness, the attraction went way beyond *liking* him. It would be all too easy to fall head over heels in love with him.

Maybe she already had...

'I reckon he's red,' her friend countered. 'They form opinions rapidly, express them boldly and choose sides quickly but may be swayed easily from one viewpoint to another.'

Nic could be red. He was certainly bold. It had felt like he'd chosen her side, too. Had he changed his mind when it had become apparent that the road might get a bit too rocky?

'Stevie's not loud enough to be red.'

'He's your boyfriend, I guess. Or he will be—if this spell works.' The girl grinned at Zanna. '*Does* it really work?'

'I haven't tried it.'

Maybe she should…

'So what do I do now that I've picked the colour?' Jen sounded breathless.

'You've got a photo of Stevie, haven't you?'

'Yeah…I cut it out of the school magazine.'

'Okay, then. You need some orange thread and an orange jellybean and the photo. You tie the thread around the photo and leave it for at least one hour to absorb his energy. Then you use the same thread to tie the jelly-bean to your phone.'

'And then what?'

'And then he rings you up and asks for a date, of course.'

'Oh…' She looked at Zanna with a hopeful expres-sion. 'Do you sell jellybeans?'

'No. There's a petrol station down the end of Rata Avenue. They'll have some.'

'Hey, thanks so much.' Jen's smile was shy. 'I'll let you know if it works.'

'Good luck.'

With the excited energy of the young girls gone, the shop became almost oppressive and time slid by even more slowly.

What did you do with massive, dying trees? Would they turn into skeletons that would make the house look like a Halloween prop or would some official person come and say that they were required to have them taken down because they could present a danger to the public?

How much would that cost?

She wouldn't tell Maggie about it, Zanna decided. She couldn't bring herself to dampen the joy her aunt was experiencing. She'd been left in charge. More than that, because Maggie had signed a power of attorney, giving her absolute control over everything to do with the house and shop while she was overseas. And the trees had probably been on death row for years. A few more months wouldn't make any difference.

It was simply another obstacle to overcome. It wasn't the final straw—not by a long shot.

Zanna picked up the book of spells the girls had left on the counter and went to put it back on the display shelf. She could close up soon and go back into the house. She needed to do some baking. The organic chocolate-chip cookies were always popular. So was the banana bread. Would it be better than being in the shop with the ghost of Nic's energy lurking?

No. It would probably be worse. There could be far more of that energy lingering in the hallway where he'd given her that first gift of knowing that her art was meaningful…

In the kitchen where she'd read his cards…

In her bedroom…

Zanna closed her eyes, trying to gather some inner strength.

And then she heard it. The roar of a powerful engine in the street.

The silence that followed was enough for her to be able to hear her own heartbeat as it picked up speed and thumped against her ribs.

He'd come back.

The joy of that knowledge took her breath away.

The bell on the door jangled.

'Hey…' Nic's tone was light but there was an underlying tension that was still making it impossible to breathe. 'You're due to close, aren't you?'

Zanna could only nod. She stared as he stepped closer. He had his helmet tucked under his arm but he had something else in his other hand. Another helmet.

'Put this on,' Nic directed. 'And come with me. There's something I want to show you.'

Zanna had never been on a motorbike. She had no idea where Nic might be planning to take her or what it was he wanted to show her.

This was crazy but she felt her hand reaching out to take the helmet.

It didn't feel like she had a choice. Or maybe that choice had already been made, in that instant when she'd invited Dominic Brabant to step into her life.

This time, Zanna could feel as well as hear the engine as Nic kick-started it into life with her sitting on the back of the bike. She'd been so sure that she'd never see him again when she'd heard it only that morning but the shocked delight of hearing him return had blown that misery out of the water.

Now she had the rich rumble of the huge machine between her legs and her arms tightly wound around Nic's waist with her chest pressed against his back. It felt dangerous and wildly exciting and incredibly sexy. She could see the road flashing past the wheels and feel the ends of her hair whipping in the wind. The first time he leaned into a corner and she felt the bike tipping was terrifying but then they were upright again and she was safe.

Because she was with Nic.

He'd come back and she felt safe again.

It took very little time to weave through the rush-hour traffic of the central city and then cut across one of the outer suburbs. This was the green belt where the wealthy could have lifestyle blocks and indulge hobbies like breeding alpacas or making boutique wines. A gorgeous, lush valley with hills and a river and pockets of native bush like small forests.

Halfway along the winding road the bike slowed and turned through some old, ornate wooden gates. They rolled past a small lake bordered by weeping willows that had a faded, wooden rowboat moored by a miniature jetty. An ancient, stone building that might have been stables long ago had a backdrop of tall, native trees but at the end of the pebbled driveway, there was nothing but a smooth stretch of grass like an inner-city park.

What on earth did he want to show her?

A perfect spot for a romantic picnic? It seemed unlikely that the small storage compartment on the bike could be hiding a hamper.

Climbing off the bike, Zanna was already missing the contact of Nic's body but his hands brushed her neck and jawline as he helped ease the helmet off her head. Even better, he then dipped his head and kissed her.

Long and slow. With that mind-blowing tenderness that had captured her heart so completely.

It was hard to suck in a breath. Even harder to think of something to say. She could feel her lips curving into a smile.

'Nice. But you could have shown me that anywhere.'

He took her hand. 'Come with me.'

They didn't stop until they'd walked up the gentle slope to reach the middle of the grassed area. Nic was still holding her hand but he wasn't looking at her. His gaze travelled slowly to take in the whole scene from top of the hill to the lake and the patch of forest and the old stables. His nod was satisfied.

'It's as good as they told me it was,' he said. 'Perfect.'

'It's certainly gorgeous,' she agreed. 'Idyllic. But what's it perfect for?'

'A house. This land is for sale. Not on the open market yet but when it is, it'll be marketed internationally. It's special, isn't it?'

Zanna blinked. Was Nic thinking of buying this property? 'You're going to build a house? You want to *live* here?'

His expression was unreadable. 'The idea of having a New Zealand summer instead of a European winter every year is certainly attractive but, no, I'm not thinking of building a house.' It looked like he was taking a deep breath. 'I was thinking of helping someone to *shift* a house.'

Zanna's jaw dropped. An image of Rata House on this land appeared in her head with astonishing clarity. With space all around instead of being dwarfed by high-rise buildings. Air to breathe that wasn't full of the fumes of inner-city traffic. A garden that could include a whole orchard instead of a couple of tired fruit trees. The serenity of a view that encompassed a tranquil lake and cool, shady forest. Stables that could be a gallery or beautiful tea rooms.

A dream scenario but…it simply wasn't possible.

The shake of her head felt violent enough to send a

painful twinge down her spine. She let go of Nic's hand as if it was burning her and stepped backwards to create more distance.

'*No...*'

'I know it's a big idea.' Nic was watching her carefully. 'You need a bit of time to get used to it.'

Zanna shook her head again. 'You're wrong. It's not a new idea. Someone suggested it years ago and Maggie was really upset about it. She said the damage would be too great and the spirit of joy from all the lives that had touched the house would be broken. It's what it is because it's *where* it is.'

'No.' His gaze was steady. Compelling. 'It's what it is because of the lives that have touched it and that's happened because of the people who live in it.' Nic's voice was quiet. As calm as his face. 'But it's dying slowly because of where it is. Getting more and more hemmed in and out of place and you must know how much it's crying out for some restoration. Wouldn't it be better to save it? Shifting it would be the ideal opportunity to repair and strengthen it. You and Maggie could still live in it. Still have the shop and the tea rooms. The people who know the house could still visit. It's not that far.'

'It's too big. It couldn't be done.'

'Anything's possible. I have a mate—Pete Wellesley —who's a specialist in shifting houses. He owes me a favour. I have tickets on hold and he could fly over from Sydney first thing tomorrow to have a look. He's already seen the photographs I took and he reckons it's doable. They'd take off the roof and turret and cut the house into pieces, separating the floors. Then they'd put new foundations down on the new site and put it all back together. With enough people on the job it would only take a few weeks.'

'It would cost a fortune.'

'The land it's on is worth a fortune. I could make sure you get enough to cover any costs.'

'Why?' Zanna's head was spinning. There was too much to think about. 'Why are you doing all this?'

He hesitated for a long moment. 'I want to help. And I know what's going to happen.'

It was what she'd wanted, wasn't it? To persuade him to help? This wasn't what she'd had in mind, though. And there was something ominous in his tone.

'What do you mean—what's going to happen?'

'I've been talking to people on the city council today.'

Of course he had. It was what he'd been employed for.

'And?'

'There's been an unofficial vote that could become official very shortly. The council feels that the house is in the way of what could be an important development for the inner city. Their words were that it was interfering with their approved developmental mission for the inner city. They could enforce a sale to them and the value they would assign is likely to be a lot less than what it would be worth if you sold it privately. Also, any legal costs of trying to object would be taken out of a compensation package.' He was holding her horrified gaze. 'The clock's ticking, Zanna. Time's running out.'

She was so scared.

Oh, she was holding herself admirably straight and the tilt of her chin suggested she would fight to the death for something—or someone—she loved but Nic could see the fear in her eyes.

The need to protect her was overwhelming. The beautiful thing was that he could do that without hurting his own interests. This was a win-win situation for everybody involved. He'd spent the day networking harder than he ever had on a project. Finding the right people to talk to and calling in favours from all over the show but he'd pulled it together. The germ of the idea he'd had that morning was coming together so smoothly that it felt like it was meant to happen.

Just as surely as Zanna Zelensky had been meant to come into his life?

Right on the heels of the need to protect came the urge to comfort and reassure. It took only a step or two to fold Zanna into his arms and hold her close. She needed time, that was all. The solution was here—for all of them. It was a stroke of extremely good fortune—and his inside contacts in the real estate industry—that had made this piece of the countryside available and Zanna had seen it without being prejudiced by knowing the agenda. She would see the location of her beloved house through a very different lens when he took her back there now because she wouldn't be able to help imagining it here.

He knew better than to push too hard. This was the time to back off. As counter-intuitive as it seemed on the surface, he needed to actually distract Zanna and let the concept take root subconsciously. He could take her out to dinner somewhere. Take her home and make love to her again. And again.

His arms tightened around her.

It might be part of an automatic game plan but it was also a bonus he wasn't about to resist, despite the niggle of the guilt that hadn't been entirely vanquished by working on this superb solution.

He hadn't said a word that wasn't the truth. He just hadn't told her the whole story—that the development the council members were so excited about was the concept of his music school. That planning permission would be a given and that enforcing a sale of Rata House would only be set into action if he had problems acquiring the necessary extra land.

He could wait and purchase the land from the council, probably for less than he intended to offer now. He was doing *this* part purely for Zanna. He'd also told the truth when he'd said the house was slowly dying. They couldn't afford the repairs it needed and they were unlikely to get council permission for any major structural work even if they could have afforded it. He did want to help. To look after her. He knew better than to put her back up by voicing the desire, however. This was a woman who could look after herself and instinct told him it was going to be tricky to win her complete trust.

While he couldn't allow it to jeopardise his project, the desire to win her trust was surprisingly strong.

And bubbling somewhere beneath the fire he'd thrown all those irons into today was the idea that it might be simple to merely fudge a timeframe. If he'd acquired the apartment block *after* buying the Zelenksy property then nobody—well, a particular somebody that he was holding close right now—could accuse him of having a conflict of interest.

Could it even be considered a conflict when it was such a perfect solution?

Yes, he was treading a fine line but it wasn't the first time. The biggest risks often generated the biggest rewards.

Time *was* running out. He'd allowed himself a week

to sort this project. It was only day two and if he could pull it off, he was on track so that everybody could win. Even better, he would have a whole week with Zanna that he could remember for the rest of his life.

'Let's go home,' he whispered into her ear. 'And sleep on it.'

Nic wouldn't let her talk about it that evening.

'Wait until you have all the information you need,' he said. 'Until the idea stops spinning in your head for long enough to see it properly. I've given Pete the nod to jump on a plane in the morning. He'll be able to answer questions better than me. Then it'll be time to talk.'

He distracted her, instead. With food and wine, at a gorgeous restaurant that had beautiful music and a dance floor.

It was no surprise that this astonishing man could dance so well. What was a surprise was the sheer bliss of drifting in his arms to the music. Of being with him.

Of wanting to be with him…for ever?

That made her head spin as much as the crazy idea of shifting her home to the most idyllic location possible.

They were dreams. Too good to be believable.

Either of them.

But, oh…it was heaven to play with them for a while.

He wasn't going to let her sleep on the concept in a hurry either, when they finally returned to Zanna's bed.

They were comfortable with each other's bodies now. Enough to touch and explore and discover new things. Nic's leisurely tracing of her body came to a halt as his fingers brushed the stone in her navel.

'I meant to ask last night,' he murmured. 'What is it?'

'A topaz,' she told him. 'My birth stone.'

'It's perfect for you. It's got the colours of flames in it. Just like your hair.' He stroked a soft curl back from her face. 'And your eyes…' He moved in to kiss her softly and she felt her lips curl beneath his.

'Why are you smiling?'

'This stone is supposed to enhance emotional balance.'

His lips were so close she could feel the word more than hear it. 'And?'

'And I'm not feeling particularly balanced right now.'

There was a moment of absolute stillness then. As if the world was holding its breath—waiting for her to tell him that she was in love with him?

She couldn't. Not yet. It was all too new to trust and too big to mess with. But it was hanging there, unspoken.

'Same,' Nic whispered.

Another moment of stillness could have made the atmosphere way too intense but then she felt his lips curl into a smile.

'I think I like it.'

Zanna was more than ready to sink into the kiss. 'Same.'

CHAPTER SEVEN

SLEEP HAD FINALLY come but the first fingers of light from a new dawn found Zanna awake again.

Her head was still spinning.

Or maybe it wasn't. Maybe her head was just fine and it was the world spinning around her. Changing its axis. Presenting her with possibilities that should be elusive and only dreams but were actually close enough to touch.

Nic was close enough to touch. Sprawled on his back with one arm flung above his head. For a long minute Zanna simply gazed at him. She loved the rumpled disorder of his wavy hair and the tangle of dark lashes kissing the top of those chiselled cheekbones. His lips were slightly parted and so deliciously soft looking amidst the dark shadowing of his jaw she had to consciously stop herself reaching out to touch them.

Instead, she slipped quietly from the bed. She needed a bit of time to herself to walk around the house and think. To compose a careful text message that wouldn't panic Maggie and make her think she had to come home but would still let her know that there was some urgency to make some big decisions.

It was Saturday, which meant she could close the shop

at midday and that would be about the time Nic returned from collecting Pete from the airport. They had the rest of the day before Pete's return flight to Sydney but the pressure was going to be on for her to make some kind of decision by the time he left, at least on whether or not she might be interested.

Of course she was interested. The idea didn't even seem so farfetched any more by the time she was introduced to Pete Wellesley. Nic's friend made Zanna think of a pirate, with his dreadlocked hair and a ring through one ear. With his easy smile and dancing eyes, it was impossible not to like him.

He had nothing like the controlled, bad-boy biker vibe that Nic had exuded at first sight but the combination of the two personalities was a force to be reckoned with. Pete's hint of mischief balanced Nic's intensity. Nic's attention to detail focused Pete's enthusiasm. She felt safe with Nic and inspired by Pete. They were both so confident and focused on the job at hand and they both seemed experts in their fields.

'We went through architectural school in London together,' Nic told her. 'And we both did a course on building heritage conservation. Pete took it further and did the thesis for his master's on relocation.'

'Did you do a thesis, too?' Zanna added a jar of olives and some cheese to the array of food she'd put together for a picnic-style lunch in the courtyard garden.

'His was on how to make money,' Pete told her.

'It was about blending modern architecture to the immediate physical environment,' Nic corrected.

'AKA how to make money.' Pete raised the bottle of beer he was holding in a toast. 'And good on you, mate. You do what you do very well.'

Zanna frowned. 'I thought you were an expert in *old* houses.'

The two men exchanged a glance. Then Nic caught Zanna's questioning gaze.

'My career has been all about developing luxury international coastal resorts and boutique hotels in the last few years but this is a special project,' he said.

His eyes added another message. That it was more than special. That he was completely invested in it because it was about someone he loved.

Her breath caught—held by the wave of emotion that swept through her. How long did it normally take two people to fall in love? If it happened this fast, did that make it an illusion?

A dream that she would have to wake up from?

The dream of saving her house might have taken an unexpected twist but, as the day wore on, it began to seem more and more possible.

'Turn of the century, you said?' With lunch and the introductory process complete, Pete had thrown himself into a thorough examination of the house, which had involved taking a lot of photographs and measurements. Having spent most of the afternoon exploring every inch, inside and out, they were finally back in the kitchen, sitting around the table as Pete entered data into his computer program. 'Do you know the exact year?'

Zanna shook her head. 'Nic seemed to think it was later than 1900 because of the Marseilles tiles. Does it matter?'

'Building styles varied a bit. If platform framing was used, which I expect it was, it means that the walls for each floor were framed separately above and below the first-floor joists. That makes it much easier to separate the floors for removal.'

Nerves kicked in again at that point. Alarm bells, even. 'I still can't believe you can chop a house up without doing enormous damage somewhere along the line.' There would be no going back if she agreed to this. No way to repair the damage if it turned out to be a mistake.

'But you saw the pictures of Pete's recent projects over lunch,' Nic reminded her, gesturing towards the tablet computer that was the only equipment Pete had brought with him other than a laser device for taking measurements. 'Even blowing up the images you couldn't tell where they'd been put back together.'

'This is a big house,' Pete said. 'It would need to go into six or maybe eight pieces. The only thing I can say for certain will get damaged are the roof tiles but you would have been looking at a replacement roof within a few years anyway.'

'That's true. There's been a leak in one of the spare bedrooms recently.' And they would never be able to afford a new roof so the damage would only accelerate.

'Slate would look good,' Nic suggested. 'Even better than the tiles.'

'It's wider than eighteen metres,' Pete continued, 'so it would need cutting twice. Where we cut depends on where the load-bearing walls are inside and any particular features that need protecting. Like the staircase.'

'And the turret,' Nic put in. 'That's got to be protected.'

'We'd remove that separately.' Pete was still tapping notes into his computer. 'Take it off with a crane. We'd separate the top storey. The ceiling of the ground floor stays with the floor of the upper storey so we'd have to put in bracing beams to hold the shape of the lower rooms together.' He stared at the screen for a long moment and then looked up to flash a grin at Zanna. 'It's doable,' he pronounced. 'And I have to say I'd relish the challenge. But you're lucky that those trees have been killed.'

Lucky? Was he serious?

'Those trees are hundreds of years old. Protected. There's nothing lucky about losing them.'

Pete raised an eyebrow in Nic's direction before turning towards Zanna. 'If they were still healthy there'd be no way you'd be allowed to take them down, and without taking them down there'd be no way of moving the house because of the high-rises around it and the big trees in the park.' He turned back to Nic. 'Are you going to give me another ride on that shiny toy you've hired and take me out to see the potential site for relocation? They're the last boxes I need to fill to get an estimate of costs.'

And then it would be a done deal.

'Sure.' Nic looked as though he was on the point of high-fiving Pete. 'And then I can drop you back at the airport. You okay with that, Zanna? I'll be a couple of hours.' He got to his feet, heading towards where he'd left the bike helmets on the floor near the French doors.

'No.' Zanna was surprised to hear the word coming out of her mouth but not nearly as startled as the two men looked.

'No,' she repeated, more firmly. 'I don't think I am okay with any of this.'

An awkward silence fell as Nic met her gaze. And then another significant glance passed between the men.

'How 'bout I meet you outside?' Pete suggested quietly.

A single nod and then they were alone.

'What's going on, Zanna?' Nic was careful not to sound impatient. 'I thought you were on board. That you liked the idea.'

It had felt like a done deal, in fact. The estimate of costs was not important. Nic was more than prepared to cover whatever it was going to cost. The goalposts were in sight and he could smell success.

'It's all happening too fast. I haven't had a chance to think about it properly, let alone talk to Maggie. I feel like I'm being railroaded. Bullied, even… And I made a promise to myself that I would never let that happen again.'

What on earth was she talking about?

'What do you mean…*again*? I'm not trying to railroad you. Quite the opposite. I didn't even talk about it last night because I wanted to give you time to think about it without feeling pressured, but…' He ran his fingers through his hair. It was a risk but if he didn't push things here, there was a real danger of all the work he'd done so far being for nothing. 'There *is* a time limit. You need my help and I can't be here much longer. We've only a few days to get it all sorted.'

'I wasn't talking about you.'

Something in Zanna's eyes gave Nic that feeling of wanting to protect her again. Of wanting to make everything all right. For a heartbeat it was actually stronger than what he wanted for himself.

Long enough for him to hold her gaze and close the gap between them. To take her hands and hold them.

'So tell me who you are talking about. Trust me, Zanna.' She wouldn't be disappointed if she did. He'd make sure of that. 'Please.'

'That's the problem,' she whispered. 'Trust…'

Nic knew that Pete was waiting for him outside beside the motorbike. Probably impatient to get going and get this project kicked into some real action. As impatient as he was himself.

But this was important.

Vital, in fact.

He led Zanna towards the table and invited her to sit. He was ready to listen and solve any problem that was about to make an appearance. He was good at that. Not that Zanna seemed in a hurry to get to the point.

'I never thought I could make a living out of my art,' she told him. 'It was a dream that seemed too good to believe in. I didn't even go to art school for years. I did a degree in art conservation first. I imagined myself working in a museum and getting up close and personal with the work of famous artists.'

Nic made an encouraging noise.

'But the more time I spent around art, the more I loved doing my own work. It was my best friend, Brie, who persuaded me to do a postgraduate art degree in London, and Maggie took out another mortgage on the house to pay for it. She'd always believed in me, she said, and when I was rich and famous I could pay her back.'

Nick waited, slotting away the information that there was more than one mortgage on the house. No problem. He could make the offer even more attractive.

'Brie came to London with me. She scored a job in a big gallery and that was how I met Simon. Brie started a campaign to get him interested in me. He was a big wheel in the European art scene and the careers of artists he picked as up and coming really took off.'

Nic didn't like the way she closed her eyes and took a deep breath. He had the feeling that this Simon was important to Zanna and he didn't like that. Good grief, was that unpleasant prickle of sensation jealousy?

'Brie's campaign worked a treat,' Zanna said. 'He chose me for more than just my art. We were living together in a matter of weeks. Talking about getting married.'

Yep. It was jealousy.

'He really wanted to help my career but he said that the kind of work I did—the flowers and cats and everything—was craft more than art. I needed to try something more contemporary. Edgier.'

Nic snorted. The man was an idiot. Had he not really looked at Zanna's paintings? Could he not appreciate how they could make people feel? Not that he knew anything much about art but surely the emotional impact was what mattered?

'It didn't feel right,' Zanna continued quietly. 'But this was my best friend and my fiancé who were trying to persuade me and I was in love so, of course, I trusted them. I let them push me in a direction I would never have chosen for myself and they pushed hard. I spent months working on a collection for an exhibition. Huge paintings. I must have gone to every old cemetery in London to choose the gravestones I based the work around.'

'Gravestones?' Nic's jaw dropped. 'You had a theme of death in your work?'

'Pretty much.' Zanna shrugged. 'It was edgy. Dark. Art, not craft.'

Nic thought of the rich colours in Zanna's paintings. The warmth. The feeling of movement and life captured in those sketches of the cats.

'They didn't know you very well, did they?'

Zanna's breath came out in a huff. 'Maybe they knew me very well. Maybe the campaign had never been about getting my career as an artist off the ground.' She shook her head. 'I'm not sure I really believe they set out to destroy me. Maybe it was a game that took on a life of its own. Or maybe it came from a subconscious need to get me out of the way. Anyway—' her voice became harsh '—it worked. They got what they wanted out of it.'

'Which was?'

'Each other, of course. The humiliation of the awful reviews my exhibition got was only part of it. I went home after a particularly horrible day to find Simon and Brie in bed together.'

'Merde...' Nic wanted to find this Simon idiot and ruin him. The way he'd tried to ruin Zanna. 'So that was why you left London?'

She nodded. 'I came home to the one person I knew I could trust absolutely. To the place I felt safe.'

Her refuge. He'd known there was something huge behind her use of that particular word. It had been that glimpse of her vulnerability that had touched something unexpected deep within him. Had been the catalyst for everything that had filled the time they'd had together since.

And he was expecting her to pick that refuge up and shake it in the hope of keeping something so precious safe. He was asking her to trust him when he wasn't even being entirely honest with her.

He could see something in himself in that moment that he wasn't proud of and the sensation was even more unpleasant than any twinge of jealousy. He'd had moments in his life when he'd hated himself and this took him back to feeling inadequate. Totally powerless. Angry instead of sad that he was losing something— no, some*one*—precious to him.

He tightened his grip on Zanna's hands. Held her gaze. If he could put this right, he might know that it was possible to do more than let her know it was okay to trust someone. He might discover that it was possible to be a better person himself and escape from a legacy that he'd thought would always haunt him. But he'd gotten in so deep—how could he even start to fix things without doing more damage? If Zanna thought she had misplaced her trust again, would she hide behind a protective barrier for the rest of her life?

She deserved better than that. How could you truly love someone if complete trust was missing? She deserved the chance to give her love without reservation and the man who was lucky enough to win that love deserved to know all of Zanna because she was so special. Unique.

'I need to take Pete out to see the land,' he said slowly. 'But that doesn't mean I'm trying to push you in a direction you don't want to go. If you decide you don't want to do this, that's fine.'

He meant every word. He might have the power to make sure he got what he wanted here but if it was at the expense of abusing the trust he was asking Zanna to put in him then he would back off. He would find another way to create a memorial to his parents.

Zanna nodded. 'I'll try and get hold of Maggie and talk to her about this. See how she feels.'

The timing of Maggie's phone call couldn't have been better.

Nic had been gone for more than two hours and Zanna had been pacing, her mind darting back and forth over a confusing spectrum.

Nic was nothing like Simon. He wasn't trying to change her into someone she wasn't. He was offering to help secure the place where she was herself most of all. He *got* her work. Unconditionally. It didn't matter a damn to him if the people who knew about art dismissed it as craft.

If she went ahead with this new plan, she would have a studio in an idyllic location that would be safe to live in for ever. With a business that could support her even if she never had the courage to try selling her work.

And he'd been right. He wasn't pushing her into agreeing with his idea. He'd backed off completely to give her space to think about it. Filled that space with the reassurance that it was safe to trust him, in fact.

To love him?

He wasn't Simon and he'd made her feel amazing things again. She would only hurt herself if she let Simon's legacy destroy something this beautiful and, if she let that happen this time, she could be setting a precedent that meant she would never truly trust anyone again.

She wanted it to happen. Both the house relocation and possibly finding a relationship that was strong enough to overcome the obvious logistical problems like living on different sides of the world, but it was terrifying to be getting this close when so much could go wrong.

What if Nic didn't feel the same way about what they'd found with each other?

What if Pete had found something about the potential site that was going to make it not doable or too expensive?

What if Maggie flatly refused to entertain the idea of such a radical sideways move to save the house?

Maybe it wasn't surprising that she burst into tears the moment she heard her aunt's voice on the phone.

Of course Maggie knew exactly the right things to say until Zanna calmed down enough to start talking. And then she listened without interrupting, other than to encourage her, as Zanna poured out everything she needed to say. Her voice was choked with tears when she told her aunt about the trees and it wobbled when she relayed the information that the council's decision to enforce the sale could be imminent.

'But Pete says it's lucky the trees have been killed,' she finished, 'because otherwise we couldn't even think about shifting it. And Nic says that the spirit of the house is about the people, not the place it's sitting, but…this is so huge, Maggie. How do I know that I can trust him?'

'You need to listen to your heart, darling. It will tell you all you need to know. You had your doubts about Simon right from the start, didn't you? You couldn't understand why he'd chosen you. You felt you had to change to deserve him. He's the one who needed to change. He didn't deserve *you*.'

A smile tugged at Zanna's lips for the first time in this conversation. Nic didn't want her to change. He wanted her to be safe to be herself. This whole plan was about protecting the things that were most important to her.

Her smile grew. 'Oh, Maggie—you should see the land that he's found for sale. It's just out of town and there's a lake and a forest and—and it's all *so* gorgeous. There's an old stable block that could become the shop and tea rooms. You'd love it.'

'*You* love it, darling, and that's all that matters.'

'It's not just up to me. This was your house long before I came to share it. It's your business. This has to be your decision and whatever you decide, I'll support you, you know that.'

'I know. So don't be upset when I tell you what I've decided, will you?'

A prickle of fear sent a shock wave down Zanna's spine. She was going to veto the project?

'I've decided to stay here,' Maggie said softly. 'Dimitry's asked me to marry him.'

'*What?* Oh, my God…' Zanna had to back up against the wall to find some support and she still found herself sinking to a crouch. '*Maggie…* You've only just met him. You can't possibly be sure about something that huge.'

'Oh, darling…' There was laughter in her aunt's voice. 'I've waited my whole life to find this. Do you think I didn't recognise it instantly? The only thing I wasn't sure of was whether Dimitry felt the same way. When it's right, you just know… Well, I did anyway. I have had a lot of practice in reading people.'

'Oh…' Zanna was closer to tears now than she had been in talking about the trees. A roller-coaster of emotions was going at full speed in her head and her heart. Happiness that Maggie had found the love of her life. Sadness that they were going to be living so far apart and that the closeness of their relationship would inevitably change. Jealousy, even, that there was someone else who would be Maggie's first priority. And running beneath all those dips and swoops were the rails of something that felt like…hope?

That Maggie was right? That there were no rules about how long it should take to know if you'd met the love of your life?

That what she'd found with Nic could be *real*…

'I gave you power of attorney, my love, and now I'm giving you more than that. The house is yours to do whatever you want to do with it. All I ask is that you take care of those cats of ours and keep the things you'll know I want to come back for safe. Now...' Even on the end of a phone line, half a world away and without the benefit of the card ritual, Maggie seemed to be able to read her mind. 'Tell me all about this Nic.'

Zanna was smiling again. 'He's French, Maggie. His full name is Dominic Brabant...'

'Brabant?' Maggie sounded startled. 'Where have I heard that name before? Oh, no...it couldn't be... Or maybe it could...'

'Here it is.' Nic pulled the folded sheet of paper from an inside pocket of his leather jacket. 'A formal estimate of the cost of shifting the house and repositioning it and a pretty generous estimate of what we think the costs of complete renovation would be.'

Was it his imagination or was Zanna sitting curiously still at the kitchen table, her fingers resting gently around the stem of a crystal glass? An open bottle of wine was beside the flickering candelabra, an empty glass beside it. Nic raised an eyebrow as he shed his jacket and her half-smile was an invitation so he poured himself a glass and sat down. He unfolded the sheet of paper and pushed it closer to Zanna.

'We got it printed out at the business centre in the airport lounge. And I've added the asking price of the land as well. See?'

'Good grief.' Zanna touched the paper as if she couldn't believe what she was seeing. 'That's nearly two million dollars.'

Nic covered her hand with his own. 'That's why I'm going to offer you three million for this property.'

This was the first step in putting things right. To make sure that Zanna understood that the dream solution he had presented was possible. That life would be secure in the future for both herself and the aunt she clearly adored.

The next step would be some honesty.

The silence that followed was unnerving. So was the way Zanna was looking at him. The way she slid her hand out from beneath his so very carefully. As if he'd done something unforgiveable.

'Why, Nic?'

'What do you mean?'

'Why would you offer me so much? The last registered valuation for this place was way less than half of that. The last offer Prime Property came up with was only six hundred thousand. Why do *you* want it so much?'

There was something in her tone that told him the game was up. That the opportunity to be voluntarily honest had been lost. His mouth suddenly dry, Nic took a long swallow of his wine.

'I've been talking to Maggie,' Zanna told him.

'Oh… She's not happy about the idea, then?'

The shake of Zanna's head dismissed his response as irrelevant. 'Was your mother's name Elise?'

CHAPTER EIGHT

IF HE WAS SHOCKED, he was hiding it well.

There was, in fact, a softening in his eyes that looked curiously like joy.

'Maggie remembers her?'

It made it worse that Nic seemed happy to have been found out. It was rubbing salt into what felt like a very raw wound.

How could he? Just a breath after she'd bared her soul and told him about how devastating Simon and Brie's betrayal had been. How hard it was for her to trust anyone's motives.

He wasn't even considering how she might be feeling right now but maybe he'd realise if she kept talking. Surely the strain in her voice was obvious?

'She said she was very beautiful, with long dark hair, but she was very shy because she thought she didn't speak English very well. And she didn't need anyone else in her life, anyway, because she totally adored her husband.'

The way she could have adored Nic. Not that he had any idea that she'd been ready to give him her whole heart. Her trust.

She couldn't go there now. No way.

Stupidly, though, her heart hadn't caught up with what her head was telling her in no uncertain terms.

And Nic was oblivious. He was hanging onto every word she spoke. This was important to him. Far more important than picking up on the sense of betrayal Zanna was fighting with because he hadn't told her about any of it.

It was a real effort to keep her voice steady. 'She remembers that she was a brilliant musician and she gave piano lessons to local children. She could sing beautifully too and your father played the guitar and she would hear them at night, singing French love songs in the garden.'

And how easy would it have been to hear that when it was coming from the garden right next door? From the people who'd lived in one of the small cottages that had been removed to make the public park.

His eyes were so dark. They caught the candlelight just then. Because of the moisture of unshed tears? The accusation that had unmistakeably laced her last words seemed to have gone as undetected as how upset she was.

'They had a baby they called Dommi. Maggie said she'd never seen such a happy little family.'

He looked away from her and his mouth tightened. Was it painful to hear this?

Good. Why should she be the only one suffering here?

'You said you were taken back to France when you were six years old.'

A single nod but Nic didn't say anything.

'You didn't tell me it was because your mother got evicted from her cottage because she couldn't manage her rent. That your father had been killed in a tragic accident at his work a year or more before that.'

'No.' The words were raw. 'I didn't tell you that.'

Her heart made her want to reach out and touch him because she knew he needed comfort. Her head made her throw an even bigger verbal spear.

'It's a bit of a coincidence that the historical protection society sent you to evaluate this house, isn't it?'

There was an accusation in her tone that grated. Zanna had no idea what fragile ground she was treading on here. How intrusive it felt to let someone else into this part of his life. To trust someone enough to share any of this story. And it was being forced on him before he was ready.

There was anger to be found there. Nobody had managed to force him to do anything once he'd been old enough to gain control of his own life.

But she knew already. The protective walls around that hidden place had been breached.

And she had trusted him, hadn't she? She'd opened her heart and shared the pain of the life she'd thought she'd had in London imploding.

Dommi. He hadn't heard that name since he was twelve years old and his mother had died. He'd become Dominic with the formalities of going into care and he'd chosen Nic when he was sixteen and found work that enabled him to become independent. To take control and steer his life towards a place where he'd never have to feel that kind of pain any more.

Nobody knew. Not even Pete—his closest friend—knew more than sketchy details of his background. And Pete had no idea why he'd decided to take on this project, although he'd guessed straight off that he'd been hiding something.

'I wasn't sent here to evaluate the house. I never told you that.'

'You knew that was what I thought. You didn't tell me the truth.'

Nic closed his eyes. 'No.'

This was it. The destruction of trust. He wasn't going to come out of this feeling like a better person. He was going to think less of himself. How on earth had this happened? He'd spent so many years building up defences against precisely this and somehow this woman had slipped under his skin and had the power to leave him unprotected and vulnerable.

'Why not, Nic?' The faint wobble in her words cut straight through his heart. 'Did you think I wouldn't understand?'

His eyes snapped open. Was it possible that she *did* understand? That she could forgive him for the deception?

She'd been through her own childhood trauma, hadn't she? She'd been lucky to have found a loving home so she couldn't know how soul destroying it was to be handed around like an unwanted parcel, but she did know what it was like to lose your parents.

'Do you remember what it was like when your parents were killed, Zanna? How you felt?'

She nodded slowly. 'It was like the world had ended. I was lost and very, very frightened.'

'It was like that for my mother and me when Papa was killed. And my world *had* ended as I'd known it. Maman couldn't get over it. She got sick. The children who came for lessons went away. She took me back to her home country but there was no way she could find work. She got really sick, with cancer that went undiagnosed until far too late. I think she wanted to die, so that she could be with Papa again.'

'Oh…*Nic*…' Zanna could hear the bewildered child behind those words. Feel the pain of thinking you couldn't make things better. That you weren't good enough or something. Her heart was definitely winning the battle over her head now and the urge to comfort was getting overwhelming. Being fuelled by an urge to forgive? 'How old were you when she died?'

'Twelve.'

'So you got taken into care?'

His nod was terse. He wasn't going to talk about those years. Ever.

'I'd already learned to stop remembering when life had been good because it only made things worse. I got very, very good at it. I hadn't even thought about any of it for years and years. Until I saw this house again. The next-door house that had the scary lady living in it.'

That brought a wry smile to Zanna's lips. 'Yeah… I thought she was pretty scary at first, too. Larger than life, that's for sure. Nothing like anybody I'd ever known.'

Zanna was nothing like anybody Nic had ever known. After watching the play of emotions on her face he had to focus again on what he needed to say.

'I did come to New Zealand for an entirely different reason,' he admitted, 'and the memories were hard to handle because I hadn't expected them. I'm ready now. To remember.' He swallowed hard. 'To honour those memories.' He met Zanna's gaze. 'I couldn't share them. They were too raw. Too personal. And…I didn't know you.'

'But you do now.'

'I do.' Her eyes were so soft. He hadn't seen an expression like that since…since his mother had told him how much she loved him. The squeeze in his chest was so painful he had to look away.

'Would you have told me—if I hadn't found out?'

'I was going to tell you tonight. I couldn't *not* tell you. Not after you told me about what happened in London. I…don't want to hurt you, Zanna.'

He was starting to gain the skill of reading her. He could see the flicker in her eyes that told him she could hear the truth in his words. The softening of something in her face that let him know that trust might have been bruised but it was still intact. Just.

He could certainly feel the tension ebbing rapidly.

'What do you want to do to honour those memories? Is that why you want to buy this property?'

'Yes.' Nic took a deep breath and then he told her about the vision for the music school. How it would sit beside the river and the park and look like it was meant to be there. How the sound of music would drift across the tiny patch of the earth where his parents had been so happy. Where he'd been so happy. He wanted to put a beautiful bench seat in the park with their names on it so that people could sit and listen to the music. He told her about the gallery he wanted to put in the foyer of the school to honour Rata House.

He wasn't sure at what point he'd taken hold of Zanna's hands. Or maybe she'd taken hold of his. It didn't matter. She listened to every word and there were tears on her cheeks when he finally stopped talking.

'That's so beautiful, Nic. We were fighting so hard to save this house partly because we knew that if it went in the future when we weren't here, something horrible might take its place—like a huge hotel or another apartment block like next door. But your music school…that's exactly what should be here. Oh, Maggie will love that.' A smile broke through the tears. 'Maybe fate kept us fighting just so that it would be here for you.'

It was hard to swallow past the lump in his throat. Hard to breathe against the constriction in his chest. And Nic had to blink hard to clear the prickle behind his eyes.

She *did* understand.

And he knew he could love her for that.

This was a gift. Did it even matter that he hadn't told her about owning the apartment block?

Yes, his head said. It could change everything.

No, his heart said. It could change everything.

Trust would not survive a second blow. Not before it had had time to get stronger. Maybe he should have told her that was what had brought him here in the first place instead of clouding it with a vague reference to an entirely different reason. If she'd asked what that reason had been, he would have told her.

But it was too late now. Saying anything else might dilute this incredible feeling of being understood. Of having someone beside him. Sharing his dream because she understood exactly why it was so important.

Or was it too late? If she understood as well as she seemed to, she would see how the purchase of the apartment block had been the catalyst for all of this and it could be dismissed along with the deception of having let her assume he'd come onto her property on behalf of the city council.

But there was a new light in Zanna's eyes now. Excitement.

'How soon can we start the ball rolling?'

'We can get the papers drawn up on Monday.' How much easier was it to buy into that excitement and silence the argument going on between his head and his heart? 'No…I've got legal contacts. Someone will be happy to work on a Sunday if they get paid well enough.'

'I'll call our solicitor,' Zanna said. 'Keith Watson. We've known him for years and years and he's helped us a lot. Given us free advice every time we've faced trouble from the council or needed to know how to handle harassment from the Scallions. He loves this house. He'll be thrilled to know it's going to be reborn.'

'Once the agreement for sale and purchase is finalised, we can give Pete the green light. If we make an immediate possession date, we can get started as soon as you're ready.'

'What am I going to do with all the stuff in the house and shop? It'll all have to come out for the removal process.'

'We'll find a storage facility. Get packers in.'

But Zanna shook her head. 'I'll need to sort everything. Maggie's going to want a lot of her things and they're precious. Like those antique instruments. I'd want to pack and shift those myself to make sure they're safe. I promised her I'd keep them safe.'

'We'll make sure they are.' The excitement was gaining force. Bubbling between them—the future so bright with the potential for amazing things to happen.

The conviction that he could do anything with Zanna by his side took Nic by surprise. He'd walked alone for ever and this feeling of shared anticipation was something new. It felt like he'd put a magnifying glass on the satisfaction he'd always felt when a new challenge was falling into place. How much greater would the joy be when it was complete?

He wanted Zanna by his side, then, too. He wanted to open the door of her restored house to take her for a tour. He wanted her holding his hand as they cut the ribbon for the opening of the Brabant Music Academy.

He couldn't imagine *not* wanting Zanna.

It was as simple as that.

And he felt like he was looking into a reflection of how he was feeling as he gazed into Zanna's eyes.

Conversation had died. Tomorrow would be soon enough to start talking through the thousands of details. Tonight was for celebrating what was going to be achieved.

Together.

Words wouldn't be enough, anyway. There was only one way that Nic could show Zanna how much it meant to him to have someone sharing this part of his soul.

Zanna couldn't tell where her body left off and Nic's started as he rose from the table to lead her upstairs. Maybe that was because she had started to move at exactly the same moment, with exactly the same destination in mind.

Any sense of betrayal had long since been extinguished. Of course he'd been unable to let a stranger into a place that he'd kept hidden for so long, even to himself. How could she blame him for taking an opportunity to protect that privacy when she'd made it so easy?

But he'd invited her in now.

He trusted her.

Maybe, this time, she could really trust her own instincts. Trust *him*. Trust the inherited wisdom that gen-
erations of seers had given Maggie.

When it was right, you just *knew*.

CHAPTER NINE

THE NEXT FEW DAYS passed in a blur.

Looking back, Zanna knew she would remember only bits of it but they were memories that she would always treasure.

The night together after he'd told her so much about what had made him into the person he was. How being invited into such a personal space had made her love him so much more.

The way Nic had looked when the contract had been signed and that first, major step had been taken. Not that she'd agreed to be paid so much more than the property was worth. Two million was enough. He could put the rest into the music school.

The surprise of discovering how well Nic could play a guitar when they were packing up Maggie's old instruments. Listening to him singing her a French love song late at night, out in the courtyard, with the chiminea and candelabra providing all the warmth and light they could need.

Knowing that this was where she always needed to be. By Nic's side.

She'd started some packing in the shop now, too. Boxes of stock were being sent to join others in the storage facility they'd hired. There was a notice on the door explaining why Spellbound would have to close in the near future but she was happy to assure customers that the business would start again before too long in an even better place.

The cats were unsettled by all the unusual activity and seemed to be always underfoot, seeking reassurance.

'It's all okay,' Zanna kept telling them. 'I know it's a worry but you guys are going to be so happy in the country. There'll be trees to climb and lots of mice to catch. You probably won't even want your tinned food any more.'

They didn't seem to want it very much at the moment. On Tuesday night, Zanna tapped the spoon against the bowl but there was no streak of black coming from any direction.

'Where are they?'

Nic glanced up from his laptop. After meetings that morning with the council planning department to apply for various permits and checking out storage facilities, he'd started preliminary plans for the music school and had been absorbed for the rest of the afternoon while Zanna had been busy in the shop. 'I haven't seen them for hours. Not even Merlin.'

'That's weird. I'd better check that I didn't lock them in the shop by mistake. They were hanging around when I was packing in there earlier.'

The cats had, indeed, been accidentally locked in the shop. Maybe they'd been asleep on the pile of clothing behind the stack of boxes Zanna had filled that day. It was Merlin who jumped into her arms as she opened the door but Marmite and Mystic glued themselves to her ankles, competing for attention with plaintive cries of having been imprisoned.

Zanna was laughing as she tried to get down the steps without the cats tripping her up but the laughter died the moment she felt the hairs on the back of her neck prickle.

She wasn't alone.

The shop was dark and empty behind her. The front door of the house was open not far away but Nic was in the kitchen at the back and probably too far away and too focused on what he was doing to hear her even if she screamed.

Maybe she was imagining things. The light of the day was almost gone and the wind had picked up so the shadows cast by the massive, dying trees and the sound of creaking branches was spooky.

Then she looked beyond the trees. The streetlights would come on at any moment now and, when they did, the figure standing beside the lamppost just outside the gate would be instantly obvious.

A male figure. Just standing there. Even without being able to see him clearly, she knew he was staring at the house.

At her.

A tourist out for a walk, she told herself. Someone had stopped to look at the curiosity the house had become.

Except that a tourist wouldn't feel like such a threat. They wouldn't be standing with such…nonchalance? And they certainly wouldn't emit a sound like low laughter. Merlin stiffened in her arms and responded with a hiss.

'Evening, Miss Zelensky.' He made her name sound like an insult. 'How's it going?'

The cats at her feet were gone in a streak, heading

for the safety of the house. Merlin's claws dug painfully into Zanna's arms as he launched himself in the wake of his siblings. Following them herself might have been a sensible option but it wasn't the way she responded to a threat. Instead, she became very still. Centring herself and gathering her strength.

'Blake. What are you doing here?'

'Happened to be in town. Just wanted a look.'

'You've looked. You can go now.'

The man Maggie had always referred to as the junior scorpion took a step closer. The rusty, wrought-iron gate was permanently ajar. Another step and he would be on the brick pathway.

'There's nothing here for you. The property's sold.' She couldn't help the note of satisfaction that coated her words. 'To someone else.'

'I know.'

Zanna felt that prickle in her spine again. A premonition of danger. She tried to shake it off. Prime Property couldn't threaten them any longer. Or was that why Blake was here? Was he angry that they'd lost their long battle?

He didn't seem angry. There was a smugness in those words.

'It's none of your business.'

He laughed again. 'You sure about that?' He turned, as if intending to walk away. 'Tell Nic I'll give him a call tomorrow. We need to talk.'

The prickle turned into a chill that sent ice into Zanna's veins. This time it was her moving to narrow the gap between them.

'Why would I do that? What makes you think he would want to have anything to do with the likes of you?'

Blake turned back. She could see the gleam of his teeth as he smiled.

'We've been partners for years, sweetheart. Dad and I were only too delighted to get rid of having to deal with you and your aunt and obviously he managed to do what we couldn't. In record time, too. What was so attractive about what he had to offer, Suzanna?' The tone was a sneer. 'As if I couldn't guess.'

'I don't believe you. Get out, Blake. I don't ever want to see you or your father again. Set foot on this property and I'll call the police. You could still be charged with malicious damage after what you did to our trees.'

'We could sue you for malicious damage right back. You've got no idea of the grief you've caused us, sweetheart. It's lucky that the heart attack didn't kill Dad. At least he'll get the pleasure of seeing you gone. Of seeing this house knocked flat.' He took another long glance upwards. 'Good riddance, I say. Good on you, Nic.'

This time when he turned he kept moving. The streetlights came on in time for Zanna to see his silhouette fade as he walked past the apartment block.

No. She couldn't believe that Nic would be in partnership with the Scallions. He would tell her how ridiculous the very idea was as soon as he heard about it. She started walking towards the front door of the house but then stopped.

It made sense.

Nic had said that his career was usually about luxury international coastal resorts—exactly the kind of developments that Prime Property was famous for.

He had hidden his connection to the property from the moment he'd walked in. Sure, she knew the story about his background was true, thanks to Maggie, but didn't that make it worse? He had come here with a single purpose in mind and perhaps the motive of knowing even a hint of association with Prime Property would have made him unwelcome to set foot in the house had been stronger than a desire to keep his background private.

And he'd gone so much further than merely setting foot in her house…

Oh…*God*…

Had she been played? Sucked into going in a direction she'd never intended? The way Simon and Brie had persuaded her to change her art? What if she was heading for an even bigger fall that she'd never be able to come back from? That she'd trusted someone enough to reveal her humiliation only to find that history was repeating itself?

Her mind raced on to imagine the worst. What if it turned out that the house fell apart when they tried to shift it? It would only be her loss, wouldn't it? They'd still have their patch of land. *Two* patches of land. Enough for the biggest hotel in town, and maybe that was the real agenda. Maybe Nic's connection to this property had just been a fortunate coincidence. That the music school would be deemed uneconomic or something before it got past the planning stage.

No. The things Nic had told her were true. They'd come straight from his heart. She *believed* him.

She'd believed Simon, too.

Maybe her instincts couldn't be trusted.

Or maybe she'd been ignoring the warnings those instincts had issued. She could hear an echo of his voice. Of hers as well, during that card reading.

'Sometimes you have to let go of an old life in order to take the opportunity of a new and fulfilling one.'

'Something I've always lived by... Do you?'

There had been a moment of warning she hadn't ignored, even then.

He may not be who he seems to be. Take care...

It was Nic who'd spotted the holes in the trees.

And who just happened to have a mate who specialised in relocating old houses. She'd noticed those odd glances between the two men that day, hadn't she?

But it had all worked, hadn't it? She'd signed legal contracts. No wonder Blake had sounded so smug.

If only Maggie was here, Zanna thought desperately. She felt so alone. She could be on the point of losing everything. Losing the house would be bad enough but she had the horrible feeling she was about to lose Nic as well.

Merlin jumped onto Nic's lap but he pushed him off as the tail cut his view of the computer screen in half. Offended, the cat started washing himself but Nic didn't notice. He'd finally got the line just right. The curve of the building as it echoed the line of the river. The software program he was using allowed him to layer the plan on top of the aerial photographs of the area that he'd already removed both Rata House and the apartment block from. He could circle it now and get an idea of how it sat from both the street side and the river side.

He heard Zanna finally come back but still didn't turn his head.

'Come and look at this. I think I've nailed it.'

It was the silence that finally broke his concentration. Nothing like the quiet serenity that Zanna was capable of generating sometimes. This was a heavy silence. Ominous. When he looked up and saw her face, he uttered a low oath.

'What's wrong? What's happened?'

Had one of the cats been run over or something? Merlin was sitting nearby, licking a paw and then scraping it over his face. And, yes…there were two cats still engrossed in eating.

Had she had some bad news about her aunt? Surely someone must have died to make her look like that. So shocked. Drained of any vestige of colour.

'Are you part of Prime Property, Nic?' Her voice was flat. 'A partner?'

'*No.*' His chair scraped on the wooden floor as he pushed it back to get to his feet. 'Hell, no…' He started to walk towards Zanna but she held her hand up and it felt like he'd hit a force field. He stopped in his tracks.

'I just found Blake Scallion standing outside the gate. He said he'd call you tomorrow because you *needed to talk*.' He could see Zanna's throat move as she swallowed. '*He* said you'd been partners for years. I didn't believe him but then I thought…it could be true. Maybe you had been sent to *deal* with the little problem that Maggie and I represented.'

'I'm not a partner of Prime Property. Yes, I've worked with them. They've used my designs to develop coastal resorts. The way other property development companies use my expertise all over the world for all sorts of projects. That was why I was in New Zealand in the first place. They've bought a huge block of land on the Hibiscus Coast and they want me on board to get another resort off the ground.'

This was the explanation he should have given her long ago but it was too late now. Way too late.

'But you've bought this property.' Zanna's expression was frozen. She wasn't prepared to believe anything he was going to say to try and explain. 'The one that Prime Property's been trying to get hold of for the last ten years. They still own the one next door. Another *coincidence*?'

'They don't own next door any more. I couldn't have started the project for the music school unless I had both properties.'

'So *you* own the apartment block now?' A wash of colour stained Zanna's cheeks. Anger…? Or maybe it was relief. He could defuse this whole situation if he took the opportunity she was offering and let her believe that he'd approached the Scallions to sell the apartment block only after he'd purchased Rata House. 'When did you buy that—or is that why Blake wants to talk to you tomorrow?'

Nic closed his eyes. Deception by omission was one thing. An outright lie was unacceptable. Yes, telling the truth could change everything but he had no choice. And maybe he needed a leap of faith. It would only be a glimmer of hope but she might understand—the way she seemed to have understood everything else about him. He opened his eyes.

'I bought the apartment block ten days ago. Before I came here.'

He had to let the silence extend as Zanna processed what he'd said. He could feel his heart thumping and it skipped a beat completely when she finally spoke again because her voice sounded so tightly controlled. Cold.

'So you came here knowing that you couldn't go ahead with your plans unless you persuaded me to sell?'

He didn't need to say anything. She could see the truth in his eyes.

And it hurt so much more than she'd tried to prepare herself for.

'Is there really going to be a music school, Nic, or was that part of the grand plan? Get me on side with the sob story of your unhappy childhood? Pete said you're good at making money. Wouldn't a really *big* apartment block or a hotel or something be more in your line of work?'

She could see that her accusation had hit home but the flash of shock in his face was quickly masked. A barrier was going up between them. A huge, impenetrable barrier.

That hurt, too.

A *sob story*? Had he really thought she understood? He'd let her into the most private part of his soul and she was dismissing it as being some sort of manipulative device.

Nic could feel his head taking over completely from his heart. Putting him in a professional mode. This was what he'd come here for, wasn't it? A business deal. And he'd succeeded. It should be enough.

Clearly, it would have to be enough.

'You're getting what you wanted out of it, aren't you? Yes, I wanted the land but when I met you and saw how you felt about the house I knew it shouldn't be simply demolished. You were right in wanting to save it but you wouldn't have won in the long run when you can't afford to even maintain it where it is. I came up with a solution that gave us both what we wanted. I made that solution possible. Do you think you could have done this without my contacts? Like Pete? Like the estate agent who told me about land that wasn't even on the market yet?'

'You were holding all the cards. You were hiding the truth. Did you just happen to spot those holes in the trees or did you already know they were there? Had you been in on those plans, too? *Years* ago?'

'No. I had no idea Prime Property had any interest in this place until I saw a file on Donald's desk two weeks ago. The picture of a house I could never forget. They have no idea why I wanted to take over the project. I haven't even told Pete what I've got in mind here. You're the only person who knows that. Knows why it matters.'

The only person who understood that he was chasing a memory. Trying to catch and preserve a fragment of how it had felt to be loved and safe. Surely she could remember how it had felt to be in each other's arms that night? That they were the only two people in the world who could share the pain of that particular loss and the joy of turning it into something meaningful?

Zanna couldn't miss the intensity of his words. She knew what Nic was trying to tap into—that shared vision of honouring both their pasts with the music school and its gallery. The trust he'd won from her by sharing his secrets.

But it wasn't going to work this time. Trust wasn't something you could keep breaking and then gluing back together. This time she was going to protect herself more effectively. And it wasn't a total disaster, was it? Maybe she wasn't going to lose the house. She might end up with that dream property in the green belt, with her house and the business intact and a place that could inspire her real work with her art.

Was that enough to make up for what she was definitely losing here?

That trust? The ability to love somebody with her entire heart and soul?

He'd come here with the same agenda that the Scal-

lions had always had. To get her out so that they could
have what they wanted. He'd lied to her. More than that…

Shame and anger curdled the grief of loss.

'Do you often have to sleep with potential sellers,
Nic?' It was hard to force the words out because every
one of them hurt. 'Get them to fall in love with you so
that they'll be only too happy to fall into line?'

That shattered the barrier for a heartbeat. Good
grief…had he really not had *any* idea how she felt about
him?

Did he think she'd been playing some kind of game,
too? *Acting?*

'Bit silly of me to persuade you to offer less, wasn't
it?' Zanna finally broke the distance she'd held between
them. She walked to the table and picked up the sheaf
of papers that was her copy of the sale and agreement
purchase. She ripped it in half.

She only had to lean a little to snap shut the lid of
Nic's laptop.

'Game over,' she said calmly. 'Get out, Nic.'

And then she turned and walked out of the room.

Into the hallway beneath the sunflower painting, but
she didn't let herself remember the way Nic's reaction
to seeing it had made her feel. Had mattered so much.

She couldn't trust anything she felt any more and,
as if demanding recognition, there were overwhelming
emotions boiling up inside. The pain of betrayal. The
grief of loss. The shame of being deceived. Broken love.
All competing with a desperate desire not to believe any
of them but to trust how she felt about Nic. Any one of
them was powerful enough to make her shake like this.

She had to keep moving so she didn't sink into a quiv-
ering heap that Nic would have to step around on his way

out of the house. She ran up the wide stairs and still she kept going. There was only one place she could go to find some sort of release from the storm. A refuge that would allow her to clear her head and start to think instead of being battered by this crashing emotional surf.

She slammed the door at the top of the spiral staircase behind her.

And then she locked it.

CHAPTER TEN

GUNNING THE ENGINE of the bike was a satisfying echo to the anger heating Nic's blood. Opening the throttle as soon as he escaped the city's speed limits and leaning into the blast of cold air finally cooled that heat enough for the shock waves to stop blasting him from all directions.

He was miles out of the city now. In a small town whose main street boasted a motel, a Chinese takeaway restaurant and a liquor store.

Perfect. A bed for the night, something to eat and a bottle of even halfway decent Scotch and he could sort this whole mess out. He could start defining exactly what was making him so damn angry and that was a very necessary first step before he decided what he was going to do next. Anger had no place in making rational decisions.

An hour or two later and being dismissed by Zanna Zelensky in the wake of her ripping up their contract was top of the list of what was making his blood boil.

The knee-jerk reaction was that *il n'avait pas d'importance*—it made no difference. It was only a copy of a legally binding contract and his solicitor held the original. He still owned the property in Rata Avenue.

Yes, it would be time consuming and expensive to have to take it to court but he would win. He would still get exactly what he'd come to Christchurch for.

But it did make a difference, didn't it? Pouring another shot of whisky into the cheap tumbler, Nic paced the soulless motel room.

The satisfaction of achieving exactly what he'd set out to achieve would always be tainted by the dispute. The planned gallery to pay homage to Rata House would be nothing more than a victory crow—an insult to Zanna.

The knock-on effects on his career were enough to anger him all on their own. He was going to have to delay meetings on projects that were starting to line up. A boutique lakeside hotel in Geneva. A warehouse redevelopment on the banks of the Thames in London. The ambitious resort planned for the stretch of beach on the Hibiscus Coast north of Auckland in New Zealand that had been the reason he'd come here for the talks with Prime Property two weeks ago.

Well…that wasn't going to happen now. He had no intention of working with the Scallions again. A short phone call to Donald was all it took to let him know that he couldn't continue to work with a company that resorted to underhanded and illegal tactics like poisoning protected trees. He left Donald in no doubt about how stupid his son had been to come here and try and put the boot in and gloat over the fact that Zanna's property had finally changed hands.

He didn't add that he would never forgive the fact that Blake had unwittingly managed to destroy the connection he'd found with Zanna because it was none of their business. But by the time he ended the call Nic knew he had identified the real core of his anger.

He couldn't win in the end on this one because he'd lost something that had nothing to do with business. Something huge. Yes, the land was the only real connection he still had with his parents and that almost forgotten life but, if that was all he had, there would only ever be memories of how special it had been. Fragments of emotion that would be fleeting echoes of how it had felt to have a home. To belong.

Pour aimer et être aimé.

To love and be loved.

When he was with Zanna, the feeling wasn't a memory. It was real. More than real because it held the magic of a promise that it could always be there. That place was irrelevant because that feeling of home and safety was to do with who Zanna was, not where she lived.

He didn't need a handful of cards spread out beneath a flickering candelabra to read his future if he lost what he'd found so recently. It might be full to the brim with professional satisfaction, public accolades and more money than he could ever spend, but on one level it would be meaningless.

That level had been safely locked away for as long as he could remember but it had been released now and it was too big and too shapeless to ever catch and restrain again.

He loved Zanna. It was as simple as that.

And hadn't she all but said that she'd fallen in love with him?

Do you often have to sleep with potential sellers, Nic? Get them to fall in love with you so that they'll be only too happy to fall into line?

With a groan, Nic reached for the bottle again and unscrewed the metal cap. Poised to pour another shot, he paused. His gaze shifted to the Formica bench of the kitchenette with its electric jug and sachets of probably dreadful coffee.

He let go of the bottle.

Strong coffee was what he needed now. And a bit more time before it was safe to hit the road again.

To go back to where he belonged.

With Zanna.

The house was no emptier than it had been ever since Maggie had set off for her journey of discovery weeks ago.

But it felt different.

Zanna could feel the cavern of that emptiness below her from the eyrie of her studio in the turret.

The spirit of joy the house had always contained was gone, destroyed by a tidal wave of anger and grief.

It was just a house in the end, wasn't it? Without the people, it was haunted by ghosts. Maggie's. Nic's. The ghost of the frightened child she had been when she'd come here and the broken person she'd been when she'd returned from London last year. Maybe the most unbearable ghost right now was the person she was when she was with Nic. The person she had wanted to be for the rest of her life.

She still needed to keep moving because, if she didn't, these emotions would suffocate her. Her hands moved of their own accord to select brushes and paints. The only available canvas was large but that was fine. She had something huge inside that needed to come out. She couldn't have consciously chosen a subject if she'd tried so she didn't spare a thought for a preliminary sketch or even a mental image of where she was headed. This was just an exercise to release some of her anguish. To channel it into a symbol of some kind, perhaps, so that she could then choose to either remove it from her life entirely or keep it as a reminder to make her future choices with more care.

The subject chose itself and it wasn't really a surprise to discover that it was going to be a portrait of Dominic Brabant. What was surprising was how well imprinted he was on her soul for the perfect shape of his face and hands and body to be emerging with such ease and precision. Cruel of her subconscious to pick the scene it had but she knew better than to mess with what was happening inside her head and her heart by trying to change what needed to be expressed.

And besides…this could quite possibly be the best painting she had ever done. As the minutes ticked into hours Zanna was aware of an excitement stealing into the turbulent mix of her emotions. It was a rare thing to find that her mind and hands and spirit were in synch enough to be producing something that felt so right from a creative point of view.

She had caught the moment perfectly and she had to blink away tears as she added the final touches to the work. The twilight of a late summer's evening. The flickering light of small logs burning in the chiminea and echoed by the candelabra on the small table. The posture and intensity of the man holding the guitar. She could almost feel the softness of the tousled waves of his hair. Hear the notes of those words of love in the most beautiful language of the world.

Feel the way those hands had touched and held her soul.

It hadn't all been an act, had it? An expert lover could have learned how to inflame a woman's desire by un-braiding her hair and touching her face as though his fingers wanted to know her features as intimately as his eyes did, but could passion be combined with such… tenderness if it was simply playing a role?

No. She didn't believe she had imagined that he felt as strongly as she did. She had felt the truth in that moment of silence when he'd admitted that he felt as emotionally unbalanced as she did.

But could she trust what she believed?

Given her track record, probably not.

Given how exhausted she was, having channelled an excess of energy into her painting, this wasn't the time to even try and decide what she could trust.

She had to sleep but the thought of going down to her own bed and sleeping alone only brought another wave of misery. Better to stay here and curl up on the antique chaise longue that had been donated to her studio when it had become too ratty to grace the formal living room downstairs. It would be softer than the floor and she was tired enough to consider that a viable option.

Zanna didn't need to leave the lights on to have the image she'd just painted as her last thought before she slipped into an exhausted slumber.

Without needing the adrenaline rush of speed to burn off anger, it took a lot longer to get back to the city.

Propping the bike on its stand, Nic pulled off his helmet and hung it over the handlebars, before turning to look at the silent silhouette of Rata House. It was completely dark from where he was standing. Hardly surprising when he checked his watch to find it was after three a.m.

Zanna would be sound asleep.

Would she be frightened by a knock on the door? He didn't want to frighten her.

Would she guess that he had come back because he couldn't stay away?

But she didn't know he loved her, did she? Would she even believe him when he told her?

Of course she'd been upset. He'd known how fragile that trust was—how it wouldn't survive an additional blow.

He'd hurt her and it was unbearable.

His feet took him, unbidden, through the wrought-iron gate and up the mossy, brick pathway. The stalk of a rough leaf, propelled by a stiff breeze, hit his cheek hard enough to sting and he could almost smell the decay of the dying trees as he veered towards the veranda of the main part of the house.

He peered through the stained-glass panels on either side of the front door, hoping to see a glimmer of light from the end of the hallway that led to the kitchen, but he could see nothing. He could still smell something, though. The musty, decayed smell of the trees seemed to be getting stronger and it was oddly pungent, as though some of those mysterious herbs in Zanna's shop were being burnt.

Sure enough, a glance towards the door of the shop entrance showed a flicker of light. The kind of light that candles would produce and Zanna was very fond of candles, wasn't she? He could remember how many of them had been burning on the counter that day he'd gone in to see her. And the way she'd held her hair back, out of danger, as she'd leaned in to blow them out.

Was she in the shop? Unpacking some of the stock, perhaps, because she believed the deal was off and she needed to reopen her business? He retraced his steps and went to knock on the shop door.

'It's only me,' he called, as he knocked. 'Nic. I need to talk to you, Zanna.'

The only response was the tapping of the 'Closed' sign on the glass of the door as it reverberated to his knock. There were stained-glass panels here, too and the candlelight was much stronger.

So was the smell.

The tendrils of smoke coming from the gap beneath the door were unmistakeable evidence that something was terribly wrong.

Spellbound was on fire.

'*Zanna*...' Nic pounded on the door with a clenched fist. He wrenched at the handle but the door was firmly locked.

Was she even inside the shop?

Down the steps again and Nic stared up at the house. Her bedroom was directly above the shop and below the turret room that contained her studio. Smoke rose and he'd heard somewhere that more people died of smoke inhalation than got burned to death in a fire.

Where was she?

The sound of a sharp crack and then a fizzing noise as though some flammable material had exploded came from within the shop and suddenly he could see the shape of flames through the coloured panels. The smoke gushed out and curled away into the night air.

Running, Nic made his way back to the house door.

He pulled out his phone and punched in the three digit emergency number.

'*Fire*,' he yelled. 'Number thirty-two, Rata Avenue. *Hurry*—there's someone inside the house.'

For a few seconds Nic made a panicked search for some kind of weapon he could use to break a window and get access to the house. A branch from one of the rata trees? The trees were virtually dead so it would be easy to break off a thick piece of wood.

Dying trees…water…the galvanised bucket. The connection took only a microsecond and it felt like Nic had the spare house key in his hand almost by the time he'd completed the thought process. Muscles in his jaw were bunched so tightly he could feel his teeth aching as he finally turned the key and shoved the door open.

The hallway was black. Even if he'd been able to locate a light switch it wouldn't have helped much but enough light was coming from behind to illuminate the thick smoke that was already obscuring half the sweep of the staircase. So much light Nic's head swivelled. Had the emergency services arrived without the use of any sirens?

No. To his horror, he saw that one of the glass panes in the bay window of the shop had blown out. It looked as though flames were hurling themselves into the night air, seeking fuel like some kind of famished, wild animal. The dry leaves and branches of one of the rata trees were close enough to provide exactly what was being sought. Spurts of flame were shooting upwards into the tree and expanding like a mushroom cloud. Illuminating the witch's hat of the turret and the dark windows beneath it.

Any thought of how dangerous it would be to go inside the house simply didn't occur to Nic. In that moment it wouldn't have mattered how quickly he might be overcome by smoke or whatever horrible fumes it might contain.

Zanna was in the house and nothing else mattered.

Nic bunched up the soft fabric of his T-shirt to try and make some protection to cover his mouth and nose. He ran into the smoke and took the stairs two at a time. The heat around him increased but there were no visible flames in here. Holding onto the carved newel post at the top of the stairs, he took a moment to orient himself.

Maggie's room. The bathroom. A spare bedroom. Zanna's room was two doors down on the right just before the spiral stairs that led to the turret. Directly over the shop and where the inferno was gathering pace. He pushed himself on. He had to take a breath and even through the bunched fabric he could taste the smoke and feel the heat and the inadequate level of oxygen the air contained.

But he was in her bedroom.

'Zanna? *Zanna*…' The effort to shout required another breath, which made him cough and draw more smoke into his lungs.

The bedroom was empty.

Smoke had now reached as far as the narrow spiral staircase and it felt thicker here than it had anywhere else. Of course it did. Smoke rose and this was the very top of the old house, in a direct vertical line from where the fire had started.

The door at the top of the stairs was closed. He had to feel for the handle. He turned it and pushed.

No…

The door was locked?

Why?

Nic banged on the wood. 'Zanna. *Zanna*… Are you in there?' She had to be in there because the door was bolted from the inside. 'There's a *fire*…'

He could hear the approaching wail of sirens now. He could hear the sound of glass breaking and then people shouting. What he couldn't hear was any sound from within the round room in the turret.

Zanna's room. Her refuge. This was where she would have gone when she couldn't bear to be in the same room as him, he just knew it.

Was she already unconscious from breathing in too much smoke?

Bracing himself, Nic gathered all the strength he could muster and slammed his shoulder against the door.

And then he did it again.

Zanna had never been so deeply asleep. So deeply drawn into the dream that had begun with the last image she'd seen before slipping into unconsciousness. She was in her courtyard garden, surrounded by the sound of the song Nic was singing as he plucked the strings of that old guitar. She was dancing by the light of the candelabra, wearing something soft and floaty—the soft velvet robe she'd been wearing the day Nic had first walked into Spellbound?

She could smell the aroma of the wood burning in the chiminea. Could feel its heat. She could even hear the words of the song Nic was singing. She knew they were in French but she could understand them so easily.

Ne me quitte pas…don't leave me…

She could hear her own name in the chorus. That was new…

Zanna…*Zanna*…

The dancing in her dream had to stop. The ground was shaking. As Zanna's mind was reluctantly dragged back into consciousness she pushed her eyelids open. Where was she?

She could make out the bare wooden floorboards that looked familiar enough but everything else was so hazy. She was surrounded by her paintings but they seemed obscured by a thick fog. The smell of the fog was weird and Zanna realised how short of breath she was. It was an effort to fill her lungs and when she tried, it was uncomfortable enough to make her cough. And that sucked more of the fog in and made her cough again even more harshly.

Nic heard the cough. The mix of relief that Zanna was in the room and fear that she might already be too overcome by the smoke somehow gave him the strength to summon a last burst of reserves. With this final punishing blow, the wood splintered around the doorhandle and Nic fell into the room, along with an enveloping cloud of thick, hot smoke.

He was on his knees but he could see the shape of Zanna, hunched on the floor beside the old couch. Pushing up with his arm sent a vicious shaft of pain through the shoulder he'd used to batter down the door. It hadn't been possible to keep his face covered while he'd been trying to break through the door and he'd inhaled enough smoke to make his lungs burn painfully as well. The coughing was constant now and a wave of dizziness assaulted him as he crawled towards Zanna to pull her into his arms.

'Fire…' He choked the word out. '*Have to…get… you out.*'

Zanna was stumbling, racking coughs making her double over. Nic kept a grip on her arms that went beyond firmness. A part of his brain registered the fact that he could be causing her pain but it couldn't be helped. Somehow, he had to get them downstairs and there was no way he could carry her down that narrow spiral staircase. Not with only one arm that was obeying commands.

There was a fire escape outside her bedroom window. A wrought-iron ladder that was attached to the weatherboards and ran down to the roof of the veranda. Or would that be unusable now? Had the flames from the burning tree crossed the gap and joined with whatever horror was rising from the shop below?

The passage down the spiral stairs was a barely controlled fall but he caught Zanna with his uninjured arm at the bottom and cushioned her impact. With one arm around her waist he crawled forward, dragging her with him. It was too difficult to breathe and Zanna seemed barely conscious. He couldn't remember what direction they needed to go in. He just knew they had to keep moving.

To stay still would mean certain death for both of them.

Zanna was only dimly aware of what was happening. She knew she was in Nic's arms. She could feel the soft smoothness of that leather jacket and the strength of his muscles as he tried to carry her. But she could feel that strength ebbing as well. The dizziness was overwhelming and her eyes were stinging so much it was impossible to open them. Fear was there, too. She knew something terrible was happening.

But she was in Nic's arms so how bad could it be? She just had to try and help him. Had to stay close.

Then she felt the grip of those arms loosen and the smoothness of that soft leather slip away. There was new pressure now. Stronger. Heavily gloved hands that were pulling her upwards. Roughly clad arms that were holding her. Alien faces obscured by masks, making sounds that resembled speech but were totally incomprehensible.

There was movement, too. Rapid and purposeful. The temperature changed and became cold. More hands were pulling at Zanna, tangling themselves in her hair painfully. Something was on her face, covering her mouth and nose. She tried to push it away because she needed to breathe. *Had* to breathe. She was suffocating.

'Leave it on.' The voice was suddenly clear. 'It's oxygen, love. You need it. You've inhaled a lot of smoke.'

Zanna tried to open her eyes. She tried to say something but the effort only provoked a new fit of coughing. She could hear someone else coughing nearby. There were sounds of people shouting and heavy activity. Generators or engines humming. Water gushing and hitting solid objects under pressure. Someone talking more quietly, right beside her.

'Just concentrate on your breathing, Zanna. I'm putting a clip on your finger so we can see what the oxygen level in your blood is doing. Then I'm going to listen to your chest. Are you hurting anywhere?'

She shook her head. How did they know her name? Who were these people? She made a new effort to open her eyes and caught a glimpse of uniformed people surrounding her. One was holding a stethoscope. Another was wrapping a cuff around her arm. She was on a stretcher and there was another one within touching distance if she reached out.

Nic was sitting on that stretcher.

Oh…thank God…Nic was here. Those patchy memories of being held so tightly in his arms hadn't been a dream. She had sent him away but he was here again.

He'd come back. The way he had that first time when she'd been so sure she wouldn't see him again.

Why had he come back this time?

To apologise, perhaps? To say goodbye?

How hard would that be?

She didn't want him to stay. She couldn't trust him. But it would have been better to have never had to see him again.

But hadn't he just saved her from something terrible? How could you not trust someone who had saved your life?

Confusion exacerbated the dizziness that was already clouding her brain.

Nic's face was blackened. He was holding a mask to his mouth and nose and coughing wretchedly. Someone was touching his arm and he gave an anguished yell of pain that Zanna was sure she could feel herself.

'Looks like it's dislocated, mate. Hang on and we'll get you some pain relief before we do anything else.'

The paramedic was blocking her view of Nic now but knowing he'd been hurt made her chest tighten and it was even harder to try and breathe.

Through the narrow windows above his head Zanna could see flashing lights. In the split second before the dizziness took hold again and forced her eyes shut, she looked out of the back doors of what she realised was an ambulance.

She could see the fire engines parked close by. A crowd of heavily uniformed figures were bustling about, dealing with equipment and hoses. And she could see the charred branches of the trees, devoid of any leaves now, and she could even see the black holes that had been the windows of Spellbound—missing teeth in a broken face.

Her house had been burned. Her home was gone.

The tears felt like overheated oil as they seared Zanna's eyes. She held them tightly shut. This was way too much to cope with.

'The cats.' Her words came out as a harsh croak and she didn't even recognise them herself. She caught the arm of the paramedic who was taking her blood pressure. The movement was agitated enough to make him abandon the task and lift the mask from her face.

'You'll have to say that again, love. I couldn't hear you properly.'

'Cats...'

'Sorry?'

'Cats.' Nic's voice came from behind the paramedic. 'There are three cats. Black.' He coughed and Zanna could hear the rasp as he sucked in a new breath. 'They would have been inside the house. You have to find them.'

'I'll pass it on. Nobody's allowed in the house yet. They're still trying to make sure the fire's contained.' The mask was fitted back to Zanna's face. 'Try not to worry. Someone will find your cats.'

She let her eyes drift shut again.

Nic was here but she didn't know why.

Her beloved house was destroyed.

Maggie was on the other side of the world.

And the M&Ms were missing. Dead?

Her brain hurt from trying to take it all in. Her lungs hurt from trying to breathe. But most of all her heart was hurting.

And it was unbearable.

CHAPTER ELEVEN

HE HADN'T FELT like this since his mother had died and they'd come to take him away.

So alone, with an unknown future that was huge and empty and forbidding.

Except this time *was* different.

He really had been alone then and he'd learned to rely only on himself. Not to let anyone close enough to make it a problem if they disappeared.

But then he'd met Zanna. How had she got so close, so fast? As if there'd been a Zanna-shaped hole in his soul that she had just slipped into?

He could have lost her last night and the enormity of facing that made everything else meaningless in comparison.

Was this love? This feeling that he could never be the best person he was capable of being without her? That an unknown future could be bright and enticing instead of something that had to be faced with grim fortitude?

Nic had the curious feeling of coming full circle. Of finding what he'd resisted searching for all his life, only to discover it had been back where he'd started. Physically and emotionally. In the only place he'd known a family. With the only person he'd ever fallen in love with.

He had to tell Zanna.

They'd been separated as soon as they'd arrived at the hospital. The first attempt to relocate his shoulder had been unsuccessful and then there'd been X-rays and drugs that had taken a long time to sleep off.

With his arm in a sling he'd finally been able to trace where Zanna was in the hospital, only to be told that she was currently asleep and not to be disturbed. When he went back again, she was awake but talking to a police detective who was investigating the fire.

'Come back in a couple of hours,' the nursing staff advised. 'Miss Zelensky's not going anywhere just yet. She needs a good rest.'

She was still asleep when Nic returned yet again but this time he wasn't going anywhere. He sat on a chair near her bed and listened to the faint rasp of her breathing.

And waited.

Sleep was the best escape.

There had been visits from doctors. A portable X-ray machine had been brought in to take images of her lungs and a respiratory technician had taken a long time to test their function. The interview with the police detective had been tiring and upsetting because nobody could tell her whether the cats were okay. It had been such a relief to drift back into unconsciousness.

Being awake meant too many things clamouring for attention. Practical things like whether she still had any clothes available and if there was enough money in the bank to cover temporary accommodation. Physical things like how long it would be before it felt easy to breathe again and how soon she would have enough of a voice to call Maggie so that she could tell her about what had happened now. The emotional things were the worst, though. That horrible feeling of knowing that something disastrous had happened and the future had changed for ever. A bit like that emotional tornado she'd found herself in after finding Simon in bed with Brie. A lot like the terrifying abyss of knowing she would never see her parents again.

She'd had Maggie then but now she had nobody. Not here, anyway. Not close enough to hold her and make her believe that it would all be all right in the end. She had a blurry memory of Nic being in the ambulance with her but she hadn't seen him since.

He'd risked his life to save her. The police detective had told her that and the nursing staff obviously thought he was a hero.

'He did come,' someone told her. 'But you were asleep. He'll be back.'

To say goodbye?

Maybe she didn't want him to come back.

She saw him the moment she opened her eyes. Sitting in the chair, slumped forward a little with his elbows on his knees and his hands shading his eyes, as if he was trying to find a solution to the problems of the world.

For a moment she just gazed at him, remembering the first time she'd seen him. When he'd walked into her shop and she'd felt the blast of testosterone and the thrill of thinking he wanted *her*.

Amazing that someone could still exude that kind of masculine power from such a relaxed position. Could still seem commanding when his clothes were streaked with grime and there was a big tear in his jeans. Could still be so incredibly sexy with a couple of days of stubble and lines of weariness etched deeply into his face.

Nobody would ever guess the vulnerable part of him that was so well hidden but, for Zanna, that knowledge would always be there. He needed her love but already she could feel it being locked away. A part of the past. Was that for the best? He might not have wanted it anyway.

Her inward breath caught and made her cough and Nic's hands dropped as he lifted his head.

For a long, long moment they simply held each other's gaze.

'Hey...' Nic's voice was quiet. A bit croaky. 'You're awake. How are you feeling?'

'Oh—okay, I think.' Her voice was still hoarse. She pushed herself more upright in the bed. 'Are you?' He had his arm in a sling.

The single nod was familiar now. 'I dislocated my shoulder. It's been put back. I just need to be careful with it for a bit.'

'No bike-riding, then.' Zanna tried to smile but it wasn't going to happen.

'No.'

A silence fell that she didn't want to continue because that could be the moment that Nic told her he was leaving. That he was giving up on his music-school project or whatever it was he'd come for because it had become all too messy and that he was going back to London. Or France. Somewhere as far away from her as he could get.

Some things had to be said, however.

'I hear you saved my life,' she managed. 'Thank you.'

'I just happened to be in the right place at the right time. It wasn't a matter of choice.'

'There's always a choice. You didn't have to put your own life at risk.'

But Nic shook his head. His look suggested she was missing the point.

'Have the police talked to you yet?'

'No. I saw an officer at the house. He was making sure nothing got looted but he let me in when I told him why I was there. I've got your bag and wallet and things. And some clothes for you. They might smell a bit smoky but they're okay.'

'You've been to the house?'

'Yes. I needed to do something while you were asleep.'

'Did you find the cats?'

'No. Sorry. I've left some food out in the courtyard for when they come back.'

'How…how bad is it?'

'I couldn't get into the shop. That's where the worst of the damage is and there was a fire investigation crew in there. As far as I can see, it's only smoke and water damage in the rest of the house but…it's not pretty, Zanna. I've called Pete. He's going to come over and see whether it makes a difference to whether it can still be moved but he can't come for a few days.'

But Zanna didn't seem to be interested in whether the project would have to be abandoned. Like she hadn't realised how stupid it had been to suggest he'd had a choice about whether or not he'd go into a burning house.

She'd been inside. Of course he'd had no choice.

'They're saying the fire was deliberately lit.'

'What?'

'There's apparently clear evidence that an accelerant was used. In the shop.' Zanna coughed again and reached for the glass of water on the bedside locker.

'I've told the police all about Blake being there. About all the trouble there's been.'

Had she told them about him as well? About the apparent deception that had led to her agreeing to sell the house?

It didn't matter. Nic's opinion of himself probably wasn't any worse than what the police would think.

'This is my fault.' He pressed his fingers to his forehead before pushing them through his hair. 'I called Don. I told him that I wouldn't be working with him again. I knew they'd be angry. I suspect the company will be in big financial strife if the new resort project gets canned. And he knew I'd bought your place. They would have made a lot of money out of that if they'd ever got hold of it.' He had to get to his feet. 'But to do *that* as some kind of revenge… You could have died, Zanna.'

'It's not all your fault, Nic.'

'What's not all his fault?'

Two police officers were standing in the door of the room. Zanna recognised one of them as the detective she'd spoken to earlier.

'Did you find him?' she demanded. 'Have you arrested Blake Scallion?'

'We've talked to him, yes.'

'And?' Nic was scowling.

'He denies any involvement. He's telling a rather different story, in fact.' The detective turned to Nic. 'You're Dominic Brabant, I assume?'

The single nod answered the query.

'And you've recently purchased thirty-two Rata Avenue from Miss Zelensky?'

'Yes.'

'And you own the adjoining property?'

'That's correct.'

'I understand you're into property development. That you've worked with the Scallions over the last few years off and on.'

'Not any more. Not after what I've learned about how they've treated Zanna and her aunt. They—'

'What did you intend to do with the house? It would be in the way of any development, wouldn't it?'

'Are you suggesting *I* set the fire?' Nic's tone was dangerous. 'When Zanna was inside?'

'And you were conveniently there to rescue her?' The detective's expression said it seemed plausible.

'That's ridiculous.' The fierceness of her words made Zanna cough again. 'We're…we're…'

What were they, exactly? Or what had they been? Friends? Lovers? Soul-mates? She didn't know what they had been and it made her feel helpless. Knowing that whatever it was wasn't there any more made it all seem irrelevant anyway. She shifted her gaze to Nic as if that could help her make some kind of sense of what had happened between them but he was glaring at the detective who was speaking again.

'The suggestion came from Mr Scallion but it's not an unreasonable scenario. I imagine the house is insured. It would be more profitable to make a claim than pay demolition costs. And hasn't a fair percentage of the contents already been put into storage?'

'Blake's lying,' Zanna said fiercely. 'He's been threatening us for years. He poisoned our trees.' She made a frustrated sound. 'You don't know what you're talking about. The house is going to be shifted, not demolished. We've bought land…'

Except that contract hadn't been signed yet, had it?

The papers had all been drawn up but the owners were overseas until next week so couldn't add their signatures.

'And of course Nic was around,' Zanna added. 'He's been staying with me since…'

Was it only last week? Would they ask how long she'd known him before she'd let him stay?

This was all crazy and she seemed to be making it worse. Zanna pressed her lips together and shut her eyes. She needed to think.

'We'd like you to come down to the station, Mr Brabant. We need to ask you some more questions and take a statement.'

'Fine. The sooner we get this sorted the better. I'd like a solicitor present as well.'

Zanna's eyes snapped open. Were they *arresting* Nic? What evidence did they have, other than circumstantial? Not for one moment had she thought he'd had anything to do with the fire but—just for a heartbeat—she could feel the roller-coaster of the doubts and perceived betrayal she had been riding for the last few days.

Was there something in what the police were suggesting?

Something she just didn't want to see because part of her still wanted to believe in Nic?

She'd ripped up the contract and potentially made it impossible for him to achieve his dream. He would have been angry about that, wouldn't he?

He'd worked with Blake before. Was it so impossible to imagine he would do it again?

But why would he have risked his own life to save her from a fire he'd started himself?

Or had he misjudged the timing of events?

Nic chose that moment to turn and look at her. He

seemed about to say something but then he met her eyes and his mouth closed.

He turned again, without saying a word, and accompanied the police officers out of the room.

Zanna was pushing her bed covers back as a nurse came into the room moments later.

'What do you need, love?'

'I need to go home,' Zanna said, her voice breaking. 'Now. Could you help me find my clothes, please?'

CHAPTER TWELVE

THE TREES WERE BARE.

Whatever leaves had still clung to their branches had either been burned away or just given up the battle and fallen to the ground. The trunk of the tree closest to the shop was blackened and the smaller branches were gone, their stumps poking into a grey sky that threatened rain at any moment. The house looked naked without the leafy screen. Exposed to the eyes of curious onlookers who stood behind the bright orange 'Police Emergency' tape that circled the front of the house and peered at the evidence of trauma with morbid fascination.

One of those figures was familiar. It was only days ago that she'd seen her solicitor, Keith Watson, and that meeting had been a celebration of a secured future for Rata House. A future that looked as if it had been snatched away.

'Suzanna.' Keith came towards her as the taxi pulled away. 'I couldn't believe it when I heard about the fire. Are you all right?'

No. Zanna was a very long way from being all right. Force of habit made her stand a little straighter, though.

'I was lucky,' she told Keith. 'I got rescued. It could have been a lot worse.'

'Indeed it could. How on earth did the fire start?'

'Apparently it was arson.'

Keith looked shocked. And then he looked around them as though worried that someone might have over-heard. 'Are you allowed inside?' He gestured towards the police officer who stood on the path on the other side of the tape.

'It's my house. Why wouldn't I be allowed inside? I need to see how bad it is.'

Keith lowered his voice. 'If they know it was arson, then it's a crime scene. Let me have a word with the officer.'

Zanna waited on the edge of the crowd, thankful for the hood of her sweatshirt giving her a perceived pri-vacy. This was hard, not being alone when she had to cope with the shock of seeing her home like this. She wasn't even sure she wanted to go inside yet.

Steeling herself, she looked past the ruined trees. The glass panes of the bay window of Spellbound were bro-ken and had been roughly boarded over. The weather-boards of the house were blackened and larger pieces of debris from the shop had been piled in a charred heap at the bottom of the steps.

Despite herself, she was drawn closer. She needed to see the worst of it.

She was closer to the rest of the onlookers now. Be-side a trio of high-school students.

'Oh, my God,' a blonde girl said. 'I can't believe this.'

'It's awful,' her companion agreed. 'Where are we going to go after school now, Jen?'

Zanna's head turned. Holding Jen's hand was a lanky youth with a flop of hair that covered one eye.

'I told you about this shop, Stevie, didn't I? It was so cool.'

'Bit of a mess now. Let's go and get a burger or something.'

'It must have been one of those candles.' Jen still sounded fascinated by the drama. 'On the counter, remember? Maybe one of them didn't get put out. It's really sad, isn't it?' She leaned closer to the boy, who obligingly put his arm around her shoulders as they turned to leave.

Zanna had to blink back tears. Maybe the jellybean spell had worked but there wouldn't be a stream of teenage girls coming into Spellbound as word of mouth spread.

There wouldn't be anyone coming in for herbal tea and organic cake either. Spellbound, as it had been, didn't exist any more.

Keith was waving at her. Holding the plastic tape up with his other hand. 'We can go in and get any necessities you might need but we can't stay long. And you can have a look but we're not to go beyond the tape or touch anything in the shop. They haven't finished the investigation yet.'

Zanna nodded. She was thankful that Keith was here. A kindly, middle-aged man who had known both her and Maggie for years. He would look after her if she couldn't cope and right now she wasn't at all sure how well she was going to cope.

They started with the shop, skirting the pile of debris and climbing the steps to look over the tape past the half-open door.

Water still dripped from intact but charred beams in the ceiling of the room. The smell of the fire was still overpowering. The dead, unpleasant odour of charred wood, wet ashes and a peculiar mixture of pungent oils and herbs. A blackened, stinking layer of rubbish covered the floor and what was left of the counter.

Zanna shut her eyes. Had she shut the door properly last night or had she been distracted by that horrible sensation of being watched and then forgotten completely when she'd gone in to confront Nic with what she'd been told? What if the cats had gone back to their favourite new sleeping place on that pile of clothing?

She choked back a sob and Keith put his arm around her shoulders.

'Let's go into the main part of the house. It can't be as bad as where the fire started.'

It wasn't as bad. Or maybe Zanna was being protected by the numbness she could feel enveloping her brain and her heart. Fatigue washed into every cell in her body and it was an effort to make her legs move to follow Keith. She just needed to get this over with and then she could find somewhere to curl up and go to sleep again for a while.

Everything looked black and dirty and smelt horrible. How could smoke do so much damage in such a short space of time? It was like someone had taken a colour image of everything and then made a very bad job of trying to turn it into an arty sepia print. The colours were all wrong on the flowers on her bedroom wall and when she touched one, all she did was make a blackened smear that obliterated the lines of the petals.

It was heartbreaking.

'Do you want to look upstairs? In the turret?'

Zanna shook her head. The last thing she remembered clearly from last night was finishing that painting—an image torn from her soul. She couldn't bear to see that ruined.

'I don't need to see any more,' she said quietly. 'I just want to check to see whether the cats have been back for any food and then I'll have to find somewhere to stay.'

'We'll organise a motel. Or you could come home with me. Janice would love to be able to look after you.'

It was a kind offer. She should feel grateful but the numbness was blunting any kind of response and Zanna was actually grateful for that. If she couldn't feel small things, maybe she'd stop feeling the huge, overwhelming things as well.

'Have you contacted your insurance company?'

'No.'

'It might be best if I do that for you. It's going to complicate things a bit that the property's been sold so recently. And that the fire was deliberate. It could get messy.'

Zanna simply nodded. She couldn't face any of the bureaucracy that this situation would create. She didn't have the energy and what was the point? Everything was ruined.

The food that Nic had left in the courtyard for the cats hadn't been touched. As if that was the last straw, Zanna sank into one of the wrought-iron chairs and closed her eyes, gathering that comforting numbness around her like a cloak.

'Have you been in touch with Maggie? Does she know about this?'

Zanna shook her head again.

'Would you like me to do that for you?'

'No. But I haven't got my phone. I don't imagine the landline will be working?'

'I wouldn't think so. They will have turned off the

services to the house after the fire. I'll have Maggie's number in my phone. Would you like to use that?'

Zanna wanted to shake her head again. She didn't want to have to tell Maggie about this. Didn't want to have anything pierce the anaesthetic cloak that was working so well to numb her emotional pain. It would be the middle of the night over there and Maggie would answer her phone already knowing that something was very wrong.

'She'll need to know,' Keith said gently. 'And I'm sure she'd want to know as soon as possible. This has been her home for a very long time and we both know how much she loves it.'

So Zanna nodded instead of shaking her head and let Keith find the number and call it. Then he handed her the phone and walked back into the kitchen to give her some privacy.

It rang and rang and went to voicemail. Hearing Maggie's voice was enough to stab a huge hole in the numbness and suddenly all Zanna wanted was to hear the voice for real and not on a recorded message so she ended the call and immediately pushed redial.

This time it was answered but then there was only silence.

'Hello? Maggie—are you there?'

She could hear something. Someone speaking faintly in a language she didn't recognise. Russian? No...it must be Romanian. Had Maggie lost her phone?

'Hello?' The query was more tentative now. 'Can someone hear me?'

'Ah...' A rich male voice was clear. 'At last. It's hard to work a different phone. Is that Suzanna?'

'Yes…' The English was perfect but heavily accented. 'Is that…Dimitry?'

'Yes. I am so pleased you called. I have been trying to find your number but couldn't access the contacts menu.'

The numbness was evaporating painfully fast, as if it was being peeled away from Zanna's skin.

'Where's Maggie, Dimitry? What's happened?'

'Maggie is in a hospital in Bucharest. I brought her here earlier in the night because I was so afraid for her and it seems that she may have had a heart attack. She is having a procedure at the moment but she gave me her phone before they took her away. She asked me to call you.'

'Oh, my God… *No…*'

Keith must have heard her agonised cry because he came out of the house swiftly. With one look at Zanna's face he took the phone from her shaking hand.

'Hello? My name's Keith Watson. I'm with Suzanna. Please tell me what's going on.'

'I do apologise for the length of time this has taken, Mr Brabant. But you understand we had several lines of enquiry to follow up.'

'So I can go now?'

'You won't be needed again until Mr Scallion's trial begins. That probably won't be for a month or so.'

'Did you get hold of Zanna? Does she know about the CCTV footage from the petrol station on Rata Avenue that shows Blake buying the can of petrol?'

'We've been unable to contact her. She left the hospital some hours ago, shortly after we brought you in for the interview. She visited the house but left in a hurry about an hour later, according to the officer we have on the scene. Her mobile phone isn't being answered. It's either switched off or dead or out of range.'

Nic could only nod. His shoulder ached abominably and it felt like days since he had slept. They'd offered him food while he'd been here at the central police station but he hadn't been hungry. The physical discomfort he was in was pale in comparison to the utter weariness of spirit weighing him down.

He would never be able to forget the way Zanna had looked at him from her hospital bed.

As if she thought he could have been responsible for the fire that had almost killed her.

He was too exhausted to feel hurt any more. Or angry, which had been the best way to deal with the hurt. Now he just felt empty.

And a bit lost.

There was only one place in this city that he felt remotely connected with and it wasn't a long walk from the city's biggest police station so it was no real surprise that he automatically headed in the direction of Rata Avenue. He would have to do something about sorting the bike still parked on the street, anyway, given that he wouldn't be riding it back to the hire firm himself.

It was late afternoon now, and beginning to rain, which made the scene of the fire all the more bleak when he arrived there. The broken and boarded windows of the shop made the house look derelict. Haunted, even.

A police officer was sheltering from the rain on the veranda.

'The owner's not here but there's a bloke in there who says he's her solicitor if you want to talk to him.'

Nic didn't bother telling him that he, in fact, was the owner. Or was he? The possession date had been yester-

day, hadn't it? Did something like this put an immediate injunction on legal proceedings? Keith would know.

He found Keith in the kitchen, finishing a phone
call.

'You can start tomorrow. Nine o'clock. I've arranged
a cleaning firm to be here at the same time, so the items
for storage can be cleaned before you transport them.
I'll be here as well. I want to make sure that everything
salvageable is removed.'

He turned to Nic as he ended the call. 'You look terrible.'

'Cheers.'

His tone was grim but Keith's face softened. He
stepped forward to grip Nic's uninjured shoulder. 'I've
known Suzanna Zelensky since she was six years old,'
he said quietly. 'A frightened little girl that Maggie was
determined to keep safe. You saved her life last night
and—on behalf of Maggie—I want to tell you how much
that means.' His voice cracked. 'Just in case Maggie
never gets the chance to tell you herself.'

He let go of Nic and cleared his throat. 'I'm sorting
out getting the house cleared for you.'

'So the property is legally mine?'

'The possession date was four p.m. yesterday so it
was well past by the time the fire started. There's a
grey area concerning insurance on the house because
nothing had been arranged to cover that separately. I'll
talk to the insurance company and we'll start working through that tomorrow. I'll have to look into the
purchase of the new land as well, but it looks as if that
might have to fall through. Suzanna's not going to be
here to sign anything.'

'Why not?' A chill ran down Nic's spine. 'Where is she?'

'Right now she's on a flight to Auckland. She's heading for LA and then London, where she can connect to a flight to Romania. It's going to take too long but it was the best we could do and the airlines have done their best to accommodate a family emergency.'

'What emergency?' Was it the mix of pain and exhaustion that was making his brain feel so sluggish?

'Maggie's had a heart attack. We have no idea how bad it was. Or even if she'll still be alive by the time Suzanna gets there.' Keith shook his head. 'As if the poor girl didn't have enough on her plate as it is. She looked a lot worse than you, Nic, but there was no stopping her.'

A smile tugged at the corner of Nic's mouth. 'She has an amazing spirit. Nobody would stop Zanna being with a person she loved who needed her.'

Keith gave him a curious glance that lingered long enough for Nic to wonder what the older man was thinking.

'I've got a few more calls and notes to make. You might want to have a wander around. I imagine you need a bit of time to decide what you need to do next.'

That was true enough. So many things would have to be put on hold. He might own the land but nothing could be started for the music school until the house was gone and that belonged to Zanna. It would be a couple of days before Pete could get here and give his opinion on whether it could still be moved but Nic didn't want to think about what would happen if it was decided that the damage was too great.

And it wasn't, surely?

With more purpose in his movements, Nic followed Keith's suggestion of wandering around. He took in the revolting mess of the room that had housed the shop but damped down the feeling of defeat the smell and sight of the damage evoked and looked more closely. The windows could be replaced and the stock certainly could. The gap in the internal wall that had let so much smoke into the main part of the house could also be repaired but how complicated that would be depended on how much damage there had been to the supporting beams.

He looked up. The solid beams would always be scarred from the charring but they looked strong enough to be structurally sound. If he went to the room above and tested the floor, he might get an even better idea of whether additional strengthening would solve any issues.

His path took him up the main stairway. He could feel his heart thumping against his ribs as he remembered the last time he'd come up here. The overwhelming fear for Zanna's safety that had driven him through the heat and smoke.

The feeling like it was his own life he was trying to save.

Being in her bedroom added a tightness to his throat that reminded him of how hard it had been to breathe. And no wonder. How much smoke had made it in here to blacken the walls like this? How sad would Zanna have felt to have been standing where he was? All that work. The painstaking hours that encapsulated the birth of a passion. The emerging talent that was such a huge part of who she was. The flowers were ruined.

Or were they?

Rubbing one gently with his finger only made the black smudge thicker but when he licked his finger and concentrated on one tiny patch, the delicate blue of a forget-me-not appeared amongst the grime as if a miniature spotlight had been focused on it. He looked around.

This could be fixed. How would Zanna feel if she could walk in here again and see them as they had been? He could imagine how still she would become. The wonder in her face that would morph into joy.

He could add a lump to the tightness in his throat as he turned away. The odds of him seeing that were virtually nil.

There was no real reason to climb the spiral staircase but maybe he needed some closure. To view the door that was responsible for the pain he was in. To see where Zanna might have died if he hadn't been able to break in.

The smoke had been thick enough to be dangerous but not as bad as it had been a floor below. The sketches and paintings weren't obscured by grimy residue. The images of the cats reminded Nic that he needed to have another look for the M&Ms before he left. The image on the easel was a different one from what had been there the last time he'd been in here.

He stepped closer. And then he stepped back again.

Something huge was squeezing the breath right out of him as he stared at the painting. At his own image that could have been a photograph except that it was too rich for that. He could hear the notes of the guitar strings being plucked. The words of the classic song he'd been singing for Zanna.

Ne me quitte pas.

Don't leave me.

How could she have captured him so perfectly without knowing him well enough to see into his soul?

And if she could really do that, there was no chance she could have believed he would ever do anything to put her in danger.

All that was needed was a chance to be together

again—without something traumatic obscuring what needed to be seen.

Of course Zanna needed time with Maggie right now but soon…

Maybe soon, what she would need would be a reason to come back.

How long would she be away?

Too long?

Or not long enough?

CHAPTER THIRTEEN

'LADIES AND GENTLEMEN, please return to your seats. We will shortly be starting our preparations for landing.'

The announcement came while Zanna was trying to freshen up in the cramped confines of the plane's toilet. She had dragged a brush through her hair, washed her face and managed to apply enough make-up to hide the physical evidence of a long and tiring journey. The train trip through Romania had been enough of a trip in itself but the ensuing roundabout connection of flights from Bucharest to Germany to Singapore and finally back to New Zealand had taken over thirty hours.

As she returned to her seat and complied with the preparation for landing instructions by putting her safety belt on and shoving her bag under the seat in front, the pilot's voice came over the engine noise again.

'Going to be a gorgeous day, folks. Light north-westerly breeze, clear skies and an expected maximum temperature of twenty-eight degrees Celsius. A real Indian summer's day.'

Just as well she'd chosen to wear her favourite orange crop top, Zanna decided—one of the few items she had grabbed during that frantic scramble to pack a bag a month ago, when she'd been so afraid she wouldn't arrive in time to see Maggie alive.

So many panicked hours with no way to communicate with anyone until she'd reached Dimitry, who had been there to meet her flight. Not only was Maggie still alive, she was back at home in Dimitry's castle. The heart attack had been minor and the treatment meant that, with a few lifestyle changes, she would probably be healthier than ever. The moment Zanna had walked into her aunt's embrace she had known that that place was exactly where she needed to be. Where she needed to stay until some healing—both physical and emotional—had taken place.

She might not have come home this soon if Keith hadn't made contact to let her know she was required to give evidence at Blake Scallion's trial for arson. The cards had told Maggie that the conclusion to the trouble was coming and she was already satisfied that karma was intact. Keith had told them that Prime Property had gone into liquidation in the last few days. The Scallions were ruined.

It wasn't the only forecast that had come from the treasured set of cards Zanna had brought over for Maggie.

'The Empress? But she's about marriage and birth...'

'Perhaps it's the birth of a creative child, darling. You might be about to start a period of artwork that will provide fulfilment. I miss your paintings so much. Especially the sunflowers under the stairs. And the ivy in the bathroom.'

That had brought tears to Zanna's eyes but she still wasn't ready to talk about it. Those paintings were gone and she missed them too. Especially that last one. She hadn't wanted to talk about Nic either. It was over. Gone, along with her dreams for the house and her studio.

The plane's wheels jarred on the tarmac and the engines howled as it slowed.

The cards had played a cruel trick, putting up the King of Pentacles as a forthcoming influence for Zanna, but she wouldn't allow herself to see it as representing a person.

Because that would always be Nic's card?

He hadn't even called.

And why would he, when he'd been left thinking that she didn't believe in him?

On top of her drama-queen performance of ripping up that contract and telling him to get out?

She'd been so hurt by the idea of him being associated with Prime Property. She'd felt so betrayed. With the benefit of hindsight she could see that it had been a necessary twist of fate that the unexpected availability of the apartment block had been the catalyst for the inspiration of the music school. If he hadn't purchased the neighbouring property first, he would never have had reason to come to a city that would never boast a coastal resort.

Where was he now? Probably on site at the location of a new project or back in London or France, waiting for decisions to be made so that they could all move forward. Of course the sale of the property hadn't been affected by her ripping up what had only been a copy of a legally binding contract.

The plane had stopped now. The snap of seat-belts being released accompanied movement as everyone began to gather their belongings.

The King of Pentacles was probably to do with all

the money that was waiting in an account after the sale had been finalised. A Midas touch, thanks to Keith, who had been taking care of everything that had needed sorting. At first unbearably weary and then feeling too sad, Zanna had let Maggie take over the intermittent conversations about what was happening and simply accepted her reassurance that things would be as they needed to be in the future. Her beloved aunt needed time to recover herself and she deserved to enjoy the happiness she'd found with Dimitry without having it tainted by worry about her niece's disastrous love life.

And it seemed that there was no hurry. Zanna could take a look while she was here for the trial and the really big decisions could wait until after that. Until she was ready.

Finally, she was. It was time to move forward, in more ways than one.

Hearing herself being paged as she emerged from customs led Zanna to an information desk.

'There's a message for you, Miss Zelensky. A Mr Keith Watson has arranged an elite taxi for you. It's the first one on the corporate taxi rank.'

Zanna smiled her thanks. It was a pleasant surprise not to have to arrange her own transport into the city. Had Maggie made the suggestion during one of those quiet conversations with their solicitor?

The walk to the taxi rank was short but there was enough time to look up and marvel at the clarity of the air here compared to the permanent haze of Europe. This was home and quality of light was something she wanted to infuse into her paintings for the rest of her life. Regular visits to the fairy-tale castle in the Transylvanian

Alps would be a must but this was where she wanted to be based.

She would just have to find somewhere to live.

The first car on the rank was a sleek, dark BMW with a discreet elite logo. Zanna opened the back door.

'Is this the taxi ordered by Watkins and Associates? Going to the Park View Hotel?'

The driver nodded into his mirror and muttered something about luggage that she had difficulty hearing. He was wearing a uniform that included a peaked cap and his mirrored sunglasses were all that she could see in the rear-view mirror.

'Don't worry about luggage. This is the only bag I have.' Sliding onto the comfortable leather upholstery, she dropped the overnight bag beside her. She fastened her safety belt as the car pulled smoothly away from the stand and then tilted her head back and closed her eyes. It was only a short ride into the central city but Zanna didn't feel inclined to engage in meaningless small talk. She needed some time to centre herself and prepare for the emotional impact that would come at some stage today when she had to go to Rata Avenue and make a decision about the final fate of her house.

The ten minutes seemed to stretch longer than even bad traffic could account for. And when she opened her eyes it took several seconds for Zanna to register what part of the city she was in. Or rather what part of the city she was *not* in. They were nowhere near the CBD. She was being driven out of town, in fact, with the last pocket of suburbia now behind them.

What was going on? Zanna's tiredness evaporated, the alarm raised by a potentially dangerous situation providing more than enough fuel to burn it off. She sat up straight as the car slowed to turn off the main road.

Maybe she wasn't being abducted. The last time she'd been on this road had been on the back of Nic's bike when he'd brought her out to see the land that would have been the perfect location for Rata House.

Had Keith arranged this, too? She'd assumed that the sale and purchase agreement for the land out here had been shelved, along with all the other plans in the wake of the fire, but maybe there was something that needed discussion. Was Keith meeting her there?

Her guess about the destination was correct, at any rate. The car slowed again at the ornate wooden gates she remembered and then rolled up a driveway newly shingled with small white pebbles. Past the lake with the willow trees and jetty and the little rowboat and there was the old stone stable building, but Zanna barely registered it. She remembered the stretch of grass like a small park and she could remember imagining Rata House in the middle of it.

Her fatigue must be a lot worse than she'd realised for her imagination to be playing a trick like this. For her to be seeing exactly what she had imagined. Her house—only it couldn't be her house because this was a younger version. Freshly painted, with a new slate roof, copper guttering and downpipes and new, wide veranda steps flanked by tubs of brilliant orange, red and yellow nasturtiums.

Even more fantastically, there were tendrils of wisteria already climbing up the wrought-iron of the veranda decoration and borders around the house were filled with the kind of old-fashioned flowers Zanna loved best. Roses and lavender and pansies. A profusion of colour that wrapped the house with a ribbon of joy. Most amazing of all were two large rata trees planted in front.

Completely lost for words, Zanna climbed out of the car very, very slowly after the driver opened the door for her. For a full minute she just stood there, completely stunned.

And then she looked around for someone to tell her what on earth was going on. How this magic had happened. But she was alone with her chauffeur.

'Do you know?' she asked. 'Who did this?'

In response, he shrugged off the uniform jacket to reveal a black T-shirt. Took off the peaked cap he was wearing. Removed the mirrored sunglasses.

And Zanna gasped.

'*Nic.*'

Oh, dear Lord, he looked exactly as he had in every dream she'd had of him in the last month. The rumpled hair and those gorgeous dark eyes. The shadowing on his jaw and that sexy hint of a slow smile that hadn't surfaced yet.

'What do you think?'

'I…' Zanna's head swerved to check that she hadn't imagined the house and then it swerved back because it was more important that she wasn't imagining that Nic was here. 'But I don't understand… How did you do this? *Why?*'

'I wanted to give you something to come back for.' The words were quiet. 'I wanted to see you again.'

'Oh…*Nic*…' Laughter was warring with tears. 'You could have just asked. If I'd known you wanted to see me I would have gone anywhere.'

She saw understanding dawn in his eyes and the lines of tension dissolve in his face. She saw the beginnings of that smile but then he was too close to see any more and she didn't need to see because she could feel. The strength of his arms around her as he held her so tightly. The softness of his lips as he kissed her and then kissed her again.

And then he took her hand. 'Come and see,' he invited. 'I want to show you everything.'

But Zanna stopped before they'd even reached the veranda steps. 'How?' She demanded. 'How on earth was this even possible?'

'It was a logistical nightmare,' Nic admitted. 'Pete and I have been working pretty much twenty-four seven since we started, which was probably about when you arrived in Romania. We've had up to a hundred contractors on site since the house was positioned, to get the renovations done. They only finished planting up the borders under floodlights last night.'

'But I hadn't even paid for the land.'

'Keith sorted it. Along with Maggie and me. She's quite some woman, your aunt, isn't she?'

'You've been *talking* to Maggie?'

'I wanted to talk to you but Maggie didn't think you were ready to listen at first. And then she came up with the idea of surprising you. Showing you that you hadn't lost as much as you thought you had.'

'Including you?'

'Especially me.' Nic kissed her again and his breath came out in a sigh that sounded like relief. 'That was why I agreed to the plan to keep it a secret. I had to know I could pull this together because I didn't want to promise something I couldn't deliver. I don't want you to ever again doubt that you can trust me.'

'I don't. I didn't… I was confused, that was all. There

were too many things happening all at once and they were too big… I couldn't take it in fast enough.'

She looked around her again. 'I still can't take *this* in. Whose idea were the nasturtiums?'

'Mine.' Nic was smiling again. 'They're the colour of flames and they make me think of you.'

'Oh, Nic… You have no idea how much I love you.'

'I don't know about that.' Nic bent to kiss her yet again. 'But I hope it's at least half as much as I love you.' When he lifted his mouth he touched his forehead to hers for a long, solemn moment.

'*Je t'adore, ma chérie.*'

She needed no translation. 'I love you, too,' she whispered back.

With her hand held within the circle of his fingers, Nic led Zanna inside. He had poured his heart and soul into this project for weeks and he'd never been so tired. Or so nervous about the result. Had he done justice to the home she had lived in for most of her life and loved so much? Changes had had to be made but that was life, wasn't it? You let go of some things and that meant you could choose the best and treasure them.

The interior walls of the house had been relined and painted in soft, pastel shades of lemon and cream. New carpets had been laid but the design and colours fitted the period of the house perfectly. New curtains graced windows with wooden framing that glowed richly after the timber had been stripped and restored.

'It feels so different,' Zanna murmured. 'So *light*…'

'It's not hemmed in by high-rise buildings any more. We've positioned it so it will get maximum sunlight, even in the winter.'

'You got everything out of storage. You've even put

the antique instruments back in the same places. And Maggie's hats… Oh, I'm glad we put them into storage before the fire. They wouldn't have survived the smoke.'

The beams in the room that had been Spellbound were the only reminder of the fire. They had been cleaned and polished but would always be misshapen and stained.

'Because you can't wipe out the past,' Nic said softly. 'And sometimes you have to honour it because it's what has made you what you are today.'

Every new surprise was a delight. Her bedroom with the painting she had done of Nic playing the guitar hanging over the head of the bed they had shared. The flowered walls intact and the blooms as bright as when they'd first been painted.

'We got lucky and found an electrician with a bit of imagination. He found places for the new plugs without having to ruin a single flower. And a plumber who looked after the ivy in the bathroom.'

Even the tiled floor in the kitchen had been saved and relaid. A new courtyard of recycled bricks lay beyond the French doors with the chiminea set amongst a collection of terracotta pots. The old rustic table and chairs were waiting. A bottle of champagne stood in an ice bucket with two stemmed glasses in invitation.

But Zanna didn't see them. Her hand gripped Nic's hard enough to cut off the circulation in his fingers as she stared at the terracotta pots filled with flame-coloured geraniums. To where there were three black shapes emerging from between the pots and coming towards her.

Letting go of Nic's hand, Zanna dropped to a crouch and gathered the wash of black fur into her arms. Tears of joy were on her cheeks as she looked up at him.

'They're alive…' she whispered.

'I found them the day we were lifting the house. Or Merlin found me.'

'He's a clever cat. He knew you were special right from the moment he met you.' Zanna was on her feet again. 'Like I did.'

He took her into his arms again. He never wanted to let her go.

'Is it all right? Is it how you imagined it could be?'

'Better. Unbelievable. I still have no idea how you could possibly have pulled this off.' Zanna's smile was misty. 'I know I really do believe in magic now.' She pulled away far enough to catch Nic's gaze. 'But I don't want to live here.'

His jaw dropped. Time stopped.

'Alone,' Zanna added. 'I couldn't live here without you, Nic. This place is perfect but…it's a house and—'

'And home is where the heart is,' Nic finished for her.

Her nod was solemn. 'Mine is with you,' she said. 'For ever.'

It was too hard to find words. Too big. All Nic could do was tilt his head in a single nod to signal his agreement. To kiss this woman he loved so much in a way that would let her know he felt exactly the same way.

For ever was going to start right now.

EPILOGUE

A year later...

THE SPEECHES WERE over and the crowd poised to applaud.

Nic's hand covered Zanna's so that they were both holding the oversized ceremonial scissors they were using to cut the wide scarlet ribbon.

The Brabant Music Academy was officially open.

The beautiful, curved building that echoed the flow of the river was being hailed as one of the most significant new assets of the city. The acoustic masterpiece of a concert hall would cater for the most discerning musicians and their fans. The numerous, soundproofed tutorial rooms would give the students what they needed to be nurtured into the futures they dreamed of. The later addition of the café and courtyard garden would encourage others to step into a world they might not otherwise have entered and the space tagged for after-school and holiday programmes might inspire members of a new generation.

Members of the symphony orchestra were playing in the concert hall as the invited guests toured the academy. Herbal tea, champagne and organic canapés were available in the café.

Nic was still holding Zanna's hand as they mingled and talked to people. So far, they hadn't made it past the foyer that housed the gallery of beautiful black and white photographs of Rata House—the captions below sharing the history of the land on which the school now stood. One of the images was in colour. And it was a painting rather than a photograph. A scene of the house reborn, with the lake in the foreground and the backdrop of the native bush.

'This is one of your paintings, Zanna?' The mayor looked impressed. 'I must get to your next exhibition. I'm told your first was a sell-out.'

'Of course it was.' The pride in Nic's voice was matched by the loving glance between the couple.

The mayor continued to admire the painting. 'It looks like it was always meant to be there. I'm delighted to see that someone had the vision to preserve such a special part of our city's heritage. And in such spectacular fashion. I suspect you're a bit of a magician, Nic.'

'No magic involved. Just a dream and a lot of hard work.'

'I'll bet. You deserve the privilege of having it as your home.'

'One of our homes.' Zanna smiled. 'We intend to spend half our year in France, where we have another house.'

'Ah…' The mayor nodded. 'I heard that was where you went to get married?'

'No,' Zanna laughed. 'We got married in a castle. In Transylvania. Let me introduce you to my aunt Magda and her husband. They've come all the way from Romania for this opening ceremony.'

Maggie was delighted to meet the mayor. 'I can't tell you what a lovely surprise it was to find the council has planted rata trees on the avenue. Such lovely, big specimens, too.'

'Mr Brabant got the biggest one available. Have you seen it out there on the lawn?'

'We're heading that way now.' Zanna linked her arm with Maggie's and smiled at Dimitry. 'Let's go and find you both a glass of something bubbly so we can celebrate properly.'

There was so much to celebrate but Zanna wouldn't be drinking anything more than a cup of herbal tea. She met Maggie's gaze over the rim of her cup a short time later.

'So the cards were right.' Her aunt smiled. 'I had a feeling the Empress was there for more than the birth of a creative child.'

It was too early for it to be any more than a guess but there was no point in trying to keep it a secret.

'We only just found out.'

'Congratulations.' Dimitry's eyes looked suspiciously moist. 'Such happy news.'

'I think it will be a girl,' Maggie pronounced.

Zanna looked up at Nic. 'If it is,' she said softly, 'I'd like to name her Elise.'

He had to take her away then. To a quiet spot away from the crowd. To the bench seat that had been placed on the river side of the rata tree on the lawn. The seat with the small brass plaque that carried his parents' names.

So that he could kiss his wife and tell her again just how much he loved her.

So that he could hear her tell him the same thing.

He'd been wrong in telling the mayor that no magic had been involved. And hadn't he told Zanna within the first few minutes of meeting her that he wouldn't believe in magic in a million years?

Well…he had just changed his mind. It was the only word to describe this—the alchemy of finding the person you wanted to be with for ever that only happened when they felt exactly the same way.

There was more magic to be found as well. Very strong magic that meant this was one spell that would never be broken.

Ever.

* * * * *

She hoped he wouldn't come closer...

Prayed he wouldn't kiss her. "We need to forget what happened tonight," she said in a rattled voice. "We agreed it'd be crazy to—"

"Nothing really happened," he said, cutting her off.

"Well, what *almost* happened. I've made a vow to myself...and it's a promise I intend to keep. I'm never going to find what I want if I get drawn deeper into this attraction. It won't go anywhere other than your bed, and I'm not prepared to settle for just sex."

Gabe stared at her. So deeply, so intensely, she couldn't breathe. The small porch created extreme intimacy. If she took one step she'd be pressed against him.

"You're right." He moved back. "You shouldn't settle for sex. You should find that middle road you want, Lauren, with someone who can give you the quiet relationship you deserve."

Then he was gone.

Her chest was pounding. Her stomach was churning. Her head was spinning.

And her heart was in serious danger.

ONCE UPON
A BRIDE

BY
HELEN LACEY

Published in Great Britain 2014
by Mills & Boon, an imprint of Harlequin (UK) Limited,
Eton House, 18-24 Paradise Road, Richmond, Surrey, TW9 1SR

© 2014 Helen Lacey

ISBN: 978-0-263-91314-9

23-0914

Harlequin (UK) Limited's policy is to use papers that are natural, renewable and recyclable products and made from wood grown in sustainable forests. The logging and manufacturing processes conform to the legal environmental regulations of the country of origin.

Printed and bound in Spain
by Blackprint CPI, Barcelona

Helen Lacey grew up reading *Black Beauty, Anne of Green Gables* and *Little House on the Prairie.* These childhood classics inspired her to write her first book when she was seven years old, a story about a girl and her horse. She continued to write, with the dream of one day being a published author, and writing for Mills & Boon® Cherish™ is the realization of that dream. She loves creating stories about strong heroes with a soft heart and heroines who get their happily-ever-after. For more about Helen, visit her website, www.helenlacey. com.

For Robert
Because you get me…

Chapter One

"You made a *what?*"

Lauren Jakowski shrugged her shoulders and bit down on her lower lip, musing whether she should repeat her words. But her two best friends' imploring looks won over.

"I made a vow," she said, and glanced at both Cassie and Mary-Jayne. "Of celibacy."

The other women snorted through the drinks they were sipping, sending liquid flying across the small poolside table. It was her brother's wedding, and once the bride and groom had cut the cake and shared their first dance, her bridesmaid's duties were officially over for the night. So she'd left the hotel ballroom and met her friends by the pool.

"Yeah, sure you did," Cassie said with a laugh, wiping her face.

"I did," Lauren insisted. "When my marriage ended."

"So you, like—" Mary-Jayne mused slowly as her dark hair swayed in the breeze "—made a commitment to never have sex again?"

"Exactly," she replied. "Not until I'm certain he's the right one."

"*He* being this dull and passionless individual you think you'll find so you can have your mediocre happily ever after?" Cassie asked, watching Lauren over the rim of her glass of soda.

She ignored how absurd it sounded. "Yes."

Cassie's brows came up. "And where are you going to find this Mr. Average?" she asked. "ReliableBores.com?"

"Maybe," Lauren said, and pretended to drink some champagne.

"So no sex?" Mary-Jayne asked again. "Even though you caught the bouquet, look sensational in that dress and there are at least half a dozen single men at this wedding who would happily throw you over their shoulder, carry you off and give you the night of your life?"

"I'm not interested in anything casual," she reiterated.

Mary-Jayne's eyes widened. "Not even with—"

"Not with *anyone,*" she said firmly.

"But he's—"

The original tall, dark and handsome...

"I know what he is. And he's not on my radar."

Which was a great big lie. However, she wasn't about to admit that to her friends. Lauren stared at the flowers sitting in the center of the small table. She *had* caught the bouquet. But she didn't want some meaningless romp at her brother's wedding.

And she certainly didn't want it with Gabe Vitali.

In the past six months, she'd been within touching distance of the ridiculously good-looking American several times. *And avoided him on every single occasion.* He was exactly what she didn't want. But since he was her brother's friend—and Crystal Point was a small town—Lauren accepted that she would be forced to see him every now and then.

"I like Gabe," Mary-Jayne said, and grinned. "He's kind of mysterious and…sexy."

Lauren wrinkled her nose. "Trouble."

"But still sexy?" Cassie laughed gently. "Come on, admit it."

Lauren let out an exasperated sigh. "Okay, he's sexy. He's weak-at-the-knees sexy…. He's handsome and hot and every time I see him I wonder what he looks like out of his clothes. I said I was celibate…not comatose."

The two women laughed, and Lauren pushed aside the idea of Gabe Vitali naked.

"Still, you haven't had sex in over two years," Mary-Jayne, the more candid of the two women, reminded her. "That's a long time. Just because you got divorced doesn't mean you can't have sex."

Lauren shrugged. "Isn't there an old saying about not missing what you don't have?"

Mary-Jayne shook her head. "Please tell me you've at least *kissed* a guy since then?"

"No," she replied. "Nor do I intend to until I know he's exactly what I've been looking for."

"You mean, *planning* for," Cassie said, ever gentle. "You know, there's no neat order to falling in love."

"Who said anything about love?" Lauren pushed back her blond bangs.

Cassie's calm expression was unwavering. "Is that really what you want? A loveless relationship without passion and heat?"

Lauren shrugged. "Marriage doesn't have to be about sexual attraction. Or love."

She saw her friends' expressions, knew that even though they were both fiercely loyal and supported her unconditionally, they still thought her thinking madness. But she wasn't swayed. How could they really appreciate her feelings? Or understand what she wanted?

They couldn't.

But she knew what she wanted. No lust, no crazy chemistry. No fairy-tale love.

No risk.

"That's just grief talking," Cassie said quietly. "When a marriage breaks down, it's natural to—"

"I'm not *mourning* my divorce," she insisted. No, definitely not. Because she knew exactly what mourning felt like. "I'm glad it's over. I shouldn't have married a man I hardly knew. I've tried being in love, I've tried being in lust…and neither worked out. Believe it or not, for the first time in a long time, I actually know what I want."

"Which is?" Mary-Jayne prompted, still grinning.

Lauren smiled at her friend. "Which is an honest, uncomplicated relationship with someone I can talk to…. Someone I can laugh with…have children with…grow old with. You know, the usual things. Someone who's a friend. A companion. And not with a man who looks as though he was made to pose for an underwear ad on one of those highway billboards."

"Like Gabe?" Mary-Jayne suggested playfully, and drank some champagne. "Okay, I get it. You want short, chubby and bald…not tall, dark and handsome. But in the meantime, how about we all get back to the ballroom and find some totally *complicated* man to dance with?"

"Not me," Cassie said, and touched her four-month-pregnant belly. Her boyfriend was a soldier currently on tour in the Middle East. "But I'll happily watch from the sidelines."

Lauren shook her head. "I think I'll stay out here for a while. You two go on ahead."

Her friends took another couple of minutes to leave, and when she was alone, Lauren snatched up the colorful bouquet, stood and walked the ten feet toward the edge of the pool. Solitude crept over her skin, and she sighed. Weddings always made her melancholy. Which was unfortunate, since she owned the most successful bridal store in Bellandale. Weddings were her life. Some days, though, she thought that to be the most absurd irony.

Of course, she was pleased for her brother. Cameron deserved every bit of happiness with his new bride, Grace Preston. And the ceremony had been beautiful and romantic. But she had a hollow spot in her chest that ached with a heavy kind of sadness. Many of the guests now inside the big hotel ballroom had witnessed her union to James Wallace in similar style three years earlier. And most knew how it had ended. Tonight, more than ever before, Lauren's sadness was amplified by her embarrassment at being on the receiving end of countless pitying looks and sympathetic greetings.

She took a deep breath and exhaled with a shudder. Somehow, her dreams for the future had been lost. But two years on, and with so many tears shed, she was stronger. And ready to start again. Only this time, Lauren would do it right. She wouldn't rush into marriage after a three-month whirlwind romance. And she definitely wouldn't be swept off her feet. This time, her feet were staying firmly on the ground.

Lauren swallowed hard, smoothed the mint-green chiffon gown over her hips and turned on her heels.

And was unexpectedly confronted with Gabe Vitali.

Stretched out on a sun lounger, tie askew and with his black hair ruffled as if he'd been running his hand through it, he looked so gorgeous, she literally gasped for breath. He was extraordinarily handsome, like one of those old-time movie stars. His glittering, blue-eyed gaze swept over her, and a tiny smile creased the corners of his mouth.

And she knew immediately…

He'd heard.

Everything.

Every humiliating word. Heat raced up and smacked her cheeks. *Great.*

Of course, she had no logical reason to dislike him… other than the fact he was good-looking and sexy and made her insides flip-flop. But it was enough to keep her from allowing her fantasies to take over. She gripped the bouquet tighter and planted her free hand on her hip in a faux impression of control, and spoke. "Whatever you might have thought you heard, I assure you I wasn't—"

"How are the knees?" he asked as he sprang up.

He was tall, around six-two, with broad shoulders and a long-legged frame. And he looked way too good in a suit. Resentment burned through her when she realized he was referring to her earlier confession.

"Fine," she replied, dying of embarrassment inside. "Rock solid."

He came around the lounger, hands thrust into his pockets. "You're sure about that?"

Lauren glared at him. "Positive," she snapped, mortified. She wanted to flee, but quickly realized she'd have to squeeze herself in between him and the sun lounger if she wanted to make a getaway. "I think I'll return to the ballroom now, if you don't mind."

His mouth curled at the edges. "You know, just because someone knows your vulnerabilities, it doesn't necessarily make him your enemy."

Lauren's skin heated. *"Vulnerabilities?"* She sucked in a sharp breath. "I don't quite know what you mean by that, but if you're insinuating that I'm *vulnerable* because I haven't… Because I… Well, because it's been a while since I was…you know…" Her words trailed off as mortification clung to every pore. Then she got annoyed as a quick cover-up. "Let's get this straight. I'm not the least bit vulnerable. Not to you or to anyone *like* you."

He grinned. "Whoa. Are you always so prickly?"

Prickly? She wasn't *prickly.* She was even tempered and friendly and downright *nice.*

She glared at him. "Do you always eavesdrop on private conversations?"

"I was simply relaxing on a pool lounger," he replied smoothly, his accent so delicious, it wound up her spine like liquid silk. "And I was here before you, remember? The fact you spoke about your sex life so openly is really no one's fault but your own." One brow rose. "And although it was entertaining, there's no need to take your frustration out on—"

"I am not *frustrated,*" she snapped, figuring he was probably referring to her being sexually starved in some misguided, macho way. Broad shoulders, blue eyes and nice voice aside, he was a jerk. "I just don't want to talk about it anymore. What I'd like is to forget this conversation ever happened."

"I'm sure you would."

Lauren wanted a big hole to open up and suck her in. When one didn't appear, she took a deep breath. "So we have a deal. I'll ignore you, and you can ignore me. That way we never have to speak to each other again."

"Since this is the first time we have actually spoken," he said, his gaze deep enough to get lost in. "I don't think it will be a hardship."

He was right. They'd never spoken. She'd made sure of it. Whenever he was close, she'd always managed to make a quick getaway. Lauren sniffed her dislike, determined to ignore the fact that the most gorgeous man she'd ever met probably thought she was stark raving mad. And she would have done exactly that. Except she turned her heel too quickly, got caught between the tiles, and seconds later, she was tumbling in a cartwheel of arms and legs and landed into the pool, bouquet flying, humiliation complete.

The shock of hitting the water was quickly interrupted

when a pair of strong hands grasped one arm, then another. In seconds, she was lifted up and over the edge of the pool and set right on her feet.

He still held her, and had his hands intimately positioned on her shoulders.

She should have been cold through to her bones. But she wasn't. She was hot. All over. Her saturated dress clung to every dip and curve, her once carefully styled hair was now draping down her neck and her blood burned through her veins like a grass fire.

"Steady," he said softly, holding her so close she could see the tiny pulse in his jaw.

Lauren tried to speak, tried to move, tried to do something, *anything,* other than shake in his arms and stare up into his handsome face. But she failed. Spectacularly. It was he who eventually stepped back. When he finally released her, Lauren's knees wobbled and she sucked in a long breath to regain her composure. Of which she suddenly had none. He looked at her, *over her,* slowly and provocatively and with just enough male admiration to make her cheeks flame. She glanced down and shuddered. The sheer, wet fabric hugged her body like a second skin and left *nothing* to the imagination.

She moved her lips. "I should…I think I should…"

"Yes," he said quietly when her words trailed. "You probably should."

Lauren shifted her feet and managed one step backward, then another. Water dripped down her arms and legs, and she glanced around for a towel or something else to cover herself. When she couldn't find anything suitable, she looked back at him and noticed he still watched her. Something passed between them, a kind of heady, intense awareness that rang off warning bells in her head and should have galvanized her wobbly knees into action. But she couldn't move.

Seconds later, he shrugged out of his jacket and quickly draped it around her shoulders. The warmth from the coat and his nearness enveloped her like a protective cloak, and Lauren expelled a long sigh. She didn't want to feel that. Didn't want to *think* that. She only wanted to escape.

"Thank you," she whispered. "I appreciate—"

"Forget it," he said, cutting her off. "You should get out of those wet clothes before you catch a cold," he said, and then stepped back.

Lauren nodded, turned carefully and rushed from the pool area, water and humiliation snapping at her heels.

One week later Gabe pulled the for-sale peg from the ground, stuck the sign in the crook of his arm and headed across the front yard. The low-set, open-plan brick-and-tile home was big and required a much-needed renovation. But he'd bought the house for a reasonable price, and it seemed as good a place as any to settle down.

And he was happy in Crystal Point. The oceanfront town was small and friendly, and the beaches and surf reminded him of home. He missed California, but he enjoyed the peacefulness of the small Australian town he now called home instead. He'd rented a place in the nearby city of Bellandale for the past few months, but he liked the seaside town much better. Bellandale, with its sixty thousand residents, was not as populated as Huntington Beach, Orange County, where he'd lived most of his life. But it was busy enough to make him crave the solitude and quiet of Crystal Point. Plus, he was close to the beach and his new job.

He liked the job, too. Managing the Crystal Point Surf Club & Community Center kept him occupied, and on the weekends, he volunteered as a lifeguard. The beach was busy and well maintained, and so far he'd only had to administer first aid for dehydration and a couple of jellyfish stings. Nothing life threatening. Nothing he couldn't handle. Nothing that made him dwell on all he'd given up.

Gabe fished the keys from his pocket, dropped the sign into the overgrown garden bed and climbed the four steps to the porch. His household items had arrived that morning, and he'd spent most of the day emptying boxes and wishing he'd culled more crap when he'd put the stuff into storage six months ago. His cousin, Scott, had offered to come and give him a hand unpacking, but Gabe wasn't in the mood for a lecture about his career, his personal life or anything else.

All his energy would go into his job and renovating the house, which he figured would keep him busy for six months, at least. After that, he'd tackle the yard, get the place in shape and put the house on the market again. How hard could it be? His brother Aaron did the same thing regularly. True, he wasn't much of a carpenter, and Aaron was a successful builder in Los Angeles, but he'd give it a shot.

He headed inside and flicked on some lights. Some of the walls were painted black, no doubt a legacy from the previous tenants—a group of twenty-something heavy-metal enthusiasts who were evicted for cultivating some suspicious indoor plants—so painting was one of the first things on the agenda. The kitchen was neat and the bathrooms bearable. And although the furniture he'd bought a few months ago looked a little out of place in the shabby rooms, once the walls and floors were done, he was confident it would all look okay.

Gabe tossed the keys in a bowl on the kitchen table and pulled his cell from his pocket. He noticed there were a couple of missed calls. One from Aaron and another from his mother. It would be around midnight in California, and he made a mental note to call them back in the morning. Most days he was glad the time difference let him off the hook when it came to dealing with his family. At least his younger brother, Luca, and baby sister, Bianca, didn't stick their nose into his life or moan about his decision to move to Crystal Point. As the eldest, Aaron always thought he knew best, and his mom was just…Mom. He knew she worried, knew his mom and Aaron were waiting for him to relapse and go running back to California.

He'd come to Crystal Point to start over, and the house and job were a part of that new life. Gabe liked that his family wasn't constantly around to dish out advice. Bad enough he got lectures on tap from Scott. Hell, he understood their motives…he might even have done the same thing had the situation been reversed. But things had changed. *He'd* changed. And Gabe was determined to live his life, even if it wasn't the one he'd planned on.

The private cul-de-sac in Crystal Point was an ideal place to start. It was peaceful, quiet and uncomplicated. Just what he wanted. A native bird squawked from somewhere overhead and he stared out the kitchen window and across the hedge to the next house along just as his cell rang. He looked at the screen. It was an overseas number and not one he recognized.

Uncomplicated?

Gabe glanced briefly out the window again as he answered the call. It was Cameron Jakowski, and the conversation lasted a couple of minutes. *Sure, uncomplicated.* Except for his beautiful, blonde, brown-eyed neighbor.

The thing about being a *go-to,* agreeable kind of person…sometimes it turned around to bite you on the behind. And this, Lauren thought as she drove up the driveway and then pulled up under the carport, was probably going to turn out to be one of those occasions.

Of course, she *could* have refused. But that wasn't really her style. She knew her brother wouldn't have called if there was any other option. He'd asked for her help, and she would always rally her resolve when it came to her family.

What she didn't want to do—what she was *determined* to avoid doing—was start up any kind of conversation with her new next-door neighbor. Bad enough he'd bought the house and moved in just days after the never-to-be-spoken-about and humiliating event at the wedding. The last thing she wanted to do was knock on his door.

Ever.

Lauren had hoped to never see him again. But it seemed fate had other ideas.

She took a breath, grabbed her bag and jacket and stepped out of the car. She struggled to open the timber gate that she'd been meaning to get repaired for the past three months and winced when the jagged edge caught her palm. Once inside her house, she dumped her handbag and laptop in the hall and took a few well-needed breaths.

I don't want to do this....

But she'd promised Cameron.

And a promise is a promise....

Then she headed next door.

Once she'd rounded the tall hedge, Lauren walked up the gravel path toward the house. There was a brand-new Jeep Cherokee parked in the driveway. The small porch illuminated with a sensor light once she took the three steps. The light flickered and then faded. She tapped on the door and waited. She heard footsteps before the door swung back on its hinges, and she came face-to-face with him.

And then butterflies bombarded her stomach in spectacular fashion.

Faded jeans fitted lean hips, and the white T-shirt he wore accentuated a solid wall of bronzed and very fine-looking muscle. His short black hair, clean-shaven jaw and body to die for added up to a purely lethal combination.

He really is gorgeous.

Memories of what had happened by the pool came rushing back. His hands on her skin, his glittering gaze moving over her, his chest so close she could almost hear his heartbeat. Mesmerized, Lauren sucked in a breath. He knew all about her. He knew things she'd told only her closest friends. He knew she'd thought about him…and imagined things.

But if he dares say anything about my knees being weak, I'll…

She finally found her voice. "I'm here…"

One brow cocked. "So I see."

"Did Cameron—"

"He called," he said, and smiled as he interrupted her. "Is he…"

"He is." He jerked his thumb over his shoulder and toward the door behind him. "Safe and sound and flaked out in front of the television."

She ignored the smile that tried to make its way to her lips and nodded. "Okay, thank you."

When she didn't move, he looked her over. "Are you coming inside or do you plan on camping on my doorstep all night?"

"All night?" she echoed, mortified that color was creeping up her neck. The idea of doing *anything* all night with Gabe Vitali took the temperature of her skin, her blood and pretty much every other part of her anatomy up a few notches. "Of course not."

He dropped his arms to his sides and stepped back.

Lauren crossed the threshold and walked into the hall. He was close, and everything about him affected her on a kind of sensory level. As much as she didn't want to admit anything, she was attracted to him. And worse luck, he knew it.

Her vow of celibacy suddenly seemed to be dissolving into thin air.

She walked down the short hallway and into the huge, open-plan living area. The furniture looked new and somehow out of place in the room. And sure enough, on the rug in front of the sofa, was her brother's one hundred and fifty pound French Mastiff, Jed. Fast asleep and snoring loudly.

"Thanks for picking him up from my brother's place," she said as politely as she could. "When Cameron called this morning, he said the house sitter had left quickly."

He nodded. "Her daughter is having a baby. She took a flight out from Bellandale after lunch and said she'd be back in a week."

Lauren bit down on her lip. "A week?"

"That's what she said."

A week of dog-sitting. Great. As much as she liked Jed, he was big, needy, had awful juicy jowls and a reputation for not obeying anyone other than Cameron. Too bad her parents had a cat that ruled the roost, or she would have dropped him off there. She had to admit the dog seemed comfortable draped across Gabe's rug.

She looked around some more. "So…you've moved in?"

"That was the general idea when I bought the house," he replied.

Lauren's teeth ground together. "Of course. I hope you'll be very happy here."

She watched his mouth twist with a grin. "You do? Really?"

"Really," she said, and raised a disinterested brow. "Be happy, or don't be happy. It's nothing to do with me."

His blue eyes looked her up and down with way too much leisure. The mood quickly shifted on a whisper of awareness that fluttered through the air and filled up the space between them. A change that was impossible to ignore, and there was rapidly enough heat in the room to combust a fire.

Warmth spread up her neck. He had a way of doing that to her. A way of heating her skin. "I need to…I need…"

"I think we both know what you need."

Sex…

That was what he was thinking. Suddenly, that was what *she* was thinking, even though turning up on his doorstep had nothing to do with her *lacking* love life or her vow to stay celibate. Lauren's cheeks burned, and her knees trembled. "I don't know what—"

"You don't like me much, do you?" he asked, cutting her off with such calm self-assurance, she wanted to slug him.

"I'm not—"

"Or is it because you *do* like me much?" he asked, cutting her off yet again. "And that's why you're so rattled at being in my living room."

Conceited jerk! Lauren sucked in some air, pushed back her shoulders and called Jed to heel. By the time the dog got up and ambled toward her, she was so worked up she could have screamed. She grasped Jed's collar and painted on a smile. "Thank you for collecting him from Cameron's."

"My pleasure."

Pleasure? Right. Not a word she wanted to hear from him. Not a word she wanted to think about in regard to him. And when she was safely back in her own home, Lauren kept reminding herself of one thing…Mr. Right was *not* Mr. Right-Next-Door.

Chapter Two

It was the dress.

That was why he'd had Lauren Jakowski on his mind for the past week.

When Gabe pulled her from the pool, the wet fabric had stuck to her curves so erotically, it had taken his breath away. She was as pretty as hell. A couple of years back he wouldn't have hesitated in coming on to her. He would have lingered by the pool, made small talk, flirted a little, asked her out and gotten her between the sheets by the third date. But he wasn't that man anymore.

Not so long ago, there had been no short supply of women in his life and in his bed. He'd mostly managed to keep things casual until he met Mona. She was the daughter of a colleague, and after dating for six months, they'd moved in together. At thirty years of age, he'd convinced himself it was time he got around to settling down. Gabe had a girlfriend, a career he loved, a nice apartment and good friends. Life was sweet. Until everything had blown up in his face.

Eighteen months later, he was in Crystal Point, working at the surf club and trying to live a normal life. A life that didn't include a woman like Lauren Jakowski.

Because she was too...wholesome.

Too...perfect.

A beautiful blonde with caramel eyes and porcelain skin. *Exactly my type.*

But by the pool, she'd made it clear to her friends what she was looking for—stability, reliability, longevity. And since he couldn't offer her any of those things, she was everything he needed to avoid. He didn't want her turning up on his doorstep. He didn't want to inhale the scent of the flowery fragrance that clung to her skin. And he certainly didn't want to remember how it felt to have her lovely curves pressed against him.

The best thing would be to ignore her...just as she'd suggested.

Damned inconvenient, then, that he'd bought the house right next door. If he'd known that before he'd signed on the dotted line, he might have changed his mind. But it was too late to think about that now. All he had to do was get through the renovation and the resale without remembering that she was merely over the hedge.

Lauren was not one-night-stand material...and he couldn't offer anything more.

Gabe dropped into the sofa and flicked channels on the television for half an hour before he thought about eating something. He headed to the kitchen and stopped in his tracks when he spotted the pile of canine accessories by the back door. Damn. He'd forgotten about that. When Cameron had called and asked him to make an emergency stop at his home to collect the dog, the vacating house sitter had thrust the bed, bowls, food and lead into his arms

along with a note listing feeding instructions. Things that
Lauren would need.

Realizing there was little point in avoiding the inevitable, Gabe shoved his feet into sneakers, swung the bag
of dog food over one shoulder, grabbed the rest of the gear
and his house keys and headed next door.

Lauren's home and gardens were neat and tidy, and the
only thing that seemed out of place was the rickety gate.
He pushed it open and headed up the steps. The porch light
was on and the front door open, so he tapped on the security screen. From somewhere in the house, he could hear
her talking to the dog, and the obvious frustration in her
voice made him smile. Maybe she was more a cat person?
He tapped again and then waited until he heard her footsteps coming down the hall.

"Oh…hi," she said breathlessly when she reached the
door.

Her hair was mussed and her shirt was pulled out from
the front of her skirt, and Gabe bit back a grin. She looked
as if she'd been crash tackled on the thirty-yard line. "Everything all right?"

She glanced over her shoulder. "Fine."

Gabe didn't quite believe her. "I forgot to give you this."

Her mouth set in a serious line. "Just leave it out there
and I'll grab it later."

"It's heavy," he said, and jangled the bag of kibble resting on his shoulder. "I should probably set it down inside."

She looked at him for a second and then unlocked the
screen. "Okay. Take it to the kitchen, at the end of the hall."

Gabe pushed the screen back and crossed the threshold.
When he passed the living room doorway he immediately
figured out the reason for her distress. Stretched out with
legs in the air and jowls drooping, the dog was rolling
around on her flowery chintz sofa.

"Jed looks as though he's made himself comfortable," he said, and kept walking.

"Yes, very comfortable."

When they reached the kitchen, Gabe swiveled on his heels and stared at her. She had her arms folded, her chin up and her lips pressed together, and even though she looked like she'd rather eat arsenic than spend a moment in his company, Gabe couldn't stop thinking about how beautiful she was.

I haven't gotten laid in a while...that's all it is.

He wasn't conceited, but he'd heard enough by the pool that night to know the attraction was mutual. He also knew she clearly thought it was as impossible as he did. Which suited him just fine. He didn't want to be stirred by her. He didn't want to spend restless nights thinking about having her in his bed.

"Where do you want it?" he asked.

"By the door will do."

He placed the gear on the floor and turned around to face her. "Would you like me to remove him from your sofa?"

"How did you know I couldn't...?"

"He's got about thirty pounds on you," Gabe said when her words trailed. "I just figured."

She shrugged. "I tried dragging him off, but he's as heavy as lead."

Gabe smiled and withdrew the note from his pocket. "Feeding instructions," he said, and dropped the paper onto the countertop. "If you want to get his food sorted, I'll get him off the sofa."

"Thank you," she said, then laid her hands on the back of a dining chair and grimaced. "Ouch."

He saw her shake her hand. "What's wrong?"

"Nothing," she replied and shook her hand again. "Just a splinter I got earlier from my gate."

"Let me see."

She curled her hand. "It's nothing."

Gabe moved around the kitchen counter. "It might become infected," he said, suddenly serious. "Do you have a first-aid kit?"

"It's nothing, really."

"It won't take a minute," he insisted. "So your first-aid kit?"

She shook her head. "I don't like needles."

"Don't be a baby."

Her eyes flashed, and she pushed her shoulders back as she marched into the kitchen and opened the pantry. "Here," she said, and tossed something through the air.

Gabe caught it one-handed and placed the kit on the table. "I'll be gentle. Sit," he said, and pulled out a chair.

She glared again, and he marveled that she still managed to look stunning with a scowl on her face. She sat down and waited while he dropped into a chair opposite.

"Hand?"

She pushed her hand into the center of the table and turned it over. "Gentle, remember?"

He smiled, opened the kit and took out an alcohol swab and an individually wrapped needle. When he took hold of her fingertips, his entire body crackled with a kind of heady electricity. Being so close wasn't helping his determination to steer clear of her.

"So what kind of work do you do?" he asked to try to get his mind off her soft skin and flowery perfume.

"I own a bridal shop in Bellandale."

He stretched out her palm. "That sounds interesting."

"Does it?"

Gabe looked up. She really did have the most amazing brown eyes. Warm and deep and intoxicating. She was remarkably beautiful, and he doubted she even knew it.

"Just making conversation," he said.

Her brows shot up. "To what end?"

"Are you always so suspicious?" he asked.

"Of what?"

"People," he replied. "Men."

She tensed, and Gabe held her hand a little firmer. "Not usually," she said quietly.

So it was just him? "I don't have any sinister intentions. So relax," he said as he extracted the splinter without her noticing at first and then gently rolled her fingers into her palm. "I'm not making a pass."

She swallowed hard. "I didn't think—"

"I would," he said quietly. "If you were looking for a no-strings, no-commitment kind of thing. But you're not. You're a commitment kind of girl, right? Abstaining from anything casual and with a clear plan for your future. Isn't that why you made your vow of celibacy?"

It felt right to get it out in the open. Maybe it would help diffuse the heat between them. Maybe it would stop him from thinking about kissing her.

She jerked her hand back and stood. "I… What I said at the wedding… It was private and personal and not up for discussion."

"I'm not mocking you," he said, and rested his elbows on the table. "On the contrary, I think I admire you for knowing what you want. And knowing what you don't."

Lauren's skin burned. He admired her? He'd pretty much admitted he wanted her, too. The awareness between them intensified, and she wished she could deny it. She wanted to dislike him. She wanted to resent him. She wanted to get away and never speak to him again.

"Thank you for the first aid," she said, and managed a tight smile. "I didn't feel a thing."

"Then we should keep it that way."

There was no mistaking his meaning. He thought it was a bad idea, too. She was happy about that. Very happy.

"So...about the dog?"

He stood up and pushed the chair back. "Get his feed ready and I'll drag him off your sofa."

Once he'd left the kitchen and disappeared down the hall, Lauren got to her feet and quickly sorted the dog's bedding and food in the laundry. A couple of minutes later, Gabe returned with Jed at his side. The dog ambled across the kitchen and into the back room and began eating.

Relieved the hound was no longer taking up her couch, Lauren took a shallow breath. "Thank you...Gabe."

He looked a little amused by her sudden use of his name and the slight tremor in her voice. His mouth twisted fractionally, as if he was trying not to smile. "No problem... Lauren."

"Well...good night."

His glittering gaze was unwavering. "I'll see you tomorrow."

Her eyes widened. "Tomorrow?"

He grinned a little. "I told Cameron I'd take the dog to work tomorrow so he doesn't destroy your yard trying to escape...until you can make other arrangements, of course."

She hadn't spared a thought to how she would care for the dog during the day. "Oh, right," she said vaguely, thinking about how the darn dog had suddenly become a reason why she would be forced to interact with Gabe. She made a mental note to call her friend Mary-Jayne and ask her to help. Lauren knew one thing—she didn't want to turn up on Gabe's doorstep again. "I'll **tie** him in the back when I leave, and you can collect him **from** there. You don't start until ten tomorrow, right?"

Gabe frowned. "How do **you know** that?"

"Cameron left me the roster," she replied. "I said I'd work the Sunday shifts while he's away if I'm needed."

"You're the fill-in lifeguard?"

"Don't look so surprised."

"I'm just curious as to why your brother didn't mention you specifically."

She shrugged a little. "I may have told him that I thought you were an ass."

Gabe laughed. "Oh, really?"

"It was after the wedding, so who could blame me?"

He raised his hands. "Because I innocently overheard your deepest secret?"

"Well, that was before I…" Her words trailed. Before what? Before she realized he wasn't quite the ogre she'd pegged him for. Now wasn't the time to admit anything. "Anyhow…good night."

Once he left, Lauren forced herself to relax. She took a long shower and changed into her silliest short-legged giraffe pajamas and made a toasted cheese sandwich for dinner. She ate in the lounge room, watching television, legs crossed lotus-style, with plans to forget all about her neighbor.

And failed.

Because Gabe Vitali reminded her that she was a flesh-and-blood woman in every sense of the word. The way he looked, the way he walked with that kind of natural sexual confidence, the way his blue eyes glittered… It was all too easy to get swept away thinking about such things.

And too easy to forget why she'd vowed to avoid a man like him at all costs.

She'd made her decision to find someone steady and honest and ordinary. No powerful attraction. No blinding lust. No foolish dreams of romantic love. Just friendship and compatibility. It might sound boring and absurd to her friends, but Lauren knew what she wanted. She wanted something lasting.

Something safe.

Since she spent most of the night staring at the ceiling, Lauren wasn't surprised when she awoke later than usual and had to rush to get ready for work. She fed the dog and then tied him on a generous lead to the post on her back patio and headed to the store. Her mother was there already, changing mannequins and merchandising the stock that had arrived Friday afternoon. Irene Jakowski had first opened The Wedding House twenty-five years earlier. Lauren had grown up around the gowns and the brides, and it had made her fall in love with weddings. During her school years, she'd worked part-time in the store, learning from her mother. When school finished, she'd studied business and accounting for two years at college before returning to the store, taking over from her mother, who now worked part-time.

Lauren dropped her laptop and bag on the desk in the staff room and headed to the sales floor. The rows of wedding gowns, each one immaculately pressed and presented on hangers, filled her with a mix of approval and melancholy.

"How's the dog?" her mother queried when she moved around the sales counter.

Lauren grimaced. "Missing his owner and slobbering all over my furniture. You know, like in that old movie *Turner & Hooch?*"

Irene laughed. "It's not that bad, surely?"

"Time will tell," she replied, and managed a rueful grin. "I don't know why he can't go into a boarding kennel like other dogs."

"You're brother says he pines when he's away from home," Irene told her. "And it's only until the house sitter returns, isn't it?"

"Yeah," Lauren said, and sighed. "Gabe is taking him to the surf club today, so at least my patio furniture is safe while I'm here."

Her mother's eyes widened. "Gabe is? Really?"

Of course her mother knew Gabe Vitali. She'd mentioned him several times over the past six months. Irene Jakowski was always on the lookout for a new son-in-law, since the old one hadn't worked out. The fact he'd bought the house next door was like gold to a matchmaking parent.

"Matka," Lauren warned, using the Polish word for *mother* when she saw the familiar gleam in her mother's eyes. "Stop."

"I was only—"

"I know what you're doing," Lauren said, smiling. "Now, let's get the store open."

By the time Gabe returned home that afternoon, he was short on patience and more than happy to hand Jed over to his neighbor. Damned dog had chewed his car keys, his sneakers and escaped twice through the automatic doors at the clubhouse.

When he pulled into the driveway, he spotted the fencing contractor he'd called earlier that day parked across the lawn. He locked Jed in Lauren's front garden and headed back to his own yard. He was twenty minutes into his meeting with the contractor when she arrived home. Gabe was in the front yard with the tradesman, talking prices and time frames, as the older man began pushing at the low timber fence that separated the two allotments and then wrote in a notepad.

She walked around the hedge and met him by the letterbox, eyeing the contractor's battered truck suspiciously. "What's going on?" she asked, looking all business in her black skirt and white blouse.

"A new fence," Gabe supplied and watched her curiosity quickly turn into a frown.

"I wasn't aware *we* needed a new one."

"This one's falling down," he said, and introduced her to the contractor before the other man waved his notepad and said he'd get back to him tomorrow.

Once the battered truck was reversing from the yard, she clamped her hands to her hips. "Shouldn't we have discussed it first?"

"It's only an estimate," he told her. "Nothing's decided yet."

She didn't look convinced. "Really?"

"Really," he assured her. "Although the fence does need replacing."

Her eyes flashed. "I know it's my responsibility to pay for half of any fence that's built, but at the moment I'm—"

Gabe shook his head. "I intend to pay for the fence, should it come to that."

She glared at him, then the fence, then back to him. "You don't get to decide that for me," she snapped, still glaring.

He looked at her, bemused by her sudden annoyance. "I don't?"

"It's my fence, too."

"Of course," he replied. "I was only—"

"Taking over? And probably thinking I couldn't possibly afford it and then feeling sorry for me, right?"

He had a whole lot of feelings churning through his blood when it came to Lauren Jakowski…pity definitely wasn't one of them. "Just being neighborly," he said, and figured he shouldn't smile, even though he wanted to. "But hey, if you want to pay for half the fence, go ahead."

"I will," she replied through tight lips. "Just let me know how much and when."

"Of course," he said.

She huffed a little. "Good. And have you been messing around with my gate?"

Ah. So the real reason why she looked like she wanted to slug him. "Yes, I fixed your gate this morning."

"Because?"

"Because it was broken," he replied, watching her temper flare as the seconds ticked by. *And broken things should be fixed.* He'd spent most of his adult life fixing things. *Fixing people.* But she didn't know that. And he wasn't about to tell her. "No point risking more splinters."

"I liked my gate how it was," she said, hands still on hips.

Gabe raised a brow. "Really?"

She scowled. "Really."

"You're mad at me because I repaired your gate?"

"I'm mad at you because it wasn't your gate to repair. I don't need anyone to fix things. I don't need a white knight, okay?"

A white knight? Yeah, right. But there was an edge of vulnerability in her voice that stopped him from smiling. Was she broken? Was that part of what drew him to her? Like meets like? He knew she was divorced, and at her brother's wedding she'd admitted her marriage hadn't been a happy one. But Gabe didn't want to speculate. And he didn't want to ask. The less he knew, the better.

"Okay," he said simply.

For a moment, he thought she might argue some more. Instead, she dropped her gaze and asked an obvious question. "What happened to your shoe?"

He glanced down. The back of his left sneaker was torn and the lace was missing. "Jed."

She looked up again, and he saw her mouth curve. "Was that the only damage?"

"Other than chewing my car keys and making a run for it whenever he got the chance."

She moaned softly. "Sorry about that. I'll get Cameron to replace them when he gets back."

Gabe shrugged. "No need. It's only a shoe."

She nodded, turned and walked back around the hedge. Gabe shook his shoulders and made a concerted effort to forget all about her.

And failed.

I really need to stop reacting like that.

Lauren was still thinking it forty minutes later when she emerged from the shower and pulled on frayed gray sweats. Her reaction, or rather her *overreaction,* to Gabe's news about the fence was amplified by his interference with her gate.

She didn't want him fixing things.

Lauren didn't want *any* man fixing things.

It was a road she'd traveled before. She knew what she wanted and white knights need not apply. Her ex-husband had tried to fix things—to fix her—and it had ended in disaster.

James Wallace had ridden into her life in his carpenter's truck, all charm and good looks. He'd arrived at The Wedding House to make repairs to the changing rooms, and she'd been unexpectedly drawn to his blatant flirting. An hour later, she'd accepted his invitation to go out with him that night. They ended up at a local bistro for drinks and then dinner, and by midnight he'd kissed her in the car park, and she was halfway in lust with him.

Three months later, she had a fairy-tale wedding.

Even though it was the wedding she'd planned to have to someone else.

To Tim. Sweet, handsome Tim Mannering. Her first love. Her only love. He had been her college boyfriend and the man she'd intended to marry. They'd made plans for the future. They'd talked about everything from building their dream home, taking an African-safari vacation, to how many kids they would have. They'd loved one another deeply and promised each other the world.

Except Tim had died three weeks before their wedding.

And Lauren walked down the aisle with another man less than two years later.

She swallowed the tightness in her throat. Thinking about Tim still filled her with sadness. And she was sad about James, too. She should never have married him. She hadn't loved him. They'd shared a fleeting attraction that had faded just months into their marriage. They'd had little in common and very different dreams. Within a year, James was gone, tired of what he called her *cold, unfeeling heart.* And Lauren was alone once more.

But she still hoped to share her life with someone. And she wanted the children she'd planned for since the day she and Tim had become engaged. Only next time, Lauren was determined to go into it with her eyes wide-open and not glazed over by romantic illusions. What she'd had with James wasn't enough. And what she'd had with Tim had left her broken inside. Now all she wanted was the middle road. Just mutual respect, trust and compatibility. No fireworks. No deep feelings. Lust was unreliable. Love was painful when lost.

There was nothing wrong with settling. Nothing at all. Settling was safe. All she had to do was remember what she wanted and why. And forget all about Gabe Vitali and his glittering blue eyes and broad shoulders. Because he was pure heartbreak material. And her heart wasn't up for grabs.

Not now.

Not ever again.

Chapter Three

Gabe went to his cousin's for dinner Wednesday night and expected the usual lecture about his life. Scott Jones was family and his closest friend, and even though he knew the other man's intentions were born from a sincere interest in his well-being, Gabe generally pulled no punches when it came to telling his cousin to mind his own business.

Scott's wife, Evie, was pure earth mother. She was strikingly attractive and possessed a calm, generous spirit. Gabe knew his cousin was besotted with his wife and baby daughter, and he was genuinely happy for him.

"How's the house coming along?" Scott asked over a beer while Evie was upstairs putting little Rebecca down for the night.

Gabe pushed back in the kitchen chair. "Fine."

"Will you stay there permanently?"

"I doubt it," he replied.

"Still can't see you renovating the place yourself," Scott said, and grinned.

Gabe frowned. "I can fix things."

Like Lauren's gate, which hadn't gone down so well. He should have left it alone. But she'd hurt herself on the thing and he didn't want that happening again. There was no harm in being neighborly.

"Job still working out?"

Gabe shrugged one shoulder. "Sure."

Scott grinned again. "And how's it going with your next-door neighbor?"

He knew his cousin was fishing. He'd told him a little about the incident at the wedding, and Scott knew he'd bought the house next door. Clearly, he'd told him too much. "Fine."

"I like Lauren," Scott said, and smiled.

Gabe didn't respond. He didn't have to. His cousin spoke again.

"You do, too, judging by the look on your face."

Gabe didn't flinch. "You know my plans. They haven't changed."

"Your five-year plan?" Scott's eyes widened. "Still think you can arrange life to order?" He looked to the ceiling, clearly thinking about his family upstairs. "No chance."

"I know what I'm doing."

It sounded good, at least. Pity he didn't quite believe it.

"You know she's divorced?" Scott asked.

"Yes."

Scott nodded. "Evie knows more about it than I do. And, of course, about the other guy."

His head came up. The other guy? "I don't—"

"He died about five years ago," his cousin said, and drank some beer. "They were engaged, that's all I know."

Gabe's insides contracted. So she'd lost someone. And married someone else. The wrong someone else. It explained the haunted, vulnerable look shading her brown eyes. But he didn't want to know any more. Hadn't he already decided the less he knew, the better?

"Not my business."

Scott's eyebrows shot up. "So no interest at all?"

He shrugged again. "No."

Scott chuckled. "You're a lousy liar."

I'm a great liar. His whole life was a lie. Gabe stood and scraped the chair back. "Thanks for the beer."

He left shortly after, and by the time he pulled into his own driveway, it was past ten o'clock. There were lights on next door, and when he spotted a shadowy silhouette pass by the front window, Gabe fought the way his stomach churned thinking about her. He didn't want to be thinking, imagining or anything else. Lauren Jakowski was a distraction he didn't need.

And he certainly didn't expect to find her on his doorstep at seven the next morning.

But there she was. All perfection and professionalism in her silky blue shirt and knee-length black skirt. Once he got that image clear in his head, Gabe noticed she wasn't alone. Jed sat on his haunches at her side.

"Am I stretching the boundaries of friendship?" she asked, and held out the lead.

He nodded. Were they friends now? No. Definitely not. "Absolutely."

She chewed at her bottom lip. "I wouldn't ask if it wasn't important."

Gabe shrugged. "What's the big emergency?"

She exhaled heavily. "He chewed off a piece of my sofa and broke the table in the living room when I left him home on Tuesday. Then he terrorized my parents' cat when I left him there yesterday. Mary-Jayne said she'd take him tomorrow and Saturday. She's got a fully enclosed yard and a dog, which will keep him company. But today I'm all out of options. I can't take him to the store and…and…I don't know what else to do."

Her frustration was clear, and Gabe knew he'd give her exactly what she wanted. Because saying no to Lauren was becoming increasingly difficult. "Okay."

"O-okay?" she echoed hesitantly.

"Yeah. Okay."

Relief flooded her face. "Thanks. I…I owe you for this."

Gabe shrugged again. He didn't want her owing him anything. Owing could lead to collecting…and that was out of the question. "No problem," he said, and took the lead.

"So dinner?" she asked and took a step back. "Tonight. I'll cook. My way of saying thanks."

His back straightened. "You don't need to—"

"I insist," she said quickly, and then looked as though she was itching to get away. "Say, seven o'clock?"

She left, and Gabe didn't go back inside until she disappeared around the hedge.

Dinner. Great idea. *Not.*
What were you thinking?

Lauren spent the day chastising herself and making sure she didn't let on to her mother that she'd somehow invited Gabe into the inner sanctum of her house, her kitchen and her solitary life. But she'd made the offer and it was too late to back out now. Besides, he was doing her a favor looking after the dog. Dinner really was the least she could do in return. He'd helped her out, and it was her way of saying thank-you. It was nothing. Just a simple meal between neighbors.

Only, simple seemed at odds with the way her nerves rattled just thinking about it.

She stopped by the supermarket on the way home, and by the time she pulled into the driveway, it was nearly six. She jumped into the shower, dried off, applied a little makeup and changed into loose-fitting cargo pants and a red knit top. By six-thirty she was in the kitchen marinating steaks and prepping a salad. And ignoring the knot in the pit of her stomach as best she could.

The doorbell rang at exactly seven o'clock.

Jed rushed down the hallway the moment she opened the door, clearly eager to get to his food bowl in the laundry.

"Hi," she said, and stepped back.

"Hi, yourself," Gabe said as he crossed the threshold.

He closed the door, and she didn't linger. Instead, she pivoted on her heels and headed back to the kitchen. By the time she'd made her way back behind the countertop, he was by the door, watching her. She looked up and met his gaze. He looked so good in his jeans and navy T-shirt, her breath stuck in her throat. She noticed a tattoo braid that encircled one biceps peeking out from the edge of his sleeve. She'd never liked ink much, but it suited him. It was sexy. Everything about Gabe was sexy. His broad shoulders, black hair, dazzling blue eyes... The combination was devastating. And dangerous.

Be immune to sexy.

He moved and rested against the door frame, crossing his arms, and Lauren was instantly absorbed by the image it evoked.

"You know, you really shouldn't look at me like that," he said, and Lauren quickly realized she'd been caught staring. Or ogling. "I might start thinking you aren't serious about that vow of yours."

Her skin warmed. "Don't flatter yourself."

His lips curled at the edges. "I never do."

"I don't believe that for a second."

"Then what do you believe, Lauren?" he asked, and met her gaze.

"I don't know what you mean."

His stare was unwavering. "I think you do."

"You're talking about what you overheard at the wedding?" She shrugged as casually as she could manage. "I thought we'd agreed not to talk about that."

He half smiled. "Did we? You said you wanted a passionless relationship."

Her breath caught. She didn't want to talk about that with him. Not when her pulse was racing so erratically. She remembered how he knew her secrets. He knew what she wanted. "Yes," she replied and hated that it tasted like a lie. "Passion is overrated."

"Do you think?" he asked quietly, his intense gaze locked with hers. "And chemistry?"

"Even more overrated."

"That's a handy line when you're in denial."

She tried but couldn't drag her gaze away. "I'm not in denial," she insisted. "About…anything."

About you. That was what she meant. And he knew it, too.

"Good," he said, almost as though he was trying to convince himself. "Shall I open this?" he asked, and gestured to the wine bottle he carried.

Lauren nodded and grabbed two glasses and a corkscrew from the cupboard, laying them on the counter. "How do you like your steak?"

"Medium rare," he replied. "You?"

She shrugged. "Same. Did Jed behave himself today? No disasters? No sacrificial sneakers?"

He grinned and grabbed the corkscrew. "It was moderately better than the last time."

She laughed softly. "He's usually very civilized when Cameron is around."

"He's pining," Gabe said, and popped the cork. "Missing the people he loves most. It's natural he would."

Lauren nodded. "You're right. And it's only for a few more days. I heard from Cameron's house sitter this morning, and she's flying back into Bellandale on Sunday afternoon."

He passed her a glass of wine, and Lauren's fingers tingled when they briefly touched his. If he noticed, he didn't show it. "How long have you lived here?" he asked.

"Just over a year."

"It's…nice. My sister, Bianca, would love it," he said easily and rested against the countertop. "She's into decorating."

Lauren pulled a couple of plates from the cupboard. "Do you have one of those large Italian-American families?"

"There are four of us. Aaron is thirty five and the eldest. He's divorced and has twin four-year-old boys. And then there's me, three years younger." He grinned a little. "Then Luca, who's thirty and married to his IT job, and Bianca, who is twenty-six and the baby of the family."

She nodded. "And your parents?"

"There's only my mom," he explained, watching her with such blistering intensity, Lauren found it hard to concentrate on preparing their meal. "My dad died fifteen years ago."

Her expression softened. "I'm sorry. Were you close?"

"Very."

She nodded again. "What did he—"

"Lung cancer."

The awful words hung in the air between them, and an old pain jabbed between her ribs. She pushed the memory off as quickly as it came.

"I'm sorry," she said gently. "I feel very lucky to still have both my parents."

"And there's only you and Cameron?" he asked.

"Yes," she replied. "And he's actually my half brother. Our mother married my dad when he was three years old. I would have loved a sister, though. I mean, we're really close, but a big family would be wonderful."

His gaze absorbed hers. "You want children?"

She nodded. "I always thought I'd like to have three kids."

He raised a brow. "With Mr. No-Passion?"

A smile tugged at his mouth, and Lauren couldn't stop her lips from creasing into a tiny grin. "Maybe. Hopefully. One day."

He looked at her oddly, as if he wanted to have an opinion about it but was holding his tongue. When he finally spoke, he surprised her. "You'll make a good mom."

"I… Thank you." The air crackled, and she avoided eye contact by feigning a deep interest in the salad she'd prepared. When he spoke again, she looked up.

"Need any help?" he asked, and took both wineglasses to the table.

"No," she replied and plated the food quickly. "I'm nearly done. Take a seat."

A minute later, she placed the plates on the table and sat down. For one crazy second she thought…no, *imagined*… that the mood between them felt a little like a date. *A first date.*

Stupid. They were neighbors. Acquaintances. Nothing more. So what if he was the most attractive man she'd ever met? Attraction hadn't done her any favors in the past. She'd been attracted to James, and that had ended badly for them both. This would be the same. And anything more than attraction was out of the question.

"So did you have a similar job in California?" she asked, determined to steer the conversation away from herself.

"Not really," he replied vaguely and picked up the utensils. "I worked as a lifeguard part-time at Huntington Beach, near where I lived."

"Cameron said the place has never run so smoothly. Do you enjoy the work?" she asked.

"Yeah…sure," he replied casually. "I like the beach," he

said, and when she raised a brow indicating she wanted him to elaborate, he continued. "And I get to teach a few classes, lifeguard on the weekends and juggle paperwork during the week." He shrugged. "It's not exactly rocket science."

She was itching to ask him more questions. Cameron had told her he was clearly overqualified for the role at the surf club. She knew he didn't talk about himself much, and that suited her fine. Most of the time. But tonight she was interested. As much as warning bells pealed, she wanted to know more about him. She wanted to know what made him tick. She wanted to know why he'd moved his life from California to Crystal Point.

"Don't you miss your old life? Your friends, your family?"

He looked up. "Of course."

"I could never leave my family like that," she said, and knew it sounded like a judgment. She shrugged and sighed a little. "I mean, I'd miss them too much to be away for too long."

If it was a dig, he ignored it. Because he was so mesmerized by her sheer loveliness, Gabe couldn't look away. He shouldn't have come around. He shouldn't have thought he could spend an evening with Lauren and not get caught up in the desire that thrummed through his blood. She was tempting. And he was…tempted.

"You really are quite beautiful."

The words were out before he could stop them. She fumbled with her cutlery, and the steak portion on the end of her fork fell back onto the plate. He watched as she pressed her fingertips against her mouth and discreetly wiped away a little sauce.

"Um…thank you. I guess."

Gabe rested back in his chair. "You don't sound convinced."

"That I'm beautiful?" She shrugged. "I've never really thought I was. Attractive, perhaps."

"No," he said quietly. "You're beautiful."

She grabbed her drink. "Are you coming on to me?" she asked bluntly.

Gabe chuckled. "No."

She met his gaze. "Because I'm not your type?"

"I'm not coming on to you because you're exactly my type."

Heat filled the space between them, and a sudden surge of blinding attraction clung to the air. But it was best to get it out in the open. He wanted her. And he was pretty sure the feeling was reciprocated.

"Is that because of what I said about you...you know... at the wedding?"

"You mean when you told your friends you've thought about me naked?"

Color quickly flamed her pale cheeks. "Is that what I said?"

"Yes."

She shrugged and smiled a little. "Well, since you were there and heard the whole conversation, there's no point denying it."

Gabe laughed. He liked that about her. She wasn't serious all the time. Even without her natural beauty, she had an energy and humor that fascinated him. For a moment, Gabe wished he could wind the clock forward, to a time in the future when he could guarantee any promises or commitment he might want to make. But he couldn't. And wishes were for fools.

He pushed some words out. "I guess not. Your friends don't seem to approve of your plans, though."

"They don't," she said, and sipped some wine. "But they support me, so that's all that matters. You know how family and friends can get sometimes…as if they know what's best, regardless of how a person might feel about it."

Gabe knew exactly. "You don't like weddings much?"

Her eyes widened. "Sure I do. Weddings are…my life."

"Really?"

She looked at him. "Well, maybe not my life. My job, at least."

He heard hesitation in her voice. "But?"

Her shoulders dropped. "Oh, you know, pretending the fairy tale exists on a day-in-and-day-out basis can be monotonous." She shook herself and picked up the cutlery again. "Sorry, I don't normally complain about it. But you're…" She stopped and looked at him. "Even though a week ago I was convinced you were simply another ridiculously handsome but conceited jerk, you're surprisingly… easy to talk to."

A good bedside manner is essential….

How many times had he heard that?

Gabe shook off the guilt between his shoulder blades. "Oh, I can be just as much of a jerk as the next guy."

She laughed, and the sound echoed around the room. "Well, thanks for the warning."

He placed his elbows on the table. "Don't thank me. I said I wouldn't make a pass. I didn't say it would be easy."

Her cheeks bloomed with color. "Oh, because I'm—"

"Because you're Commitment 101."

"And you're not?" she queried.

"Exactly."

"Have you ever been tempted? Or close?" she asked and pushed her barely eaten meal aside.

"Once," he replied and took a drink. "It didn't work out."

She stared at him, as if she was trying to figure out why. But she never would. He didn't talk about it. Ever. She took a second, swallowed hard and then spoke. "Did you love her?"

"It didn't work out," he said again, a whole lot quicker than he would have liked. "I guess there's your answer."

Her brows arched. "So you didn't love her? Not even a little bit?"

Gabe's mouth twisted. "I didn't realize there was such a thing as being a little bit in love. I cared for her, sure. But like I said, we didn't work out. There's no great mystery to it."

He wasn't about to tell Lauren that she was right—he hadn't really loved his ex-girlfriend. He'd done her a favor by letting her go. He was sure of it. And besides, Mona hadn't put up much resistance. Once she'd known she had an out clause, she'd left their relationship as quickly as she could.

Lauren bit her bottom lip, watching him. "So you got burned?"

He shrugged. "Not exactly."

"Then what, exactly?" she asked.

"We split up," he replied. "We went our separate ways. Neither of us was heartbroken."

"Which leaves you where?" Her eyes were full of questions. "Working at the surf club and having casual relationships and sex with women who are equally uninterested in commitment?"

"Ah...I suppose."

"Well, that sounds...like fun."

Not.

That was what she was thinking. Shallow and meaningless and hollow. Gabe thought so, too...even though he'd drilled himself to accept his present and future. But he suddenly lost his appetite.

"It is what it is," he said, and pushed back in his seat. "I'm not looking for...anything."

She watched him, her brown eyes darkening. "I've always believed that we're all looking for something...love or sex, belonging, companionship. Or maybe something more complicated, like peace of mind…or even isolation."

Which one are you looking for?

That was the question in her words. Gabe shrugged a shoulder casually. She was so close to the truth. "Is that why your marriage didn't work out?" he asked, shifting the focus back to her. "Because you wanted different things?"

She gripped her wineglass. "My marriage failed because my husband and I had nothing between us but fleeting physical attraction. Which isn't enough," she added.

It explained why she wanted a passionless relationship… sort of. "And now you're looking for more?" he asked. "Or maybe less?"

"Sometimes less *is* more," she replied. "Which is why I'm determined to think with my head next time…and not my—" she paused, smiling "—libido."

Gabe tensed. Thinking of *her* libido didn't do his any favors. "Or your heart?"

She smiled. "Precisely," she said.

He remembered what his cousin had said to him the night before. She'd lost someone. She'd lost love and settled for sex. The fact that she now wanted a middle road made perfect sense. "Someone did get it, though?"

Her gaze was unwavering. "You mean my heart? Yes. Someone did."

"Who was he?"

Silence stretched between them. He shouldn't have asked. He shouldn't want to know. The more he knew, the harder it would be to stay away from her.

"My first love. My only love, I guess."

She said the words so quietly and with such raw honesty, his insides contracted. He didn't want to hear any more. "You don't have to—"

"His name was Tim," she said, cutting him off. "We met

in college. I was nineteen and studying business. He was across the hall in engineering. We fell in love. A few years later we got engaged. And then…"

Gabe knew what was coming, but he asked anyway. "And then, what?"

She drew in a sharp breath. "And then he died."

"Was it an accident?"

She shook her head. "No. He was sick."

Sick…

Gabe's stomach churned uneasily, and he forced the next words out. "What kind of illness did he have?"

"Primary glioblastoma," she replied. "It's a—"

"I know what it is," he said quickly and pushed his chair back some more.

Brain tumor…

An aggressive, unforgiving kind of cancer that usually left a patient with months to live rather than years. It was all he needed to hear. It was time to go. He needed to finish eating and leave.

"I'm sorry," Gabe said, and spent the following few minutes pretending interest in his food. Even though he felt sick to his stomach. He pushed the meal around on the plate, finished his wine and declined the coffee she offered to make.

"I need to get going," he said as soon as he felt it was polite to do so, and stood.

"Oh…sure." She got to her feet. "Thanks again for looking after Jed."

"No problem. Thanks for dinner."

Once they reached the front door, he lingered for a moment. He liked her. A lot. She was sweet and warm and funny and so damned sexy, he could barely think of anything other than kissing her perfectly bowed mouth. He wanted Lauren in his bed more than he'd wanted anything for a long time.

But he wouldn't pursue it.

She'd lost the man she'd loved to cancer.

And he'd bet his boots it wasn't a road she'd ever want to travel again.

He needed to forget all about Lauren. And fast.

Chapter Four

Spending the evening with Gabe confirmed for Lauren that since her divorce, she'd gone into a kind of lazy hibernation. She'd quit volunteering at the surf club, rarely joined her mother for the tai chi classes she'd always loved and avoided socializing regularly with anyone other than her two closest friends. It hadn't been a deliberate pulling away, more like a reluctance to go out and put on her happy face.

That needed to change.

Lauren knew if she was going to find someone to share her life with, she actually needed to start having a real *life*.

But that real life didn't include her sexy neighbor.

On Friday night she went to the movies with Cassie and Mary-Jayne, stayed out afterward for coffee and cake and got home by ten.

There was a light on next door. Lauren ignored the fluttering in her stomach and headed inside. As soon as she'd crossed the threshold, she heard Jed's whining. Minutes later she discovered her great plan of leaving him locked in the laundry was not such a great plan. It was, in fact, a disaster. He'd somehow chewed a hole in the back door, and his big head was now stuck between the timbers. Lauren groaned, cursed her brother under her breath for a few seconds and then attempted to pull the dog free. But he was lodged. His neck was wedged around the cracked timber, and she didn't have the strength to pull him free.

Surprisingly, the dopey dog was in good spirits, and she patted him for a moment before she grabbed her phone. She could call her father? Or perhaps Mary-Jayne might be able to help?

Just get some backbone and go and ask Gabe.

She reassured the dog for a little while longer before she walked next door. The porch light flickered and she sucked in a breath and knocked.

Gabe looked surprised to see her on his doorstep.

"Lauren?" He rested against the door frame. "What's up?"

He wore faded jeans that were splattered with paint, and an old gray T-shirt. There was also paint in his hair and on his cheek. She wanted to smile, thinking how gorgeous he looked, but didn't. Instead, she put on a serious face.

"I need help."

He straightened. "What's wrong?"

"It might be better if you just see for yourself."

He was across the threshold in seconds. "Are you okay?"

"I'm fine. Jed, on the other hand..."

"What's he done now?" Gabe asked as they headed down the steps.

"Like I said, you need to see this for yourself."

A minute later they were in her house. They moved to the laundry and were facing Jed's bouncing rear end. And Gabe was laughing loudly. Really loudly. In fact, he was laughing so hard he doubled over and gripped the washing machine.

"It's really not that funny," she said crossly and planted her hands on her hips. "He could be hurt."

"He's not hurt," Gabe said, still chuckling as he moved across the small room and knelt down beside the dog. "The goofy mutt is just stuck."

"Exactly. He's wedged in and I can't pull him free."

He examined the door. "Do you have a hammer?"

"A hammer?"

"I need to knock a bit of this plywood out the way," he explained.

She nodded and grabbed the small toolbox under the sink. "I think there's something in here."

He opened the box, found the small hammer and got to work on the door. Jed whined a little, but Lauren placated him with pats and soothing words while Gabe made the hole large enough for the dog's head to fit back through. It took several minutes, but finally Jed was free and immediately started bounding around the small room, whipping Lauren's legs with his tail.

"Oh, that's good," she said on a relieved sigh. "Thank you."

"He looks okay," Gabe said, smiling. "But your door's not so lucky."

Lauren glanced at the door. The hole was bigger than she'd thought. "I'll need to call someone to fix it on Monday."

He nodded as he rose to his feet. "Sure. I'll board it up for you now so you'll be safe over the weekend."

Lauren's insides contracted. The way he spoke, the way he was so genuinely concerned about her, melted what was left of her resentment toward him.

Admit it…you like him.

A lot.

Too much.

"Ah—thanks," she said quietly and moved Jed out of the small room.

Gabe followed her. "Be back soon," he said as he strode down the hallway and headed out the front door.

He returned five minutes later with a large square piece of plywood, a cordless drill and a box of screws, and quickly repaired the hole. Lauren watched from her spot near the door, absorbed by the way he seemed to do everything with such effortless ease. Nothing fazed him. He was smart and resourceful and sexy and warmed the blood in her veins. Gabe made her think of everything she'd lost. And everything she was determined to avoid.

"Lauren?"

His voice jerked her back to earth. He was close. They were sharing the space in the narrow doorway, and Lauren's gaze got stuck on his chest and the way the paint-splattered T-shirt molded his chest. Her fingertips itched to reach up and touch him, to feel for herself if his body was as strong and solid as it looked. She remembered how he'd pulled her from the pool at the wedding and how his hands had felt upon her skin. It had been a long time since she'd felt a man's touch. Longer still since she'd wanted to.

Memories of Tim swirled around in her head. She'd loved him. Adored him. She'd imagined they would spend their lives together, loving one another, having children, creating memories through a long and happy marriage. But he'd never, not once, made her knees quiver and her skin burn with such blistering, scorching awareness. Even the fleeting desire she'd felt for James seemed lukewarm compared to the way Gabe made her feel. Her sex-starved body had turned traitor, taunting her…and she had to use her head to stay in control.

"I was…I was thinking…"

Her words trailed off when she looked up and met his blistering gaze. There was so much heat between them. Undeniable heat that combusted the air and made her stomach roll.

"Thinking?" he asked softly. "About what?"

Lauren willed some movement into her feet and managed to step back a little. "Your jacket," she muttered and turned on her heels and fled through the kitchen and toward the guest bedroom.

When she returned, Gabe was in the hallway, tools in hand.

"I forgot to return this," she explained and passed him the dinner jacket he'd given her the night of the wedding and which she'd since had dry-cleaned. "Thank you for lending it to me."

"No problem." He took the garment and smiled. "Well, good night."

"Ah—and thanks again for freeing Jed.... Your saving me from disaster is becoming something of a habit."

"No harm in being neighborly," he said casually.

Too casually. She knew he was as aware of her as she was of him. But they were skirting around it. Denying it.

"I guess not. Good night, Gabe."

He left, and Lauren closed the door, pressing her back against it as she let out a heavy sigh. Being around Gabe was wreaking havoc with her usual common sense. He wasn't what she wanted. Sure, she could invite him into her bed for the night. But that was all it would be. He'd called her Commitment 101, and he was right. He'd told her he didn't do serious. He didn't want a relationship. They were too different.

When she arrived at The Wedding House the following morning, her mother was there before her, as was their part-time worker, Dawn.

"You look terrible," her mother remarked, clearly taking in her paler-than-usual skin and dark smudges beneath her eyes. Lauren wasn't surprised she looked so haggard—she hadn't slept well. Instead, she'd spent the night fighting the bedsheets, dreaming old dreams, feeling an old, familiar pain that left her weary and exhausted.

"Gee—thanks," she said with a grin. "Just a little sleep deprived because of Jed, but I'll tell you about that later."

Irene smiled. "Are you heading to the surf club this afternoon? Or do you want me to go? We have to have the measurements for the stage and runway to the prop people by Monday, remember?"

She remembered. There was a fund-raiser at the surf club planned for two weeks away, and although Grace was the event organizer, Lauren volunteered to help in her sister-in-law's absence. Since she was organizing a fashion parade for the night anyway, it wasn't too much extra work liaising with the staging and entertainment people and the caterers.

"I'll go this afternoon," she said, and ignored the silly fluttering in her belly. All she had to do was measure the area for the stage and change rooms for the models. It was not as if she would be hanging around. It was not as if she had a reason to *want* to hang around.

"If you're sure," her mother said, her eyes twinkling.

Her übermatchmaking mother knew very well that Gabe might be there.

"I'm sure," she insisted. "And stop doing that."

Her mother raised both brows. "What? I just want to see my only daughter happy."

"I want to see me happy, too," Lauren said, and instructed Dawn to open the doors.

"I'm concerned about you," Irene said, more seriously.

"I'm fine, Matka," she promised. "Just tired, like I said."

The models for the parade had started coming into the store for their fittings, and that morning Carmen Collins crossed the threshold and held court like she owned the world. They'd gone to school together, and the self-proclaimed society princess made it her business to insult Lauren at every opportunity. But the other woman knew people with deep pockets, and since that was what the fundraiser was about, Lauren bit her tongue and flattered Carmen about the tight-fitting, plum-colored satin gown she was wearing in the parade.

"I do adore this color," Carmen purred and ran her hands over her hips. "So are you modeling in the parade?"

"No," Lauren replied and saw her mother's raised brows from the corner of her eye. "I'll be too busy with the show."

"Pity," Carmen said with a sugary laugh. "You do look so sweet in a wedding dress."

Lauren plastered on a smile and pulled back the fitting room drapes. "Maybe next year," she said, clinging to her manners as though they were a life raft. "I'll have the dress pressed and ready for the show."

The other woman left by eleven, and her mother didn't bother to hide her dislike once Carmen was out the door.

"Can't bear that woman," Irene said, and frowned. "She was an obnoxious teenager and hasn't improved with age."

"But she married a rich man and knows plenty of people who'll donate at the fund-raiser," Lauren reminded her mother. "That's all that matters, right?"

Her mother huffed out a breath. "I suppose. Anyway, we've only got three more of the models to come in for a fitting and we're done. So off you go." She shooed Lauren and smiled. "I'll close up."

Lauren grinned, hugged her mother, quickly changed into gunmetal-gray cargo pants, a pink collared T-shirt and sneakers and then headed to the Crystal Point Surf Club & Community Center to measure the space she'd need for the catwalk.

The holiday park was filled with campers and mobile homes, and she drove down the bitumen road that led to the clubhouse. Almost a year earlier, the place had been gutted

by fire, and the renovated building was bigger and better
with much-improved facilities. She parked outside, grabbed
her tape measure and notebook and headed through the automatic doors on the ground level.

And came to an abrupt halt.

Gabe was there.

Wet, laughing and clearly having a good time in the
company of a lifeguard, a young woman who Lauren
vaguely recalled was named Megan.

"Lauren?" he said as he straightened from his spot leaning against the reception desk. "What brings you here?"

She held up the tape. "Benefit stuff," she said, and tried
to ignore the way the safety shirt he wore outlined every
line and every muscle of his chest and shoulders at the same
time as the little green-eyed monster was rearing its head.

Snap out of it.

"Do you know Megan?" he asked and came toward her.

She nodded. "Hello."

"It's Mimi," the girl corrected cheerfully, showing off
perfectly white teeth and a million-dollar smile to go with
her athletic, tanned body. "No one calls me Megan except
my parents." She laughed and gazed at Gabe a little starry-
eyed. "And you." Then she turned her attention back to
Lauren. "So Gabe said you might be filling in for Cameron
while he's away if we get too busy. The beaches have been
crazy today.... Gabe just pulled an old man in from the rip."

Lauren smiled and looked at Gabe. That explained why
his clothes were wet and why he had sand on his feet. "Is
the man okay?"

"Shaken up, but fine," he replied and smiled. "But I
wouldn't call him old. He was probably only forty."

Perfectly toned and tanned *Mimi* laughed loudly. "Ancient," she said, and grabbed Gabe's arm, lingering a lot
longer than Lauren thought appropriate. "Well, I'd better
get back on patrol. See you."

She breezed out of the room with a seductive sway that Lauren couldn't have managed even if she'd wanted to.

"Do you need help with that?" Gabe asked, looking at the tape in her hand.

Lauren shook her head. "No."

"So you're organizing the benefit with Grace?"

She looked at him. "The fashion parade. Why? Are you interested in modeling?"

He laughed. "Ah, no thanks. I did promise your brother I'd help out setting up, but that's all."

Lauren placed the retractable tape at one end of the room, and when it bounced back into her hand, he walked over and held it out straight for her. "Thanks," she said, and pulled the tape out across the room.

"If you need models, perhaps Megan can help?" he suggested and came across the room.

"Mimi," she corrected extrasweetly, and placed the notebook on the desk. "And I think I have all the models we need." Lauren remained by the desk and raised a brow. "She's a little young, don't you think?"

He frowned. "No. She's a strong swimmer and a good lifeguard."

Lauren flipped the notepad open without looking at him. "That's not what I meant."

The second he realized her meaning, he laughed loudly. "She's what, nineteen? Give me *some* credit."

Lauren glanced sideways. "She's perky."

"And a teenager." He moved closer. "Why all this sudden interest in my love life?"

"I'm not interested," she defended, and shrugged as she faked writing something on the notepad. "You can do what you like. Although, everyone knows that interoffice romances can be tricky and—"

Lauren was startled when he touched her arm gently. Mesmerized, she turned to face him. Side by side, hips against the desk, there was barely a foot between them. She tilted her head back and met his eyes. His gaze traveled over her face, inspecting every feature before settling on her mouth. It was intensely erotic, and her knees quivered. The hand on her arm moved upward a little, skimming over her skin, sending jolts of electricity through her blood.

Her lips parted...waiting...anticipating...

It had been so long since she'd been kissed. Too long. And she knew *he* knew that was what she was thinking.

"I'm not going to kiss you," he said softly, his gaze still on her mouth. "Even though I want to, and it would certainly stop you talking nonsense about Megan."

"All I—"

"Shh," he said, and placed two fingertips against her lips. "Keep talking, and I *will* kiss you."

Lauren knew she had to move. Because if she didn't, sanity would be lost, and she'd fling against him and forget every promise she'd made to herself. The fleeting attraction she'd experienced the first time they'd met six months ago had morphed into heady, hot desire that was slowly becoming all she could think about.

And it's not what I want....

Mindless passion was dangerous.

And if I'm not careful, I'm going to get swept up in it all over again....

"You promised," she reminded him on a whisper. "Remember? No making passes."

"I know what I promised," he said, and rubbed his thumb against her jaw. "I did warn you I could be a jerk, though."

Lauren took a deep breath. "You know what I want."

"And you seem to be of a mind to tell me what I want," he said, still touching her lips. "Which is not, I might add, a teenager with a silly crush."

"She's more woman than teenager, and—"

He groaned. "You really do talk too much."

If the automatic doors hadn't whooshed open, Lauren was certain he would have kissed her as if there was no tomorrow. And she would have kissed him back. Vow or not.

"Gabe," Mimi's squeaky voice called frantically from the doorway. "I need your help."

He dropped his hand and stepped back. "What's wrong?"

"There's a lady on the beach who's had a fall, and I think she might have broken her ankle."

Gabe moved away from her and grabbed the first-aid bag. "Okay...show me where."

He was out the door in a flash, and Lauren took a few seconds to get her feet to move and follow. By the time she reached the first crest of the sandbank, Gabe was already attending to the elderly woman. He was crouched at her side, one hand on her shoulder and asking her questions while Mimi unzipped the first-aid bag.

Lauren moved closer to assist. And took about ten seconds to realize that Gabe didn't need her help. He knew exactly what he was doing.

It wasn't broken, but his patient, Faye, had a severe sprain and probably tendon damage, and as he wrapped her ankle, he instructed Megan to call for the ambulance. The woman was well into her eighties, and her tender skin was bruising quickly. She needed X-rays and the type of painkillers he couldn't administer.

Gabe wrapped her in a thermal blanket to ensure she didn't go into shock and stayed with her and her equally elderly husband until the paramedics arrived. The beach was busy, and he sent Megan back onto patrol and remained with the couple...excruciatingly aware that Lauren was watching his every move.

Once the ambulance arrived, it was about a fifteen-minute process to get Faye from the beach and safely tucked inside the vehicle. Her husband chose to travel in the ambulance, and Gabe accepted the old man's car keys for safekeeping and was told their grandson would be along to collect the car within the hour.

His shift was over by three o'clock, but he lingered for a while to ensure the remaining bathers were staying between the boundary flags, as the water was choppy. Megan took off for home, and Gabe headed back to the clubhouse to lock up. He found Lauren in his office, sitting at the desk and writing in her notebook. He watched her for a moment, thinking that an hour earlier, he'd been on the brink of kissing her. It would have been a big mistake. Definitely.

"Did you get your work done?" he asked when he came into the room.

"Yes," she replied and collected her things together.

"I gather this benefit is important?"

She nodded. "It will raise money for the Big Brothers Big Sisters program. Cameron said you've been working with the program, too."

"A little," he replied, reluctant to tell her any more. Like the fact he volunteered his time to help coach an under-twelve's swimming and lifesaving team twice a week.

"You and Cameron put me to shame."

"How so?"

She shrugged and stood. "He's always been community focused. Not…self-focused. You're like that, too, otherwise you wouldn't be doing this job you're clearly overqualified for, or do things like volunteering with the kids from the Big Brothers program."

Discomfiture raced across his skin. So she knew. "It's nothing, really. Just a couple of hours twice a week."

"It's more than most people do," she qualified. "More than I do."

"You're helping with the benefit," he reminded her. "Raising money for the program is something important."

She shrugged again. "I guess. You know, you were

amazing with that elderly lady. Cameron was right about you…you have a talent for the first-aid side of things in this job."

Gabe's insides crunched. He could have told her the truth in that moment. He could have told her that she was right. But that it wasn't talent. It was experience. He could have told her that for ten years he'd worked as a doctor in the E.R. at the finest hospital in Huntington Beach. But if he did, she'd want to know why he left.

Why I quit…

And how did he tell her that? One truth would snowball into another.

And Gabe wasn't ready.

He wasn't ready to admit that an innocent woman and her baby had died on his watch.

Chapter Five

Lauren dropped Jed off at her brother's house on Sunday afternoon. The house sitter was back and would be in residence until Cameron and Grace returned from their honeymoon. It was past five by the time she got home, and by then she only had half an hour to shower, change and prepare an array of snacks for the girls' night she was having with Cassie and Mary-Jayne.

It was impossible to *not* notice the bright yellow car parked at the entrance of Gabe's driveway.

She'd spotted the same vehicle outside the surf club. Megan's car. Obviously.

So what? He can do what he likes.

But Lauren had to force back the swell of jealousy burning through her veins.

She'd never *done* jealous. Not even with Tim. And she certainly wasn't going to waste time thinking about her neighbor and the perky *Mimi* doing *whatever* over the hedge.

When her friends arrived, Lauren headed through the front door to greet them and immediately heard a woman laughing. She noticed that Megan and Gabe were now outside and standing by the yellow car, clearly enjoying one another's company. And her stupid, rotten and completely unjustified jealousy returned with a vengeance. She willed it away with all the strength she could muster. When Cassie and Mary-Jayne reached the porch steps, they must have noticed the scowl on her face, because they both had raised brows and wide smiles on their faces.

"Trouble in paradise?" Cassie asked and walked up the steps.

Her friends knew what had happened at the wedding. They'd called it fate. Kismet. *Providence.* The fact he'd moved in next door simply added fuel to their combined romantic foolishness.

Mary-Jayne blew out a low whistle. "That's some serious competition you have there."

Of course she meant Megan. Young, perky, chirpy… Everything she wasn't. Lauren's scowl deepened. Her friends were teasing, but she felt the sting right through to her bones. For Gabe's no-commitment, casual-sex-only lifestyle, the effervescent Megan was no doubt perfect. She was pretty and uncomplicated. She probably wasn't haunted by memories of a lost love. She almost certainly wasn't looking to settle down and raise a family. So, perfect.

"Glaring at her over the hedge won't make her turn to stone, you know," Mary-Jayne said, and grinned.

Worse luck.

She jabbed her friend playfully in the ribs. "I need a drink," Lauren said as she turned on her heels and followed the two other women back inside.

Ten minutes later they were settled in the living room, a tray of snacks on the coffee table and a glass of wine in hand. Except for Cassie, who made do with sparkling grape juice.

"Have you heard from Doug?" Lauren asked her pregnant friend as she settled back in the sofa. "Has he warmed to the idea of the baby?"

The fact that Cassie's much older soldier boyfriend hadn't taken the news of her pregnancy very well had become a regularly talked about subject between them. It had been a month since Cassie had told him the news about the baby, and Lauren was concerned for her friend.

"He said we needed to talk about it," Cassie explained, her eyes shadowy. "I know he'll come around and consider this baby a blessing. But I don't want to distract him while he's on a mission."

"He's a total jerk," M.J. said bluntly, and tossed her mass of dark curls. "You know that, right?"

Lauren quickly took the middle ground. Something she often had to do. Cassie was a calm, sweet-natured woman who avoided confrontation and drama, while effervescent M.J. attracted it like a bee to a flower. Lauren figured she was somewhere in between. As different as they were, she knew they shared one common trait—unfailing loyalty to one another and their friendship.

"Perhaps we shouldn't judge him too quickly," she said, and ignored M.J.'s scowl.

"He should be judged," M.J. said, and grunted. "Do you even know where he is at the moment?"

Cassie shook her head. "Not really."

Lauren tapped Cassie's arm. "His brother might know. Perhaps you should—"

"Tanner's in South Dakota," Cassie said quietly. "And he and Doug rarely talk. Besides, Doug will come around. You'll see."

Lauren hoped so, for her friend's sake. And if not, she'd

be there to support Cassie, just as her friends had rallied around her when she'd needed them.

Cassie smiled. "So let's talk about you, not me. What's been going on between you and Mr. Gorgeous from next door?"

"Nothing," Lauren replied, and drank some wine. She wasn't about to tell them about the near-miss kiss at the surf club the previous afternoon. They'd be all over that information in a second. It wasn't as though she really wanted to exclude them. She knew they worried about her. They'd been her rocks after Tim died. And then again when James had walked out. But they didn't really understand her determination to avoid those kinds of feelings…even though they supported her. But Gabe was a complication she didn't need to discuss with her friends. The more time she spent with him, the less she felt she knew.

And she had to get him out of her system once and for all.

Only, she had no idea how she was supposed to do that when he had a habit of invading her thoughts…and her dreams.

It was ironic how much Gabe had come to avoid hospitals. At one time, the four walls of Huntington Beach's largest health-care facility had been his life. But then everything changed. Funny how some lingering fatigue and a small lump in his armpit could so quickly alter his fate.

Biopsy…cancer…surgery…chemo…radiation therapy…

The disease had been caught early, and with a bit of luck he'd been assured of a long life, but that didn't mean he could avoid the necessary follow-up examinations every six months. The specialist asked the usual invasive questions on his visit—questions he'd never considered invasive until he'd been on the other end of the conversation. Being a cancer patient had certainly altered his perspective on

having the right kind of bedside manner. If he did decide
to practice medicine again, he would do it with a renewed
respect for what the sick endured.

If...

Gabe missed his career more than he'd ever imagined
he would. Becoming a doctor had been his dream since he
was twelve years old, and getting into medical school had
been the realization of years of study and hard work. But
things changed. Life changed.

And then one arrogant decision had altered everything.

He'd gone back to work too soon. Everyone around him
said so. His family. His colleagues. His oncologist. But after
a bad reaction to the treatment and medication, and after
six weeks in bed chucking his guts up, he'd had enough.
He was determined to reclaim his life and return to the
job he loved.

Two weeks later a young mother and her baby were dead.

Perhaps technically not his fault, but he knew in his heart
that the blame lay at his feet. Nauseated and tired from that
day's round of treatment, Gabe had left a second-year resident alone in the trauma room for a few minutes and headed
for the bathroom. While he was gone, a patient had been
brought into the E.R. and the young doctor didn't have the
experience to handle the emergency. The young woman,
who was seven months pregnant, had hemorrhaged, and
both she and her unborn child died.

Plagued by guilt, after the inquiry, an undercurrent of
uncertainty had shadowed him and he'd stuck it out for
another month before he bailed on his career, his friends
and his family.

His life as he knew it.

And Crystal Point was as far away from all that as he
could get.

It was a place where he could wrap himself in anonym-
ity. A place where he could forget the past and not feel de-

fined by his illness or the tragedy of that terrible night in the E.R.

"Gabe?"

He stopped beneath the wide doorway of the specialist's rooms. Lauren stood a few feet away. Discomfort crawled along his skin. She was the last person he'd expected to see. And the last person he wanted to see outside the specialist's office.

"Hello," he said quietly, and wondered how to make his getaway.

She came to a stop in front of him. "What are you doing here?"

He took a second and considered all the things he wouldn't say. "What are *you* doing here?"

She frowned. "My friend Cassie works on reception in Radiology. I'm meeting her and Mary-Jayne for lunch."

She had a friend who worked at the hospital? One who might recognize him when he came in for testing? His discomfort turned into an all-out need to get away from her as quickly as possible before she asked more questions. Before she worked things out.

"I have to go," he said, and stepped sideways.

Her hand unexpectedly wrapped around his forearm and she said his name. Her touch was like a cattle brand against his skin, and Gabe fought the impulse to shake her off. Being this close didn't help his determination to stay away from her.

"Is everything okay?" she asked, and glanced up at the signage above his head. The word *oncology* stuck out like a beacon.

Any second now she's going to figure it out.

Dread licked along his spine. The thought of Lauren looking at him with sympathy or pity or something worse cut through to his bones. "Everything's fine."

She didn't look convinced. But Gabe wasn't about to

start spilling his guts. He wanted to get out of there as fast as he could.

She half smiled and then spoke. "I'm just surprised to see you here. Are you visiting someone or—"

"Last I looked I wasn't obligated to inform you of my movements."

His unkind words lingered in the space between them, and he wanted to snatch them back immediately. Even though he knew it was better this way. For them both. He knew she was struggling with the attraction between them, just like he was. He knew she wanted someone different... someone who could give her the picket-fence life she craved. And that wasn't him. She'd lost the man she'd loved to cancer. Of course she wouldn't want to risk that again.

"I'm...sorry," she said quietly. "I shouldn't have asked. I was only—"

"Forget it, Lauren," Gabe said sharply, and saw her wince as he pulled his arm away. "And I...I didn't mean to snap at you." The elevator nearby dinged and opened, and he wanted to dive inside. "I have to go. I'll see you later."

Gabe moved away and stepped through the doors. Away from her. And away from the questions in her eyes.

But by the end of the week, he was so wound up he felt as though he needed to run a marathon to get her out of his system. He needed to, though...because he liked being around her too much. He liked the soft sound of her voice and the sweet scent of her perfume. He liked the way she chewed her bottom lip when she was deep in thought. He liked how her eyes darkened to a deep caramel when she was annoyed, and wondered how they'd look if she was aroused. He wondered lots of things...but *nothing* could happen.

She'd lost her fiancé to cancer...making it the red flag of the century.

And Gabe had no intention of getting seriously involved

with anyone. Not until he was sure he could offer that some-one a real future. He had a five-year plan. If he stayed cancer-free for five years, he'd consider a serious relation-ship. Maybe even marriage. Until then, Gabe knew what he had to do. He had to steer clear of commitment. He had to steer clear of Lauren.

Cameron returned from his honeymoon midweek and stopped by the surf club Saturday morning just as Gabe was finishing off first aid to a pair of siblings who'd be-come entangled with a jellyfish. He reassured their con-cerned mother her children would be fine, and then joined his friend at the clubhouse.

"Busy morning?" Cameron asked, looking tanned and relaxed from his weeks in the Mediterranean, as he flaked into a chair.

"The usual summer holiday nonsense," he replied. "Sun-burn and dehydration mostly."

Cameron nodded. "Thanks for helping my sister out with Jed. She told me what happened to her door."

Gabe shrugged. "No problem," he said quickly, and tried to ignore the way his pulse sped up. He didn't want to talk to his friend about Lauren. He didn't want to *think* about Lauren. "Gotta get back to work."

Cameron stood and shook his head. "Thanks again. And don't forget to swing by my folks' house tonight, around six," he reminded him. "My beautiful wife is trying out her newly learned Greek cooking skills in my mother's kitchen, so it should be mighty interesting."

Gabe experienced an unexpected twinge of envy. His friend looked ridiculously happy. Cameron had the same dopey expression on his face that Scott permanently car-ried these days. He was pretty sure he'd never looked like that. Not even when he'd been with Mona.

"Sure," he said, thinking the last thing he wanted to do

was spend an evening at Lauren's parents' home, because he knew Lauren would be there, too. "See you then."

When he got home that afternoon, he changed into jeans and a T-shirt and started painting the main bedroom. It kept him busy until five-thirty. Then he showered, dressed and grabbed his car keys.

When he reversed out of the yard, he realized that Lauren was doing the same thing. Their vehicles pulled up alongside one another at the end of their driveways. He stopped, as did she. Their windows rolled down simultaneously.

"Hi," she said. "Are you going to my—"

"Yes," he said, cutting her off.

"My brother mentioned you were coming. Probably foolish to take both cars?"

She was right. He should have offered to drive her. But he hadn't seen her since their meeting at the hospital. He'd behaved badly. Rudely. Gabe nodded. "Probably."

"So…" Her voice trailed. "Yours or mine?"

Gabe sucked in some air. "I'll drive."

Her mouth twisted. "Be back in a minute."

He watched as she moved her car back up the driveway, got out and came around the passenger side of his Jeep. When she got in, the flowery scent of her perfume hit his senses. She buckled up and settled her gaze to the front.

"Ready?" he asked.

"Yes."

He backed the car onto the road and then came to a halt. He had something to say to her. "Lauren, I want to apologize again for being so dismissive the other day." He invented an excuse. "I was late for an appointment and—"

She waved a hand. "Like you said, not my business."

Gabe was tempted to apologize again. But he didn't. He nodded instead. "Okay."

She flashed him a brief look. "Just so you know, when we turn up together my mother is going to think it's a date."

"It's not, though," he said, and drove down the street. "Right?"

"Right," she replied.

Gabe reconsidered going to the Jakowskis'. He didn't want Lauren's mother getting any ideas. Or Cameron. Whatever he was feeling for Lauren, he had to get it under control. And fast.

Lauren knew the moment she walked into her mother's kitchen that she was going to get the third degree. Irene had greeted them at the door, explained that Cameron had been called into work and would be joining them later and quickly shuffled Gabe toward the games room to hang out with her father.

Her mother ushered Lauren directly into the kitchen. Grace was there, standing behind the wide granite counter, looking radiant. Her new sister-in-law was exceptionally beautiful. In the past, she'd always considered the other woman frosty and a little unfriendly, but Lauren had warmed toward Grace since it was clear her brother was crazy in love with her, and she with him.

Lauren stepped in beside Grace and began topping her mother's signature baked lemon cheesecake, a task she'd done countless times. Her sister-in-law remained silent, but her mother wasn't going to be held back.

"It's nice that Gabe could join us this evening. He really is quite handsome," Irene said as she busied herself pulling salad items from the refrigerator. "Don't you think? And such a lovely accent."

Lauren's gaze flicked up briefly. *"Matka,"* she warned, and half smiled. "Don't."

But she knew her mother wouldn't give up. "Just stating the obvious."

"His ancestors are Roman gods," Lauren said, and grinned. "So of course he looks good."

Irene laughed softly. "That's the spirit…indulge my matchmaking efforts."

"Well, there's little point fighting it," Lauren said with a sigh. "Even though you're wasting your time in this case."

"Do you think?" her mother inquired, still grinning as she grabbed a tray of appetizers. "Don't be too quick to say no, darling. He might just be the best of both worlds," Irene said, and smiled. "When you're done decorating that cake, can you grab the big tureen from the cabinet in the front living room?"

Lauren smiled. "Sure," she replied, and waited until her mother left the room before speaking to her sister-in-law. "See what I have to put up with?"

"She just cares about you," Grace replied, and covered the potato dish she'd prepared. "And he seems…nice."

He is nice. That was the problem. He was also sexy and gorgeous and not the *settle-down* kind of man she was look-ing for. He'd said as much. And she'd had nice before. Tim had been the nicest, most sincere man she'd ever known. Even James had been nice in his own charming, flirta-tious way. The kind of nice she wanted now didn't come with a handsome face and the ability to shoot her libido up like a rocket.

The best of both worlds…

What exactly did her mother mean? That Gabe was at-tractive, charming, funny and smart and just what any sen-sible woman would call the *perfect package?*

Too perfect. No one was without flaws. Secrets.

Lauren placed the cheesecake in the refrigerator and ex-cused herself. The big living room at the front of the house was rarely used. It housed her mother's treasures, like the twin glass lamps that had been in their family for four gen-erations, and the cabinet of exquisite crockery and dinnerware. Lauren stopped by the mantelpiece and stared at the family photographs lining the shelf. There were more pictures on the long cabinet at the other end of the room. Her mother loved taking pictures.

She fingered the edge of one frame and her insides crunched. It was a snapshot of herself and Tim. He looked so relaxed and cheerful in the photo. They were smiling, pressed close together, his blond hair flopping over his forehead. Had he lived, he would have been soon celebrating his thirtieth birthday. She looked at his face again. It was Lauren's favorite picture of him. Memories surged through her. Memories of love. And regret. And...anger. But she quickly pushed the feeling away. Anger had no place in her heart. Not when it came to Tim.

"You looked happy."

Lauren swiveled on her heels. Gabe stood behind her. Engrossed in her memories, she hadn't heard his approach. "Sorry?"

"In the picture," he said, and stepped closer. "You looked happy together."

"We were," she said, intensely conscious of his closeness. "That's...Tim," she explained softly and pointed to the photograph. "He was always happy. Even when he was facing the worst of it, somehow he never lost his sense of humor."

Gabe's eyes darkened. "Did he pass away quickly?"

She nodded. "In the end...yes. He died just a few weeks before we were due to be married."

"And then you married someone else?"

"Not quite two years later," she replied and immediately wondered why she was admitting such things to him. "It was a big mistake."

Gabe nodded a little. "Because you didn't love him?"

"Exactly," she said, and sucked in a short breath.

"There must have been something that made you marry him?"

Lauren's skin grew hotter. "Sex."

His blistering gaze was unwavering. "That's all?"

"I'd had love," she admitted, so aware of his closeness she could barely breathe. "And I'd lost it. When I met James, I thought attraction would be enough."

"But it wasn't?"

She sighed. "No."

"And now you don't want that, either?" he asked.

Lauren raised a shoulder. "I don't expect anyone to understand."

"Actually," he said quietly. "I do. You lost the love of your life, then settled for something that left you empty, and now you want to find that no-risk, no-hurt, middle road."

Middle road? Could he read her mind? "That's right. I married my ex-husband after only knowing him for three months. It was a foolish impulse and one I regret…for his sake and mine."

Gabe looked at the mantelpiece. "Which explains why there are no pictures of him."

"My mother was never a fan of James," she said, and felt his scrutiny through to her bones. "Once we divorced, the wedding pictures came down." Lauren looked down to her feet and then back up to his gaze. "Ah…what are you doing in here? I thought you were out on the back patio with my dad."

"I was," he replied, and grinned fractionally. "But your mother sent me on a mercy dash to help you carry some kind of heavy dish."

Lauren rolled her eyes and pointed to the tureen in the cabinet. "My mother is meddling."

He smiled, like he knew exactly what she meant. "To what end?"

Lauren raised a shoulder. "Can't you guess? I told you she'd think this was a date."

His gaze widened. "Should I be worried?"

She laughed a little. "That my mother has her sights set on you? Probably."

Gabe laughed, too, and the sound warmed her right through to the blood in her veins. He was so…likable. So gorgeous. And it scared her. With James, she'd jumped in, libido first, uncaring of the consequences. Still grieving the loss of the man she'd loved, Lauren had found temporary solace in arms that had soon left her feeling empty and alone. Although she'd thought him good-looking and charming, she'd realized soon after they'd married that they had very little in common. But the attraction she had for Gabe was different. The more time she spent with him, the less superficial it felt. Which put her more at risk.

"I shall consider myself warned," he said, and chuckled.

Lauren walked toward the cabinet and opened the door. "Thanks for being so understanding," she said, still grinning.

"I, too, have a meddling, albeit well-meaning mother who wants to see me…shall we say, *settled*. So I understand your position."

For a second, she wondered what else they had in common. He clearly came from a close family, as she did. "Doesn't she know you're not interested in commitment?"

His gaze locked with hers. "I don't think she quite believes me."

Lauren's breath caught. "Have you…"

"Have I what?"

She shrugged, trying to be casual but churning inside. "Have you changed your mind about that?"

Lauren couldn't believe she'd asked the question. And couldn't believe she wanted to know. Her elbow touched his arm and the contact sent heat shooting across her skin.

She should have pulled away. But Lauren remained where she was, immobilized by the connection simmering between them.

"No," he said after a long stretch of silence. "I haven't."

Of course, it was what she needed to hear. Gabe wasn't what she wanted. Because he made her feel too much. He made her question the choice she'd made to remain celibate until she found someone to share her life with. He didn't want what she wanted.

He's all wrong for me....

Even though being beside him, alone and in the solitude of the big room, seemed so unbelievably normal, she was tempted to lean closer and invite him to kiss her. His gaze shifted from her eyes to her mouth, and Lauren sucked in a shallow breath. Her lips parted slightly and he watched with such searing intensity, her knees threatened to give way. There was heat between them, the kind that came before a kiss. The kind of heat that might lead to something more.

"Gabe..." She said his name on a sigh.

"We would be crazy to start something," he warned, unmoving and clearly reading her thoughts.

"I know," she agreed softly.

Crazy or not, she was strangely unsurprised when he took hold of her hand and gently rubbed his thumb along her palm. He was still watching her, still looking at her mouth.

"Do you have any idea how much I want to kiss you right now?"

She shivered at his question, despite the warmth racing across her skin. Lauren nodded, feeling the heat between them rise up a notch. "Do you have any idea how much I want you to kiss me right now?"

His hand wrapped around hers. She was staring up, waiting, thinking about how she hadn't been kissed for such a long time. And thinking how Gabe had somehow, in a matter of weeks, become the one man whose kiss she longed for.

Chapter Six

Gabe could have kissed her right then, right there. He could have lost himself in the softness of her lips and sweet taste of her mouth. He could have forgotten about his determination to keep away from her and give in to the desire he experienced whenever she was near. And he would have. But a loud crash followed by an equally loud shout pushed them apart immediately. The dish from the china cabinet was quickly forgotten as they both hurried from the room.

When they reached the kitchen, he saw there was glass and water on the floor and also a pile of tattered flowers. Lauren's father was sitting on the ground, knees half-curled to his chest.

"Dad!" Lauren gasped as she rushed to his side.

Irene and Grace came through the doorway and stood worriedly behind Gabe as he quickly moved between them to settle beside the older man. Franciszek Jakowski was holding up a seriously bleeding hand, and Gabe quickly snatched up a tea towel from the countertop and wrapped it around his palm.

"I knocked the darn vase off the counter," Franciszek explained as Gabe hauled him to his feet. "Cut myself when I fell."

"Can you walk?" Gabe asked, knowing he needed to look at the wound immediately.

Franciszek winced as he put weight on his left foot. "Not so good."

He looked at Lauren. "Hold your father's hand up to help with the bleeding, and I'll get him to a chair."

She did as he asked, and Gabe hooked an arm around the other man's shoulder and soon got him settled onto the kitchen chair. Blood streamed down his arm and splattered on Gabe's shirt. He undid the towel and examined Franciszek's hand. The cut was deep and would need stitches. Irene disappeared and quickly returned with a first-aid kit. Gabe cleaned and dressed the wound, conscious of the scrutiny of the three women hovering close by. Within minutes, he also had Franciszek's left ankle wrapped with an elastic bandage.

"The cut definitely needs stitches," he said, and wiped his hands on a cloth Lauren passed him. "And it looks like you've only sprained your ankle, but an X-ray wouldn't hurt just to be sure."

Irene extolled her gratitude and was on the telephone immediately, making an appointment to see their local doctor within the next half hour.

"I'll drive you," Lauren volunteered, but her mother quickly vetoed that idea.

"Grace can drive us," she said, and looked toward her daughter-in-law, who nodded instantly. "You can stay and clean up. And I need you to keep an eye on dinner. We won't be too long."

"That's for sure," Franciszek agreed cheerfully, although Gabe was pretty sure the older man was in considerable pain. He patted Gabe's shoulder. "Thanks for the doctoring, son. Much appreciated."

Gabe's stomach sank. Being reminded of who he was, even though no one but his family knew the truth, hit him like a fist of shame between the shoulder blades. He glanced at Lauren and then looked away. There were questions in her eyes. Questions he had no intention of answering.

It took several minutes to get Franciszek into the car, and when Gabe returned, Lauren was in the kitchen, picking up pieces of shattered glass from the floor. She was concentrating on her task, looking shaken and pale.

"Are you okay?"

She glanced up. "Just worried about my dad."

"He'll be fine."

Her small nose wrinkled. "Thanks to you," she said as she rose to her feet and walked around the countertop. "You might want to consider switching careers."

His gut sank. "What?"

"You'd make a good paramedic," she said, and grabbed a banister brush from the cupboard beneath the sink. "You clearly have a knack for it. You know, I have a friend who's an admin in emergency services. I could probably arrange for you to—"

"No…but thank you," he said, cutting her off before she said too much about it. "Need some help with this?"

She held his gaze for a moment, and then passed him the broom. "Sure. I'll get the mop and bucket." She propped her hands on her hips and looked at his blood-stained shirt. "I'll find you something to wear and you can pop that shirt in the machine before it permanently stains. I think Cameron has some clothes in one of the guest rooms. I'll go and check."

She disappeared, and Gabe stared after her. Guilt pressed

down on his shoulders. He wanted to tell her the truth about himself. But one would lead to another and then another. And what was the point? There were already too many questions in her lovely brown eyes.

When she returned with the mop and bucket, she placed a piece of clothing on the table. "I'll finish up here. You can go and change."

He met her gaze. "Okay."

Gabe left the room and headed for the laundry. Once there, he stripped off his soiled shirt and dumped it in the washing machine. He added liquid, cranked on the start switch and rested his behind on the edge of the sink. Then he expelled a long breath.

Damn.

He wanted to kiss her so much. He wanted to touch her. He wanted to feel her against him and stroke her soft skin. He wanted to forget every promise he'd made to himself about waiting to see if his illness returned before he'd consider being in a relationship. But it wouldn't be fair to any woman. More than that, it wouldn't be fair to Lauren. He couldn't ask her to risk herself. He *wouldn't*. He'd seen firsthand what it had done to his mom when his father had battled cancer for three years. He'd watched his mom lose the light in her eyes and the spirit in her heart. He'd watched her grieve and cry and bury the man she'd loved.

And Lauren had been there, too. He'd heard the pain in her voice when she'd spoken of her lost love. It should have been enough to send him running.

She thought he'd make a good paramedic? The irony wasn't hard to miss. There were questions in her eyes, and they were questions he didn't want to answer. But if he kept doing this, if he kept being close to her, he would be forced to tell her everything.

And admitting how he'd bailed on his life and career wasn't an option.

Pull yourself together and forget her.

He needed to leave. And he would have if Lauren hadn't chosen that moment to walk into the laundry room.

When Lauren crossed the threshold, she stopped dead in her tracks. Gabe stood by the sink in the small room with the fresh shirt in his hands. And naked from the waist up. He turned to face her.

It had been so long since she'd been this close to a man's bare skin. And because it was Gabe, he was thoroughly mesmerizing, as she'd known he would be. She'd known his skin would look like satin stretched over steel and that his broad shoulders and arms would be well defined and muscular. The smattering of dark hair on his chest tapered down in a line and disappeared into the low waistband of his jeans, and Lauren's breath caught in her throat.

His gaze instantly met hers, and she didn't miss the darkening blue eyes and faint pulse beating in his cheek. Somehow, she moved closer, and when Lauren finally found her voice, they were barely feet apart.

She dropped the bucket and mop. "I...I'm sorry...I didn't realize you were still in here."

Heat swirled between them, coiling around the small room, and she couldn't have moved even if she wanted to. She tried to avert her gaze. Tried and failed. He had such smooth skin, and her fingers itched with the sudden longing to reach out and touch him.

"You..." Her voice cracked, and she swallowed. "You were right with what you said before. We'd be...crazy...to start something...to start imagining we could..."

Her words trailed off, and still he stared at her, holding her gaze with a hypnotic power she'd never experienced before. Color spotted her cheeks, and she quickly turned and made for the doorway. Only she couldn't step forward because Gabe's hands came out and gently grasped her shoulders. She swallowed hard as he moved in close behind her and said her name in that soft, sexy way she was becoming so used to. The heat from his body seared through her thin shirt, and Lauren's temperature quickly spiked. His hands moved down her arms and linked with hers. She felt his soft breath near her nape, and his chest pressed intimately against her shoulders.

His arms came around her and Lauren pushed back. One hand rested on her hip, the other he placed on her rib cage. The heat between them ramped up and created a swirling energy in the small room. Her head dropped back, and she let out a heavy sigh as his fingertips trailed patterns across the shirt. It was an intensely erotic moment, and she wanted to turn in his arms and push against him. She wanted his kiss, his touch, his heat and everything else. She wanted him to plunder her mouth over and over and then more. Flesh against flesh, sweat against sweat. She wanted his body over her, around her, inside her. She wanted *him*... and not only his body. Lauren tilted her head, inviting him to touch the delicate skin at the base of her neck with his mouth. But he didn't. Instead, Gabe continued to touch her rib cage with skillful, seductive fingers, never going too high and barely teasing the underside of her breasts.

She could feel him hard against her. He was aroused and not hiding the fact. Lauren moved her arms back and planted her hands on his thighs. She dug her nails against the denim and urged him closer. His touch was so incredibly erotic, and she groaned low in her throat. Finally, he kissed her nape, softly, gently, and electricity shimmered across her skin.

"Lauren," he whispered against her ear as his mouth trailed upward. "I'm aching to make love to you."

Lauren managed a vague nod and was about to turn in his arms and beg him to kiss her and make love to her when she heard a door slam. The front door. Seconds later, she heard her brother's familiar voice calling out a greeting.

Gabe released her gently and she stepped forward, dragging air through her lungs. "I should go."

"Good idea," he said softly as he grabbed the shirt and pulled it quickly over his head. "I should probably stay here for a minute."

She nodded and willed some serious movement into her legs and was back in the main hallway seconds later. Cameron, dressed in his regulation police-officer uniform, greeted her with a brief hug and ruffled her hair.

"Hey, kid...what's happening?" he asked once they were in the kitchen and saw the pan of broken glass on the countertop.

She quickly filled him in about their father's mishap, and once she was done, he immediately called Grace. Her brother was still on the phone when Gabe walked into the room. Her body still hummed with memories of his touch, and their gaze connected instantly. If Cameron hadn't turned up, she was sure they'd be making love that very minute. And it would have been a big mistake. When the moment was over, there would be regret and recrimination, and she'd hate herself for being so weak.

When her brother ended his call, he explained that their father was being triaged, and that they'd be home as soon as he was released. In fact, they returned close to an hour and a half later. By then, Lauren had shuffled the men out of the kitchen and finished preparing dinner.

It turned out that Gabe was right. Her father had needed stitches for his hand, and his foot was only sprained. By the time they settled her dad at the head of the table, crutches to one side, it was nearly nine o'clock. Lauren was seated next to Gabe and felt his closeness as if it was a cloak draped across her shoulders.

Once dinner was over, she headed back to the kitchen

with Grace and began cleaning up. Gabe and her brother joined them soon after, and Grace tossed a tea towel to each of them.

"Idle hands," her sister-in-law said, and grinned when Cameron complained. "Get to work."

Lauren laughed and dunked her hands into a sink full of soapy water. Like with everything he did, Gabe ignored Cameron's whining and attended the task with an effortless charm that had both Lauren and Grace smiling. It would, she decided, be much better if he had the charisma of a rock. But no such luck. Aside from the insane chemistry that throbbed between them, Lauren liked him so much it was becoming impossible to imagine she could simply dismiss her growing feelings. Sexual attraction was one thing, emotional attraction another thing altogether. It was also hard to dismiss how her mother, Grace and even her brother watched their interaction with subtle, yet keen interest.

By the time they left, it was past eleven o'clock, and then a quarter past the hour when Gabe pulled his truck into his driveway. She got out, and he quickly came around the side of the vehicle.

"Well, thanks for the lift," she said, and tucked her tote under her arm.

He touched her elbow. "I'll see you to your door."

"There's no need," she said quickly.

"Come on," he said, and began walking down the driveway, ignoring her protest.

Lauren followed and stepped in beside him as they rounded the hedge that separated their front lawns. He opened the gate and stood aside to let her pass. By the time she'd walked up the path and onto the small porch, she was so acutely aware of him she could barely hold her keys steady.

Open the door. Say good-night. Get inside. Easy.

Lauren slid the key in the screen door and propped it

open with her elbow while she unlocked the front door. "Um…thanks again," she said, and turned on her heels. "And thanks for what you did for my dad. I'm glad you were there to—"

"Lauren?"

She stilled, clutching her tote, hoping he wouldn't come closer. Praying he wouldn't kiss her. "We…we need to forget what happened tonight," she said in a voice that rattled in her throat. "We agreed it would be crazy to—"

"Nothing really happened," he said, cutting her off. "Did it?"

Lauren took a breath. "Well, what *almost* happened. I've made a vow, a promise to myself…and it's a promise I intend to keep. And I'm never going to find what I want if I get drawn deeper into this…this attraction I have for you. We both know it won't go anywhere other than your bed, and I'm not prepared to settle for just sex. Not again."

He didn't move. But he stared at her. He stared so deeply, so intensely, she could barely breathe. The small porch and dim light overhead created extreme intimacy. If she took one tiny step she would be pressed against him.

"You're right," he said, and moved back a little. "You shouldn't settle for sex. You should find that middle road you want, Lauren, with someone who can give you the relationship you deserve."

Then he was gone. Down the steps and through the gate and quickly out of view. Lauren stayed where she was for several minutes. Her chest was pounding. Her stomach was churning. Her head was spinning.

And her heart was in serious danger.

Gabe knew he was right to leave Lauren alone. He hadn't seen her all week. Deliberately. He left for work earlier than she did and returned home before her small car pulled into the driveway each afternoon. Not seeing her helped. A lot. Or more like a little. Or not at all.

Unfortunately, not seeing her seemed to put him in a bad mood.

Something his cousin took pleasure in pointing out on Thursday afternoon when Gabe dropped by the B and B.

"You know, you'll never get laid if you don't ask her out," Scott said with a wide grin, and passed him a beer.

"Shut up," he said, and cranked the lid off.

His cousin laughed. "Hah. Sucker. Just admit your five-year plan is stupid and that you're crazy about Lauren."

Gabe gripped the bottle. "I know what I'm doing."

"Sure you do," Scott shot back. "You're hibernating like a bear because you don't want to admit you like her. That's why your mom has been calling my mom and my mom has been calling me. You haven't been taking any calls from your family for the past two weeks."

"They worry too much," he remarked, and shrugged. "They think I'm going to relapse and die a horrible death. And maybe I will. All I know is I don't want to put anyone in the middle of that. Not anyone. Not Lauren."

"Maybe you should let her decide that for herself."

"Will you just…" Gabe paused, ignored the curse teetering on the end of his tongue and drank some more beer. "Stop talking."

Scott shrugged. "Just trying to see my best friend happy."

"I'm happy enough," he shot back. "So lay off."

His cousin laughed, clearly unperturbed by his bad temper. "You know, not every woman is going to run for the hills if you get sick again."

"Mona didn't run," Gabe reminded the other man. "I broke it off with her."

Scott shrugged again. "Another example of you needing to control everything, right?"

Tired of the same old argument, Gabe finished his beer and stood. "I have to bail."

"Hot date?"

Gabe grabbed his keys off the table. "A wall that won't paint itself."

"Sounds riveting," Scott said drily. "Renovating that house won't keep you warm at night, old buddy."

His cousin was right, but he had no intention of admitting that. He took off and was home within a few minutes. Once he'd dropped his keys on the hall stand, he rounded out his shoulders. Pressure cramped his back, and he let out a long breath. He needed to burn off some of the tension clinging to his skin. There was easily over an hour of sunlight left, so he changed into his running gear and headed off down the street.

Gabe reached The Parade quickly. The long road stretched out in front of him. He crossed the wide grassy verge and headed for the pathway leading to the beach in one direction and to the north end of the small town to the other. He vetoed the beach and headed left, striding out at an even pace and covering the ground quickly. It was quiet at this end of town. Without the holiday park, surf club and kiosk there was only a scattering of new homes, and the waterfront was more rock than sand. He spotted a pair of snorkelers preparing to dive close to the bank and waved as another runner jogged past.

Up ahead, he spotted someone sitting alone on one of the many bench seats that were placed along the line of the pathway. It was Lauren. He'd recognize her blond hair anywhere. He slowed his pace and considered turning around. But he kept moving, slowing only when she was about twenty feet away. She was looking out toward the ocean, deep in thought, hands crossed in her lap. An odd feeling pressed into his chest. As though he suddenly couldn't get enough air in his lungs. God, she was beautiful. He stopped a few feet from the seat and said her name.

Her head turned immediately. "Oh, hi."

She was paler than usual. Sadder. The tightness in his chest amplified tenfold.

He stopped closer. "Are you okay?"

"Sure," she said quietly, unmoving.

Gabe wasn't convinced. He moved around the bench and sat down beside her. "I'm not buying. What's up?"

"Nothing," she insisted.

"It's four-thirty on a Thursday afternoon. You're not at the store," he said pointedly. "You're sitting here alone staring out at the sea."

She shrugged a little. "I'm just thinking."

He knew that. "About what?"

She drew in a shallow breath. "Tim."

Of course. Her lost love. "I'm sorry, I shouldn't have—"

"It's his birthday," she said quietly, and turned her gaze back to the ocean. "I always come here on this day. It's where he proposed to me."

Gabe immediately felt like he was intruding on an intensely private moment. Big-time. He got up to leave, but her hand came out and touched his arm.

"It's okay," she said, her voice so quiet and strained it made his insides twinge. "I could probably use the company."

"Do you usually?" he asked. "Have company, I mean?"

She shook her head and dropped her hand. "Not usually."

Gabe crossed his arms to avoid the sudden urge to hold her. He looked out at the sea. "You still miss him?"

"Yes," she said on a sigh. "He was one of the kindest people I've ever known. We never argued. Never had a cross word. Well, that is until he…"

Her words trailed, and Gabe glanced sideways. "Until he what?"

She shrugged again. "Until he was dying," she said, so softly he could barely hear. "It sounds strange to even say such a thing. But I didn't find out he was sick until a few weeks before the wedding."

"His illness progressed that quickly?"

She shook her head. "Not exactly. He knew for over six months. He just didn't tell me."

Gabe's stomach sank. But he understood the other man's motives. The unrelenting guilt. The unwanted pity. Gabe knew those feelings well. "He was trying to protect you."

"So he said. But all I felt was…angry."

The way she spoke, the way her voice cracked and echoed with such heavy pain made Gabe wonder if it was the first time she'd admitted it out loud. Her next words confirmed it.

"Sorry," she said quietly. "I don't ever whine about this stuff to anyone. And I don't mean to criticize Tim. He was a good man. The best. When we met we clicked straight-away. We were friends for a few months, and then we fell in love. Even though it wasn't fireworks and insane chemistry and all that kind of thing."

"But it was what you wanted?" Gabe asked quietly, his heart pounding.

"Yes," she replied. "But then he was gone…and I was alone."

Gabe uncrossed his arms and grasped her hand, holding it tightly within his own. She didn't pull away. She didn't move. Silence stretched between them, and Gabe quickly realized that despite every intention he'd had, his attraction for Lauren had morphed into something more. Something that compelled him to offer comfort, despite the fact he had to fight the sudden umbrage coursing through his blood when she spoke about the man she'd loved. He wasn't sure how to feel about it. He wasn't sure he should even acknowledge it.

Thankfully, a few seconds later, she slid her hand from his and rested it in her lap. Gabe sucked in some air and tried to avoid thinking about how rattled he'd become by simply sitting beside her.

"You don't like being alone?"

"No," she replied. "Not really. I guess that's why I married James. And exactly why I shouldn't have." She took a long breath. "I wanted the wedding I was denied when Tim passed away."

"And did you get it?"

She nodded. "Yes. I had the same venue, the same guests and the same themed invitations." Her voice lowered. "I even wore the same dress I'd planned on wearing two years earlier."

The regret and pain in her voice was unmistakable, and Gabe remained silent.

"When I was engaged to Tim, I was so wrapped up in the idea of being married," she admitted on a heavy sigh. "Up to that point my life, my world, had been about the store and weddings and marriage and getting that happily ever after. I was so absorbed by that ideal, I didn't realize that he was sick…that he was *dying*. When he was gone, I felt lost…and I turned that grief into a kind of self-centered resentment. Afterward, I was so angry at Tim for not telling me he was ill. And then James came along, and he was handsome and charming and…and *healthy*. Suddenly, I glimpsed an opportunity to have everything I'd ever wanted."

Gabe's chest constricted. Any subconscious consideration he'd ever given to pursuing Lauren instantly disappeared. She was looking for a healthy, perfect mate. Not a cancer survivor. "But you still want that, right? Even though your marriage didn't work out?"

"I want my happily ever after," she confessed. "I want someone to curl up to at night. I want someone to make me coffee in the morning. And I really want children. It doesn't have to be wrapped up in physical attraction or even some great love story. In fact, I'd prefer it if it wasn't. It just has to be real…honest."

Her words cut him to the quick. "I hope you find what you're looking for," he said, and got to his feet. "I'll walk you home."

"That's okay," she said, and twisted her hands together. "I think I'll stay here for a while longer."

"Sure."

"And, Gabe," she said as he moved to turn away. "Thanks for listening. I needed a friend today."

He nodded. "Okay."

On the run back home, Gabe could think of only one thing. Lauren had needed a friend. The thing was, he didn't want to be her friend. He wanted more. Much more. And he couldn't have it.

Not with his past illness shadowing him like an albatross.

He was broken physically. She was broken emotionally.

And he was stunned to realize how damned lonely that suddenly made him feel.

Chapter Seven

With the benefit at the community center only hours away, Lauren really didn't have time to dwell on how she'd literally poured her heart out to Gabe just days earlier. It was better she didn't. Better…but almost impossible. Her dreams had been plagued by memories of all she'd lost. Of Tim. And more. She dreamed about Gabe, too. Dreams that kept her tossing and turning for hours. Dreams that made her wake up feeling lethargic and uneasy.

But she had to forget Gabe for the moment. Tonight was about the benefit. Her sister-in-law had done an amazing job organizing everything. It was a black-tie event, catered by the best restaurant in Bellandale. On the lawn outside the building, a huge marquee had been set up to accommodate a silent auction of items ranging from art to fashion and jewelry and a variety of vacation destinations. Under a separate marquee, there were tables and chairs set out for dinner, and a dance floor. There was also a band in place to provide entertainment. Inside the building, the runway was decorated and ready for the models to begin the fashion parade. Lauren stayed behind the scenes, ensuring hair and makeup were on track before the models slipped into their gowns. She'd also changed into a gown—a stunning strapless silk chiffon dress in pale champagne. It was shorter at the front, exposing her legs to just above the knees and then molded tightly over her bust and waist, flaring off down her hips in countless ruffled tiers that swished as she walked. She'd ordered the gown months ago and had never had occasion to wear it. Other than Cameron's recent wedding, it had been too long since she'd dressed up. Too long since she'd felt like making an effort. But tonight was special. The money raised would help several children's charities, including the Big Brothers Big Sisters program that was so important to her brother.

She hadn't seen Gabe but knew he had been there earlier, helping out with the marquees and the staging setup. Avoiding him was her best option. Avoiding him made it possible to function normally. Avoiding him was what she needed to do.

"Lauren?"

She was alone in the foyer of the community center. She'd been checking the stage and working out the music cues with the DJ, who'd since disappeared. The models were upstairs; so were Mary-Jayne and Cassie, as they'd volunteered to help with the gown changes.

Lauren turned on her high heels. Gabe stood by the door. He wore a suit, probably the same one he'd worn to her brother's wedding, and he looked so gorgeous, she had to swallow hard to keep a gasp from leaving her throat.

"Need any help here?" he asked.

Her brows came up. "Changed your mind about strutting on the catwalk?"

He laughed. "Not a chance. But I hear you roped my cousin, Scott, into it."

"Not me," she said, and placed her iPad onto the stage. "He's Mary-Jayne's brother-in-law, so she did all the convincing."

Gabe's gaze rolled over her. "You should be modeling tonight…you look beautiful."

She shrugged. "What? This old thing," she said, and laughed softly. "Thanks. You know, you don't look so bad yourself."

He grinned in that sexy, lopsided way she'd become used to. "So, need any help?" he asked again.

Lauren shook her head. "I don't think so. Grace has everything under control. She's *very* organized."

He chuckled. "You mean the consummate control freak? Yeah, I kinda figured."

Lauren relaxed her shoulders. "Well, it's good to have someone like that at the helm for this kind of event. Actually, I…"

"You…?" he prompted when her words trailed.

"Oh…nothing…I was just thinking how I should apologize for the other day."

"No need," he said quietly.

"It's only that I don't usually talk about those things. It probably sounded like I was blaming Tim for dying. I wasn't," Lauren assured him, unsure why she needed to explain herself. But she did. "Sometimes…sometimes the grief gets in the way."

His eyes darkened and he nodded as if he understood. It struck her as odd how he could do that. It was as though he knew, somehow, the depth and breadth of the pain in her heart.

"I remember how my mom was after my dad died," he said quietly. "I don't think she ever really recovered."

"Sometimes I feel like that," she said. "I feel as if the pain will never ease, that I'll be grieving him forever. And then…and then there are times when I can't remember the sound of his voice or the touch of his hand." She stopped, immediately embarrassed that she'd said so much. "I don't know why I do that," she admitted. "I don't know why I say this stuff to you. It's not like we're…" She stopped again as color rose up her neck. "The truth is, I'm very confused with how I should feel about you."

"You shouldn't be," he said softly. "We're neighbors. Friends. That's all."

If she hadn't believed he was saying it to put her at ease, Lauren might have been offended. She drew in a long breath then slowly let it out. "After what happened at my parents' house the other night, I think we're both kidding ourselves if we believe that."

"What *almost* happened," he reminded her. "There's no point getting worked up over something that didn't happen, is there?"

Annoyance traveled up her spine. He thought she was overreacting? Imagining more between them than there actually was? She pressed her lips together for a second and gave her growing irritation a chance to pass. It didn't. "Sure. You're right. There's no point. Now, if you don't mind, I have to finish getting ready for the parade."

He didn't budge. "You're angry?"

"I'm busy," she said hotly.

As she went to move past him, one of his arms came up to bar the doorway. "Wait a minute."

Lauren pressed her back against the doorjamb. He was close. Too close. "No. I have to—"

"I'm trying to make this easy for you," he said, cutting her off.

Lauren's gaze narrowed. "I think you're trying to make this easy for yourself."

He moved, and his other arm came up and trapped her in the doorway. "Maybe I am," he admitted softly. "Maybe I'm just crazy scared of you."

Scared? She wouldn't have pegged Gabe to be a man scared of anything. Especially not her. "I don't understand what you—"

"Sure you do," he said, and moved closer. "You feel it, too. Don't you know I can barely keep my hands off you?"

Lauren had to tilt her head to meet his gaze. "So it's just about attraction?" she managed to say in a whisper. "Just...sex."

Their faces were close, and his eyes looked even bluer. Lauren sucked in a shaky breath, feeling the heat rise between them against her will. She wanted to run. She wanted to stay. She wanted to lock the door and strip off her dress and tear the clothes from his body and fall down onto the carpet and make love with him over and over. She wanted him like she'd never wanted any man before.

"I wish it was," he said, and inched closer until their mouths were almost touching. "I wish I didn't like spending time with you. I wish I didn't keep thinking about you every damned minute I'm awake, and could stop dreaming about you every time I go to sleep."

The frustration in his voice was both fascinating and insulting. He wanted her but resented that he did. Thinking of his struggle ramped up her temperature. And it made her mad, too.

"Sorry for the inconvenience," she said with way more bravado than she actually felt.

"Are you?"

She glared, defiant. "You're an ass, Gabe. Right now I wish I'd never met you."

He didn't believe it. Nor did she. He stared at her mouth. Lauren knew he was going to kiss her. And she knew *he knew* she wanted him, too. There was no denying it. No way to hide the desire churning between them.

"My vow..." Her words trailed as she struggled for her good sense. "I promised myself I'd wait until—"

"Forget your vow," he said, cutting off her protest. "Just for right now, stop being so sensible."

A soft sound rattled in her throat, and Gabe drew her closer, wrapping his arms around her as he claimed her lips in a soft, seductive and excruciatingly sweet kiss. She went willingly, pressing her hands to his chest, and she felt his heart thunder beneath her palm. His mouth slanted over hers, teasing, asking and then gently taking. Lauren parted her lips a little as the pressure altered and the kiss deepened. Everything about his kiss, his touch, was mesmerizing, and Lauren's fingertips traveled up his chest and clutched his shoulders. He was solid and strong and everything her yearning body had been longing for. When he touched her bare skin where the dress dipped at the back, she instinctively pressed against him, wanting more, needing more. He gently explored her mouth with his tongue, drawing her deeper into his own, making her forget every coherent thought she possessed.

"Hey, Lauren, have you seen the—" Cassie's voice cut through the moment like a bucket of cold water. Gabe dragged his mouth from hers and released her just as Cassie came into view, emerging through the open doorway on the other side of the room. "Oh, gosh! Sorry."

Gabe stepped back, his breathing a little uneven. He stared at her, through her, into a place she never imagined she'd ever let any man into again. "Good luck with the show," he finally said to Lauren, and slipped through the doorway.

She watched him disappear then took a deep breath and faced her friend. Cassie's eyes were wide and curious. "Did you need me for something?"

Cassie grinned. "Ah, the models are getting restless. Especially Carmen Collins. I said you'd come upstairs and give them a pep talk before the parade starts."

"Sure," Lauren said, and grabbed her iPad.

Cassie cleared her throat. "Sorry about that...I didn't mean to interrupt. But the door was open and—"

Lauren raised a hand. "Please, don't apologize. I shouldn't have let it happen."

"Why not?" her friend asked. "You're single. He's single. You're awesome. He's gorgeous. You like him. He *clearly* likes you. You're friends. Neighbors. Sounds perfect."

Lauren's brows shot up. "Have you been watching *When Harry Met Sally* or *Love Actually* again?"

"Don't disregard old-fashioned romance so easily," Cassie said, and grinned.

"I don't," Lauren said. "But you know that's not what I'm looking for." *Gabe's not what I'm looking for.* But her lips still tingled. Her skin still felt hot where he'd touched her. Lauren ignored the feelings and smiled toward her friend. "Come on, let's get the models ready."

The fashion parade was a success. And Lauren was so busy for the next four hours that she didn't have a chance to think about Gabe. Or talk to him. Or remember his kiss.

The models did a splendid job, and by the time the last gown had been paraded up and down the catwalk and the entire cast returned for one encore lap, Lauren was exhausted. Her mother was on hand passing out business cards, and made several bridal-fitting appointments for the following week.

The silent auction was also a hit, and Lauren put a modest bid on a vacation up north and was outdone by her brother. Dinner was served underneath the huge marquee, and thankfully, she wasn't seated at Gabe's table. He was with Scott and Evie and some of Evie's family, while she spent the evening at a table with her brother and parents. Grace was a fabulous emcee and the auction raised thousands of much-needed dollars.

By the time dessert was served, several couples had taken to the dance floor. Lauren turned to Cassie, who was seated beside her, and immediately took note of her friend's pale complexion.

"You know, you don't look the best."

Cassie shrugged one shoulder and drank some water. "It's nothing. I'm a little tired. It's just baby hormones."

Lauren frowned. "Are you sure?"

"Positive."

She was about to get started on her dessert when she noticed someone standing behind her. Lauren knew instinctively it was Gabe. He lightly touched her bare shoulder, and the sensation set her skin on fire.

"Dance with me, Lauren?"

She looked up and met his gaze, ignoring how Cassie bumped her leg under the table. "I really shouldn't leave Cassie alone."

"I'll be fine," her friend, the traitor, assured them. "Go ahead. I insist."

He held out his hand. She took it and got to her feet. He led her to the dance floor and drew her into his arms. The woodsy scent of his cologne immediately assailed her senses and she drew in a shuddering breath. His broad shoulders seemed like such a safe haven, and she was almost tempted to imagine for one foolish moment that they were *her* safe place. Hers alone. Where no one could intrude. The place she'd been searching for. But that was a silly fantasy. She knew the rules. She'd made them. She wanted commitment and he didn't.

Like with everything he did, he moved with an easygoing confidence, and Lauren followed his lead when the music suddenly slowed to a ballad.

"You can dance," she said, and relaxed a little.

"I'm half Italian," he replied against her ear, as though that was all the explanation he needed to offer.

She couldn't help smiling. "Are you one of those men who is good at everything?"

He pulled back a little and Lauren looked up. His mouth twisted. "I guess I'll let you judge that for yourself."

His words wound up her spine like a seductive caress. Suddenly, she sensed they weren't talking about dancing. With the beat of the music between them and the memory of their kiss still hovering on her lips, Lauren was drawn into the depths of his dazzling blue eyes. As a lover, she imagined, he'd be passionate and tender and probably a whole lot of fun. Of course, she'd never know. But still…a little fantasy never hurt anyone.

"I'm sorry about before," he said, and held her close.

He regretted their kiss? "Sure. Forget about it. I have."

His breath sharpened. "I meant that it was hardly the place to start something like that. I hadn't planned on kissing you for the first time while two hundred people were within watching distance."

"So you *planned* on kissing me at some point?"

"After what happened at your brother's wedding, and all the time we've spent together since, I really don't think we could have avoided it."

Her brother's wedding? Was he referring to what he'd overheard her say to her friends? How she'd thought about him naked? Conceited jerk. "You're not irresistible, you know."

"I'm not?" he queried, and rested a hand on her hip.

Lauren could feel him smile as her forehead shadowed his chin. "No."

He chuckled. "So I guess that means you won't want me to kiss you again?"

Her belly fluttered. "Exactly. You have to remember that we want different things."

"That's right. You're still looking for Mr. Reliable?"

"Yes. And not Mr. Roll-in-the-Hay."

"Too bad for me, then," he said, still smiling. "Incidentally, have I told you how beautiful you look tonight?"

"You mentioned it."

Lauren couldn't help smiling. Their banter was flirty and harmless. Nothing more would happen unless she wanted it to. Gabe was charming and sexy, but he also oozed integrity. And she might have been tempted to sleep with him. If she didn't like him. But she did like him. A lot. Too much. And with her heart well and truly on the line, a night in his bed wouldn't be worth the risk, despite how much she wanted it.

"You're easily the most beautiful woman here tonight."

It was a nice line, even if she did think he was being overly generous. The song ended and Lauren pulled back a little. "Thank you for the dance."

"My pleasure."

As he walked her back to her table, Lauren was very aware that her mother was watching them. She could almost see Irene's mind working in overdrive. Cassie wasn't at the table, and she immediately asked after her friend.

"I think she went inside to collect her bag," her mother explained, and then patted the vacant seat, inviting Gabe to sit down.

"Be back in a minute," Lauren said, and walked from the marquee.

She found Cassie in the clubhouse upstairs, sitting on the small couch in the corner of the same room the models had used earlier as a dressing room. There were rails filled with gowns along one wall and shoes were scattered across the floor. Her friend looked up when she came through the doorway.

"Everything all right?" Lauren asked.

Cassie had her arms wrapped around her abdomen and grimaced. "It's nothing. I'm sure it's nothing."

Lauren's gaze moved to Cassie's thickened middle, and she walked across the room. "Are you in pain?"

"I'm fine," Cassie replied, and then clutched at her abdomen with both hands.

Suddenly, her friend looked the furthest from fine that Lauren had ever seen.

"What is it?" she asked and dropped beside the sofa. "What can I do?"

Cassie shook her head. "I don't know…I don't know what's wrong. It might be the baby."

There were tears in her friend's eyes, and Lauren quickly galvanized herself into action. Falling apart wouldn't help Cassie. "You need to see a doctor. I'll get Cameron to carry you into my car, and then I'll take you to the hospital."

She turned on her heels and headed for the door. Evie, Grace and Mary-Jayne were at the top of the stairs talking. "What is it?" Evie, the original earth mother, asked, and stepped toward the room.

"Cassie's ill."

The three women were in the room in seconds, and Evie touched Cassie's forehead with the back of her hand. "She has a temperature."

Cassie doubled over and gripped her belly. "It hurts so much. I'm scared. I don't want to lose my baby."

"It's okay, Cassie, you'll be fine. I'll ask Cameron to—"

"Grace, M.J.," Evie said quickly, and cut her off. "You'd better go and find Gabe."

Gabe?

Both women nodded and backed out of the room. Lauren waited until they'd disappeared and turned her attention back to Evie.

"Evie, I'm sure Cassie would prefer my brother to get her to the hospital."

Evie shook her head. "She needs a doctor. Right now."

"I agree. But I can't see how—"

"Lauren, Gabe *is* a doctor."

When Gabe entered the room, he spotted Lauren standing by the narrow sofa, comforting her friend. She looked at him, and his chest instantly tightened.

She knows....

Damn. But he'd known it was bound to come out eventually.

He wavered for a second before quickly turning his attention to the woman on the sofa. He asked Cassie a series of questions, such as how severe was the pain, was it constant or intermittent, was she spotting. And as Cassie quietly answered, he felt Lauren's gaze scorching the skin on the back of his neck.

It was hard to stay focused. Memories of that terrible night in the E.R. flooded his thoughts, and panic settled in his chest. *Just do it.* That night another pregnant woman had needed his help, and he'd failed her. But he couldn't fail Cassie. Not when Lauren was watching his every move. This was Lauren's closest friend. She'd be inconsolable if anything happened to her.

It was all the motivation Gabe needed to pull himself together. Instinct and experience quickly kicked in, and he asked Cassie to lie back on the sofa. He gently tilted her to her left side and asked questions about the position and intensity of the pain. He then quickly checked her abdomen. After a minute he spoke. "Okay, Cassie, I need you to relax and take a few deep breaths."

Cassie's eyes were wide with fear. "Do you think it's the baby? I don't want to lose my baby. I can't...I just can't... Not when Doug is so far—"

"You'll be okay. Both of you," he assured her and patted her arm. "We'll get you to the hospital." He turned toward Evie. "Call an ambulance. Tell them we have a patient in her second trimester with probable appendicitis."

Cassie let out a sob. "Do I need an operation?"

He nodded and squeezed her hand. "It'll be all right. You and your baby will be fine."

By the time the ambulance arrived, Gabe had Cassie prepared, and they were ready to go. Lauren volunteered to collect some of her friend's things from her home and meet them at the hospital. Gabe spoke to the paramedics as they carefully loaded Cassie onto the stretcher, and then he followed in his truck.

By the time he reached the hospital, Cassie was already being transferred to the surgical ward and was being prepped for an emergency appendectomy.

He'd been in the waiting room for about forty minutes when Lauren walked through the doorway. She'd changed into jeans and a blue shirt and carried a small overnight bag in one hand. She came to a halt when she spotted him.

"Is she in surgery?" she asked quietly.

Gabe got to his feet. "Yes. Is there someone we should call?"

"Only Doug, her boyfriend," she replied and placed the bag on the floor. "He's a soldier on tour, and I don't know how to contact him. I guess I could check the numbers stored in her phone. She doesn't have any real family of her own other than her grandfather, and he's in an aged-care home and suffers dementia. Doug has a brother in South Dakota, so I could call him if anything...I mean, if something..." Her eyes shadowed over. "If something goes wrong with Cassie or the baby."

"She'll pull through this," he said, fighting the urge to take Lauren into his arms.

"Do you know what's happening to her?" she asked coolly.

"You mean the surgery?" He drew in a breath. "They'll probably give her an epidural or spinal anesthesia as it's safer than general anesthesia."

"And the baby?"

"The safest time for a pregnant woman to have surgery

is during the second trimester. Cassie is seventeen weeks along, so she and the baby should be fine."

"Should?" Lauren's brows shot up. "Is that your professional opinion?"

It was an easy dig. "Yes."

She dropped into one of the vinyl chairs and sighed heavily. "I feel like such a fool."

"Lauren, I wanted to—"

"It's so obvious now," she said, and cut him off dismissively. "That first night when I picked up Jed and I got the splinter. And the old lady on the beach. And then when my dad sprained his ankle." She made a self-derisive sound. "How stupid I would have sounded to you, prattling on about how you'd make a good paramedic. What a great laugh you must have had at my expense."

Guilt hit him squarely between the shoulders. She had a way of making him want to tell her everything. "I wasn't laughing at you."

She met his gaze. "No? Then why all the secrecy?"

Gabe shrugged one shoulder. "It's a little complicated."

"Handy cop-out," she said, clearly unimpressed. "I thought we were…friends."

I don't know what we are. But he didn't say it. Because he didn't want to be her friend. He wanted to be more. And less. He wanted to take her to bed and make love to her over and over. He also wanted to stop thinking about her 24/7.

"I lost a patient," he said, and heard how the hollow words echoed around the small room. "So I took some time off."

Her expression seemed to soften a little. "Oh…" He could see her mind ticking over, working out a way to ask the next question. "Was it because of something you did wrong?"

"Indirectly," he replied and sat down opposite her. "It was around midnight and I'd worked ten hours straight.

I left the E.R. for a while, and when I was gone, a young woman was brought in. She was pregnant and hemorrhaging, and a second-year resident treated her. Unfortunately, the patient and her baby died."

She stared at him. "How awful."

"Yes," he said, remembering the event like it was yesterday. "It was a terrible tragedy. And one I will always regret."

"You said you weren't there at the time," she said, and frowned. "Which means it wasn't actually your fault."

Guilt pressed down. "It was. Even though I wasn't the only doctor in the E.R. that night, I was the attending physician on duty, and I should have been there when I was needed the most. A less experienced resident was forced to handle the situation and because of that, a woman and her child died."

It wasn't an easy truth to admit. And it sank low in his gut like a lead weight. It didn't matter how many times he replayed it over in his mind. He should have been there. His arrogance and self-importance had been the reason he'd failed the patient. The blame lay at his feet. And his alone. If he'd followed his own doctor's advice, he wouldn't have returned to work so quickly. Instead, he'd ignored everything and everyone and done it his own way. With fatal consequences.

Her eyes widened. "Were you sued?" she asked. "Was there some kind of malpractice suit? Is that why you quit being a doctor?"

Gabe's stomach tightened. *Quitter.* He'd called himself that over and over. But it had been easier leaving medicine than swallowing the guilt and regret he'd experienced every time he walked through the hospital corridors.

"There was an inquiry," he said, and ignored how much he wanted to haul her into his arms and feel the comfort of her touch, her kiss, her very soul. "The hospital reached a settlement with the woman's family. I wasn't implicated."

"And the other doctor?"

"She was suspended and left the hospital soon after."

Lauren twisted her hands in her lap. "Would you have saved the patient if you were there?"

Gabe took a deep breath. "I believe so."

"But you don't know for sure?"

He shrugged lightly. "Who can know anything for certain?"

Her gaze was unwavering. "But as a physician, wouldn't you be trained to deal with absolutes? Life or death. Saving a patient or *not* saving a patient. There are no shades of gray. It's one or the other, right?"

Her words cut deep, and he wanted to deny the truth in them. "I can't—"

"So tell me the truth," she said, and raised her brows. "Why did you really quit being a doctor?"

Chapter Eight

Lauren pushed aside the nagging voice in her head telling her to mind her own business. She couldn't. He was a mystery. A fascinating and infuriating enigma. She wanted to know more. She wanted to know everything.

Because…because she liked him. As hard as she'd tried *not* to, she was frantically drawn toward Gabe. The kiss they'd shared earlier that evening confirmed it. She hadn't planned on having feelings for him. But now that she had them, Lauren was curious to see where it might lead. He was attracted to her…. Perhaps it might turn into more than that. Maybe he'd reconsider his no-commitment position. Just as she'd begun to rethink her own plans for wanting a relationship based on things other than desire or love.

Love?

Oh…heavens. *I'm in big trouble.* The biggest. *Desiring. Liking. Loving.* Her once broken and tightly wrapped-up heart had somehow opened up again. And she'd let him in. Even if he didn't know it.

"I told you why," he said, and got to his feet.

Lauren watched him pace around the room. The tension in his shoulders belied the dismissive tone in his voice. "You told me you felt responsible for losing a patient that wasn't directly *your* patient. How is that your fault? How is that a reason to throw away your career?"

He stilled and stared at her for the longest time. Lauren knew she was way out of line. He would have been well within his rights to tell her to go to hell. But she knew he wouldn't. There was something in his expression that struck her deeply, a kind of uneasy vulnerability she was certain he never revealed. Not to anyone.

"Walking away from that life was one of the hardest things I've ever done," he said quietly. "I don't expect you or anyone else to understand my reasons."

Lauren drew in a shaky breath. "I'm sorry. I don't mean to sound like I'm judging you. I'm not," she assured him. "It's just that I…I guess I…care."

He didn't budge. His blue-eyed gaze was unwavering. Only the pulse in his cheek indicated that he understood her meaning.

"Then, don't," he said, and crossed his arms. "We've been through this before, Lauren. You want something else, something and someone who won't give you grief or pain or disappointment. That's not me. If you waste your heart on me, I'll break it," he said, his voice the only sound in the small room. "I won't mean to…I won't want to…but I will. I'm not the middle road you're looking for, Lauren."

Humiliation and pain clutched at her throat. But she wouldn't let him see it. "Sure. Whatever." She stood and grabbed the bag at her heels. "I'm going to check on Cassie."

She left the room as quickly as she could without looking as if she was on the run. Once she was back in the corridor, Lauren took several long gulps of air. Her nerves were rattled. Her heart felt heavy in her chest. She made her way to the cafeteria and stayed there for the next hour. She was allowed to see Cassie when she came out of surgery, but her friend was groggy and not very talkative. By the time Lauren headed home, it was past midnight.

Gabe's truck was not in the driveway, but she heard him return about twenty minutes after she did. She didn't want to think about him.

If you waste your heart on me, I'll break it....

It was warning enough. She'd already had one broken heart when she'd lost Tim. Lauren wasn't in the market for another. He'd made his feelings, or lack thereof, abundantly clear.

After a restless night where she stared at the ceiling until 3:00 a.m., on Sunday morning, Lauren headed off to the hospital. Seeing Cassie lifted her spirits.

"You look so much better today."

"Thanks," Cassie replied, and sighed.

Lauren placed the flowers she brought on the small bedside table. "When are you getting out of here?"

"Tomorrow," her friend replied. "The surgery went well, and the baby is okay."

There was a huge look of relief on Cassie's face, and Lauren smiled. "I'm so glad to hear it. Did you manage to reach Doug?"

She shook her head. "But I left a message."

Lauren could see her friend's despair. "I could try to call him. Or perhaps you should contact Tanner, and he could try to get in touch with his brother."

Cassie sighed. "I haven't spoken with Tanner since the last time he came home, which was a couple of years ago. Last I heard, he was still horse whispering in South Dakota. Doug will call me," Cassie said assuredly. "He will. I know it. I left a message and said it was important. He'll call me," she said again.

Lauren hoped so. Doug's reaction to the baby had been lukewarm at best, and she knew Cassie hadn't heard from him since.

"So," Cassie said, and grinned. "About Gabe. I think—"

"Let's not," Lauren pleaded.

"Indulge me. I'm the patient, remember?" she said, and patted her IV. "I'm guessing you didn't know he was really a doctor?" she asked. "And a pretty good one, by the way he reacted yesterday."

"I didn't know," she admitted.

"I guess he had his reasons for keeping it a secret."

Sure he did. He was emotionally unreliable and therefore unattainable. She'd get over him soon enough. For the moment, he was just a distraction, and her fledging feelings would recover. Lauren was sure of it.

It didn't help that the object of her distraction chose that moment to enter the room.

With Mary-Jayne at his side.

Of course, she knew he was acquainted with her friend. He was Scott's cousin, and Evie was Mary-Jayne's sister. Still…a little burst of resentment flooded her veins.

She met his gaze. He looked so good in jeans and a black polo shirt, and walked with the easy swagger she'd come to recognize as uniquely his. Lauren tried to smile and failed.

"Look who I found outside," Mary-Jayne announced with a big grin.

"Ladies," he said easily, and stepped into the room. "Am I interrupting?"

"Not at all," Cassie was quick to say. "I'm so glad you're here. I wanted to say thank you for yesterday."

Gabe shrugged. "No thanks necessary. As long as you're feeling better."

"Much," Cassie said, and beamed a smile. "Are they for me?" she asked of the bunch of flowers in his hand. When he nodded, her friend's smile broadened. "Daffodils are my favorite. Thank you."

Lauren fought back a surge of jealousy and drew in a deep breath. So he met Mary-Jayne in the hallway, and Cassie was a little starstruck? *It means nothing to me.* One kiss didn't amount to anything. She had no hold on him and shouldn't care that her friend might have a harmless crush on the man who'd potentially saved her and her baby. Besides, Cassie was devoted to Doug.

She hopped up from her chair and took the flowers, careful not to touch him. He said hello, and she managed to reply and then disappeared from the room in search of a vase.

"What's up with you?"

Lauren came to a halt and waited for Mary-Jayne to catch up. "Nothing."

Her friend grabbed her arm. "We met in the hall, that's all."

"I don't know what you mean."

Mary-Jayne's slanted brows rose up dramatically. "Sure you do. Dr. Gorgeous in there only has eyes for you."

"That's…that's ridiculous," Lauren spluttered. "We're just neighbors."

"You can deny it all you want, but I know what I see."

If you waste your heart on me, I'll break it….

His words came back again and sat like lead in her stomach.

The nurses happily obliged her with a vase, and when they returned to the room, Gabe was sitting beside Cassie's bed, and her friend's hand rested against his forearm. The scene looked ridiculously intimate. Resentment bubbled, and Lauren pushed it away quickly.

"I was just telling Gabe how grateful I am," Cassie said, and patted his arm one more time before she placed her hands in her lap and grinned at him. "Again."

He shrugged in a loose-shouldered way, but Lauren wasn't fooled. "I'll get going. Good to see you all."

Once he was gone, Cassie blew out a low whistle. "Boy, could you two be any more into each other and less inclined to admit it?"

Lauren colored wildly. "That's ridiculous."

"Yeah, right," Cassie said, and grinned. "I'm not the most observant person in the world, but even I can see that you have some serious feelings for him."

"And I think right about now is the time for me to leave," Lauren said gently, and grabbed her bag. She loved Cassie. But now wasn't the time to have a discussion about her feelings for Gabe. Feelings he'd made perfectly clear he didn't want and couldn't return.

"You know, I'm sure he had his reasons for not telling you he was a doctor," Cassie said, ignoring her indication to leave. "If that's what's bugging you. Some people don't like talking about themselves."

I know...I'm one of those people.

"I'll see you tomorrow. Make sure you let me know when you're leaving so I can pick you up. My mother is insisting you stay with her and my dad for a couple of days."

She hugged both her friends goodbye, and by the time Lauren arrived home, it was past midday. She got stuck into some cleaning and sorted through a few cupboards in the kitchen. It was menial, mind-numbing work that stopped her dwelling on other things. Or at least gave the impression. Later she did some admin work for the store and spent an hour in the backyard, weeding and repotting some herbs. Gabe wasn't home, and that suited her fine.

When she was done, it was well past five, and Lauren headed inside to clean up. She took a long bath and dried herself off before cozying into candy-pink shorts and matching tank shirt. She called Cassie and arranged to pick her friend up the following morning. With that done and the store organized for next day, Lauren ignored the idea of dinner and mooched around the cupboards for something sugary. Being a usually health-conscious woman, the pantry was bare of anything she could call junk, and she made do with a bag of organic dried apples.

She was sitting on the sofa, watching television with her knees propped up and dipping in for a third mouthful of apple when the doorbell rang. Lauren dropped the bag and headed up the hallway. When she opened the door and found Gabe standing on her porch, Lauren took a deep breath. He looked tired. As though he hadn't slept for twenty-four hours.

Well, too bad for him.

"What do you want?"

He had an envelope in his hand. "I got the estimate for the new fence. You said you wanted to—"

"Sure," she snapped, and held out her palm.

He placed the note in her hand. "You're under no obligation to pay half. The fence is my idea and I'd rather—"

"I said I'd pay for it," she said, cutting him off.

He threaded his fingers through his hair, and she couldn't stop thinking how mussed and sexy he looked. "Okay. If you're sure. Check out the estimate and if you agree, I'll get the contractor to start work in the next week or so."

Wonderful. A great high fence between them was exactly what she needed.

"I'll let you know," she said through tight teeth.

He nodded, shrugged a little and managed a smile. "I'll talk to you later."

He turned and took a few steps. Lauren wasn't even sure she'd spoken his name until he turned back to face her.

"Yes, Lauren?"

She pushed herself out of the doorway, and the light above her head flickered. He was a few feet away, but she could still make out every angle of his handsome face. A question burned on the edge of her tongue. Once she had her answer, she'd forget all about him.

"Why did you kiss me last night?"

The words seemed to echo around the garden, and the sound of insects chorused the silence that was suddenly between them. He took a couple of steps until he stood at the bottom of the stairs.

"If you think this is such a bad idea," she went on, getting stronger with each word. "If you believe there's nothing going on here...why did you even bother?"

He let out a heavy breath. "Because I had to know."

She shivered, even though it was warm outside. "You had to know what?"

"I had to know what your lips tasted like just one time."

Her shiver turned into a burn so hot, so rampant, Lauren thought she might pass out. She grabbed the screen door to support her weakened knees. No man had ever spoken those kinds of words to her. Tim had been sweet and a little shy. James's flirtatious nature had been obvious and overt. But Gabe was somewhere in between. Not shy. Not obvious. He was a seductive mix of reserve and calm, masculine confidence.

"And that's all it was? Just...just a single kiss?"

"What do you want me to say to you?" he shot back. "Do you need to hear that I want to kiss you again? That I want to make love to you? Of course I do. I've told you that before. I've never denied that I'm attracted to you, Lauren. You're...lovely. You're smart and beautiful and the more time I spend with you, the more I want you. But I can't give you the kind of commitment you want. Not...not right now."

Not right now?

What did that mean? A possibility popped into her head.

"Are you married?" she asked. "Or separated? Is that why you—"

"Of course not," he cut her off tersely.

"I had to ask," she said, and sighed. "You're so hot and cold, Gabe. You say one thing to me and then do another. I'm confused, and it seemed plausible."

"Well, it's not. I've had three semiserious relationships and a few one-night hookups. But I've never been married. I thought about it when I was with my last girlfriend, but we never got around to making any firm plans. In between, I was busy with my career."

"A career you then gave up?"

His expression turned blank. And she'd never wanted to read him more. But couldn't.

"I have to go," he said. "Good night."

She watched him leave and waited until he rounded the hedge before she returned inside and closed the door.

On Tuesday morning, Gabe noticed five missed calls on his cell. Two from his mom. Three from Aaron. His brother had then reverted to text messaging.

What's going on with you?

He sent one back when he arrived at work.

Nothing.

Aaron responded immediately.

Mom's worried about you. Call her.

Sure.

Gabe knew his one-word replies would irritate his interfering older brother.

Ten minutes later, he received another message.

Just do it, Gabriel.

Gabe ignored the deliberate use of his full name in his brother's message and stuffed the phone in his pocket. Well-meaning relatives with advice he could do without.

Megan arrived, and he plastered on a smile. It would be best if he kept his lousy mood to himself. No one needed to know that he was so wound up, so frustrated, he could barely string a sentence together. She had her older sister with her, a remarkably attractive girl in her mid-twenties whose name he couldn't recall but who looked him over with barely concealed approval.

The teen dumped a few books on his desk. "Thanks for these," she said chirpily.

"They helped?" he asked, and pulled another medical textbook from the desk drawer.

"Yeah," she replied. "I sit the nursing entrance exam next week."

Megan had borrowed a few of his old medical texts to help with her studying and hadn't asked why he had them. Not like Lauren would have. She'd ask. She'd want to know everything. And the damnable thing was, he'd want to tell her.

"Well, good luck," he replied. "Just drop it back when you're done with it."

Megan grabbed the book and sashayed out of the room, but her sibling hovered in the doorway, brows raised suggestively. In another time, he might have been tempted to ask for her number, to take her out and get her into bed after a few dates. But he wasn't interested in the pretty brunette with the wide smile. Gabe cursed to himself. He was so wrapped up in Lauren that nothing and no one else could shift his distraction. Nothing could ease the unexpected ache in his chest and the unrelenting tension cramping his shoulders. Kissing her had been like nothing on earth. And he wanted to feel that again. He wanted to take her in his arms and make love to her over and over and somehow forget he couldn't offer her the future she deserved.

The cell in his pocket vibrated again. It was another message from his brother.

You said you'd call. Get to it.

Gabe ignored the message and got back to work.

But by two he'd had enough, and since no one was booked in to use the upstairs rooms that afternoon, he locked up and headed home. Back at the house, there was painting to be done, drywall to replace and plaster, and the lawn needing mowing. But he ignored every chore. Instead, Gabe started unpacking some of the boxes in the spare room. The box marked Personal Items got his full attention. Gabe rummaged through the papers and soon found what he was looking for. His diploma of medicine. Still in the frame his mother had insisted upon. He looked at it, and shame hit him squarely behind the ribs.

Quitter...

Like he'd rarely allowed himself to think in the past eighteen months, Gabe wondered what would have happened had he stuck it out. What would have ensued had he ignored the guilt and regret tailing him around the hospital corridors? Would time have healed his fractured spirit? Would it have lessened the remorse? Would he have been able to practice medicine with the self-belief it demanded? Right now, he felt healthy. His last round of tests had come back clear. He was cancer-free.

Perhaps it was time to take his life back?

A first step. A giant step. But one he had to do if he was ever going to be truly happy.

Gabe shoved the diploma back in the box and resealed the lid.

He needed a run to clear his thoughts and stretch out the muscles in his back and limbs. He changed his clothes and headed out. When he returned, he showered, pulled on jeans and a T-shirt and grabbed his keys. If he wanted to take his career back, there was no time like the present to start.

He had a patient to check on.

Lauren sat on the edge of the bed in the spare room at her parents' house and chatted to her friend. It had been her bedroom once. Back then, the walls had been pink, and posters of rock gods had covered the walls. Since she'd moved out, her mother had redecorated in the more subtle tones of beige and white.

"This isn't necessary, you know, for me to stay in bed," Cassie insisted, and patted the mattress. "I feel fine."

"Good," Lauren said, and smiled. "But humor us all anyway, and rest for a few more days. You had surgery, and you need to take it easy."

Her friend had resisted coming to stay at her parents' home to recuperate. But since Lauren's dad was now retired, it meant that someone would be able to watch Cassie around the clock. Cassie meant a great deal to her family. She was like another daughter to her parents and as close to Lauren as a sister could be. She wasn't about to allow her friend to be alone.

"Okay," Cassie said, and grinned. "I'll be a model patient. As long as I know Mary-Jayne is looking after my dog, I'll relax."

"She is," Lauren told her. "I'll go and make some tea and bring it up with dinner."

"What time are your folks getting back?" Cassie asked.

Lauren checked her watch. It was just after seven. "Matka is at mah-jongg and will be back by nine-thirty, and Dad's helping Cameron supervise a bowling expedition with a group of kids from the Big Brothers program tonight. So you'll have to put up with me until then." She grinned. "But I promise I won't smother you."

Cassie chuckled. "Good. Um...I think I heard the doorbell. You might want to get that."

Lauren had heard it, too. She left the room and headed downstairs and was stunned to find Gabe on the other side of the door when she swung it back on its hinges.

"Oh...hi."

"Hey," he said, looking gorgeous beneath the overhead light. "I just stopped in to check on Cassie. I called her earlier, and she said she was here."

She did? Lauren needed to have a talk with her friend. She'd bet her boots Cassie had deliberately arranged this meeting. Her friend wasn't averse to a little matchmaking. Too bad it was pointless. "I didn't realize you had her number."

His mouth twitched. "I got it from Cameron."

"Oh, right. Well, she's upstairs...third room on the right."

Lauren turned on her heels and headed back down the hall. He could close the door. He could make his own way upstairs. She didn't want to spend any more time with him than was necessary. It was the only way she'd succeed in getting him out of her system.

But damn it if she couldn't hear them talking and laughing from her spot in the kitchen. The sound traveled down the stairway and managed to spur on her mounting jealousy and resentment.

She was about fifteen minutes into preparing dinner when she felt Gabe's presence in the room. Lauren looked up and noticed him in the doorway, arms crossed and one shoulder resting against the doorjamb.

"How does she seem?" she asked stiffly, slicing cucumber as though it was the enemy.

"Good," he replied, and pushed himself off the door frame. "Recovering well."

"So nice of you to make a house call." She turned toward the sink. "You know the way out."

But he stepped closer. "Is every conversation we have going to be a battle from now on?"

She harrumphed. "Probably. I should have stuck to my guns that night at my brother's wedding and ignored you. My life was simpler then."

"We couldn't ignore one another if we tried," he said, and was suddenly behind the counter.

"Oh, I can try," she assured him. "And I will."

He turned and rested his behind on the countertop. "I don't know what it is about you, Lauren... You make me think about things. You have a way of getting under my skin."

"Like a burr?" She wasn't going to be nice to him. Lauren finished the salad and soup she'd prepared for Cassie and placed it on a tray. "I'm going to take this upstairs. When I come back down, I'd prefer it if you weren't here."

By the time she was upstairs, her knees were wobbling so much she had to quickly place the tray on the bed. She looked at her smiling friend.

"I figure this is your doing?"

Cassie shrugged innocently. "Maybe a little. I thought it was sweet that he wanted to make sure I was okay. He's very nice. You shouldn't give up so easily."

"I'm not giving up," she said, and propped another pillow behind her friend. "I'm just not going to waste time dreaming about something that will never happen."

She lingered in the room for a few more minutes, giving Gabe plenty of time to leave. But when she returned to the kitchen, he was still there, still standing by the counter.

She heard his phone buzz.

"I think you just missed a call."

"I didn't miss it," he said, and shrugged a shoulder. "I didn't answer it."

"Girl trouble?" she inquired, hurting all over just thinking about it.

He half smiled, as though he knew she hated imagining him with some faceless woman. "My mom," he explained. "Or my brother Aaron…checking up on me."

"Do you need to be checked on?"

"They seem to think so," he said, and pushed himself off the counter.

"Well, I guess it's natural for a mother to worry when one of her kids lives on the other side of the world. I don't imagine my mother would be any different. She likes that Cameron and I both live close by. It makes her feel as though everything is right in her world. I don't think it matters how old we get…she just needs to know we're safe and happy, because that makes *her* feel safe and happy."

His gaze darkened, and he looked at her oddly. "You know, I don't think I've ever thought about it quite like that before."

Lauren's knees wobbled again. She was trying hard to stay strong and ignore him. But staring into Gabe's brilliant blue eyes wasn't helping. Hearing the seductive tone of his voice wasn't helping, either.

She shrugged. "I don't think we ever fully understand how hard it is for parents to let us live our own lives. They want to protect us from being hurt and from enduring life's disappointments. Even though it can sometimes feel like being wrapped in cotton wool and then be overprotected."

"Is that what happened to you?" he asked quietly. "After Tim died?"

Lauren nodded. "And again when my marriage ended. With Tim… I think because it happened so quickly, I was in shock. One moment I was planning my wedding, the next I was dressed in black and standing beside his grave. There was no time to prepare…to say goodbye. I was so mad at him for shutting me out that I didn't spend time telling him the important things…like how much he meant to me and how much I would miss him."

"Maybe he didn't want to hear that," Gabe said, his voice soft and husky. "Maybe he couldn't have borne your sadness, and it was all he could do to control what was happening to him. Maybe he didn't want your pity and didn't want to witness your grief and your tears. And perhaps you being mad at him for shutting you out…well, maybe that made him feel *normal*…as though he wasn't defined by his illness. Like he was still the person you loved, still a healthy and strong man and not only a terminally ill cancer patient."

Lauren's throat burned. The raw truth in his words cut deep. Everything Gabe said made sense. Somehow, he knew how to reach into the depths of her soul.

She blinked to avoid the tears that threatened to spill. "Tim never got angry with me for reacting like I did. But *I* was angry with me. For a week I walked around in a daze. All I could think was how my wedding plans were ruined. I was so selfish."

"No," Gabe said gently. "Despair has many faces, Lauren. Focusing on your wedding plans was simply a coping mechanism. It's not so hard to understand."

She nodded, agreeing with him with her heart, even though her head told her to forget him and find someone who truly wanted her back. "I guess you would have seen grief like that before. I mean, dealing with patients and their families."

"I… Yes," he said quietly. "Of course."

His unwavering gaze was deeply intense and made Lauren's heart race. Heat and awareness coiled through the space between them, somehow drawing them closer, even though they were two feet apart. They weren't touching, but Lauren *felt* his presence like a lover's caress.

Suddenly, the middle road she'd been longing for seemed passionless and bland.

And the man in front of her was the one man she wanted for the rest of her life.

Chapter Nine

"Has Gabe gone home?"

Lauren picked up the tray from Cassie's bedside table and ignored the way her heart beat faster simply at the mention of his name. He'd left with the barest of goodbyes, and she'd breathed a sigh of immense relief once he'd walked out the door.

"Yes," she replied. "But he said he'd check on you in a couple of days."

"That's sweet of him," Cassie said, and grinned. "Although I'm not sure he's actually dropping by to see me."

Lauren frowned. "You're as obvious as my mother."

Her friend began ticking off his attributes on her fingers. "He's handsome, charming, single and a doctor...what more do you need?"

Commitment and love...

She wanted exactly what she'd been saying she didn't want. And neither she was likely to get from Gabe Vitali.

"He doesn't want a relationship. He's commitmentphobic." Lauren sighed heavily. "Looks, charm and medical degree aside, he's emotionally unavailable."

"I'm not so sure," Cassie said. "Maybe he's just been unlucky in love and is wary of getting close to someone again."

That's not it.

But there *was* something…some reason why he pulled back and made it clear he wanted to avoid commitment. And Lauren was sure it had nothing to do with a failed relationship. It was something else…something deeper. Something that was somehow wrapped up in the patient he lost, his decision to quit being a doctor and then choosing to move his life to Crystal Point.

"Perhaps," she said, and shrugged. "It doesn't matter anyway. He's not for me."

"Settling isn't the answer," Cassie said quietly. "I know you have this idea that you want an uncomplicated, painless relationship…but relationships *are* complicated. And they can be painful and messy. Just because things ended so tragically with Tim and then you married a man you didn't love, it doesn't mean you have to make do with ordinary."

But ordinary won't break my heart.

And Gabe would.

Hadn't he already told her as much?

"I don't believe in the fairy tale anymore," she said, and knew it was a lie. "You should rest. My folks will be home soon. I'll see you tomorrow."

She headed downstairs, and once the dishes had been done, Lauren made her way to the front living room. As always, the photographs on the mantel drew her closer. Dear Tim, she thought as she looked at his picture with a familiar sadness. Was Gabe right? Had Tim kept his illness a secret so she wouldn't pity him…so he wouldn't have to deal with her thinking of him as sick? As somehow less than a man? In the years since his death, she'd thought of his reasons countless times and always ended up believing he'd wanted to protect her from the inevitable grief and loss. But what if it was more than that? Had she been so blind? So self-centered, she hadn't considered that Tim was protecting himself, too?

When her mother arrived home, she was still sitting in the front room, still thinking about the man she'd loved and lost. And she thought about Gabe, too…and wondered how she'd managed to develop feelings for someone she hardly knew. It was different to the way she'd fallen for James. Her ex-husband hadn't made her think…want…need. He hadn't stirred her mind and body the way Gabe did. James had been an escape from the terrible anguish of losing Tim. Nothing more. She was ashamed to admit it to herself. He'd deserved better. And so had she.

By the time she returned to her house, showered and changed and rolled into bed, it was past ten. There were lights on next door, and she wondered if Gabe was up late working on the renovations in the house. Once the work was done, she was sure he'd sell the place. What then? Would they see one another as infrequently as they had before he'd moved next door?

Sleep eluded her, and after staring at the shadows bouncing off the ceiling for most of the night, Lauren snatched a few restless hours before she pulled herself out of bed at seven, dressed and drove into Bellandale. She swapped her car for the store's van and then headed back to Crystal Point Surf Club & Community Center to collect the gowns that had been left there after the benefit. She'd borrowed Cameron's key and hoped she could get the task done before Gabe arrived for work.

No such luck.

He turned up just as she was trekking the third armload of gowns down the stairs.

He stood at the bottom of the stairway. "Need some help?"

Lauren brushed past him and clutched the gowns. "No, thank you," she said as she stomped through the doorway and loaded the dresses neatly into the back of the van. When she returned inside, he was still by the stairs.

"How did you get in?" he asked.

"I borrowed my brother's keys. I didn't think it would be a big deal."

"It's not," he replied, and followed her up the stairs. "Stop being stubborn and let me help you."

Lauren glared at him. "I'm not stubborn."

He raised one dark brow. "Yeah, right," he said, and held out his arms. "Give me what needs to be taken downstairs."

Lauren's mouth tightened, but she did as he asked. It only took another twenty minutes to get everything in the van, including the three metal hanging rails he quickly pulled apart and loaded in the back of the vehicle.

"Thanks. I appreciate your help," she said as she closed the back door to the van.

"No problem. Do you want me to follow you and carry this stuff back into your store?"

"Ah, no," she said quickly. "My mother will be there to help. Thanks again."

"Do you like working with your mom?" he asked unexpectedly, and followed her around to the driver's door. "And running your own business?"

"It's what I've always done," she replied.

"Which isn't exactly an answer, is it?"

Lauren shrugged. "My mother opened the store twenty-five years ago. I took over when I graduated from business college. Do I like it?" She sighed deeply. "It's all I know. I like it well enough."

But his glittering gaze saw straight through her facade. "Sometimes it makes you unhappy."

"Some days," she admitted. "Other days it's not so bad. When I was younger, I guess I was wrapped up in the romance of it all. The gowns…the tradition… Back then it seemed to have a purpose. Now…not so much."

Because Tim died, and I discovered that not everyone gets their happy ending….

His phone beeped, and he ignored it like he had before. Lauren's eyes widened. "So did you end up calling your mother and brother?"

Gabe stared at her for a second and then grinned a little. "Not yet."

Lauren grunted under her breath. "I didn't peg you to be the inconsiderate type."

"Inconsiderate?" He repeated the word and frowned. "I'm not."

"You might want to remind your family of that the next time you speak with them," she said, and smiled ultra-sweetly. "If you ever get around to it."

Lauren watched as his resentment grew. To his credit, he kept a lid on his rising annoyance. She wasn't usually driven to lecture someone she hardly knew. He'd accused her of getting under his skin…. The problem was, he did exactly the same thing to her.

And no one had ever made her so reactive.

Gabe challenged her thoughts and ideals. He made her really *think* about things. And he had, in a matter of weeks, forced her out of the self-absorbed routine she'd disguised as her life. Even her plans to find someone to share her life with had been tainted with the memories of all she'd lost. But who was she kidding? Settling for a passionless, loveless relationship was no way to live. And in her heart, she knew she could never honor Tim by settling for less.

Looking at Gabe, it was easy to get lost in his blue eyes and handsome face…but there was so much more to him than that. And that was what she found so hard to resist. He was charming, certainly. And sexy. But he was also kind and generous, and despite her silly accusation, clearly considerate and helpful. Hadn't he come to her aid countless times? Like when she was forced to look after Jed. Or how he'd helped her dad after his fall. And he'd shown incredible concern for Cassie and her baby. There was something elementally *good* about Gabe. And that was what she was so attracted to. That was why her heart pounded whenever he was close.

That's why I've fallen in love with him....

She shivered, even though the breeze was warm.

Oh, God...it's true.

"Lauren?" His voice seemed to whisper on the wind. "Are you all right?"

She nodded, shell-shocked at the unexpected intensity of her feelings. How ironic that she'd done exactly the opposite of what she'd planned after her divorce. She'd derided attraction and desire and now found herself craving Gabe's touch more than she had ever wanted any man before. And love? She'd put it out of her head, too. Because it scared her so much to want love again.

"I'm...I'm fine," she stammered. "I have to go."

Another car pulled up just as she opened the door to the van. Two people emerged from the small yellow car. Megan and another equally pretty and sporty-looking woman in her mid-twenties. It took Lauren two seconds to notice how the other woman looked at Gabe as if she wanted to devour him.

"You could stay," he said with a grin as they approached. "For protection."

Lauren's mouth twisted. "I'm sure you're capable of protecting yourself."

"That's Megan's older sister," he explained.

"That's a woman with her eye on the prize," Lauren

said as she hopped into the van and drove off, drowning in jealousy.

And feeling like the biggest fool of all time.

It took Gabe twenty minutes to extract himself from the clutches of Megan's persistent sibling. She reminded him that her name was Cara and asked for his number. He avoided answering her, pleading a pile of urgent paperwork on his desk.

Once she left and Megan headed to the beach for her patrol shift, Gabe wrote a list of things he needed to do for the day.

Thing number one: stop thinking about Lauren.
Thing number two: stop dreaming about Lauren.

He snatched a glance at his cell phone on the desk. He really should call his mother. And Aaron. But he just wasn't in the mood to talk. Or to be talked *at*. His mom would know something was up. She'd dig and dig until he admitted that he'd met someone. That he *liked* someone. And that his beautiful next-door neighbor was driving him crazy.

Then Claire Vitali would want to know everything.

And he had nothing to say.

Lauren was broken emotionally. He was broken physically. It could never work. The more he knew her, the more it served to strengthen his resolve. Even though he could have easily talked himself into it. The way she looked at him, the way she'd responded to his kiss at the benefit, the way she argued and contradicted him at every opportunity... It was like pouring gasoline on a bonfire. Everything about Lauren drew him in. Her face, her body, the sweet floral scent of her skin...every part of her connected with every part of him.

Which was as inconvenient as hell.

Even more inconvenient was the sight of Megan's sister standing on his doorstep at seven o'clock that evening. He'd been home for several hours. He'd changed and gone for a run, then returned home to work on painting one of the guest rooms. He'd just emerged from showering and pulling on fresh jeans and a T-shirt when the tall brunette had arrived on his doorstep clutching the textbook he'd loaned to Megan. Returning the book had been her excuse for dropping by, and he made a mental note to query Megan about handing out his address.

His visitor managed to wheedle her way up the hall and into the front living room, and Gabe was just about all out of patience when he heard another knock on his front door. Gabe told Cara to stay put and headed up the hallway.

Lauren stood beneath the porch light. In a long floral skirt and pale blue T-shirt she almost stole his breath. Gabe quickly pulled himself together.

"Hey…what's up?" he asked.

She held out an envelope. "The estimate for the fence looks reasonable. There's a check in there with my half of the initial payment."

"Thanks for getting back to me," he said quietly and took the note. "I'll let the contractor know he can start as soon as possible."

She shrugged, and the T-shirt slipped off her shoulder a little. "Okay."

The sight of her bare skin heated his blood, and he swallowed hard. "If you like, I'll—"

"Gabe?"

Great.

His unwelcome guest chose that moment to come sauntering down the hall, hips swaying, calling his name. He saw Lauren's expression tighten. And as stupid as he knew it was, he didn't want her thinking he was entertaining some random woman in his home.

"Sorry," she said, breathing harder than usual. "I didn't realize you had company."

"I don't," he said, and her brows shot up instantly. It was stupid. They weren't together. They weren't dating. They weren't sleeping together.

One kiss…that was all it was…

And even though there was nothing going on with the unwanted woman in his hallway, Gabe still felt like an unfaithful jerk.

"You can do what you like," Lauren shot back, and swiveled on her heels.

She quickly disappeared down the garden, and Gabe let out an impatient sigh.

"You have to go," he said to the woman now at his side. "Good night."

Minutes later, after quickly packing Cara into her car and waving her off, Gabe walked around the hedge and tapped on Lauren's door. The screen was locked, but the door was open, and he could hear her banging pots in the kitchen.

He called her name. She responded with more banging. She was mad. And she was jealous. The notion made him grin stupidly.

"Lauren, come out here and talk to me."

"Go away."

"Not until you let me explain."

"I don't want to hear it," she said, and banged some more.

Gabe expelled a heavy breath and leaned against the door. "She was just returning a book I loaned to—"

"Yeah, I'm sure it's her reading skills that you like," she said loudly, cutting him off.

"I don't like anything about her," he said, and sighed. "I hardly know her. She was returning a book I loaned to her sister. Now, will you come to the door so we can stop yelling?"

Pots banged again. "I said, go away."

Exasperated, Gabe straightened his back. "I hardly know her, like I said. You've no reason to be jealous."

The banging stopped. Gabe waited, but she didn't come to the door. The sudden silence was almost eerie. After a few minutes, he gave up and headed down the steps. He'd been back in his own house for about ten minutes when he heard the sharp rap on his front door. Lauren stood on the other side of the screen, cheeks ablaze, chest heaving.

He pushed the screen back and watched, fascinated and suddenly wholly aroused as she glared at him, hands planted on her hips.

"I. Am. Not. Jealous."

Oh, yeah, she was.

Gabe raised a brow. "No?"

Lauren pulled the screen out of his grasp and held it back farther. "No."

"I think you are."

"And I think you're an egotistical jerk," she shot back. "I've no interest in anything you do."

Every feeling, every ounce of desire he had for her rose up, and in that moment, Gabe was powerless to do anything other than smile broadly. "Then why are you on my doorstep?"

Lauren's resolve crumbled a little. Damn him. She shouldn't have let her temper get the better of her. Coming to his door was crazy thinking. "Because…we're arguing and I—"

"No, we're not," he said, and reached out to take her hand. "I think…" He paused, looking deep into her eyes. "I think this is more like foreplay than an argument."

Lauren flushed and pulled back. "Of all the conceited—"

"Let's not have this discussion on the doorstep, okay?" he said as he turned and walked down the hall.

Lauren stayed where she was for a moment. *I should turn around and go home.*

I really should.

Instead, she crossed the threshold, closed the door and followed him into the living room. When she entered the room, she saw he was standing by the sofa. And he was smiling. Lauren wasn't sure if she wanted to slug him or kiss him.

"Come here," he said softly.

She took a deep breath and stepped toward him. "You are the most—"

"That woman who was here earlier is Megan's sister, Cara. She returned a book I loaned to Megan," he said, cutting her off again. "Megan is sitting a nurse's entrance exam next week," he said quietly, cutting her off again. "And that's all. She may have had another motive, but I'm *not* interested in her...okay?"

Her heart raced.

Oh, sweet heaven. She tried to ignore the heat that traveled across her skin as well as the seductive sound of his voice. But failed. Every sense she possessed was on high alert.

"I shouldn't care what you do..." When he grasped her hand, she crumbled some more. "Gabe...I...I just..."

He lightly shrugged his magnificent shoulders and gently urged her closer until there was barely a whisper of space between them. "I can't fight this anymore," he admitted hoarsely. "I want to. I know I need to, for your sake, because you deserve more than the empty words of a future I simply can't promise you. And I've really tried to stop wanting you...but I can't."

There was such raw passion in his words, and Lauren's breath was sucked from her lungs. She moved closer and they touched, chest against breast. Gabe wound his arms around her, urging her against him.

"I've tried, too," she said through a sigh.

Gabe touched her face and kept his gaze connected with hers as he rubbed his thumb gently across her chin. Lauren tilted her head back and smiled. In all her life, she'd never experienced anything like the sensation of being near Gabe, or his soft, mesmerizing touch.

Their mouths met, and Lauren's head spun. His kiss was like nothing on earth. His hands were warm against her back, his mouth gentle as he coaxed a response. Lauren gave it willingly. She would give him anything. Everything. And the revelation rocked her through to the core.

I am so in love with him. Completely, irrevocably, crazily.

She opened her mouth, tasted his tongue against her own, felt a rush of pleasure coil up her spine and across her skin. She whispered his name against his lips, and Gabe urged her closer. Lauren sighed deeply from that way-down place, which was fueled by need and longing and a powerful rush of desire.

"I want to make love to you," he whispered raggedly, moving his mouth from her lips to her cheek. "So much."

Lauren moaned, all resistance gone. *Just for tonight. I can have this. I can have him. I can pretend it will work out.* "I want that, too."

Gabe grasped her hand and led her down the hall and into his bedroom. He released her and flicked on the bedside lamp. The big bed was covered in a patterned blue quilt, and she swallowed hard as nerves spectacularly set in. His gaze never left her, and she felt the heat of his gaze through to her bones.

"So...here we are."

Lauren didn't move. "Here we are." She managed a tiny smile. "I'm a little nervous."

"You don't need to be."

There was desire and passion and tenderness in his eyes. He wouldn't rush her. He wouldn't coerce or manipulate her with empty words. He opened the bedside drawer, found a condom and dropped the packet on the mattress, and even that made her long for him all the more. He was sweet and considerate. He was everything she wanted.

"Lauren, come here."

She moved toward him and stopped about a foot away. Desire and heat swept through the room with seductive force. She wished she'd had a chance to change into something sexy and filmy. The skirt and T-shirt seemed way too ordinary.

She rested her hands against his chest and then trailed down to the hem of his shirt. "Take this off," she said boldly, and saw him smile.

Gabe pulled the shirt over his head and dropped it on the floor. "Better?"

Lauren nodded. "Much," she replied, and traced her fingertips down the middle of his bare chest and twirled her fingers through the dark hair. She noticed a faded crisscross of small scars near the curve of his armpit and instinctively reached up to outline a finger along the skin there.

He tensed instantly.

"What's this from?" she asked softly.

"It's...nothing," he replied, equally as quiet. "Forget about it."

"Gabe, I—"

"Shh," he said, and placed two fingers gently against her lips. "Later. Right now, let's forget about the past. Let's be in *this* moment."

Lauren's eyes widened as she slid out of her sandals. She liked the sound of that. She dropped her hands and deliberately took her time as she gripped the edge of the T-shirt and slowly lifted it up and over her shoulders. Then she tossed it onto the foot of the bed and inhaled deeply. The white lace bra she wore was modest, but beneath the smoldering brilliance of Gabe's blue eyes, she felt as though it was the sexiest piece of underwear on the entire planet.

Heat charged between them, and she pushed past any lingering insecurity. He wanted her. That kind of look couldn't be faked. He had no agenda. She sucked in a breath and spoke. "Your turn."

He quickly flipped off his shoes and grinned in such a sexy way, her legs trembled. "Back to you."

She sucked in more air, willed strength into her knees as she unzipped her skirt and hooked her thumbs into the waistband. She heard his breath catch, saw the hot desire in his eyes. And waited. Took a breath. Then met his gaze head-on and slowly stripped the garment over her hips. She pushed it aside with her foot and rounded out her shoulders. Her briefs were white cotton and lace high-cuts. Not nearly seductive enough. Not the kind that aroused desire. Except Gabe looked hotly aroused, and it made her want him all the more.

"So," Lauren said, way more steadily than she felt. "You?"

Gabe's hands stilled on his belt, and his smile was pure sexual heat. He released the buckle and slid the belt from the loops. "Done," he said, and dropped it on the carpet. "Next?"

At a distinct disadvantage, Lauren smiled and backed up toward the bed. She reached around and slowly unclipped her bra, then eased herself from the shoulder straps and pulled the garment free. The bra fell from her fingertips and landed at her feet.

He looked at her and let out a ragged groan. Her nipples peaked instantly. "Okay…enough."

Lauren wondered what he meant for a microsecond, wondered if he found her lacking. But then he was in front of her, reaching for her, wrapping his arms around her. His mouth hovered over her eager lips, waiting to claim, waiting for her surrender. She gave it, completely and wholly and pressed against his chest. He captured her mouth in a searing kiss and gently fisted a handful of her hair. There was no force, no reticence, only need and desire and the realization it was the perfect kiss. The perfect moment. And all other kisses were quickly forgotten.

They tumbled onto the bed, mouths still together, hands moving over skin. He cupped one breast, and Lauren moaned low in the throat. His fingers were firm yet gentle, his mouth hot against her as he trailed down her cheeks, to her neck and then lower still, to where she ached for his touch. There was magic in his hands and mouth, and Lauren experienced a surge of feeling so intense, so deep, that it warmed her through to her bones. For the first time in forever, she was exactly where she wanted to be, and she sighed heavily as she shook in his arms.

"What is it?" Gabe asked and looked up. "Are you okay?"

Lauren smiled and touched his face. "I'm fine. Don't stop," she pleaded, and grabbed his shoulders.

"I have no intention of stopping," he said, and kissed her hungrily.

It was what she wanted to hear. What she needed to hear. The kissing went on, soft and hard, slow and fast, mesmerizing and wholly arousing. Lauren pushed against him, felt the abrasive denim rub across her thighs. "You're still wearing too many clothes," she whispered, and placed a hand on the band of his jeans.

He smiled against her skin. "You, too," he said, and pushed her briefs over her hips in one smooth movement. The way Gabe looked at her was real and heady and made her spin.

Naked and without inhibitions, Lauren curved against

him and popped the top button on his jeans. She tugged at the zipper and laughed delightfully when he rolled her over and kissed her again.

"Please," she begged softly, and grabbed the waistband again.

"Relax, Lauren," he said, and curved a hand down her back and over her hip. "There's no need to hurry."

He was wrong. There was a need to hurry. She wanted him desperately. She wanted to feel his skin against her, taste his kiss over and over and have the weight of his strong body above her, inside her. It was a need unlike any Lauren had ever known. "I want you," she said against his mouth. "Now."

"Soon," he promised, and moved his hand between them, stroking her where she longed to be touched with skillful, gentle intimacy. Tremors fluttered across her skin, and Lauren responded instantly. The heat grew as her breath quickened, and she let herself go, up and up, shaken by a white-hot, incandescent pleasure so intense, she could barely draw breath. She'd forgotten that feeling—forgotten how good it felt to experience such powerful release. Gabe kissed her again and smothered her soft groans and whispered pleas.

She laid her hands on his jeans and felt him hard against the denim. "You really are wearing too many clothes."

He nodded and swung his legs off the mattress. As he watched her, the connection between them shimmered. Then he smiled that lovely smile she longed for more than any other. Seconds later, his remaining clothes were off, and once the condom was in place, he was beside her on the big bed. They kissed again, long, hot kisses, tongues dancing together, skin on skin. She touched him as she'd wanted to do for weeks—his thighs, his arms, his back. His smooth skin burned beneath her fingertips, and when his mouth found her breast and he gently toyed with the nipple, she arched her spine off the bed. He moved above her and Lauren lay back, urging him closer. She wrapped her arms around his strong shoulders, opened herself for him and waited for that moment. He rested on his elbows, hovered above her and looked into her face with scorching intimacy.

The moment was achingly sweet and unbelievably erotic at the same time.

He nudged against her until finally they were together. Lauren sighed deep in her throat. She loved the feel of him. Being with Gabe felt right. He didn't move for a moment, didn't do anything other than stare deeply into her eyes.

"You're so beautiful, you take my breath away," he said softly.

It was a lovely, romantic notion, and Lauren absorbed his words right though to her heart. No one had ever spoken to her with such quiet tenderness. She blinked back tears and shuddered, feeling every part of him against her in a way she'd never experienced before.

He moved, and she went with him, up and over into that place where only they existed.

Chapter Ten

Gabe stirred, stretched out and took a deep breath. The soft scent of flowers played around in his memory. Lauren. He snaked an arm across the sheets, expecting to find her asleep beside him. But he was alone.

The digital clock on the bedside table read 4:00 a.m. A thin sliver of streetlight shone through a gap in the curtains, and he heard a dog barking in the distance.

Gabe swung off the bed, grabbed his briefs and jeans from the floor and pulled them on. He left the bedroom, padded down the hall and found Lauren in the kitchen, sitting at the table with a mug between her hands. Her tousled hair and T-shirt was enough to stir his blood. He could easily make love to her again. And again. And every day for the rest of his life.

Whoa.

He couldn't promise that. What if he didn't have a rest of his life? Only now. This moment. If his illness returned, he wasn't about to drag Lauren into what that would mean.

She'd been through enough. She already buried the one man she'd loved. How could he do that to her again?

She looked up when he entered the room and smiled. "Hi. Tea?" she offered, and tapped the mug.

"Sure," Gabe said, even though he didn't really care for the stuff. He watched her get up, move around the counter and flick on the kettle. "Couldn't sleep?" he asked.

She shook her head and grabbed a mug from the cupboard. "Not really. Sorry if I woke you."

Gabe walked into the galley. "Everything all right?"

"Sure," she said quietly, and popped a tea bag into the mug. "I'm not a sound sleeper. Comes from living alone, I guess."

"You're not alone now, though."

The kettle dinged, and she poured the water. "For the moment...no."

An odd twitch caught him behind the ribs. He stepped closer and touched her arm. "Lauren, forget the tea."

She inhaled and turned toward him. "You mean you want to have *the* talk? Before you skedaddle me back home?"

There was a familiar spark in her eyes, and it was a look he knew. She was annoyed with him. "I mean, forget the tea and come back to bed."

She twisted back to the sink. "I thought we'd have—"

"A postmortem?" He reached across and touched her cheek. Unable to help himself, he smiled. "Let's not do that. You think too much."

"I don't," she insisted. "And it's insensitive of you to laugh at me."

Gabe gathered her in his arms, kissed her forehead and spoke gently. "You're being a little ridiculous, you know that?"

She sagged against his chest, and he tightened his grip. "I know. I'm just not used to feeling like this. I'm not used to *doing* this. We hardly know one another. I was looking for something else, and then you move in next door with your blue eyes and nice smile and I was…I was…"

He pulled back and softly grasped her chin. "You were what?"

She let out a long breath. "Done for."

Gabe's insides contracted. What was she saying? That it was more than a developing friendship and blinding physical attraction? That she loved him?

Sure, he had feelings for Lauren. A lot of feelings. And making love with her had been out of this world. But falling in love wasn't part of his plan. Hell, it was out of the question at the moment. Not when he didn't know if he actually *had* a future. He had a five-year plan and intended to stick to it. Lauren deserved more than empty promises. Or another casket to grieve over.

"Lauren, we're friends and I'd—"

"Friends with benefits?" she said, and cut him off as she pulled away. "I really hate that expression. It's a convenient line to avoid commitment."

Gabe bit back a frustrated sigh. "The only thing I'm trying to avoid is hurting you."

She blinked hard. "Well, you're not doing so great."

He knew that. There were tears in her eyes, and he'd put them there. "If I'd thought you wouldn't be—"

"Forget the condescending speech, Gabe," she said, cutting him off again. "I'm sorry I'm not able to take the emotion out of sex. Blame it on my traditional upbringing, but I've always thought that making love should mean exactly that."

She was right. It should. "I agree. And there was nothing casual about last night for me, Lauren. But I can't promise you more than this…." He paused and took a breath. "More than now. I can't say what the future will bring, and I don't know where I'll be."

She pulled herself from his embrace. "Are you leaving? Going somewhere? Are you going back to California? Is that why you—"

"No," he said quickly, and urged her close again. "Of course not."

"Then what do you mean?"

Guilt hit him between the shoulder blades. *Tell her the truth....*

But he couldn't. "Forget it. Come back to bed, Lauren."

Her eyes glistened, and she nodded.

Back in his bedroom they made love again. This time it was quicker, hotter, as though they had a need that had to be sated. Afterward, Lauren stretched and sighed and curved against him. And he was, Gabe realized as he drifted back to sleep, happier and more content than he could ever remember being before in his life.

At seven, Lauren rolled out of bed and met Gabe in the kitchen, wearing only a navy blue bathrobe he'd offered. He'd made pancakes, and she'd agreed to try them before she returned home to shower and change and head to the store. Despite her earlier display of emotion, there was an easy companionship between them, as if they'd done it before, as if they knew one another deeply and intimately.

Which they did, she figured, coloring a little when she remembered the way they'd made love just hours ago. Being with Gabe was like nothing she'd experienced before. He was an incredibly generous lover. He was thoughtful and attentive, and they were well matched in bed.

What about out of bed?

Was there enough between them to stand up to the test outside the bedroom? She hoped so. He'd made no promises, offered no suggestions that their relationship would go beyond one night together. But there was no doubt in her mind that what they'd shared was more than simply sex.

"Are you okay?" he asked, watching her as she mulled over her second mug of tea.

Lauren looked up and smiled. "Fine. Just thinking I should get moving. I have to open the store this morning, and if I'm late, my mother will ask a thousand questions."

He grinned. "Can I see you tonight?"

Lauren's insides jumped. "Are you asking me out on a date?"

"Yes."

Her brows arched. "That's quite a commitment. You sure you're ready for that?"

He came around the table and gently pulled her to her feet. "I guess we'll find out as we go."

He kissed her with a fierce intensity that had *possession* stamped all over it. And Lauren didn't mind one bit. They made out for a few minutes, and when he released her, Lauren was left breathless and wanting him all the more.

"I'll just grab the rest of my clothes," she said with a smile as she left the kitchen.

Back in his bedroom, she gathered up her clothes and quickly changed back into her underwear, skirt and T-shirt. She found her shoes at the foot of the bed and slipped into them before she walked into the en-suite bathroom to return the robe. She hung it on a hook and turned toward the mirror. Only to be faced with her pale complexion and mussed *bed* hair.

She moaned and finger combed her bangs. There were remnants of mascara clinging to her lashes, and she looked for a tissue to wipe beneath her eyes. When she found nothing on the counter, Lauren opened the overhead cabinet. And stilled immediately.

A long row of medication bottles caught her attention. Serious medication. Very serious. She'd seen similar medication bottles before. Along the same shelf, there were vitamins and several homeopathic tonics. Lauren's blood ran cold. Why would a strong, healthy man like Gabe need so much medicine? It didn't make sense. She suppressed the urge to examine one of the bottles, but her mind continued to race. A rush of possibilities scrambled in her head. He was a doctor...perhaps it was something to do with that?

It's none of my business.

But she still longed to know.

Immediately embarrassed that she'd even noticed the bottles, she was about to shut the cabinet when she heard a sound from the doorway.

"Lauren?"

Gabe's voice. Marred with concern and query. She turned to face him and found his expression was completely closed off. Unreadable. Guarded.

Her mouth turned dry. "I was...I was looking for a tissue." She stopped speaking and looked at him. "I'm sorry, I shouldn't have opened the—"

He stepped forward and closed the cabinet door. "You should leave if you're going to open your store on time," he said flatly.

Lauren's stomach lurched. He looked solemn. He looked annoyed; he looked as though she'd invaded his privacy in the worst possible way.

"What's going on, Gabe?" she asked, stepping out of the en suite and into the bedroom. "Why are you—"

"I'll see you out," he said, and swiveled on his heels.

Lauren followed him out of the room and was halfway down the hallway when she said his name. He stopped and turned.

"What?" he asked.

"Exactly," she said. *"What?"*

They were now both in the living room doorway, neither moving. He was tense, on edge, and Lauren resisted the urge to reach out and touch him. He looked as if he wanted her gone. And the notion hurt through to her bones.

"It's nothing," he said quietly. "We should both get ready for work."

Lauren shook her head. "Don't do that. Don't shut me out."

Silence stretched between them like a piece of worn, brittle elastic. Somehow, the incredible night making love with one another and the lovely relaxed morning sharing pancakes and kisses had morphed into a defining, uncomfortable moment in the hallway.

All because she'd seen medication in a bathroom cabinet.

An odd feeling silently wound its way through her blood and across her skin. And a tiny voice whispered in the back of her mind. As the seconds ticked, the whispering became louder, more insistent. Something was wrong. Had she missed signals? Had she been so wrapped up in herself she hadn't really seen him? And without knowing how or why, Lauren suspected the answer was within her grasp.

Just ask the question.... Ask him.... Ask him, and he'll tell you....

"Gabe…" Her voice trailed off for a few moments and she quickly regathered her thoughts. "Are you…sick?"

Shutters came down over his face. She'd seen the look before—that day at the hospital when they'd met near the elevator. He'd been coming from the direction of the specialist offices. *The oncology specialist.* Lauren scrambled her thoughts together. Suddenly, she wasn't sure she wanted to hear his reply.

"No," he said finally.

"But…"

"I was," he said when her query faded. "Eighteen months ago."

A sharp pain tightened her chest. A terrible, familiar pain that quickly took hold of her entire body. It was hard to breathe, and she didn't want to hear any more. But she pressed on.

"What did you—"

"Hodgkin's lymphoma," he said impassively, cutting her off.

Cancer...

Lauren's knees weakened. He'd had cancer.

Just like Tim.

She swallowed the thick emotion in her throat. Every memory, every fear, every feeling of despair and pain she'd experienced with Tim rose up and consumed her like a wave. Tears burned the backs of her eyes, and she struggled to keep them at bay as a dozen questions buzzed on her tongue.

And then, like a jigsaw in her mind, the scattered pieces of the puzzle came together.

Gabe seemed to understand the despair she'd experienced at losing Tim. And he also seemed to understand the other man's motives better than she ever had. Gabe didn't want commitment. He wasn't interested in a relationship.

If you waste your heart on me, I'll break it....

She put her hand to her mouth and shuddered. It was too much. Too hard. Too familiar. And then she ran. Out of his bedroom. Out of his house. Out of his life.

By midday, Gabe was silently thanking Lauren for doing what he couldn't. For walking away.

For racing away...

It was better than facing what he'd expected—the reflection, the realization. *The pity.*

Of course she'd taken off. What sane, sensible woman wouldn't? It certainly hadn't taken Mona long to find the door once he'd given his ex-girlfriend an opportunity to bail on their relationship. She hadn't wanted to waste her life on a man with a death sentence.

And neither would Lauren.

Which is what he wanted, right? No involvement, no feelings, no risk.

Now he just had to convince himself.

Last night had been incredible. The best sex he'd ever had. But it had been a mistake. And wholly unfair to Lauren. From the beginning, she'd been clear on what she wanted, and Gabe knew he'd somehow ambushed that goal by allowing himself to get involved with her. He had a five-year plan, and he still intended sticking to it.

He got a text message from Aaron around two o'clock.

You still haven't called Mom.

He replied after a few minutes and got back to work.

I'll get to it.

When?

Gabe snatched the phone up and responded.

When I do. Back off.

He turned the cell to mute, logged off the computer and sat deep in his chair. He was, he realized as he stared at the blank screen, out-of-his-mind bored with his job. Shuffling paperwork during the week and attending to jellyfish stings and sunstroke on the weekends simply didn't cut it. He wanted more. He needed more.

During the night, in between making love with Lauren and holding her in his arms, they'd talked about his career. For the first time since he'd left Huntington Beach, Gabe admitted how much he missed practicing medicine. As he sat at the desk that had never felt like his own, Gabe knew what he had to do.

It was after four, and he was just finishing a promising call with the human resources director at Bellandale's hospital when there was a tap on the door. It was Lauren.

She entered the room and closed the door.

"Hi," she said quietly. "Can we talk?"

Gabe's stomach tightened. She looked so lovely in her sensible black skirt and green blouse. She'd come to end it. Terrific. It was exactly what he expected. *And* what he wanted. They'd stay friends and neighbors and that was all. Perhaps *friends* was stretching it, too. A clean break—that was what they needed.

He nodded. "Sure."

Her hands were clasped tightly together. "I wanted to... I'd like to..."

Gabe stood and moved around the desk. "You'd like to what?"

She sighed and then took a long, unsteady breath. "To apologize. I shouldn't have left the way I did this morning. I think I was so...so...overwhelmed by it all, by what you told me...I just reacted. And badly. Forgive me?"

Gabe shrugged. "There's nothing to forgive. Your reaction was perfectly normal."

"Don't do that," she said, and frowned. "Don't make it okay. It's not okay."

"I can't tell you how to feel. Or how to respond to things." He perched his behind on the desk. "Considering what you've been through in the past, it makes sense that you'd react as you did."

"It's because of what I've been through in the past that I should *not* have reacted that way. I'm ashamed that I ran out this morning without asking you anything about it. But I'm here now. And I'd like to know." Her concerned expression spoke volumes. Gabe knew that look. He knew what was coming. He waited for it. "Would you tell me about your illness?"

And there it was.

Pity…

His illness. As though it suddenly defined him. As though that was all he was. The ultimate unequalizer. Healthy people to one side. Sick people to the other.

Gabe took a breath. Best he get it over with. "There's not much to tell. I was diagnosed with lymphoma. I had surgery and treatment. And I still take some medication. End of story."

She nodded, absorbing his words. "And you're okay now?"

"Maybe."

She frowned. "What does that mean?"

"It means there are no guarantees. It means that my last round of tests came back clear. It means that without a recurrence within five years, I should be fine."

Should be. Could be. Maybe.

If she had any sense, she'd turn around and run again.

"And that's why you don't want a serious relationship?" she asked, not running.

Gabe met her gaze. At that moment, he didn't know what the hell he wanted other than to drag her into his arms and kiss her as if there was no tomorrow. But he wouldn't. "Exactly."

"Because you might get sick again?" Her hands twisted self-consciously. "Isn't that a little…pessimistic?"

"Realistic," he corrected.

She stepped a little closer. "Then why did you make love to me last night?"

Because I'm crazy about you. Because when I'm near you, I can't think straight.

"I'm attracted to you," he said quietly.

"And that's all?"

"It's all I can offer," he said, and saw her eyes shadow. He didn't want to hurt her, but he wasn't about to make any grand statements, either. She'd be better off forgetting him and resuming her search for Mr. Middle-of-the-Road. "You know what you want and that's not…me. I care about you, Lauren, too much to lead you on."

Her eyes widened, and she laughed shrilly. "You're joking, right?"

"No."

"That's a convenient line for a man who's *afraid* of commitment."

Gabe squashed the annoyance snaking up his spine. "I'm not afraid of—"

"Sure you are," she shot back quickly, and waved her arms. "You work here instead of the job you're trained to do, even though you're clearly a skilled doctor. You won't even commit to a phone call to your family. And let's not forget the meaningless one-night stands."

"That's an interesting judgment from someone who can't bear to be alone."

As soon as he said the words, Gabe knew he'd pushed a button. But damn, couldn't she see that he wanted to make it easier for her, not harder?

Her eyes flashed molten fire. "I *can* be alone. But I'd prefer to not be. And maybe you think that makes me weak and needy." She cocked a brow. "And you know what—perhaps it does. But I'd rather be like that than be too scared to try."

Gabe's gut lurched. He didn't want to admit anything. She was right when she said he was scared. But he couldn't tell her that. Because she'd want to know why. "You don't know what you're asking."

She shook her head fractionally. "I'm not asking anything. I never have. I like you, Gabe. I…I more than *like* you. I wouldn't have spent last night with you if I didn't feel—"

"You want a future, Lauren," he said, and cut her off before she said something she'd inevitably regret. "A future that includes marriage and children and a lifetime together." He inhaled deeply. "It's a future we all take for granted. Until you're told you might not have it."

"But you said you were okay now."

"The cancer could still come back. I wasn't given a one hundred percent chance of making it past five years," he said, and ran a hand through his hair. "Not exactly dead man walking, but close enough that I knew I had to make a few decisions."

Her mouth thinned. "Decisions?"

"About my life," he explained. "About how I wanted to *live* my life. I left my home, my career and my family because I'd had enough of people treating me as though I was somehow changed…or that having cancer had changed me. Because despite how much I didn't want to admit it, I was changed. I am changed. And until I know for sure that I have a future, I'm not going to jump into a relationship." He stared at her. "Not with anyone."

"Jump?" She shook her head. "Most of the time I feel as though you've been dragged into this by your ankles. So, I guess *jumping* into bed with me doesn't count?"

"Of course it counts, and that's exactly my point," he replied. "But I can't give you what you want. I can't and won't make that kind of promise. It wouldn't be fair to you, Lauren. I've had eighteen months to think about this, and I didn't come to the decision lightly. I'm not going to get involved here, only to…"

"To what?"

He sucked in a breath. "To die."

Lauren stepped back and wrapped her arms tightly

around herself. He knew she heard fear in his voice, and he hated the sympathy in her eyes. But she kept on, relentless.

"I don't need that kind of promise, Gabe."

He shook his head. "You do. You would. If we got serious, you'd want it. Hell, you'd deserve it. And I couldn't give it to you."

"How do you know?" she asked. "You're imagining the worst when—"

He made a frustrated sound. "Because I just know. Because I've lived with it for eighteen months. I know what being sick did to the people around me. As a doctor, I saw sickness every day and didn't have one clue what my patients went through until I found myself on the other side of the hospital bed."

"I wasn't one of those people."

"No, you weren't. But you know how this could work out." He raised a hand dismissively. "You've been through it, you grieved...you're *still* grieving for Tim and that life you'd planned for."

"This isn't about Tim," she said quickly. "This is about you. Tim had a terminal illness. An inoperable brain tumor. He was dying...you're not."

"I might," he said flatly.

"So could I. No one can expect that kind of guarantee."

"Isn't that why you married a man you didn't love?" he asked. "Because he was healthy and could give you that kind of assurance?"

"I was—"

"You were looking for your happily ever after," he said, frustrated and annoyed and aching inside. "You were looking for a man who could give you the life you'd dreamed about. I can't do that. Damn it, I don't even know if I could give you the children you want so badly."

Her face crumbled. "Oh, I hadn't thought about—"

"About the possible side effects of chemotherapy and radiation." Gabe expelled a heavy breath. "Well, think about this…there are *no* guarantees. And as much as you say you don't want them, we both know you do. Go home, Lauren," he said coldly, knowing he was hurting her, and knowing he had to. "Go home and forget about this."

Forget about me.

Seconds later, she was gone.

Chapter Eleven

Lauren left the store early on Thursday afternoon and arrived home to find two battered trucks in Gabe's driveway and one in hers. The fence between the two properties, which had long since been hidden by the overgrown hedge, was now in piles of broken timber on both front lawns. She maneuvered her small vehicle around the truck and parked under the carport.

One of the workers came around to her car and apologized up front for the noise they were making and said they'd be finished for the day within a couple of hours.

"But that tree has got to go," he said, grinning toothlessly.

The tree was a tall pine that sat on the fence line and often dropped its branches on her roof. It wasn't much of a tree, and her brother had offered several times to remove it for her.

"Oh, really?"

"The root system will wreck the new fence. We'll get started on it this afternoon, if that's okay?"

Lauren shrugged. "No problem."

Once inside, she changed into jeans and white T-shirt and set her laptop up on the kitchen table. She had invoicing and wages to do and preferred to do it without the inevitable distractions at the store. She poured a glass of iced tea and sat down to work.

By four-thirty, the contractors were still at it. And they were noisy. They were digging new post holes along the fence line with a machine that made a loud *clunk* sound with every rotation. And the buzz of dueling chainsaws didn't help her concentration.

Not that she was in a concentrating mood. For two days, she'd been walking around on autopilot, working at the store, talking to her mother, pretending nothing was wrong when she was broken inside.

Gabe's words still haunted her. His admittance that he might not be able to father children played over and over in her mind. In her heart, she knew that didn't matter to her. Sure, she wanted children. She longed for them. But she wanted Gabe more. Even though he didn't want her back.

At the store that day, she'd arrived early and took inventory on a range of new arrivals. When that was done, she'd dressed two of the windows with new gowns and played around with matching accessories. When she was finished, she'd stood back and examined the results. Not bad, she thought. How long had it been since she'd enjoyed her work? *Years.* Too long. After Tim died, she'd lost interest in the fashions and could barely tolerate the enthusiasm of the clients looking for their perfect gown. Her own fairy tale was over, and Lauren took little pleasure in anything related to weddings or the store. It had stopped being fun and instead became a duty.

Perhaps it was time to sell the business and try something new?

She'd once had dreams of taking a break from the store when she was married and had a family of her own. But Tim's death had changed everything, and now that dream seemed as unreachable as the stars around some distant planet. Because despite how much she'd convinced herself it was what she wanted, her plans for a loveless, passionless relationship were stupid. If falling for Gabe had shown her nothing else, Lauren now knew what she wanted. Along with friendship and compatibility, love and passion were vital. In fact, she wanted it all. Everything. A full and complete relationship.

Maybe a vacation was in order. She hadn't been on a holiday for years. Perhaps that would quell her discontented spirit. In the meantime, she'd talk with her mother about putting on another part-time employee so she could take some time off. She thought she might even go back to college.

And she'd get over Gabe. She had to.

Lauren was just about to get herself a second glass of iced tea when she heard an almighty bang, followed by several loud shouts and then a crash and the booming sound of timber cracking. Another sound quickly followed—this one a hollow rumble that chilled her to the bone. The roof above creaked and groaned, and suddenly parts of the ceiling gave way as tiles and branches came cascading through the gaping hole now in her roof. She dived under the table as prickly branches and sharp barbs of shattered timber fell through the gap. Plaster from the ceiling showered across the room in a haze of dust and debris, and she coughed hard as it shot up her nose and into her lungs.

When it was over, she heard more shouts and the sound of heavy boot steps on the roof. She coughed again and wiped her watery eyes. Still crouching, she shuffled backward but quickly moved back when she felt a sharp sting on her left arm. A jagged branch had sliced her skin, and she clamped her right hand across the wound to stem the flow of blood. When that didn't help she noticed her T-shirt was ripped in several places, so Lauren quickly tore off a strip from the hem and made a makeshift bandage to wrap around her arm.

She moved forward and tried to make another exit point, but the branches were thick and too heavy for her to maneuver out of the way. Lauren swallowed the dust in her throat and coughed again. The kitchen table was completely covered in branches and debris from the ceiling support beams, shattered roof tiles and plaster. Her legs started to stiffen in their crouched position, and she stretched forward, looking for a way out from under the table. She tried to push a few of the smaller branches out of the way, but the sharp ends pinched her hands.

She could have been badly injured. Or worse. But she quickly put that thought from her mind and decided to wait for workers to come and help her. And finally, she heard a voice and heaved a relieved sigh.

"Lauren!"

Gabe. Her heart thundered in her chest when she heard footsteps down the hallway and then the sound of tiles crunching beneath his feet. She could see his jeans-clad legs through the twisted branches.

"Where are you?" he asked urgently, coming closer.

"I'm under here," she said, and rattled one of the branches. "Under the table."

"Are you hurt?"

"A few scratches," she replied, coughing again and ignoring the throbbing sting from the gash on her arm. "But I think I'm mostly okay. I have a cut on my arm."

"Stay still, and I'll be there as quickly as I can."

He immediately made his way through the room, easily hauling fallen plaster and timber out of his path. The branches around the table shook and swayed, and she heard him curse under his breath. Within seconds, he'd made a space large enough for her to crawl through. He crouched down, and relief coursed through her veins. She pushed back the swell of emotion rising up.

"Give me your hand," he said, and she reached out.

His fingers clasped around hers, warm and strong and lovely and safe. Lauren stifled a sob as he gently drew her out through the space and got her to her feet. And without a word, he folded her into his arms and held her close.

"I've got you," he whispered into her hair as he gently stroked her scalp. "You're okay now."

Relief pitched behind her ribs, and as Lauren glanced around, the enormity of the destruction struck her like a lash. The room was wrecked. Plaster and timber were strewn over the floor, and benches and dust from the shattered ceiling plaster covered every surface. The huge branch that had fallen through the roof covered the entire table, and there were broken branches and foliage everywhere.

"Oh...what a mess."

Gabe held her away from him. "Forget that for a minute. Let's check your injuries."

He quickly examined her and looked underneath her bandage. "I don't think it needs stitches, but you should probably see a doctor."

She smiled. "Isn't that what I'm doing right now?"

He stared at her for a moment, and then smiled back. "I guess so. I have a medical kit at home, so I can dress that for you. Now let's get out of here."

And then he lifted her up into his arms as though she were a feather.

"I can walk," she protested.

"Humor me, okay?"

Her legs did feel shaky, so she nodded. Seconds later, he

was striding down the hallway and out the front door. The contractors were all hovering by the bottom steps.

"I'm fine," she assured them when she saw their worried faces.

"Don't go inside," Gabe told the workers. "There could be structural damage. I'll be back soon, so wait here."

She smiled at his bossiness and then dropped her head to his shoulder. It felt nice being in his strong arms. When he rounded the hedge, she noticed how his front door was wide-open, as if he'd left the house in a hurry.

"I really can walk," she said once he'd carried her up the steps.

But he didn't put her down until they reached the kitchen. Then he gently set her to her feet and pulled out a chair. Once she was settled and he'd grabbed a first-aid kit, he undid the makeshift bandage and examined the wound.

"It's not deep," he said, and cleaned the area, applied a small bandage around her forearm and then circled it in plastic wrap. "That should keep it dry when you shower."

"Thanks," she said, and fought the urge to fall into his arms again. "I need to get back to my house and call my insurance company."

"Later," he said. "I'll go and check it out while you rest here."

"There's no need to—"

"There's every need," he said, and grabbed her hand. "You've just been through a frightening ordeal, and you're injured. Plus, there's a great gaping hole in the roof and there could be structural damage to the house."

Lauren ran her free hand down her torn T-shirt and jeans. "I need some fresh clothes, so I'll go home and change and then call the—"

"Stop being so damned obstinate," he said impatiently. "Let me check out the house, and I'll get your clothes while I'm there."

She pulled her hand free. "I'm not sure I want you rummaging through my underwear drawer. It's private and—"

"Lauren, I have seen you naked," he reminded her. "Remember? It's a little late for modesty. Go and take a shower, and I'll be back soon."

"A shower? I don't know why you—"

"Once you look in the mirror, you'll see why," he said, and smiled. "I'll be back soon."

He left the room, and Lauren tried not to be irritated by his high-handedness. She cradled her sore arm and headed for the en-suite bathroom. And worked out why he'd insisted she shower. She was covered in grime and plaster dust. Her face and hair were matted with the stuff, and her clothes were speckled with blood and dirty smudges.

Lauren stripped off the soiled clothes and stepped beneath the warm water, mindful of the plastic-covered bandage. She washed her hair as best she could, and by the time she emerged from the cubicle, wrapped her hair up in a towel and slipped into his bathrobe, she heard him striding down the hallway.

He paused in the doorway carrying a short stack of clothes. "Let me know if you need anything else," he said, and placed them on the bed.

She nodded. "Thank you. How does my house look?"

"Redeemable," he said, and half smiled. "I've told the contractor to tarp the roof so there's no more damage overnight. And I've arranged to have a certified builder assess the damage in the morning. Get dressed, and I'll make you a cup of that tea you like."

Lauren had to admit he'd done a fair job at choosing her clothes. Gray linen pants and a red collared T-shirt, a sensible black bra and brief set and slip-on sandals. As she stepped into the briefs, she didn't want to think about his lean fingers touching her underwear. Gabe's take-charge attitude should have made her as mad as ever, but she was actually grateful for his kindness. What had been a frightening experience was eased by him coming to her rescue. When she was finished dressing, she headed for the kitchen. He'd made tea, as promised, and was staring out the long window, mug in hand.

"I think I inhaled a bucket of plaster dust," she said when she entered the room.

He turned and met her gaze. "If the cough keeps up, let me know."

"I will. Thanks for the tea." She saw her handbag, dusty laptop and house keys on the counter. "Oh, that's good. I wasn't sure the computer survived the tree crashing on top of it."

"It seems okay," he said quietly. "I found your bag but couldn't find your cell phone."

She shrugged. "That's fine. I don't need it, anyhow."

"So how are you feeling now?" he asked.

"Pleased I dived underneath the table."

"Me, too," he said, and set the mug down. "I'd just gotten home when I saw the pulley snap and then saw the branch nosedive into your roof."

"Apparently, that tree was going to mess with the fence," she said, and grinned. "They didn't warn me about what it might do to my house, though."

He chuckled, and the sound warmed her blood. "I'm glad you're okay. I was worried about you."

He sounded uncomfortable saying it, and Lauren tensed. He might have been worried, but he clearly didn't want to be. She'd accused him of being hot and then cold, and that certainly seemed to sum up the way he acted around her.

"Thanks for coming to my rescue," she said as flippantly as she could manage.

His mouth flattened, and he passed her his phone. "You can call your parents if you like. Or your brother."

She shook her head and placed the phone on the table. "They'll only worry."

"Well, they'll know something's up when you stay with them tonight."

"I'm not going anywhere," she said, and pushed her shoulders back. "I'm sleeping in my own bed, in my own house."

"No," he said quietly. "You're not."

"Ah, yes I am."

"I'm not going to argue with you about this, Lauren. You stay with your parents or your brother, or if you like I'll drive you to Cassie's. But you're not spending the night in a potentially compromised building that has a huge hole in the roof."

She crossed her arms. "You don't get to tell me what to do."

"Right now, when you're being stubborn and disagreeable, I'll do whatever I have to do to keep you safe."

His words had *ownership* stamped all over them, and the fact he had the audacity to say such a thing when he'd made it clear they had no future only amplified her resentment. He really needed to stop interfering. Sure, she was grateful he'd gotten her out from under the table, but that didn't give him open season on deciding where she would sleep.

"I'll be perfectly safe."

The pulse in his cheek throbbed. "No, you won't...so you stay with your family, or you can stay here. Those are your only options."

Of all the bossy, arrogant, bullheaded...

"Fine," she said quickly, and saw the startled look on his face. "I'll stay here."

No way...

Gabe's stomach landed at his feet. She wasn't staying with him when she had a bunch of perfectly good relatives to rely on. She was simply being provocative. He was just about to say as much when the challenge in her eyes silenced any protests.

Instead, he called her bluff. "Okay…but you still have to call your parents and tell them what happened."

Her brows came up. "That's interesting coming from a man who won't pick up the telephone to call his own family."

"We're talking about you," he quipped, "not me."

She shrugged. "So where's my bedroom?"

"I'll sleep in the guest room. You can have my room. You'll be more comfortable there."

"Familiar surroundings, you mean?"

His body tensed. "I haven't finished painting in the guest room," he said, and grabbed his cell. "I can order pizza if you're hungry?"

She nodded. "Sure. No anchovies, please. And extra mushrooms."

He half smiled. "Why don't you rest in the living room, and I'll place the order."

She did as he suggested, and once the pizza had been ordered, Gabe grabbed a couple of ginger beers from the refrigerator and headed for the living room. He found her on the sofa, legs curled up, arms crossed, staring at the blank television.

"Everything all right?" he asked, and passed her a bottle.

"Just thinking about my wrecked house."

"It's a house, Lauren," he said quietly, and sat on the other end of the sofa. "Houses can be fixed."

"Not like people, right?" she shot back, and sighed. "Once broken, always broken."

The tremor in her voice made his insides contract. "Is that how you feel?"

"Sometimes," she admitted. "Lately more often than not. I think I just need to…make some changes."

"Changes?"

She raised her shoulders. "I was thinking of selling the store."

He didn't hide his surprise. "That's a bold move. Are you sure it's the right one?"

"Not really," she replied. "I'm not sure of anything. If I do decide to sell, I know my mother will be disappointed. But I don't know how much longer I can keep pretending that it makes me happy. I've been pretending since... since..."

"Since Tim died?"

She nodded slowly. "Yes. Some days I find it so stifling. And then other days I can't believe I'm having such ungrateful thoughts. I mean, what's not to like about being around people who are looking to create the perfect, most special day and then sharing in that joy? But all I feel is tired and weary of plastering on a wide smile every time a bride comes into the store looking for the gown of her dreams."

Her pain reached deep into his soul. "You've had a bad day...don't make a hasty decision when you might not be thinking clearly."

"Spoken from experience?" she asked softly.

"Yes," he replied.

She shrugged. "I won't."

The doorbell rang, and Gabe got to his feet. "Our dinner. Back in a minute."

They ate in the kitchen, and by eight-thirty were lingering over coffee.

"Are you okay?" he asked when he noticed her frowning.

"Tired," she replied. "And sore. I think I strained my back when I darted underneath the table. Which is a small price to pay considering what could have happened."

Gabe pushed his mug aside. "I don't want to remember what I thought when I saw that tree crash."

"I'm glad you were there to rescue me."

Was she? Was he? It seemed as though there was no escaping the pull that drew them together. It had a will of its own, dragging him back toward her at every opportunity.

"Nothing's changed," he said, and hated how cold his voice sounded.

"Everything's changed. I can't pretend and just switch off my emotions."

"Can't? Or won't?"

Her gaze was unwavering. "What are you so afraid of?"

Gabe sucked in a breath. "Hurting you."

"People get hurt all the time. You can't always control it."

"I can try," he said, and stood. "I won't mislead you, Lauren. I won't make promises I can't keep. I've told you how I feel about you and—"

"Actually," she said, cutting him off. "You haven't said how you feel about me at all…only how you feel about relationships and commitment."

Discomfiture snaked up his spine. "It's the same thing."

Her brows rose tellingly. "That's a man's logic," she said, and got to her feet. "And I'm a woman, Gabe. I think and feel deeply. And I know what I want. For the first time in a long time, I actually know what will make me happy. And who."

Guilt pressed onto his shoulders. "Don't pin your hopes on me, Lauren. I can't make you happy…because I can't promise you a future."

She stared at him, eyes glistening. "Is it because you think you might not be able to give me a baby?"

The burn in his stomach intensified. "You can't deny that's important to you."

"It was," she admitted. "It is. But there are other options, like IVF and adoption. I mean, no two people know if they'll be able to produce a child until they try. And you said it was a possibility, not an absolute."

Her relentless logic was butchering him.

"It's just one more complication, Lauren. One that you don't need."

"But I'm right?" she asked. "So now you're hiding behind this idea of potential infertility to keep me or any other woman at arm's length?"

"I'm not hiding. I'm laying out the facts."

"The facts?" she echoed. "You're like a vault when it comes to the facts. Right now, in this moment, you're well and strong and *here*...why isn't that enough?"

"Because it's not. Because it might not last," he replied, frustrated and angry.

"But you don't know what will happen...no one does."

"I know what the medical data says. I know what the odds are of it coming back. If I can stay healthy for five years and not relapse, then I'll consider my options. But until then—"

"Five years?" She cut him off and shook her head. "You can't organize feelings to order like that."

"I can. I will."

"So you plan to avoid getting close to anyone for the next few years just in case you aren't around to seal the deal? That's absurd. What made you so cynical?"

"Facing the prospect of death."

"I don't believe you," she said hauntingly. "There's more to it. You had a career where you saw death all the time, a career that obviously called out to you because you're mentally strong and compassionate and able to deal with grief and despair and hopelessness. I don't believe that all that strength disappeared because you were faced with the challenge of an illness you've now recovered from."

His chest tightened. "I can't talk about—"

"What happened to you?" she pleaded. "Tell me...what happened that made you so determined to be alone?"

Gabe's heart thundered, and he fought the words that

hovered on the end of his tongue. He didn't want to tell her; he didn't want to admit to anything. But the pained, imploring look on her face was suddenly harder to deny than his deep-seated determination to say nothing.

"My dad died when I was seventeen," he said flatly. "And I watched my mom become hollow inside. At first, I watched her become headstrong in her denial and refuse to admit the inevitable. I watched her use every ounce of strength she had to give him hope and keep him alive. I watched her argue with doctors and oncologists about his treatment and try every holistic and natural remedy she could to give him more time. And then when the treatment stopped working and he relapsed, I watched her care for him and feed him and bathe him, and then I watched her cry every day when she thought no one was looking. And when he died, part of her died, too. She was heartbroken. She was sad, and there was nothing anyone could do for her...there was nothing *I* could do for her."

He drew several gulps of air into his lungs. It was the first time he'd said the words. The first time he'd admitted how helpless he'd felt watching his mother fall apart.

"And I'm never going to put anyone through that...not ever."

She shuddered. "So instead you'll shut the world out?"

"Not the world," he said quickly. "Just..."

"Just me?" she asked, eyes glazed. "Or any woman who wants to be with you for more than a one-night stand?"

"Exactly," he said woodenly.

She shook her head. "It wasn't your job to fix your mother. No one can fix that kind of pain...only time can truly heal," she said quietly. "Believe me, I know. If your mother didn't recover, it's not your responsibility or job to question why. And it must be that your dad was the true love of her life."

"Like Tim was yours?"

Did he sound as jealous by that idea as he felt? He didn't want to feel it. Didn't want to think it. Didn't want to be so conflicted and confused that all he wanted to do was haul her into his arms and kiss her over and over and forget every other wretched thought or feeling.

Her mouth softened. "I did love Tim, very much. But I didn't honor that love when I married James. And when my marriage ended, I was determined to find someone who wouldn't make me feel anything that might dishonor those feelings again. And I tried," she said as tears filled her eyes. "And failed."

"And that's exactly why I won't do this, Lauren. That look you have when you talk about Tim… My mom had that same look. You've been through it, too. You know how it feels to lose someone you care about. Why the hell would you potentially put yourself through that again? It doesn't make sense. You need to walk away from this. And me."

"So you're doing this for me. Is that what you're saying?"

He shrugged. "I'm doing this for us both."

She inhaled resignedly. "I'm going to bed. Are you coming?"

Bed? He groaned inwardly. "No."

Her mouth twitched. "You're not going to make love to me tonight?"

Gabe's entire body tightened. She was pure provocation, and he wanted her so much, his blood felt as though it were on fire.

"No." It was close to the hardest thing he'd ever said.

Her eyes shadowed. "Would you just…hold me?"

Pain and longing sat in his gut like a lead weight. But she didn't know what she was asking. If he stayed with her tonight, there would be no turning back. He wanted her… he wanted her so much he ached inside thinking about denying that feeling. But Gabe wouldn't allow that wanting to turn into needing. Needing meant giving everything. Everything meant loving. And that was impossible.

"I can't." His voice sounded hollow and empty. "I can't give you what you want."

She looked at him, and he saw the disappointment and regret in her eyes. She was hurt.

"No, I guess you can't," she said, and left the room.

Chapter Twelve

"And that's it?"

Lauren dropped her gaze to the floor. If she kept looking at Cassie and Mary-Jayne, they'd see the tears in her eyes. And she wouldn't cry anymore. She'd cried enough over lost love throughout the years. She'd cried for Tim. She'd cried when he'd finally told her he was dying and wouldn't be able to give her the future he'd promised. She'd cried over his grave and in the years since. She'd even cried for James when he'd walked out the door. She'd cried for lost dreams and for the children she'd never borne.

And not once, during all those tears and anguish, did she ever think she'd love again. Nor did she want to. She'd planned on friendship and companionship and then marriage and children to help ease her aching heart. And instead had tumbled headlong into something that was all desire and heat and a longing so intense it physically pained her. She loved Gabe. And she knew, deep down to her soul, that it was the one love she would never recover from.

But she had to try.

And she would.

"That's it," she replied, and pretended to enjoy the glass of wine she'd been cradling for the best part of an hour. She managed a smile. "Looks like I'm back to trawling ReliableBores.com."

Mary-Jayne made a huffing sound. "Did he give you a reason?"

Sure he did. But Lauren would never betray Gabe's confidence and tell them about his illness. Now she had to concentrate on forgetting all about her fledging feelings and put Gabe Vitali out of her mind. And show a little more enthusiasm for her friends' company. But she wasn't in the mood for a Friday-evening movie and junk-food marathon. She simply wanted to lick her wounds in private.

"Don't forget it's my sister's birthday party tomorrow night," Mary-Jayne reminded them. "I'll pick you both up."

Lauren nodded and noticed that Cassie, who still hadn't heard from Doug, looked about as unenthused as she felt. An evening with Scott and Evie Jones was one thing... knowing Gabe would be there, too, was another thing altogether. However, she was determined to put on a brave face and go. Avoiding Gabe was pointless. They shared several of the same friends and were bound to run into one another occasionally. She might be able to steer clear of him over the hedge that separated their homes, but becoming a hermit to her friends wasn't an option.

"How's the house look?" Cassie asked.

"The repairs will take the best part of the weekend, but I should be back in by Tuesday."

"Well, you can stay here as long as you like," her friend offered.

And she was glad she had such loyal friends. She'd gone to bed the night before with a broken heart and awoke with more resolve than she knew she possessed. Gabe was gone by the time she pulled herself out of bed, and had left a cursory note telling her a builder would be at her house at seven-thirty to check for structural damage. By eight she was back inside her own house, cleaning up with the help of the fencing contractor and his crew, who'd arrived with sheepish faces and good intentions. And while the repairs to the roof were being done, she'd stay with Cassie and try to stop thinking about Gabe.

"Thanks, I appreciate it."

"That's what friends are for," Cassie assured her, then smiled. "You know, there's this man at work I think you might like."

Lauren groaned. "A blind date? Ah, no thanks."

"What's the harm? He's nice. He's in the pathology department. Want me to set you up?"

"No chance."

On Saturday morning, Lauren headed to the store early. She gave her mother an abridged version of what had happened with the house, leaving out how she'd stayed at Gabe's that night and only telling her she was bunking in with Cassie until the repairs were done. She didn't mention her thoughts about selling the store. She'd think about that later. When her heart wasn't breaking. When she was whole and was certain she'd finished crying wasted tears.

Late that afternoon, Lauren dressed in a pale lemon sundress in filmy rayon that tied at her nape. The garment fitted neatly over the bodice and flared from the waist. She matched it with a pair of silver heels and kept her hair loose around her shoulders. Mary-Jayne picked her up at six, and since Cassie had decided to give the party a miss, they drove straight to Dunn Inn. The big A-framed home was set back from the road, and the gardens always reminded

Lauren of something out of an old fairy story. There was a wishing well in the center of the yard, surrounded by cobbled paths and tall ferns, and it had been a bed and breakfast for over a decade.

Gabe's car wasn't out front, and she heaved a relieved sigh. She grabbed Evie's birthday gift from the backseat and followed Mary-Jayne inside. Evie was in the kitchen, as was Grace. Lauren had always envied the three sisters' relationship. They were as different as night and day and yet shared a formidable bond. Of course, she adored her brother, but sometimes wished she'd had a sister, too.

"Scott's running an errand," Evie explained, and Lauren wondered if she imagined how the other woman glanced in her direction just a little longer than expected. "He'll be back soon."

Mary-Jayne laughed. "Oh, with some big birthday surprise for you?"

Evie raised her steeply arched brows. "Well, it's certainly a surprise. Not for me, though. And since I'm not sure I really want to be celebrating the fact I'm only two years off turning forty, I'm more than happy about that."

"The gifts are all on the buffet in the front living room," Grace said as she cradled Evie's six-month-old daughter in her arms.

Her sister-in-law was glowing, and Lauren wondered if she was pregnant. It would certainly explain why her brother had sounded so chipper on the phone that morning when he'd called after hearing about her tree mishap from her mother. She was achingly happy for Cameron and knew he deserved every ounce of happiness that was in his life. But part of her envied him, too. He'd put his heart on the line when he'd pursued Grace, and it had paid off.

Not like me....

Her heart was well and truly smashed. Gabe was out of reach. As unattainable as some remote planet. He'd made it abundantly clear that he wasn't interested. He'd rejected her, wholly and completely. And she had to stop wasting her energy hoping he'd come around. There would be no fairy-tale ending.

Lauren offered to take the gifts into the living room and left the sisters alone to catch up. The big room was formal and furnished with a long leather chaise and twin heavy brocade sofas. A collection of Evie's artwork covered the walls, and a thick rug lay in front of the fireplace and hearth.

She'd just laid the gifts out when she heard the wide French doors rattle. A second later, Gabe was in the room. In black trousers and white shirt, he looked so handsome, it was impossible to arrest the breathless gasp that escaped her throat. But he looked a little tired, too, and she wondered if he'd had as much trouble sleeping as she'd had. She almost wished sleeplessness upon him. She wanted to share everything with him…including her misery.

He didn't say anything. He only looked at her, taking his time to rake his stare from her sandaled feet to her freshly washed hair. A gust of awareness swept into the room like a seductive wind, and she couldn't have moved even if she'd tried. Heat coursed up her limbs and hit her low in the belly. In a flash of a second she remembered every touch, every kiss, every moment of their lovemaking. And she knew, by the scorching intensity of his gaze, that he was remembering it, too.

It was hard to stop from rushing into his arms. Because they were the arms she loved. She wondered how it had happened…how she'd managed to fall in love with a man who didn't love her in return. Who wouldn't risk loving her in return. A man who was everything she'd sworn off and yet was everything she craved. A man who openly offered her nothing but heartache.

"Lauren," he said finally, breaking the thick silence. "You look lovely."

She swallowed hard and shrugged. "Thank you."

"How are you feeling? Is your arm getting better?"

"Yes," she said, and touched the narrow bandage. "Healing well."

"How's the house?"

"Good," she replied. "Actually, I wanted to thank you for getting the builder to come around and assess the place. He's been very accommodating and will have the repairs finished by next week."

"No problem. He's the father of one of the kids in the junior lifeguard program at the surf club. He was happy to help out."

"Well, I appreciate your concern. I didn't see your truck out front so I wasn't sure you would be here today."

"I'm parked out back," he explained. "If you'd rather I left, then I'll go."

"No," she said quickly. "It's fine," she lied, dying inside. "It's Evie's birthday, and Scott is your cousin. You should be here with your family."

He stepped closer. "I've been thinking about you."

She shrugged. "I can't imagine why."

His gaze was unrelenting. "We left things badly the other day and I—"

"It's fine," she assured him with way more bravado than she felt. "You said what you had to say. I'm over it."

I'm over you....

Liar.

He nodded slowly. "That's...good. You know, I never planned on hurting you."

Humiliation coursed through her blood, and she had to dig herself out of the hole she was in. "You didn't, so spare yourself the concern. I'm perfectly okay. We had one night together. The sex was great. The pancakes were not so great." She shrugged again and plastered on a tight smile as she counted off a few fingers. "And I'm back to day three of my new vow of celibacy."

"So...you're okay?"

Her smile broadened. "Never better. Don't worry on my account, Gabe. We had sex...it's not a big deal. People have sex all the time. We had an itch, we scratched it."

His mouth thinned. "An itch? Is that what it was?"

"Sure," she said, and shrugged. "What else? I mean, we really don't know one another very well, and we always seem to end up arguing. It's better we slept together early on rather than drag the whole thing out for an age. My plans haven't changed, and yours seem set in stone... so no harm done."

He stared at her, long and hard, and finally he crossed his arms and shook his head. "I don't believe you, Lauren. I think...I think you're saying what you imagine I want to hear."

She laughed loudly. "Maybe I just wanted to get laid... like you did."

"Is that what you think I wanted?" he asked quietly. "To get laid?"

"Sure," she replied, and shrugged. "You told me as much that night you came over for dinner, remember? You called me Commitment 101 and said you have casual and meaningless sex."

His brows came up. "I said that?"

"Words to that effect."

He smiled. "Well, I haven't had as much meaningless sex as you've clearly been imagining. And before you go accusing me of doing that with you, be assured there was nothing meaningless to me about the night we spent together. You told me you don't make love casually, and I believe that." He said the words with such arrogant confidence, she wanted to slug him. "But I think you're hurt and I think you're angry. And I also think—"

"And I think you're the most conceited jerk of all time," she said hotly, cutting him off. A door closed in the house, and she heard voices, but Lauren pressed on, battling with the humiliating fury she felt in her heart. He didn't want her. He didn't need her. Why couldn't he simply leave her alone? "I don't care how much I want to get laid in the future, I will steer well clear of your bed. One night in the sack with you isn't enough to—"

Lauren stopped ranting when she heard someone clearing their throat and noticed that three people were standing in the doorway. It was Scott and two others. A man, tall and handsome with fair hair and blue eyes just like Gabe's, and a woman whose eyes were equally as blue and who looked to be around sixty. She heard Gabe groan as he turned on his heels and faced the group.

When he spoke, Lauren almost fainted on the spot.

"Hi, Mom."

Seeing Claire Vitali in the doorway, with his brother Aaron hovering close by, was enough to quell any urge he had to kiss Lauren's amazing mouth. Since he'd walked into the room and spotted her by the buffet, it was all he'd wanted to do. With her temper flared and her cheeks ablaze with color, he'd never seen her look more beautiful or more desirable. But she was hurting, too, and even though she denied it, Gabe knew he was responsible for the unhappiness in her eyes. He hated that he'd done that…even though he felt certain it was for the best.

The group moved into the room, and before he had a chance to make introductions, his mother was clutching at him in a fierce and long embrace. Once she'd finished hugging, she kissed his cheek and stepped back.

"It's good to see you, Gabriel," she said, using his full name for deliberate effect, and smiled.

Despite his shock, he was genuinely pleased to see his parent. "You, too, Mom."

His mother noticed Lauren immediately and held out her hand. "Hello, I'm Claire Vitali."

Lauren took her hand and introduced herself. "It's nice to meet you."

Gabe saw the gleam in his mother's eyes. "And you."

"Well, I'll leave you all to catch up," Lauren said, and moved across the room as if her soles were on fire. He noticed she smiled at Aaron and Scott on her way out but didn't spare him a glance.

"I'll go, too," Scott said, and grinned.

"Yeah," Gabe said. "Thanks so much for the heads-up."

His cousin shrugged. "Our mothers swore me to secrecy. And don't be too long. It's my wife's birthday, and there's cake."

Once he was gone, Aaron stepped toward him. "That's one pretty girl," his brother said with a grin, and went for a bear hug. Gabe ignored the comment about Lauren and hugged him back.

When the hugging was over and they were settled on the two sofas, he asked the obvious question. "So what are you two doing here?"

"I'm here because she insisted I come," Aaron said, and grinned.

"I wanted to see my son," his mother replied. "And since you weren't returning my calls..."

Gabe glanced at his older brother, looking his usually cocky self on the opposite sofa, and scowled. "I did text and say I was busy."

"Mom didn't believe me," Aaron said, and grinned again. "She wanted to see for herself."

He looked to his mother. "See what?"

"I needed to make sure you were okay," she said, and gave him a look of concern.

"I'm fine," he said. "As you can see."

His mother's mouth thinned. "Are you really? You can tell me if you're not."

"You came all this way because you thought I'd had some kind of relapse?"

She sighed crossly. "I came all this way because you're my son, and you and your brothers and sister are the most important thing in my life. I won't apologize for caring."

Guilt pressed between his ribs. "I'm sorry I worried you. But I'm fine."

"You don't look fine," she said, and frowned. His mother never was one to pull punches. "You look tired and annoyed, and you're clearly not happy that we've turned up unannounced. So what's going on with you?"

Sometimes Gabe wished he came from one of those families where everyone didn't know everyone else's business. Was there such a thing as caring too much? When he'd been diagnosed with lymphoma, his mother and siblings had closed ranks around him, almost to the point of smothering him with concern. And it hadn't taken long for resentment to set in. Since then, they'd treated him differently, and it irritated the hell out of him. It was as though they'd wanted to wrap him in cotton wool and *fix* everything.

"Nothing," he assured her, feeling about sixteen years old. "Everything's fine. I'm healthy. I have a job I like, friends… You don't need to worry, Mom. I'm a grown man, and I can take care of myself."

"I'll always worry," she said, still looking grim. "It's a given that a mother worries about her children, regardless of how old they are." She sighed and patted his arm affectionately. "But if you say you're fine…then I believe you. You still look tired, though."

"I'm just not sleeping great at the moment. Otherwise, I'm in perfect health and have the results of my latest tests to prove it. Please, stop fretting."

"So," Aaron said, and stretched back in the sofa. "You're fine. Which doesn't explain why you've been avoiding our calls for the past month or so." His brows rose questioningly. "What's the story with the pretty blonde with the big brown eyes who you clearly got into bed but who now wants nothing to do with you?"

"Aaron," their mother chastised. "That's enough."

Gabe's mouth pressed tight. "My relationship with Lauren is no one's business and I don't—"

"Relationship?" His brother laughed and cut him off. "Ha…of course. Now I get it." Aaron propped forward on the seat and grinned broadly. He looked at their mother. "Mom, he's not sick…he's *lovesick*."

Gabe found the urge to crash tackle his big-mouthed brother. "Shut up."

"Aaron." Their mom said his brother's name again, this time quietly. "Go and eat some cake. I'd like to talk to your brother alone."

"I'm right," Aaron said with a grin as he stood. "I know I'm right."

Once Aaron left, Gabe faced his mother's stare. "Is that true?" she asked gently.

"Is what true?"

She made a face. "Lauren… Are you in love with her?"

Gabe got to his feet and paced around the sofa. "No."

"But you're involved with her?"

"Not exactly. It's complicated," he said, and shrugged. "And I don't want to talk about it."

"Well, that's always been your problem, really…not talking," his mom said, and sighed. "Just like your father. Not talking about your illness…not talking about what happened at the hospital when you went back to work…not talking about why you broke up with Mona…not talking about why you needed to put an ocean between your old life and your new one."

His shoulders tensed. "You know why I left."

"Because you blamed yourself for that woman and her baby dying," she said gently. "Even though it wasn't your fault. Even though you weren't there."

"I *should* have been there. I was on duty."

"You were sick," his mother reminded him.

"Yes," he said hollowly. "I was. And I went back too soon. I did everything I would have told a patient to *not* do. I ignored what was best and did exactly what I wanted, and because of that a young woman and her baby died. I am to blame, Mom. It doesn't matter how many times I try to get it clear in my head, or how often I'm told the inquiry didn't find me culpable." He pointed to his temple. "In here I feel the blame. In here I see her husband weeping over her body. Because I was arrogant and thought I could trick my broken body into being what it once was." He sighed heavily. "But it's not. And it might never be. I won't pretend anymore. And I certainly won't drag anyone else into that place if I do end up back where I was."

His mother's eyes glistened. "You mean Lauren?"

"I mean anyone," he said pointedly. "I saw what it did to you, Mom…watching Dad slowly fade away. It was hard to sit back and for a time watch you fade away, too."

"Gabe, I didn't—"

"We should get back to the party," he said, and held out his arm. "Before that lousy brother of mine eats all the birthday cake."

She blinked a couple of times. They weren't done. But his mother knew not to push too much. Gabe led her into the dining room and noticed that everyone was there, standing around the table as Evie prepared to blow out the birthday candles…everyone except Lauren.

Had she left?

He ducked out of the room and headed outside. She was in the front yard, standing on the cobbled pathway by the wishing well, partially hidden by large ferns, arms crossed and clearly deep in thought. Everything about her reached him deep down, into a place he'd never let anyone go.

Are you in love with her?

His mother's words came rushing back. He'd denied it. Because he didn't want to face what it would mean to truly love a woman like Lauren. Aaron had called him love-sick, and in a way that's exactly how he felt. He couldn't define it, couldn't put into words what he was feeling when he was around her. It was like a fever that wouldn't break. A pain that wouldn't abate. His chest hurt simply thinking about her. And his damned libido seemed to be on a kind of constant red alert.

Was that love?

He hoped not. He didn't want it to be. He was no good for Lauren.

"Are you making wishes?" he asked as he approached.

She shook her head. "I don't think I believe in them."

"You're going to miss out on cake," he said.

She turned her head sideways. "I'm going to skip the cake. And the party."

"Are you planning on walking home?" he asked, stepping a little closer.

"It's not far," she replied. "A few blocks."

"In those heels?" He stared at her feet for a moment. "I'll drive you home if that's what you want."

"No," she said quietly. "You should stay here with your family." She uncrossed her arms and turned toward him. "Your mother seems nice."

"She is nice."

"And clearly worried about you," she said, and smiled wryly. "I told you to call her."

Gabe shrugged. "I know you did. I should have listened. She was convinced I had...you know...relapsed."

"Well, she must be relieved to know you're fine. And I'm sorry if your mother and brother overheard our conversation before," she said, and Gabe noticed her cheeks were pinkish. "I shouldn't have lost my temper."

"My mom's cool. And don't worry about Aaron. He's a jerk, too," he said, and grinned a little. "You'd probably like him."

Lauren rolled her eyes. "I've decided to give up on handsome and charming men. Too much trouble."

"Maybe there's something safe in that middle road you were looking for."

"Maybe," she agreed. "Anyhow, I'm going home now."

Gabe reached for her instinctively. He took her hand and wrapped his fingers around hers. "I'm...I'm sorry, Lauren."

She didn't pull away. She didn't move. She only looked up at him, and in the fading afternoon light, he could see every feature. The morning after the night they'd made love, he'd watched her sleep, and in that time he'd memorized every line and curve of her face. He wanted to make love to her again. And again. He wanted to hold her in his arms and kiss her beautiful mouth. But she wasn't his to kiss.

"I know you are," she said so quietly, her voice whispered along the edge of the breeze. "I am, too. I'm sorry you think you're not worth the risk. And I'm sorry you think I'm not strong enough to handle whatever might happen. I guess after what happened with Tim, you have your reasons for believing that. But you're doing exactly what Tim did. He didn't trust me enough to try.... He didn't trust me enough to let me in and share the time he had...and you don't trust me, either."

Gabe's insides jerked. "It's not about trust."

"It is." She pulled her hand from his and reached up to gently touch his face, eyes glistening. "But do you want to know something, Gabe? I would have rather had five years, one year, one month with you…than a lifetime with someone else."

Chapter Thirteen

Lauren moved back into her house on Wednesday afternoon, and since the new fence was now complete, she had less chance of seeing Gabe. Which was exactly what she wanted.

She also made a few decisions. She talked with her mother about The Wedding House and agreed that they'd look to finding a buyer within the next twelve months if she was still keen to sell. In the meantime, Lauren had decided to cut back her hours at the store and return part-time to college to get her accounting degree.

And after much convincing from her meddling, albeit well-meaning friends, she agreed to go on a date with Cassie's pathologist on Friday night. She also made a commitment to walk Cassie's dog, Mouse, since her friend was still feeling the effects of her appendectomy, and at nearly five months pregnant, wasn't keen to be on the end of the leash of the huge Harlequin Great Dane. He was well mannered, though, and incredibly quiet and not unruly like Jed.

On Friday morning, she took him for a long walk, and was heading back along the pathway when she saw Megan jogging toward her. The teen's long limbs stretched out, and her tiny sports shorts molded her toned thighs. Lauren felt about as sporty as an old shoe in her baggy cotton shorts and sensible racer-back T-shirt when the girl came up to her.

"Hey, there," Megan said cheerfully. "Nice dog."

"Thanks," she said, and tried to be as equally cheerful.

"So," the other girl said, jogging on the spot. "Are you the reason why Gabe's in such a bad mood?"

Lauren's skin prickled. "I don't know what you mean."

She shrugged. "It was just something my sister said. But she can be pretty catty when she wants to be. She had this idea that you and Gabe were together."

"No, we're not."

Megan grinned. "Have you met his brother? He's hot. But then, I've always had a thing for blonds. Anyhow, if you're not the reason why he's in a bad mood, someone is, 'cause he's been unbearable all week." Megan laughed shrilly. "Gotta run. See ya!"

She watched the other girl jog away, and then turned Mouse back onto the path. She was about twenty feet from passing alongside the surf club when she spotted Gabe's brother outside the building, phone pressed to his ear. He was handsome, she thought, but not as classically good-looking as his younger brother. Lauren was hoping to pass by unnoticed, but he waved to her when he realized who she was.

Seconds later, he walked over. "Nice to see you again," he said, and smiled. "Although I don't think we were actually introduced. I'm Aaron. That's some dog you have there."

"He's on loan from a friend. So are you enjoying Crystal Point?"

"I like the scenery," he said, and grinned. "And nice weather. It's a lot like California."

She asked him about his twin sons, and was about to excuse herself when she saw Gabe standing on the second-story balcony, watching them. Or more to the point, glaring at them.

"Uh-oh," Aaron said, and waved to his brother. "He doesn't look happy. Can't figure why. Can you?" he asked with a devilish grin.

Heat seeped up her neck, and Lauren shrugged. "No idea."

"He can be a little uptight about some things."

She'd never considered Gabe to be uptight. Bossy and hardheaded, perhaps. And stubborn. And handsome and sexy, and she'd always thought him to be rather charming and easygoing. Stupidly, she didn't like that his brother was so openly criticizing him.

"I suppose we can all be like that," she said quietly. "Under certain circumstances."

He laughed loudly. "Ah, so you, too, huh?"

"Me, too, what?" she asked, puzzled.

He laughed again. "Nothing…just go easy on him, okay? He's been through a lot. And I don't think he quite knows what to do about you, Lauren."

Reject me…that's what.

She'd laid her heart on the line. She'd told him how she felt in the garden at Dunn Inn and he'd only turned around and walked away. No words. No comfort. No acknowledgment.

His silence had told her all she needed to know.

"Oh, I'm pretty sure he does. Nice talking with you. So long."

She walked off and felt Gabe's gaze follow her the entire way up the path until she disappeared from his view. He could stare all he wanted. She'd had nearly a week to pull herself together and had so far had done a good job. He was out of her thoughts.

Now all she had to do was get him out of her heart, as well.

Gabe missed Lauren like crazy. He missed talking to her. He missed how the scent of her perfume always seemed to linger on his clothes for ages after they'd spent time together. And he missed kissing her.

And he hated that he'd hurt her.

I would have rather have had five years, one year, one month with you...than a lifetime with someone else.

Her words haunted him. They were honest and heartfelt and much more than he was worthy of. And he'd been so tempted to take what she offered. More than tempted. He'd wanted it. Longed for it. *Ached* for it.

He'd wanted to wrap her in his arms and hold her there forever.

Except...he might not have forever to offer her. And she deserved that. She deserved more than an empty promise and his broken, defective body.

He headed back downstairs and started work. It was mind-numbing admin stuff, but at least it kept him busy. And gave him a chance to stop thinking about Lauren.

"That's one seriously gorgeous woman."

Gabe turned around. Aaron was hovering by the door. He knew his brother was talking about Lauren. "Aren't you supposed to be packing for your flight tomorrow?"

"Change of plans," he quipped. "Mom and I were just talking... We're staying another week."

Gabe groaned to himself. Another week? He wasn't sure he'd cope with another week of his well-meaning mother and annoying older sibling. "Why? Don't you have a life and two kids to get back to?"

Aaron smiled, walked into the office and plunked into a

chair. "You know very well that my ex-wife has the boys, and my business partner is running things while I'm away. And anyway, I wouldn't miss this chance to see you squirm for anything."

Gabe called him an unflattering name and pretended to work.

"You didn't answer my question," Aaron said.

He stared at the paperwork on his desk. "It wasn't a question," he reminded his brother. "It was a statement. And I'm not squirming."

Aaron laughed. "Oh, you sure as hell are. And I must say she's very pretty and kind of wholesome looking...but sexy underneath that whole girl-next-door thing, if you know what I mean."

Gabe knew exactly what he meant. He jerked his head up. "Haven't you got somewhere else to be? Someone else to irritate?"

Aaron linked his hands behind his head and stretched. "Nope...just you."

"I'm working."

"You're ignoring my question...got it bad, huh?"

Gabe scowled. "What I've got is work to do and no time to waste. I'll see you tonight, around six."

His family was staying at Dunn Inn for the duration of their trip, since Gabe had insisted his house wasn't ready for guests, and the B and B was more comfortable. But he'd put off having them around all week until they'd invited themselves over for dinner that night.

His brother left shortly afterward, and Gabe spent the day moving from bad mood to foul mood and in no particular order. Not even the news that he'd been successful in his interview with the hospital had lightened his spirits. There were licenses and insurances to renew, but he'd been offered a job in the E.R. and would start the following month. It meant he had time to hand in his resignation and help find a replacement.

By the time he returned home, it was well after five. He took a quick shower, dressed in jeans and T-shirt and was just marinating the steaks when he heard Scott's dual-cab truck pull up outside. He headed outside and walked down the steps. By the time he reached his brother and mother, another car had pulled up next door. He could see over the fence, and when he spotted Lauren walking down her driveway and then the male driver of the car get out, Gabe's body stilled. They were saying hello. She was smiling. The man opened the passenger door and she got into the car.

Aaron was now out of the truck and was also watching. He clamped Gabe on the shoulder and chuckled. "Looks as though you've got yourself some competition."

"Don't be an ass," Gabe said, and opened the door for their mother.

He greeted his mom and kept one eye on the car as it drove off down the cul-de-sac.

She's on a date....

It shouldn't have made him madder than hell. It shouldn't have made him feel anything. He'd made the rules. She'd opened her heart, and he'd refused to take it. But a date?

He was burning inside just thinking about it.

Over dinner, he stayed silent and let his brother and mom talk. Tension pressed down on his shoulders, and he couldn't quell the uneasy feeling in his gut. He'd told her to find someone else, and she'd done exactly as he'd suggested. It should have eased the guilt. But it didn't. It only amplified the confusion and discontent rumbling through his system and settling directly in the region of his heart.

When Aaron took a phone call and wandered off to the living room for some privacy, his mother cornered Gabe by the kitchen counter.

"So now that you've had a few days to calm down, would you like to tell me about Lauren?"

He shook his head. "No."

His mother sighed. "Do you know what I think? I think you're very much in love with her, and it scares you like you've never been scared before."

I'm not in love with her. I'm not in love with her. I'm not in love with her....

"Nonsense," he said, and started stacking plates in the dishwasher.

"Are you worried she'll leave like Mona did, should your health change?"

"Lauren is nothing like Mona," he replied, and continued stacking. "Actually, I'm concerned she'll do exactly the opposite."

His mother shook her head. "Gabe, isn't that her choice to make?"

"Not if I can help it." He straightened and placed his hands on the counter. "Please stay out of it, Mom. That means no interfering, no meddling… Promise me you'll just leave it alone."

"I can't do that," she said, and smiled. "When one of my kids is in trouble, I'll always interfere."

"I'm not in trouble," he insisted. "And I know what I'm doing. She's grieved for one man already. I won't be responsible for her having to do that over another."

"Another man? Who?"

He briefly explained about Tim. "Now, can we drop it?"

His mother nodded. "Yes, of course."

Gabe made coffee, and when Aaron returned, they sat around the table for a while, telling old tales about things they'd done as kids. Like the time Aaron got caught making out with the local minister's daughter, or when geeky, sixteen-year-old Luca got suspended from math club because he'd followed Gabe and Aaron and gotten a tattoo on his arm. The stories made him laugh and put him in a marginally better mood. He waved them off at nine-thirty but was back on the porch fifteen minutes later when he spotted a car return next door.

She got out and walked up the driveway as the car pulled away. So her date didn't see her to the door. *Schmuck.* Mounting dislike and rage festered in his gut for a few more minutes, and before he had a chance to stop himself, Gabe was striding around the fence, the hedge and then through the gate and up the steps.

He tapped on the door and waited. He heard her heels clicking on the timber floor, and when she pulled the door open, she looked genuinely surprised to see him.

"Oh…Gabe."

He shifted on his feet. She was so beautiful. Her hair was down, framing her perfectly lovely face, highlighting the deep caramel eyes that haunted him. She wore a little black dress that flipped over her hips and made every ounce of desire and longing he possessed surge to the surface in a wave.

"Who the hell was that?" he demanded once she'd opened the security door.

She moved back a little. "You mean my date?"

"Yeah," he shot back, so agitated he could barely get the word out. "Your *date.*"

She actually smiled. Like she thought him hilarious. Or the biggest fool of all time. Or both. "His name is Steve. Although I'm not quite sure how that's any of your business."

It wasn't. *She was on a date with someone named Steve.* Steve who? He hated the name, anyhow. *Forget about it… she can do whatever she likes. And with whomever she likes.* But be damned if the very idea of that didn't make every part of his flesh and bones ache.

"I was only…" He stopped, realizing nothing he could say would make him look like anything other than exactly what he was—a stupidly jealous idiot. It was a sobering realization. Had he ever been jealous before? Had he ever cared enough about anyone to garner such an emotional response?

No. Never.

I think you're very much in love with her, and it scares you like you've never been scared before....

His mother's words beat around in his head.

She made an impatient sound. "Goodbye, Gabe."

He didn't move. He stared at her. Long and deep. And the more he stared, the more he knew her impatience increased. And before he had a chance to question why, he reached out and pulled her close. She looked startled for a microsecond and then tilted her head and glared up at him. Body to body, breath to breath, Gabe experienced a connection with her that was so intense, so acute, it almost knocked him unconscious. Had her date kissed her? Had another man kissed those lips he'd somehow come to think of as his own? His arms tightened around her frame, drawing her against him so intimately, he could feel every lovely rise and curve.

She shook her head. "Don't you so much as think about—"

He claimed her lips, driving his own to hers with blatant passion and little finesse. He found her tongue and toyed with it, drawing it into an erotic dance as old as time. It took her seconds to respond, and she kissed him back, winding her tongue around his, and the sensation pitched an arrow of intense pleasure from his mouth to his chest and stomach and then directly to his groin. He urged her hips closer and groaned. She felt so good, and he wanted her so much. He wanted to strip her naked and feel every luscious curve and dip of her body. He wanted to lose himself in her sweet loving and forget he couldn't give her what she deserved.

Gabe was about to ease them both across the threshold

when she suddenly wrenched free. She pulled away from him and stumbled back on unsteady feet, dragging in big gulps of air.

She pressed the back of her fingers against her mouth. "Don't do that again."

"Lauren, I—"

"Leave me alone, Gabe. Don't kiss me. Don't touch me. Don't come over. Don't call. Don't so much as leave me a note in my letterbox. I'm done. You got that? *Done.*"

Then she closed the door in his face.

Lauren didn't sleep that night. She tossed in her bed and stared at the ceiling. How *dare* Gabe turn up on her doorstep and demand to know who she'd been out with. How *dare* he act all jealous and wounded. And how *dare* he kiss her like that! It was a kiss that had *possession* stamped all over it. And he didn't own her. Her broken heart had now turned into an angry one. He'd forfeited any rights she may have given him. She'd date whoever she wanted to. Even Steve, who had been the perfect gentleman over dinner and was polite and friendly and had done all the right things for a first date. And since he'd called her only ten minutes after dropping her off and asked if he could see her again, he was clearly emotionally available. Unlike Gabe, who obviously only wanted to kiss her and confuse her. So maybe Steve didn't make her pulse race.... He might, over time.

She finally dropped off to sleep after two and woke up with a headache. Saturday morning was busy at the store. Lauren had a gown fitting around ten and put on a smile when the exuberant client arrived with her wedding party. The dress was a beautiful concoction of ivory organza and lace, and it fitted the bride like a glove. By midday the last client had left, and Lauren closed the doors while her mother attended to the cashiering.

"Everything all right?"

Irene Jakowski was too smart to fool. Lauren had been on autopilot for most of the day, doing and saying the right thing, when inside she was confused and hurting and angry.

"Fine, Matka," she said when her mother repeated her question.

Her mother nodded and touched her arm. "There's someone special out there for you, I know it."

Lauren sighed. "I think I've already had my someone special."

"You mean Tim?" her mother asked. "Are you sure about that?"

She frowned just a little. "Of course. You know what he meant to me."

"I know," Irene said. "But you were young when you met, and teenage love can sometimes have you looking through rose-colored glasses."

"Are you saying Tim might not have been as perfect as I imagine he was?"

Irene nodded. "He was a nice young man, and I know you were compatible in many ways. And you might have been happy together. But sometimes easy isn't necessarily what will *keep* you happy. You married James on the rebound. All I'm saying is don't *settle* simply because you think you have to. And not when something wonderful might be within your reach."

She knew what her mother was suggesting. In her mother's romantic eyes, Steve was settling, and Gabe was Mr. Wonderful. "It was one date, Matka," she reminded her. "A nice date, but one date."

"That's how it starts."

No, it had started with heated looks, an argument and an unexpected fall into a swimming pool. Now she had to get him out of her system, her head and her heart.

"I'm not going to settle, I promise you. I've had enough of thinking I want the middle road. I told myself I would be happy with that because I felt so guilty about marrying James. I mean, the way I did it, the way I had everything the same as when I'd planned to marry Tim, only the groom was different. *That's* when I settled, when I married a man I didn't love because I was so wrapped up in having a big wedding. And it didn't make either of us happy. If my brief relationship with Gabe has shown me anything, it's that I want to be *in love*. Truly, madly and deeply. Because I know what it feels like now, and anything less simply won't be enough."

There were tears in her mother's eyes when she'd finished speaking. "I'm glad to hear you say that. I'm glad to hear you want to be happy. After Tim's death and then with James…I wondered if you'd ever risk your heart again. But you did. And I'm very proud of you."

Lauren shuddered out a long breath. "I did risk my heart, Matka. He just didn't want it."

On Saturday night, Gabe paced the rooms of his house like a caged bear. She'd gone out again. The same car had arrived to collect her at six o'clock. It was now close to ten, and she wasn't home. He tried painting the last of the bedrooms to take his mind off Lauren and her date and imagining her doing who knows what. When that didn't work, he poured bourbon he didn't drink, ordered pizza he didn't eat and ignored the two calls from Aaron on his cell.

He fell asleep on the sofa and woke up at midnight with a cramp in his neck. The lights were off next door and the realization that Lauren might have decided to stay out all night cut through him with the precision of a knife. By morning, Gabe was so wound up that he pulled on sweats and sneakers and ran for a solid hour, only caving when he got a stitch in his side. He jogged home, showered and changed into worn jeans and T-shirt and downed two cups of strong coffee.

When his mother arrived at ten, minus Aaron, he knew he was in for a sermon. He sat in the kitchen, cradling a mug of coffee and waited for it.

And got it in spades.

"I've been talking with Irene Jakowski," she said so matter-of-factly, she got his immediate attention. "And we've decided that we need to knock some sense into the pair of you."

Gabe actually laughed. "Mom, I think you and Mrs. Jakowski should stop colluding and accept the inevitable."

"And what's that? You're unhappy. Lauren's unhappy. The only thing that's inevitable is that it's going to stay that way unless you do something about it."

"She's moved on," he said, and pushed the mug aside. "Which is how it should be."

"Stubborn as a mule," his mother said, and tutted. "Just like your father."

"Realistic and sensible," he replied, and half smiled. "Just like you."

"Gabriel," she said with deliberate emphasis. "I'm going to say something I never thought I would ever have to say to you." She drew in a long breath. "Stop being such a coward."

"Mom, I—"

"All your life you've done the right thing. As a child, you never got into any serious trouble. You did well at school. You studied hard. You stayed away from the wrong crowds. You really were a pillar of strength when your dad died. Afterward, you pulled the family together. You were the glue, Gabe. I was so very proud when you got into medical school and then even more so when you became such a wonderful doctor. But I was so busy being proud, I failed to see that I'd relied on you too much."

His throat thickened. "You didn't, Mom."

"I did," she said. "And all that responsibility took a

heavy toll on you. While Aaron was acting wild and chasing girls and Luca was sticking his head into a computer to avoid thinking about what we'd all lost, you worked hard and got on with things. And I think a part of you closed down because of that responsibility. Aaron is charming and says whatever's on his mind, and Luca is all moody and mysterious and cross...but you don't let anything or anyone touch you."

She sighed and reached across the table to grasp his hand. "You got sick. And you should have shouted and complained and blamed something or someone...but you never did. You kept it inside and locked everyone else out. We were all falling apart at the idea of losing you, and you kept us at arm's length. Then you went back to work and something terrible happened." She squeezed his fingers. "You're not to blame, son. But the only way you're ever going to believe that is if you talk about it and share it and forgive yourself. And to do that, you need to let someone in."

Someone. *Lauren.*

"I can't," he said quietly. "I can't do that to her. Not after what she's been through. I can't promise her everything and potentially leave her with nothing. Not like Dad—"

"Nothing?" his mom said, and cut him off. "Do you think your father left me with nothing?" Her eyes glistened. "Gabe, your dad left me *everything.* He left me four incredible children and the memories of a wonderful life. Do you honestly think our marriage was defined by those last few years?"

Did he? Had he been so wrapped up in making sure they still worked as a family that he'd forgotten what it was like before his father became ill?

"I don't, not for one minute," his mother said earnestly, "resent a single moment of the time I spent caring for your dad when he was sick. He was my husband and the father of my children. He was my rock. My center." Tears welled in her eyes. "And I was honored that he trusted me when he was at his most vulnerable and let me care for him right up until the end."

Gabe swallowed the emotion in his throat. He remembered what Lauren had said to him about trust. She'd said Tim hadn't trusted her. She said he didn't trust her, either. And she was right. He didn't trust easily. Because he was afraid. Of being really seen. Of being considered less than strong and whole. Of being weak. And Lauren saw through that. She saw it all and had still wanted him. And like a fool, he'd pushed her away.

He looked at his mother. "You asked me a question a week ago, and I lied to you."

Her eyes widened. "What question?"

"You asked me if I was in love with her."

Claire Vitali smiled. "And are you?"

Gabe took a breath, felt the air fill his lungs and give him strength and nodded. "Yes, I'm completely and hopelessly in love with Lauren Jakowski."

Chapter Fourteen

Lauren was with a client on Monday afternoon and had finished lacing up the back panel on a beautiful beaded lace gown when a deliveryman arrived, carrying an extravagant floral arrangement. Her first thought was that they were from Steve, and although she considered it a bit too much after only two dates, flipped open the card and looked for his name.

Wrong.

No name. Just a message and an initial.

"Can we talk? G."

Not from Steve. He wasn't trying to change her mind about seeing him again. He'd texted her that morning to arrange another date. A text she'd put off replying to because she didn't want to lead him on. Then he'd called, and she'd declined his offer to go out that week. He was nice. But that was all. He'd taken her refusal easily and wished her well for the future.

She looked at the message again. Gabe. And he wanted to talk? As far as she was concerned, she'd said all she intended saying. They were done and dusted. She tossed the note in the trash and told Dawn, the salesclerk, to take the flowers home.

There was a note pinned to her door when she arrived home. "I would really like to talk with you." More talk? She scrunched the note in a ball and tossed it over the hedge and onto his front lawn.

Flowers arrived again the following day. Her mother and Dawn thought it was incredibly romantic. So did Cassie, when she relayed the story to her best friend. Mary-Jayne called her, too. And Grace. But she wasn't going to be swayed. She didn't want to talk to him. He'd had his chance, and he'd blown it.

On Wednesday, the flower deliveryman had a huge smile on his face when he entered the store. Lauren sent the young man away, flowers in hand, and felt an odd burst of triumph that she'd stuck by her guns. Of course, when she arrived home and found Gabe sitting on her porch steps, flanked by Jed, who wore a silly white bandana around his neck while Gabe held up a tiny white flag, her icy reserve thawed for a brief moment. Until she remembered he'd pushed her away time and time again.

"What's this?" she demanded, and flung her bag over her shoulder.

Gabe smiled and patted the dog on the head. "I borrowed him from your brother. I needed an ally."

She raised a brow and looked at the ridiculous flag. "You're looking for a truce?"

"I was thinking more along the lines of a complete surrender."

Her heart pounded. It was a romantic notion. But she wasn't falling for it. "I hear your family's still in town?"

"Yes," he replied, and got to his feet. The dog followed and rushed toward Lauren. "My mother would very much like to meet you properly."

"I can't imagine why." Lauren laughed loudly. "Since I intend to forget all about you, there's no point."

"You'll never forget me," he said, and stepped closer. "I'll bet that you'll remember me for the rest of your life."

Lauren laughed again. Egotistical jerk. "Have you been drinking?"

"I'm perfectly sober. Why did you send my flowers back today?" he asked.

"Because I don't want flowers or anything else from you."

He reached out and touched her hair, twirling the strands through his fingers. "The flowers are just a place to start."

"A place to start what?" she asked suspiciously as she pulled back from his touch.

"Our courtship."

"Courtship?" She laughed at the old-fashioned word and thrust her hands on her hips.

He *was* drunk. There was no other explanation. And he looked as if he was thinking of kissing her. Which was out of the question. She stepped back and frowned. "Why on earth would I want to do that?"

Gabe smiled that killer smile. "How about because you're in love with me?"

She laughed again, because she didn't know what else to do amidst the madness. "You're out of your mind. I'm going inside. Don't even think of following me."

"You didn't deny it."

"Because…because it's too ridiculous, and because I'm tired of this conversation."

She raced up the steps and fiddled with the door lock. She looked around, hoping he was gone. But no such luck. He stood at the bottom of the steps. Her body shook thinking about how handsome he looked, even holding the silly flag.

"I'll be here tomorrow," he said quietly. "Just in case you change your mind."

She frowned. "Don't you have to work?"

"I quit," he said softly. "I'm going back to medicine. I start in the E.R. at Bellandale Hospital next month."

"Good for you," she said extra sweetly.

"Don't you want to know why?"

She shrugged. "It's not my business."

He stared at her and didn't bother hiding the wounded expression. But she had no intention of backing down. He didn't have the right to simply snap his fingers and expect her to come running.

"I want to be the best man I can be…for you."

"What's the point?" she said flatly.

"Because I…I…"

"Good night, Gabe," she said exasperatedly. She unlocked the door. "And incidentally, I think courtship is meant to start before two people sleep together. We've had this back to front from the very beginning, and that's all the sign I need. And stop sending me flowers. I don't want them or anything else from you." Then she headed inside without looking back.

"Have you tried talking to her again?"

Romantic advice seemed to come out of the woodwork, Gabe discovered, when it became obvious to everyone he knew that Lauren wasn't about to forgive him anytime soon. This time it was his mother, who'd decided to hang around in Crystal Point for another week and dispense counsel about his failures to get Lauren's attention at every opportunity.

"Maybe it's time I had a talk with her," she suggested, and pushed her tea aside.

"You need another approach," a voice said from the doorway.

It was Cameron. *Great.* He was in for the big-brother talk. "Your point?"

Gabe figured he'd tried every approach he knew. He'd been on her doorstep each afternoon for the past four days, and she'd simply ignored him and gone into her house and locked the door. There were calls she wouldn't return, notes she wouldn't read and flowers she sent back. And he had a diamond ring in his pocket he wanted to give her, but was convinced she'd toss it in the trash. Total emasculation wasn't in his plans.

He'd wait. And hope she'd come around.

"No risk, no prize."

Cameron again. And this time, Scott and Aaron were behind him. Gabe looked up and scowled. "What?"

"Is she worth it?"

It was a stupid question, and with his patience frayed, Gabe dismissed the question with a barely audible grunt.

"Is she worth risking everything for?" Cameron asked again, relentless.

Gabe straightened in his seat. "Yes."

"Then tell her that."

In that moment, Gabe realized that he'd been so busy trying to woo Lauren with flowers and dinner invitations, he'd neglected to do the one thing he should have done an age ago.

Tell her the truth. Risking everything meant telling her everything. Like she'd told him time and time again. She'd trusted him. First with her past, then her body and then her heart. It was time he did the same. Because she knew what he'd been through and hadn't turned away. She accepted and wanted him. No questions. No prejudice. *No fear.* When, because of what she'd been through with Tim, she'd had every reason to run and not look back. But she hadn't. She'd put her heart on the line and he'd smashed it. Instead of applauding her courage and embracing that love, he'd brought up a whole load of excuses and reasons why they couldn't be together.

And one reason in particular.

Because he was scared of dying. Scared of living.

He let out a deep breath and looked at her brother. "So what's your big suggestion?"

Cameron grinned. "Well, asking her to forgive you for being a stupid ass hasn't worked, has it?"

Gabe thought about the flowers and the notes and the restrained effort he'd shown during the week. He talked about caring and wanting, and laughed at her attempts to ignore him. But he hadn't told her what she wanted to hear. "Not so far."

"Well, I reckon it's time for you to start begging and prove to her you'll do anything you have to do to win her heart."

And that, Gabe thought with a weary laugh, might just work.

Lauren was ever thankful that Saturday mornings were always busy at the store. It kept her mind away from thinking about anything else. Or anyone else. Or someone in particular.

A bridal party arrived at ten for their final fittings, and when the bride emerged from the changing room in her dress, Lauren set to work, fluffing the three layers of tulle and organza before she adjusted the straps and stepped away so the client's mother and attendants could admire her. When the fitting was complete and the bride was out of her gown, Lauren handed the client over to Dawn to process the sale and bag up the goods.

The bell above the door dinged and Lauren smiled when Cassie and Mary-Jayne entered the store.

"Hi, there," she said, and looked at her friends. "What are you both doing here?"

Cassie grinned. "Reinforcements."

"Huh?"

Her friend shrugged and kept smiling. "Trust me."

"You know I—" The door opened again. The bell dinged. And Gabe's mother walked into her store.

"Good morning, Lauren," she said before Lauren had a chance to move. "I'm not sure if you remember me from last week—I'm Claire Vitali." She grabbed her hand and squeezed it gently.

Lauren stared at the older woman. She had the same eyes as her son, the same smile. There was kindness in her expression and warmth in her hand. Her resolve to stay strong wavered. But she wasn't about to be easily swayed.

"It's nice to meet you," she said, and withdrew her hand. "I'd like to stay and talk but I have to—"

"It can wait," Mary-Jayne said with one of her famous grins.

The door opened again, and Grace and Evie entered.

Lauren frowned. "What's going on?"

"Reinforcements, like I said," Cassie explained.

Panic rushed through her blood. Something was wrong. "Has something happened? Is it my dad, or Cameron or—"

"You're father is fine," her mother said as she emerged from the stockroom.

"So is your brother," Grace added.

Lauren backed up. "I don't think—"

"That's just it, Lauren," Cassie said gently. "Stop thinking. At least, stop *overthinking*. We're all here because we care about you."

She stilled as realization dawned. "So this is, what, an intervention? That's why you're all here?"

"Actually, I think they're all here to stand point and make sure I do the right thing."

Gabe...

She hadn't heard him come through the door. He moved around Evie and Grace and stood near the counter. Lauren remained rooted where she was. Her legs turned to Jell-O. Her heart raced like a freight train. She looked at her family and friends. They were smiling, all hopeful, all clearly wondering what she would do next.

I wish I knew.

It was hard not to stare at Gabe. He looked so good, and she'd missed him. But he'd hurt her. And she didn't want to be hurt again.

"This isn't the right time or place to have this discussion," she said, and tried to politely ignore the bridal party hovering behind her.

"Since you won't talk to me, I reckon it's the only time," he said, and flashed her customers a breathtaking smile. "I'm sure everyone will understand."

The bride nodded, and before Lauren had a chance to protest, her mother had subtly ushered the bridal party from the store.

"What do you want?" she asked as stiffly as she could once the customers were gone.

He took a breath. "First, to apologize."

Lauren shuttled her gaze to her mother, Claire Vitali, Cassie and the other women and saw they were all smiling. Like they knew exactly what was going on. "Okay—apology accepted. You can *all* go now."

But they didn't move.

"I mean it," she said crossly. "Don't think just because you'd managed to swindle everyone into coming here today that I'm going to simply forget everything you've said and done and—"

"They volunteered," he said.

She looked at the sea of faces. "I don't believe it."

"You should. They care about you and only want to see you happy."

"Exactly," she said, and frowned. "Which has nothing to do with you."

"It has everything to do with me," he shot back. "I make you happy."

"You make me mad," she snapped.

"Well, I'd make you happy if you'd let me."

She forced her hands to her hips. "And how do you propose to do that?"

"I'll get to the proposing in a moment. Now, where were we? Oh, yes, I was—"

"What?" Her eyes bulged. "You're going to propose?"

"Well, of course I'm going to propose. But back to what I was saying. Oh, yes…and second," he said, and came a little closer, "I'd like to tell you a story."

"A story?" she echoed vaguely, certain she'd just imagined that he said he was about to propose. "I don't know what—"

"It's a story about a man who thought he was invincible." He spoke so softly she almost strained to hear, but she was quickly mesmerized by the seductive tone of his voice. "He thought nothing and no one could touch him. He went to medical school and became a doctor and spent his days trying to fix people who were broken. But underneath that facade of caring and compassion, he was arrogant and stubborn and always did what he wanted because he thought he knew best. And then one day he was told he was sick and everything changed. He wasn't strong. He wasn't healthy. Now he was broken but he couldn't fix himself. He had the surgery and the treatment, but because he was stubborn and arrogant, he went back to work before he should have."

Lauren's throat closed over. Her heart was breaking for him. His pain was palpable, and she longed to fall into his arms. She had been so attuned to him, she hadn't noticed that their mothers and friends had somehow left the store. Everyone was outside and they were alone. She could see them through the big front window. They were smiling. And suddenly, she almost felt like smiling, too. Right now, in front of her, lay her future. But she didn't smile. Because he was opening up, and she wanted to hear everything.

"Gabe, I—"

"I went back to work too early," he said, his voice thick. "I didn't listen. I didn't want to hear it. I just wanted to prove that I was the same. That I wasn't damaged and somehow less than the man I once was. Less than the doctor I once was. But while I was in the bathroom throwing up from the side effects of the medication I was on, the woman and her baby came into the E.R. I wasn't there. And she died, along with her baby. All because I wouldn't admit that I *was* changed. That I was suddenly not just a man. Not just a doctor. I was a cancer patient. And it felt as though those words defined me, made me, *owned* me."

Her entire body shuddered. The raw honesty in his words melted her. "That's why you quit being a doctor? Because you believed that patient died because you were sick? Because you were somehow less than who you used to be?"

"Yes."

Her expression softened. "But you're not."

"I know that now," he said, and smiled. "I know that because when you look at me, I know you don't see a patient. You don't see a man who was sick. You just see…me."

He stepped closer, and Lauren swayed toward him. "Of course I do."

"Doesn't anything scare you, Lauren?" he asked, and took her hand. "After what you went through with Tim, doesn't the very idea of being with me make you want to run?"

"I've only ever seen you, Gabe. Not the doctor, not the patient. The man…the man who has listened to me and comforted me and makes me feel more alive than anyone else ever has. A man who's kind and considerate and has never judged me. And I'm not scared."

He pulled her gently toward him.

"The only thing I'm scared of is waking up and finding that this is a dream."

"It's no dream," he said softly. "You must know that I'm in love with you."

Did Gabe just say he loved me?

She shook her head, not quite prepared to believe him. "No, you're not."

"I am," he said, and touched her cheek. "I love you. I love

that you make me laugh. I love that you tell me when I'm being an egotistical jerk. And I love that you had the courage to let me into your heart when you had every reason not to."

Lauren blinked back tears. "But...you said you had a plan and wouldn't—"

"A stupid plan," he said, and grasped her hand. "I was wrapped up in self-pity and afraid to get involved, and you knew it. You saw through me, Lauren, and still...still wanted me. Even when you knew there was a chance it might not be forever, or I could get sick again. Or I might not be able to give you the children you want." He linked their fingers. "You talk straight and make the complicated simple. You told me how you felt and it spooked me. I'm not proud of my behavior these past weeks, and I promise I'll always be honest about my feelings with you from this day. You have such incredible strength...a strength you don't even know you possess."

Lauren swayed, felt his arms beckoning her. He looked solemn, sincere and wholly lovable. "I don't know...I'm not sure I can."

He squeezed her fingers. "You can, Lauren. Trust me...I won't hurt you again."

"Trust you?" She looked at the sea of faces peering through the windows. "Even though you dragged my friends and family here today to give you an advantage?"

He smiled. "It was Cameron's idea. He thought if I made a big enough fool out of myself in front of our families, you just might just show mercy and forgive me for being an idiot." He came closer until they were almost touching. "I love you, Lauren. I think I've loved you from the moment I pulled you from that swimming pool. And I'm sorry I haven't said it sooner."

He really loves me? Her legs wobbled, and he took her in his arms. "You're not going to completely ruin my reputation and kiss me in front of all these people who are staring at us through the window, are you?"

"I certainly am."

She heard whoops and sighs from the people outside, and Lauren laughed. It felt good. She thawed a little more. Gabe's love was what she wanted. *All* she wanted. And suddenly having the whole world know it didn't bother Lauren in the slightest. He was right—she was strong. Strong enough to open her heart again. And strong enough to cope with whatever the future brought them. He'd pushed past his fears to claim her, and she loved him all the more for it.

"But first," he said, and stepped back a little, "I have to ask you a question."

"What question is that?" she teased, and grinned foolishly.

Gabe dropped to one knee in front of her. "Marry me?" he asked, and pulled a small box from his pocket. The lid flipped open and she saw the perfectly cut diamond, which glittered like his eyes. "When you're ready, when you trust me enough, marry me, Lauren?"

Lauren touched his face and held out her left hand and sighed. "I think you've made a big enough fool out of yourself today for me to know I can trust you, Gabe. And my answer is yes. I'll marry you. I love you." She grinned. "And I kind of like the idea of being a doctor's wife."

Gabe got to his feet, slipped the ring onto her finger and kissed her. "I have you to thank for making me see sense, for making me realize how much I've missed my work. I was afraid to go back. I was afraid to try to recapture what I'd lost. But knowing you and loving you has made me stronger. You make me whole."

Lauren returned his kiss with every ounce of love in her heart. "You're the love of my life, Gabe."

His gaze narrowed. "I thought—"

"You," she said, and touched his face. "Only you. I did love Tim, but honestly, anything I've felt in the past feels a bit like kid stuff compared to the way I love you. And want you. And need you."

His eyes glistened. "Thank you. And while I may not be the first man you've loved, I'm honored to be the one you love now."

"Now and forever." She pressed against him and smiled. "But, Gabe, where are we going to live? Your place or mine?"

"How about neither?" he suggested. "How about we find somewhere new? A new home for a new beginning."

"I like the sound of that," Lauren said, and accepted his kiss. "And I'd like to get a dog," she said breathlessly when the kissing stopped.

He grinned. "Anything you want."

Lauren curved against him. "And babies?"

His arms tightened around her, and he smiled. "I'll see what I can do."

She sighed. "I'm not worried, Gabe. I want to marry you and have your baby. But if there's only ever us, that will be enough."

"You're sure?"

"Never surer."

She kissed him again, knowing she finally had her happy ending.

* * * * *

Don't miss Cassie's story,
Coming in early 2015!

MILLS & BOON®

Why shop at millsandboon.co.uk?

Each year, thousands of romance readers find their perfect read at millsandboon.co.uk. That's because we're passionate about bringing you the very best romantic fiction. Here are some of the advantages of shopping at www.millsandboon.co.uk:

* **Get new books first**—you'll be able to buy your favourite books one month before they hit the shops

* **Get exclusive discounts**—you'll also be able to buy our specially created monthly collections, with up to 50% off the RRP

* **Find your favourite authors**—latest news, interviews and new releases for all your favourite authors and series on our website, plus ideas for what to try next

* **Join in**—once you've bought your favourite books, don't forget to register with us to rate, review and join in the discussions

Visit **www.millsandboon.co.uk**
for all this and more today!